BEAUTIFUL BROKEN THINGS

'*Beautiful Broken Things* is the book I've been waiting for. It made me want to go and rugby-tackle my best friends and give them a giant hug. It's a beautiful tale of the power and complexities of female friendship' Holly Bourne, author of *Am I Normal Yet?*

'*Beautiful Broken Things* is a book that the YA world desperately needs – a book about the beauty, passion and extremities of female friendship' Alice Oseman, author of *Solitaire*

'Starkly realistic and ultimately uplifting, *Beautiful Broken Things* is a compelling tale of pain and redemption, growing up and growing together, and finding empowerment and growth in friendship' Catherine Doyle, author of

'Stories about female friendsh.
ones with no romance, but *Bea*
in an intensely compelling and   James,
author of *The Next Together*

'A gorgeous, bluntly honest story of friendship, hardships and rebuilding. This book captures that feeling of be-all and end-all best-friendship so brilliantly' charlieinabook.weebly.com

Sara Barnard lives in Brighton and does all her best writing on trains. She loves books, book people and book things. She has been writing ever since she was too small to reach the 'on' switch on the family's Amstrad computer. She gets her love of words from her dad, who made sure she always had books to read and introduced her to the wonders of second-hand bookshops at a young age.

Sara is trying to visit every country in Europe, and has managed to reach thirteen with her best friend. She has also lived in Canada and worked in India.

BEAUTIFUL BROKEN THINGS

SARA BARNARD

MACMILLAN

First published 2016 by Macmillan Children's Books
an imprint of Pan Macmillan
20 New Wharf Road, London N1 9RR
Associated companies throughout the world
www.panmacmillan.com

ISBN 978-1-5098-0353-8

Copyright © Sara Barnard 2016

The right of Sara Barnard to be identified as the
author of this work has been asserted by her in
accordance with the Copyright, Designs and Patents Act 1988.

1 3 5 7 9 8 6 4 2

A CIP catalogue record for this book is available from
the British Library.

Printed and bound by CPI Group (UK) Ltd, Croydon CR0 4YY

For Lora, my very best.

'If I could tell you only one thing,
My message would be this:
The world would be a lonely place
If you did not exist.'

Erin Hanson

Before

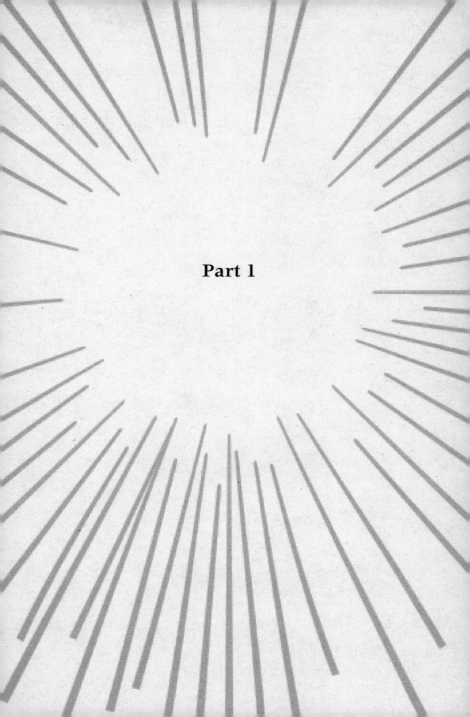

Part 1

I thought it was the start to a love story.

Finally.

The boy, who looked to be around my age or slightly older, had skidded to a stop in front of me. He gave me a quick, obvious once-over and then switched on a wide, flirtatious grin. His friend, better looking but very much not grinning flirtatiously at me, rolled his eyes.

'Heeeey,' the boy said, just like that. Heeeey.

'Hi,' I said, sending up a quick prayer that my bus wouldn't arrive before the conversation ended. I tried to flick my hair casually – difficult to do when it's a touch on the bushy side – and lifted my chin, like my sister once showed me when she was trying to teach me how to act confident.

'What flavour have you got?'

'What?'

He gestured to the ShakeAway cup in my hand. 'Oh,' I said, stupidly. 'Toblerone.' I'd only had a few sips of the milkshake. I liked to let it melt a little before I started drinking it properly, and the cup was heavy in my hand.

'Nice.' The boy carried on grinning at me. 'I've never tried that one. Can I have a sip?'

Here is what I was thinking as I handed over my milkshake: He likes ShakeAways! *I* like ShakeAways! This is a MOMENT. This is the START.

And then his back was to me and he and his friend were running away, their laughter lingering after them. When they were a few feet away, the boy turned, waving my cup triumphantly at me.

'Thanks, love!' he bellowed, either not realizing or not caring that he was not old enough – not to mention suave enough – to pull off 'love'.

I just stood there with my hand holding nothing but air. The other people at the bus stop were all staring at me, some hiding smirks, others clearly pained with second-hand embarrassment. I adjusted my bag strap as nonchalantly as I could, avoiding anyone's gaze, seriously considering stepping in front of a passing bus.

Three days ago I had turned sixteen – the first of my friends to hit this particular milestone, thanks to my early-September birthday – and my parents had rented out a hall for my birthday party. 'You can invite boys!' my mother had told me, looking more excited by this prospect than anyone. The problem wasn't that I didn't want boys (definitely not), the problem was that I went to a girls' school, and I could count the number of boys I knew well enough to speak to on one hand. Despite the efforts of my best friend, Rosie, who went to the mixed comprehensive and had plenty of boy/friends, the gender mix at the party was hopelessly unbalanced. I spent most of the night eating cake and talking with my friends rather than flirting wildly and dancing with what Rosie called potentials, like sixteen-year-olds are supposed to do. It wasn't a bad way to see in a new age, but it wasn't exactly spectacular either.

I mention this so my OK-have-my-milkshake-stranger idiocy has some context. I was sixteen, and I honestly believed that I was due a love story. Nothing epic (I'm not greedy), but something worth talking about. Someone to hold hands with (etc.). The milkshake meet-cute should have led to that. But instead I was just me, standing empty-handed, and the boy was just a boy.

When the bus pulled up just a couple of minutes later and I retreated to the anonymity of the top deck, I made a mental list of milestones I *would* have reached by the time my next birthday rolled around.

1) I would get a boyfriend. A real one.
2) I would lose my virginity.
3) I would experience a Significant Life Event.

In the following year I achieved just one of these goals. And it wasn't the one I expected.

'So he just *took* your milkshake?' Rosie's voice was sceptical. It was nearly 9 p.m., and she'd called me for our traditional last-night-before-school-starts chat.

'Yeah. Right out of my hand.'

'He just snatched it?'

'Um. Yes?'

There was a pause, followed by the sound of Rosie's laughter tickling down the line. Aside from my grandparents, Rosie was the only person I spoke to using the landline. 'Oh my God, Caddy, did you *give* it to him?'

'Not deliberately,' I said, already wishing I hadn't brought up the milkshake story. But it was always hard to stop myself telling Rosie everything. It was just second nature.

'I wish I'd been there.'

'Me too – you could have chased after him for me.'

Rosie and I had spent the day together, another before-school-starts tradition, and had actually bought a milkshake each before going our separate ways. She would definitely have chased after him, had she been there. When we were four, not long after we'd first met at a ballet class we both hated, an older boy had snatched my bow (I was the kind of kid who wore bows in her hair) and Rosie had sprinted after him, taken back the bow and stamped on his foot. Our friendship had followed a similar pattern ever since.

'Why didn't *you* chase him?'

'I was surprised!'

'You'd think after all this time in separate schools you'd have learned to chase your own bullies,' Rosie said, her voice light and teasing.

'Maybe Year 11 will be the year.'

'Maybe. Do they even have bullies in private school?'

'Yes.' She knew very well that they did. She was the one I'd cried to for several straight months in Year 8 when I'd been the target. My school, Esther Herring's High School for Girls, had more than its fair share of bullies.

'Oh yeah. Sorry. I mean boy bullies. Obviously you don't get those at Esther's. Those are the ones I chase for you.'

I let her tease me about teenage boy thieves for a few minutes more until we hung up. I headed back upstairs in the direction of my bedroom, walking past my mother, who was ironing in front of the TV.

'I've got your uniform here,' she called after me. 'Do you want to come and get it?'

I trudged reluctantly back towards her. My uniform was hanging on the cupboard door, the pleats on the skirt perfect, the blazer practically shining. I'd avoided looking at my uniform all summer. It was even greener than I remembered.

'All freshly ironed,' Mum said, looking pleased and proud. No one was happier that I was at Esther's than her. When she found out I'd got in, she cried. Actually we both cried, but mine were not happy tears.

'Thanks,' I said, taking the hangers.

'Are you excited about tomorrow?' She was smiling, and I wondered if she was being oblivious on purpose.

'Not really,' I said, but I injected a note of humour into my voice, to avoid a long 'don't disparage your opportunities' speech.

'It's a big year,' Mum said. The iron made a loud, squelching hissing noise, and she lifted it up. I suddenly realized she was ironing my father's pants.

'Mmmm,' I said, edging towards the door.

'It'll be a great one,' Mum continued happily, not even looking at me. 'I can already tell. Maybe they'll make you a prefect.'

This was unlikely. Being well behaved and getting good grades was not enough to set you apart at Esther's. The two prefects likely to be selected from my form were Tanisha, who'd started a feminist society in Year 9 and wanted to be prime minister, and Violet, who headed up the debating team and had campaigned successfully to get the school to go Fairtrade. Esther's was made for people like Tanisha and Violet. They didn't just achieve, which was expected to be a given for everyone, they thrived.

'Maybe,' I said. 'Don't be disappointed if I'm not though, OK?'

'I'll be disappointed at them, not you,' Mum replied, like this was any better.

Great, I thought. Another thing to worry about.

'I really hope you'll be focusing on your goals this year,' Mum said, looking up at me just as I tried to make my escape from the room. She was always big on goals.

I thought of the milestone list I'd mentally penned earlier on the bus. Boyfriend. Virginity. Significant Life Events.

'I am,' I said. 'Completely focused. Goodnight.'

Here's my theory on Significant Life Events: everyone has them, but some have more than others, and how many you have affects how interesting you are, how many stories you have to tell, that kind of thing. I was still waiting for my first one.

Not that I'm complaining, but my life up to the age of sixteen had been steady and unblemished. My parents were still married, my best friend had been constant for over ten years, I'd never been seriously ill and no one close to me had died. I'd also never won any major competition, been spotted for a talent (not that I had a talent) or really achieved anything beyond schoolwork.

This wasn't to say I hadn't been on the fringe of these kinds of events for other people. Rosie herself had had two, both bad. At two and a half her father walked out on her and her mother, never to be seen again. When she was eleven, her new baby sister, Tansy, was a cot-death victim. My older sister, Tarin, had been diagnosed with bipolar disorder at the age of eighteen, when I was ten, and the entire period of her diagnosis had been marked by dark clouds and tears and Serious Discussions. I'd experienced these latter two events from the middle of the storm, and had seen how they'd shaped the lives of two of my favourite people in the world.

Rosie and Tarin both thought my significant-life-event theory was ridiculous.

'Don't wish tragedy on yourself,' Tarin said. 'Or mental illness.' She didn't get it when I tried to explain that significant life events could be happy things as well. 'Like what?'

'Like getting married?' When her eyes went wide I added quickly, 'I mean in general, obviously, not for me any time soon.'

'God, Caddy, I hope you dream bigger than marriage as your life's significant event.'

Rosie was dismissive. 'They're just horrible things that happened, Cads. They don't make me more interesting than you.'

But the thing was, they did. The only interesting story I had to tell about my own life was that of my birth, which aside from my starring role as The Baby really had nothing to do with me. My parents, holidaying in Hampshire several weeks before my estimated arrival day, were stuck in a traffic jam in a little village called Cadnam when Mum went into labour. She ended up having me on the side of the road, with the help of a nurse who happened to be in another car.

This made a great story to pull out of the hat if I ever needed to, and I'd told it so many times ('Caddy's an interesting/weird/funny name. What's it short for?') I knew what kind of facial expressions to expect from the listener and the jokes they'd likely make ('Good thing they weren't driving through Croydon/Horsham/Slough! Ha!'). But that still didn't make it *mine*. I couldn't remember it, and it had no effect on my life. It was a significant event for my parents, not for me.

If anyone asked me for a story from my life in the present tense, I always went blank.

Of course I wasn't trying to invite tragedy into my life. I knew the takeaway from pain is sadness, not anecdotes. But everything about me and my life felt ordinary, hopelessly average, even clichéd. All I wanted was something of some significance to happen.

And then, so slowly at first I almost didn't notice it happening, it did.

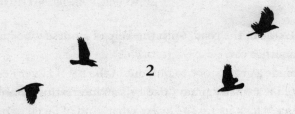

<u>Tuesday</u>

Rosie, 09.07: New girl alert.

Caddy, 10.32: ??

10.34: We have a new girl!

10.39: Really? Details please.

10.44: Her names Suzanne. Seems very cool. More later, maths now.

13.19: She just moved here from Reading. Takes same options as me! V funny.

13.20: I mean shes v funny, not the options thing.

13.28: Cool. How's everything else?

13.33: Same as. Call me tonight for chattage x

13.35: Will do x

<u>Wednesday</u>

08.33: I am on the bus and I just realized I forgot to brush my teeth.

08.37: Lovely!

10.38: Guess who isn't a prefect?

10.40: Is it you?

10.42: Yes.

10.43: WOOOHOOOOOO! *streamers*

10.44: Your support means the world to me.

13.01: You will always be PREFECT to me!

13.05: Um, thanks?

13.06: Geddit?

13.09: Yes!

13.11: HAHAHAHAHA. Suzanne says I shouldn't laugh because maybe you wanted to be prefect.

13.29: You told her?

13.33: Yeah! I told her you def didnt want to be prefect and I'm laughing in a good way.

13.35: Sz says all of the best people she knows aren't prefects.

13.40: Cads?

13.46: I def didn't want to be prefect. Mum wanted me to be though.

13.48: :(

13.49: We'll be not prefects together xx

Thursday

13.19: Nikki has clocked that Suzanne is cool. She tried to get her to sit with her at lunch.

13.25: Successfully?

13.27: No. Suzanne said she was good with me. Nikki said, you must have noticed she's a loser by now. Sz was like, wtf? and Nikki goes 'SERIOUSLY. I'm SAVING YOU.'

13.28: Bitch!!! Are you OK?

13.29: No. I'm crying in the toilets.

13.30: Want me to call you?

13.31: No.

13.31: Yes please.

Friday

09.01: What did you have for breakfast this morning?

09.02: Um, cereal?

09.03: Mum made me pancakes. I WIN!

13.12: Idea. How about I bring Suzanne with me when I come to yours after school? Then you can meet her!

13.42: Sure, OK.

13.43: Yay! You'll love her, she's amazing. We'll come straight over, probs be at yours at about 4.

13.58: See you then x

15.33: WEEKEND!!!

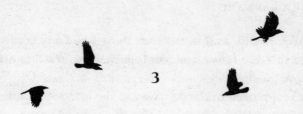

I'd planned to make it to my house before Rosie and Suzanne arrived, mainly because I tried to keep the amount of time Rosie saw me in my school uniform to an absolute minimum. She was lucky enough to have an ordinary uniform – black skirt, white shirt, black cardigan – and she had a tendency to laugh in my face if she ever caught me in mine.

So it was just my luck that I was pushing my key into my front-door lock when I heard the stamp of feet behind me and then there was Rosie, throwing herself up against the still-closed door and pushing her face right up close to mine.

'Hello!' she shouted, all smiles.

I had to laugh. 'Hi,' I said, twisting the key and opening the door. 'Any chance I can persuade you to stay out here while I go change?'

'Nope!' Rosie said, pushing herself in front of me and blocking the doorway. 'It's too late. We've both seen you now.' She gestured behind me. 'Suze, didn't I tell you it would be the greenest thing you've ever seen?'

I glanced behind me at the new girl, who was smiling. When our eyes met, she grinned. 'Hi!' She was effortlessly friendly, her voice upbeat and her face open. 'I'm Suzanne.'

'*Obviously* you're Suzanne,' Rosie said, rolling her eyes before turning and heading into my house, leaving the two of us on the doorstep. 'Who else would you be?'

'Hi,' I said, trying to match Suzanne's bright tone and failing. 'Um. I guess you know I'm Caddy.'

She nodded. 'Your house is really nice.'

'Thanks,' I said, as if it was something I had any control over. I stepped into the house and she followed me, moving aside so I could close the door.

Rosie reappeared in the doorway to the kitchen, holding three red cans. 'You drink Coke, right?' she said to Suzanne, waving one at her.

Suzanne glanced at me, as if wondering if she should ask permission.

'Don't mind her,' I said, taking one of the cans for myself and starting up the stairs. 'She thinks this is her house too.'

'It basically is.' Rosie sounded far more cheerful than she usually did after her first week back at school. By this point the previous year, she'd collapsed on my living-room sofa and refused to move.

In my room, Rosie pulled over my beanbag chair and sank into it, for some reason choosing not to take her usual spot beside me on my bed. Suzanne sat down next to her, her eyes flitting around. I saw her glance land on my battered poster from the old Disney film *The Rescuers* – a present from Tarin several years ago as a nod to a treasured childhood joke – and a bemused smile skittered across her face.

I tried to study her surreptitiously, this possible pretender to my best-friend throne, who was so not who I'd expected from Rosie describing her over the phone.

This was probably because, for all her talking over the last few days – and there had been a lot – she'd neglected to mention what for me was the most noteworthy thing: Suzanne was gorgeous. Not just pretty, or cute, or any other standard word, but full-on stunning. It wasn't just the blonde hair – far more natural looking than mine, to the point where it might even *be* natural – or the blue eyes, or even the fact that she was model slim. It was also her make-up and even the way she carried herself. I felt daunted by her, painfully aware of my unbrushed hair and my tendency to slouch, not to mention my hideous caricature of a school uniform. No wonder Rosie had described her as so confident. How could she not be, when she looked like that?

'So how do you like Brighton so far?' I asked, choosing the easiest question to start with and hoping it would be enough to fulfil my duty as friend of a friend.

'It's great,' Suzanne said, looking back at me and smiling. 'I was saying to Roz, you're both so lucky to have grown up here.'

I registered the use of 'Roz' and bit down on the inside of my lip to stop myself making a face.

'I told her it's overrated,' Rosie said.

'You've got a *beach*!' Suzanne replied with a laugh.

'A *pebble* beach!'

'There are worse places to grow up,' I said. 'You're from Reading, right?'

Suzanne raised her hand and wiggled it from side to side. 'Sort of. From when I was eight.' Anticipating my next question, she added, 'I was born in Manchester.'

That explained the not-Southern tinge to her accent.

'So how come you moved here?' I asked. 'Was it, like, a job thing?'

Her brow crinkled in confusion.

'I mean, did your parents get a new job or something?' I elaborated.

'Oh.' She looked uncomfortable. 'Actually it's my aunt that I live with.'

'Oh,' I said, not sure what to say next, apart from the obvious. I glanced at Rosie to see if this was news to her. Her unconcerned expression suggested not.

Another silence. I waited, hoping she'd reveal a bit more, but she said nothing. Rosie, apparently enjoying watching the two of us fumble for conversation, raised her eyebrows at me. I could see the ghost of a grin on her face.

'What does your aunt do?' I asked finally.

'She's a chef,' Suzanne said, brightening. 'She owns one of the cafes on Queen's Road. Muddles?'

'Oh yeah, I know it.' I'd walked past it once with my parents and my mother had commented that Muddles was a stupid name for a cafe. Dad, in a jaunty mood, had said it was a cosy name. We hadn't gone in.

'What do *your* parents do?' Suzanne asked me.

'My dad's a doctor,' I said, 'a consultant at the hospital. My mum's a communications manager for the Samaritans.'

Her eyebrows lifted, as people's tended to do when I mentioned my parents' respective careers. People assumed a lot when they heard 'doctor' or 'the Samaritans'. Words like 'saint' and 'hero' and 'selfless' and 'if only everyone was like them' tended to crop up.

The truth was more along the lines of a distracted and rarely glimpsed father and a world-weary, seen-it-all-before mother. From the evidence, they were great at their jobs. But that didn't necessarily make them golden human beings.

'What kind of consultant is your dad?' Suzanne asked, the kind of question people asked when they either couldn't think of anything else to say or just wanted to be polite.

'A & E,' I said.

She looked instantly impressed. 'Wow.'

'It's not as interesting as it sounds,' I said.

'All the best hospital shows are set in A & E,' Suzanne said knowledgeably. 'He must have some great stories.'

'If he does, I never hear them,' I said. 'He works a lot. Like, night shifts and stuff? So I don't really see him much.'

Suzanne made a face, no doubt because she had no response

to this as much as out of sympathy. There was another awkward pause, at which point Rosie finally took pity on us both and spoke up. 'Caddy's parents are great.' I looked at her, surprised. 'You know those people and you're like, oh yeah, you've got how to be human figured out.'

I laughed. 'Um, OK.'

'Seriously.' Rosie raised her eyebrows at me. 'I hope you're grateful.' She turned to Suzanne. 'When I was eleven, my baby sister Tansy died —' Suzanne's eyes went wide at this — 'and my mum had trouble coping, so I came to live with Caddy for a few weeks. So I know.'

'Rosie,' I said, 'that's very heavy information to just drop into a sentence.' Suzanne was still looking stunned.

'Your baby sister *died*?' she echoed. 'That's horrible.'

'Yeah, it was,' Rosie said, and even though her voice was casual I saw her shoulders square and her jaw tighten. These are things you only notice on a best friend. 'But the point of the story was Caddy's parents.'

'Roz,' I said.

'That's horrible,' Suzanne said again, her voice quiet. She was looking at the floor.

'Do *you* have any horrible life stories to tell?' Rosie asked. Her voice was cheerful, but it had a definite edge. For all her deliberate nonchalance, I knew she didn't like talking about Tansy. 'Caddy calls them Significant Life Events.'

'*Roz*.' My voice was sharper this time. She looked at me, pulling a deliberate innocent face. Sometimes I felt like I was *her* parent. Reining in Rosie.

Suzanne looked from me to Rosie, clearly wondering if she should speak. Finally she said, 'What counts as significant?'

'Moving house probably counts,' I said, trying to be generous. 'Nothing significant has ever happened to me. I'm dull.'

Suzanne looked at me a little oddly, and I realized too late that describing myself as dull on first meeting probably wasn't a good way to make friends. I opened my mouth to try to redeem myself, but my mind had gone blank. Oh well, I thought, resigning myself to her inevitable opinion of me. She's only Rosie's school friend. Who cares what she thinks?

4

'So. Got a boyfriend yet?'

Tarin arrived home on Sunday evening, tanned and beaming, sporting presents and a new tattoo (three birds in flight on the side of her left wrist). She'd been on a last-minute holiday with her own boyfriend, Adam, in Turkey and so had missed both my birthday and my first week of school.

'No,' I said flatly. 'I promise that I will text you if that happens.'

'When,' Tarin corrected promptly. '*When* it happens.'

I rolled my eyes, but I was smiling. It was hard not to smile around my sister when she was in a good mood. Erratic and vibrant, Tarin filled any room she was in. My most vivid memories of her from my childhood were whirlwinds of colour and excitement, punctured by impenetrable clouds of darkness, when nothing would bring her out of herself. She was calmer and more stable now, six years on from her diagnosis, but she was still Tarin, sister extraordinaire.

'Here,' she said, holding out a bag to me. 'It's not wrapped, sorry. Happy birthday.'

The bag contained a scarf: purple and silver, soft, beautiful. I pulled the material gently through my fingers. 'It's gorgeous. Thanks.' I lifted the scarf to my neck and tried to figure out how to wind it the way she always wore hers.

'Sixteen's a big one,' Tarin said. 'I can't believe you're sixteen. In my head you're still five years old.'

'Oh, great, thanks.' I had no idea what I was doing with the scarf. I leaned back to check my reflection to see if my attempt looked as stupid as it felt. My whole head seemed to have suddenly ballooned as my hair – a constant source of frustration – had bunched up underneath it. Said hair, of the slightly bushy variety, was artificially brightened with highlights, from the mousy colour it had dulled to from the blonde I was born with. No length seemed to distract from the bushiness; short made me look like I had a mane (and not in a good way), while long just gave me more to try and tame. As with so much else in my life, I'd settled for the that'll-do end of the spectrum and kept it shoulder-length. Usually I tied it back from my face and tried to forget about it.

I sighed. After I'd pulled my hair from under it, the scarf had become lopsided. I flicked it in annoyance and Tarin leaned across to adjust it for me. Tarin had a tendency to act more like a parent than a sister, given the eight-year age difference and my general lack of worldliness.

'Has Rosie got a boyfriend?'

'Not a proper one. She had a thing with some guy in her form, but that was only a few weeks.'

'I guess she's got more options than you.' She made a mock-sympathetic face. 'You poor thing, all cooped up in that oestrogen prison.'

I laughed. 'It's not that bad.'

'You're being deprived. It's an outrage. I told Mum and Dad, I said to them, don't make Caddy grow up without boys. It's a cruelty. But did they listen? Noooo.'

Tarin had gone to normal school, and by normal I mean neither single-sex nor private. Nobody had made Tarin wear a bright green blazer and knee-high socks. She'd been free to wear too much make-up and thread ribbons through her hair.

'I've decided that I'm definitely going to get one this year though,' I said, hoping that saying it out loud would somehow make it happen. 'A boyfriend.'

'Oh yeah?' Tarin's face broke into a grin. 'You've decided?'

I nodded. 'That's my goal for the year. And I'm going to have sex. And do something significant.'

'Don't all three of those count as the same goal?' she asked. 'Three birds, one stone? One boy to unlock the set of achievements? With his penis of significance?'

'You're teasing me.'

'I am. Well spotted.' She gave my hair an affectionate tug. 'So what are you going to do to make this happen?'

I paused.

'Because it's great that you've decided that that's what you want, but you should be trying to make it happen as well.' This was easy for her to say. Tarin never had to try to make anything happen.

'Mmm,' I said, starting to regret bringing it up.

'Not that I think you'll have any trouble,' she added quickly. 'Look, maybe you should do more out-of-school stuff. Meet new people.'

'Speaking of new people,' I said, seeing my opportunity to change the subject and taking it, 'there's a new girl in Rosie's form.'

'Yeah?' Tarin had taken my scarf and wound it around her own neck, fluffing out her light brown hair over it. It suited her far better than it did me.

'Rosie *loves* her,' I said.

'Does she?' She gave me a look, a small, knowing smile dancing on her face. 'Are you jealous?'

'Is it that obvious?'

She laughed. 'No, but I know you. You and Rosie are as inseparable as it is possible to be, and you managed it being in different schools for ten years. Now a new girl arrives right near the end of your educational chapter and Rosie likes her?' She made an exaggerated 'oh dear' face, then grinned. 'New people are always exciting. I wouldn't worry. It's the novelty, you know? Have you met her?'

'Yeah, on Friday.'

'What's she like?'

I hesitated. 'Nice.'

She made an incorrect buzzer noise. 'Try again with a word that means something.'

'She's very confident. But in a relaxed kind of way, not in a showy way.' I realized as I was speaking that this was close to identical to how Rosie had first described her over the phone. 'And funny. Sarcastic kind of funny. Oh, and she's really pretty.'

'Sounds unbearable.'

I had to laugh. 'She is *much* cooler than me.'

Tarin slapped my arm. 'Don't say things like that! As if cool matters.' Only people to whom cool comes easy, like Tarin herself, ever say things like this. 'Did you like her?'

I thought about it. 'I didn't *not* like her.'

'Did you *want* to like her?'

'Not really.'

'Maybe give her a chance at least? If Rosie likes her, she must be all right. And remember, it's only one week into the school year. They might not even be talking in a few weeks' time.'

I tried to remind myself of this later that evening, when I clicked on to Facebook and rolled my finger over my laptop's touchpad to look at my feed. I let my eyes follow the updates without really taking them in until they snagged on one. *Rosie Caron and Suzanne Watts are now friends.*

My chest gave a kick of completely irrational jealousy. Of course they'd be friends on Facebook. In fact it was kind of a surprise that it had taken this long. But still. I moved the cursor to hover over Suzanne's name, hesitated, and then clicked. This turned out to be pointless, as I could see absolutely nothing of her information, except her profile picture. I leaned forward to look at it more closely. She was with a girl and a boy, all of them dressed in an unfamiliar school uniform, and they were clinging on to each other in an overly exaggerated embrace. The photo had captured them mid-laugh.

I clicked back to Rosie's page and saw that Suzanne had posted a video on her wall. Feeling ridiculously nervous, I clicked on it. It was a puppy trying to get out of a tent, defeated by its own short legs. It was a cute video, but it made me relax because I knew – and Suzanne clearly *didn't* know – that Rosie didn't really like dogs. She should have chosen a video of a cat.

Feeling brighter, I shut my laptop and went to the bathroom to brush my teeth. I had ten years on this girl, and however interesting or cool she was, time was surely the biggest upper hand of them all.

5

By Wednesday, it was like the summer holidays had never happened. Daily life at Esther's was back in full swing and my homework schedule was already suffocatingly full. My supposedly optional after-school activities had once again taken over my free time. The old allegiances and grudges, built up over the last four years and sometimes even longer, had been reinstated.

My own friendship group had remained pretty much the same since Year 7, a somewhat disparate group of girls who didn't quite belong to any of the cliques. This suited me perfectly, because I already had Rosie and all I really wanted was a group I could fade comfortably into during school hours. Mishka, Allison, Kesh and I had formed our friendship in the first few days of Year 7 and had clung to each other ever since.

'The thing that you want to think about,' Kesh was saying as we waited in line at the canteen, 'is whether he's actually better than any of the other guys out there. And if he's not, what's the point?'

'That's irrelevant,' Mishka said. 'Other guys, whether they're "better" or not – and what does that even mean? – aren't viable options.'

'Why not?' Kesh demanded.

'Because they're not interested?' Mishka said, like it was obvious. We were talking about Ty, the boyfriend she'd spent most of her summer with despite the fact that he sounded like a bit of a prick.

'I'm sorry?' Allison said, her eyebrows raised. 'Are you

actually saying that the only reason you're with him is because there's no one else?'

'Obviously,' Mishka said flatly, and I laughed.

'Don't you like him at all?' Allison pressed.

Mishka shrugged. 'He's not bad. But I mean, I'm not going to marry him or anything. Caddy, can you pass me that chicken-salad wrap?'

I leaned over, grabbed the last wrap and handed it to her. A girl behind us let out a groan.

'It makes sense to me,' I said.

'Oh, not you too.' Kesh looked disappointed. 'You're supposed to have standards and force them on the rest of us.'

I rolled my eyes. Two years ago I'd refused the weed offered to me at Kesh's birthday party and had made sure none of my other friends smoked any. That had been during my pious phase and I probably wouldn't say no now, but none of them had ever let me forget it. I had become the moral one, and it was a reputation I couldn't figure out how to shake off.

'I'd take anyone who showed any interest in me,' I said. 'I'll start having standards when I'm lucky enough to have choices.'

'Exactly,' Mishka said. 'Thank you, Caddy.'

'You're all crazy,' Kesh declared.

'Excuse me, *I'm* not crazy,' Allison said. She'd been with her boyfriend for almost two years, and usually listened to these kinds of conversations with an annoying smile on her face.

'Well, can you tell Mish that she shouldn't waste time on little boys like Ty?' Kesh said, taking a bottle of water from the cabinet.

'Is that all you're having for lunch?' Allison asked instead, pointing at the side salad, which was the only other thing on her tray.

'You know what,' Mishka said quickly, when Kesh's face dropped ominously, 'you're probably right. Maybe Ty is a waste of time. But that's fine with me for now, OK?'

'Speaking of wasting time,' Allison said brightly, 'do you guys have plans this Friday? We could go to the cinema.'

'I'm seeing Rosie,' I said.

'Of course you are.' Allison made a face. 'What about you two?'

They made plans together as I dug my fork into my spaghetti. I'd never felt much like I was missing out when they spent social time together without me. Rosie had been around long before they'd entered my life, and I knew she'd be there after they'd left it. That was the security of a best friend, and that meant everything.

On Thursday, ten minutes before her 9 p.m. phone curfew, Rosie called. 'Hey!' she said when I took the phone from my mother. 'Just a quick one.'

'Hey,' I said. 'How are—'

'Can't talk long,' Rosie interrupted. 'Just wanted to tell you there's a change of plans for tomorrow night. Luke's parents are away for the weekend so he's having a party. Me and Suze are going, and she's going to stay at mine after.'

'Oh,' I said.

'I'll see you on Saturday evening maybe? Or Sunday?'

'OK. Um, who's Luke?'

'From our form. His brother is in the sixth form, so it should be amazing.' She sounded giddy.

'I thought you hated those kinds of things.'

'No, you're thinking of you.' *Ouch.* 'There'll be alcohol, so it'll be fine. Hey, you want to come? You should come!'

'I won't know anyone.' I'd tried going to parties with Rosie's friends in the past, and it hadn't exactly gone well. I was too anxious and awkward around people I didn't know, and so usually ended up trailing after Rosie for the whole night. It was not fun for either of us. She hardly ever asked me any more.

'You mean except me, Suze and all my other friends you've met loads of times before?'

'I've got Service on Saturday morning,' I said, referring to a compulsory Esther's community-service initiative and feeling a jolt of relief for having come up with a legitimate excuse. 'I can't really turn up hungover.'

'So don't drink.'

'Roz.' *As if.*

'OK, OK. Are you sure? It'll be fun. Plus, how do you think you're going to get a boyfriend sitting at home?'

That's the downside of telling your best friend everything. They remember it. 'Maybe next time.'

'Are you OK? Are you pissed off?'

'No, it's fine.' *I'll just watch TV with my parents.*

'Hey, how about you come round to mine after school tomorrow while we get ready? We'll order pizza, and we won't be leaving till about nine, so . . .'

A pity invite.

'Um, maybe. I'll think about it.'

'Think about it quickly. I've literally got about a minute left.'

Pity pizza versus TV with my parents.

'OK, sure,' I said finally, already regretting it.

'Great, come here at about five. Hey, go with Suze! Her aunt is driving her, and I bet she'll pick you up. I'll tell her.'

'Wait—'

'OK, time's up. See you tomorrow! Bye!'

For all Rosie had said about them getting ready together, Suzanne was already dressed to the nines when she and her aunt Sarah picked me up. I was wearing a hoodie and black capris, and I eased into the back seat feeling foolish and plain.

'You look nice,' I said to her.

Suzanne turned in her seat and beamed at me, her fingers on the headrest. 'Thanks!' The seat belt strained at her shoulder. 'Did you change your mind yet?'

'Nope,' I said, feeling even worse. Had she thought I was going to? It hadn't even occurred to me.

Sarah reached out and tapped Suzanne's knee. 'Can you sit properly? You're making me nervous.'

'I'm fine,' Suzanne replied without moving. 'I trust your driving skills.' She leaned further against the back of her seat, glancing around me. 'Didn't you bring any stuff?'

'What stuff?'

Her face fell. She looked genuinely disappointed. 'Are you really not coming?'

'No,' I said awkwardly. 'I'm just coming for the pizza.'

'Oh.' She looked confused. Obviously the idea that someone wouldn't jump at the chance to go to a party full of strangers was alien to her. We were clearly never going to be friends.

'I don't know anyone,' I said, feeling like I needed to explain myself. 'Plus I've got Service tomorrow.'

'Service? What's that?'

'It's a programme that Esther's runs,' I explained. 'It's like community service.'

She looked appalled. 'And you have to do that *every* Saturday? Aren't you allowed to have a *life* at that school?'

'Suzie,' Sarah said chidingly, but there was a laugh in her voice.

'It's just one Saturday a month,' I said quickly. 'But no, now you mention it.'

The car jolted to a stop at the traffic lights, and Suzanne's head jerked forward. 'Ouch,' she said.

Sarah reached out her hand again and pushed her palm

playfully against Suzanne's face until she gave in and sat properly. For the last few minutes of the drive, I watched the back of Suzanne's head. Her hair had been mussed slightly by Sarah's fingers, causing blonde wisps to escape from her high ponytail. Just below the ponytail, partially hidden by the thin straps of the top she was wearing, I could see a scar snaking from the back of her neck, curving towards her right shoulder.

'Call me tomorrow when you want me to pick you up,' Sarah said to Suzanne as we pulled up outside Rosie's house.

'I'll just get the bus,' Suzanne said lightly.

'No,' Sarah said, patient but firm. 'Call me and I'll pick you up.'

Suzanne made a face as if she was about to protest, then thought better of it. 'Fine. But don't blame me if I drag you away from something more exciting.'

'What's more exciting than you?' Sarah asked teasingly. I wondered how old she was. Somewhere in her thirties maybe? Something about the way they talked to each other made me feel like they didn't know each other that well, as if they were just practising their niece and aunt roles. 'Hey, have a good time, OK?' She reached into her pocket and produced a ten-pound note. 'Emergency money. Which I expect back when I see you tomorrow.'

Suzanne pocketed the cash, turning in her seat to me. 'Ready?'

'Thanks for the lift,' I said to Sarah, opening the car door.

'No problem. Nice to meet you, by the way.'

Unsure what to say to this, I smiled and nodded on my way out of the car. Suzanne swung her bag over her shoulder and looked expectantly at me. She was wearing tight dark jeans with a glittery cami top and heels. She could have passed for eighteen easily.

'You look amazing,' I couldn't help saying, even though a

second compliment really wasn't necessary.

'Thanks!' she said again, unfazed. I started towards Rosie's house and she followed.

'How did you learn to do your make-up like that?'

Suzanne shrugged. 'YouTube videos? I just experiment a lot really. It's easy.'

It is not easy.

'I can show you,' Suzanne offered. 'I used to do my friends' make-up all the time.'

'Maybe,' I said vaguely.

Rosie was still wearing her school uniform when she opened the door to let us in. Skipping any greetings, she brandished a Papa John's menu at us, beaming. 'Mum says so long as we get a Veggie Supreme for her, we can have whatever we want.' She stopped waving the menu and looked at me. 'You didn't bring clothes?'

'I told you I'm not going out,' I said, trying to quash a rising irritation.

'I thought you might change your mind.' She jutted out her bottom lip in an exaggerated pout. Then she glanced at Suzanne. 'Oh my God, I love that top. You both have to help me decide what to wear.'

The 'both' was generous. It seemed unlikely to me that I'd have anything to offer in this area. Why would she ask me when Suzanne was right there? It would be like choosing an emu over a flamingo.

I was right. While Suzanne and Rosie played dress-up with Rosie's entire wardrobe, I sat on the bed and fattened myself up on pizza, reading an old issue of *Glamour* magazine and contributing nothing but 'hmmms'.

To her credit, though probably more to do with best-friend loyalties than my dazzling fashion sense, Rosie tried, pulling a sequinned top out of the wardrobe and holding it up in my direction. 'Do you think I can wear this again so soon after your birthday?'

'Sure,' I said. 'It's not like it's the same people.'

'Good point. Jeans or a skirt?' She directed the question at Suzanne, who shrugged.

'What do you feel like?'

'Jeans.' Rosie said, as I'd known she would. She took a pair from the wardrobe shelf and shook them out. 'Turn around, Suze. And just don't look, Cads.'

Suzanne turned away obediently, met my gaze and made a ridiculous face. Despite myself, I laughed.

'You better not be laughing at me,' Rosie said over her shoulder. 'OK. What do you think?' She spread out her arms and leaned slightly so I could see the full outfit. Suzanne turned back around.

'Perfect,' she said, smiling.

Rosie looked at me hopefully. I gave her a thumbs up. 'Great!' She looked relieved. 'I'm going to get shoes. Be right back.'

When she was gone, Suzanne sat carefully down on the bed next to me and took a slice of pizza. 'What are you going to do tonight?'

Nothing. 'I'm not sure,' I hedged, trying to think of an answer that wasn't pathetic. *Oh God, maybe I should just go.* Maybe it would be better this time, now I was sixteen. Maybe . . . an image came into my head of me trailing awkwardly after Rosie, except this time she was giggling and talking to Suzanne, who was not trailing after anyone and was definitely not awkward. *God, no.* It wouldn't be better. It would be even worse.

'You should come next time. When you don't have your Service thing the next day.' Her face was open and friendly, but I felt a surge of annoyance. Why did she get to be the one inviting me places? Shouldn't it be the other way around?

'I definitely will,' I lied.

She smiled at me, but a jolt of paranoia stopped me smiling back. Had Rosie told her I didn't like parties? Was she pitying me? Or worse, secretly laughing at me? Before I could say anything else, Rosie came back into the room, carrying a pair of glittery silver flats. 'Do you think I should straighten my hair?'

'No,' I said. Rosie's small, bird-like face needed all the volume it could get. When she straightened her curls it made her head look even smaller.

'It looks nice wavy,' Suzanne said. 'Do you have any mousse?'

'Mum might,' Rosie said thoughtfully, fluffing up her hair in the mirror.

The two of them began an animated conversation about hairstyles and I zoned out, watching my best friend talk. Rosie was twirling a few dark strands around in her fingers speculatively and it occurred to me that the two of us rarely had conversations like this. Maybe she'd been missing it.

By the time they were ready to leave, Suzanne had put Rosie's hair up into an elaborate plaited bun and done her make-up, transforming her into a completely different person. If she could work that kind of magic on me, maybe she was worth having around.

Later Rosie's mother drove the three of us first to my house to drop me off. She kept catching my eye in the rear-view mirror and smiling as Rosie and Suzanne giggled beside me, as if she could see right into my head.

'I'll talk to you tomorrow?' Rosie said to me as we pulled up at my house.

'Sure,' I said. 'Have fun!'

'You have fun too,' she grinned at me, her voice teasing.

'Ha ha,' I said, shutting the door.

Before they'd even driven away, Rosie had already turned

back to Suzanne and they were both laughing. I looked at my house, sighed and headed in for a fun night alone.

22.47: CADNAM OH MY GOD
22.49: What?
22.52: WHAT????
22.57: I LOVE YOU!!
22.59: OK. I love you too.
23.01: xxxxxxxxxx
23.29: Suze thinnks you dont like herr
23.31: Of course I like her
23.32: Thats what i said!!!
00.19: Ommmgggghh im a bit drunk
00.22: Yes you are.
00.36: shit mums comin and i cant find suze.
00.38: do u kno where she iss?
00.39: No
00.48: in the car goin home. found suze. SLEEPY.
00.50: Night night, talk to you tomorrow x
00.53: NIGHT x

When I woke up in the morning, I had five missed calls and three voicemails. Snuggling deeper into my pillow, I put my phone to my ear to listen.

'Caddddyyyy! Oh my God, why is your phone on silent, you LOSER? We want to talk to youuu! WAKE UP.'

'HI, it's Suze. Rosie says wake up, wake up. HEY – maybe she's waking up right now and she can't call us back 'cause we're on the phone. Maybe we should—'

'It's us again!' Rosie's voice. 'We are just saying, "HELLO, SLEEPY," and "GOOD MORNING" for when you wake up! LOVE YOU, night night night!'

I looked at my screen again after I'd finished listening. Just gone 9 a.m. I was pretty sure they'd both still be sleeping, but I rang Rosie anyway.

When it clicked through to voicemail, I put on my loudest, brightest voice. 'Good MORNING. How is your HEAD? Hope you had fun! Call me later. And I love you too, even when you're a drunken moron.'

At half past ten I arrived at Pathways, the assisted-living facility I'd never even heard of before I got it as my Service assignment for the term. I spent most of my morning making tea for the real members of staff and watching the news. I left at lunchtime, my Service timetable dutifully signed by the manager, who didn't even know my name, and headed home, pulling out my phone and calling Rosie, who picked up on the second ring.

'Hey!' I said. 'I'm done with Service.'

'How did it go?'

'Oh, fine. How was last night? Is Suzanne still with you?'

'It was good. No, she left about an hour ago.'

'Did you have fun?'

'Yeah! More when we first got there and we were getting drunk and stuff. But she kind of disappeared after an hour or so. I still had fun though.'

'What do you mean, disappeared?' I stopped at the traffic lights, tapping the button with my fingers, watching the light change.

'She went off with Chris, this guy from the sixth form.'

'She left you on your own?'

'Oh no, I was with Lev and Maya.' Levina and Maya were, before Suzanne at least, Rosie's closest friends from school. 'And Ollie was hanging around a bit.'

'Oh, was he now?' I said, raising my eyebrows even though she couldn't see me. 'I hope you told him to get lost.'

There was a silence.

'Rosie!' I scolded.

'I'd had a lot to drink, OK?' she said, defensive. 'And it was kind of nice to have him being all interested for once. Anyway, that's not what I was going to tell you.'

'I think you getting off with your sort-of ex is worth talking about,' I said, stepping around an unnecessarily large pram that a harassed-looking woman had pushed directly into my path.

'Oh please. He's hardly an ex. When I have an ex worth talking about I hope I'll have done more than kiss him. Anyway. When we were drinking, before she went with Chris, me and Suze talked a lot and *she –*' she paused dramatically – 'has had *sex*.'

'Really?' I tried to figure out what I should do with my voice. Should I be surprised? Impressed? Was I either of these things?

'With *more than one guy*.'

'Wow,' I said, and then felt ridiculous. I sounded like a twelve-year-old.

'I know!' Rosie said, making me feel better. 'I'm not sure she'd have told me if we hadn't had tequila.'

'You had tequila?' I *was* surprised now. When we drank, it was usually alcopops and fruit ciders, or syrupy sweet shots that tasted mostly of sugar. Straight spirits were still too much for me.

'Yes, and it was disgusting. I almost threw up.' She paused. 'I actually kind of did. Anyway! She was a lot more chatty after that; usually she's quite guarded.'

'Did she tell you why she lives with Sarah?' I asked.

'No, I didn't ask.'

That would have been the first thing out of my mouth. 'Why not?'

'Because we were talking about sex, Caddy!'

'All right, sorry. So, how many guys?'

'Two.'

'Oh, when you said more than one guy I thought you were going to say it was five or something.'

'No, she's not like that.'

I thought of all the girls I knew who'd had sex. There were the girls at my school, like Olivia, who wore their skirts as short as humanly possible and snuck cigarettes outside the school gates and did everything they could to prove they weren't private girls' school clichés, seemingly unaware they were ticking every clichéd box. I only knew two girls my age who weren't virgins and didn't fit that same mould: Allison, who'd been with her boyfriend Sammy for almost two years, and Chessy, my cousin, who was also in a long-term relationship.

'Did you get the losing-virginity story?' I asked, trying to decide which category Suzanne would fit into.

'No, we're not that close, and she wasn't that drunk. She did say she's never had a proper boyfriend though.'

I squinted into the empty space in front of me, trying to revise my categorizations to make them fit.

'I can hear you being judgemental,' Rosie said suddenly, and I had to laugh.

'I was just thinking about Chessy.'

'You don't have to be "I-love-you-forever" in love to have sex, you know,' Rosie said, her voice annoyingly preachy, as if this was something I didn't already know. 'Sometimes liking a guy is enough. And sometimes you just want to get it over with.'

'So Suzanne got it over with twice?' I snarked, surprising myself. Maybe I really was judgemental. Or jealous. I'd had to set myself a goal to even *try* to have sex, and she'd already been there done that with two different guys.

'Caddy! Don't make me wish I hadn't told you.'

'As if you wouldn't tell me,' I laughed. 'So, anyway.' It seemed like a good time to change the subject. 'Where did you leave things with Ollie?'

'Nowhere, it was just a silly drunk thing. Hey, want to come over for dinner? Mum's making enchiladas, and we can watch crappy TV.'

'I can't tonight. Seeing my gran, remember?'

'Oh.'

'Tomorrow?'

'Mum wants to take me to a talk at the Dome. It's on feminism. Want to come? There might be tickets left.'

'Um. No, thanks.' As far as I was concerned, I got enough of that at school. 'I guess I'll see you next weekend?'

'OK.'

The disappointment in her voice was a relief. I hadn't been entirely replaced yet.

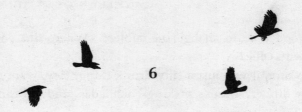

6

Despite what Tarin had said, Suzanne's novelty showed no signs of wearing off for Rosie over the next few weeks and, to make things worse, Rosie seemed to be trying her hardest to push the two of us into friendship. On one of my rare afternoons with no after-school clubs or activities to endure, Rosie suggested we played badminton, and then blindsided me by bringing Suzanne with her. And, just to make things worse, they were late.

As if bringing a third person along for what was most definitely a two-player game wasn't bad enough, it turned out Suzanne couldn't even play. Rosie seemed oblivious to my annoyance, but Suzanne caught on almost immediately.

'I can just watch,' she offered, looking nervous. 'Is there somewhere I can sit and watch?'

'On badminton courts?' I asked, hearing the snide tone in my voice, unfamiliar and unkind.

'Don't be silly,' Rosie said easily. 'We'll teach you to play. It's really easy, right, Cads?' She smiled at me. 'It'll be fun to do something a bit different. It'll be way better than just the two of us.'

She had taken to saying things like this a lot, and I wished she'd stop.

One particularly low point came in early October. I stayed after school until almost 6 p.m. working on the set design for the school production – *My Fair Lady* – with Mishka and a few other girls from my art class. Just before I left, I tripped over the stepladder and spilled paint down myself. When I got home, Mum shouted at me for being clumsy and careless, and I eventually ended up sulking in my bedroom. All of this aside, my real mistake was logging on to Facebook, where Suzanne had just tagged Rosie in a series of pictures with her and other classmates at the Globe theatre. They were decked out in full Shakespearean gear and they looked ridiculous, but utterly happy.

I was clicking through the pictures, my throat getting tighter on each, until I landed on one of Suzanne and Rosie, arms around each other, beaming. A gigantic turquoise hat with an unnecessarily large feather was balanced across their two heads, which were bent towards each other. Suzanne had tagged the photo 'Lady Rosanna Caronforth and Lady Susannah Wattsimus'. Rosie had commented, '17th century besties.' Suzanne added, 'Innit. Forsooth.'

I bawled until I was hoarse.

Here's the really stupid thing: I didn't actually dislike Suzanne. In fact, I probably would have *liked* her if I wasn't so terrified about losing my best friend to her. She was sarcastic and hilarious and fun to be around, but she was also friendly – far friendlier to me than I'd been to her, and probably friendlier than I deserved. I could see why Rosie wanted the three of us to be friends, but I resented her trying so hard.

And there was something else. For someone as extroverted and chatty as Suzanne, she was surprisingly reticent when it came to talking about herself. Or, more accurately, herself pre-Brighton. I still had no idea why she'd even moved here. Not that I was expecting her to offer this information to me – still a relative stranger – but I couldn't even get it second-hand, because Rosie didn't know either.

I couldn't shake the feeling that something was off, even though Rosie claimed not to care. Why did Suzanne live with her aunt, and why did she never mention the rest of her family? If the subject came up she'd answer whatever question it was so casually it was easy to miss – 'Siblings? Yeah, a brother, he's twenty.' – and then change the subject or make a joke. It always took me at least a minute to catch up with what she'd just said, and by then it was too late to go back. It was the artful way she did this, so clearly practised and finely tuned, that really got to me. She had to be hiding something big, and what could be so bad that she couldn't just tell us what it was?

Half-term seemed to come out of nowhere, like always. My two-week holiday felt long overdue, but I was still impatient for the first week to pass, so I could be joined by my non-private-school friends. The extra week off was definitely a perk, but sometimes I felt, like with so many perks of the private-school life, that it was wasted on me.

Towards the end of the first week of freedom I went to a party at Luca Michaelson's house. He was one of the St Martin's private-school boys everyone knew, and his parties were the stuff of adolescent legend. I'd never been to one, mainly because I'd never been invited, but this time Kesh practically forced me into a dress and dragged me along with her, Allison and Mishka. The really shocking thing in all of this was that I had a good time. I drank vodka and Coke and knocked back shots when they were handed to me. I kissed a skinny boy called Jonny who tasted of cigarettes but had told me I was pretty. I sat in the bathroom with Mishka while she sobbed about her ex and held back her hair when she threw up. I thought, in one of those moments of drunken clarity, Maybe I'm good enough by myself.

In the morning, waking up on Luca's living-room floor with Kesh using my legs as a pillow, I tried to hang on to this feeling. I imagined cutting myself loose from Rosie, leaving her with

Suzanne. I could add the prefix 'best' to my friendship with Mishka and Kesh, and even Allison. It would be easy.

But then I looked at my phone.

22.09: Hope your having a gd time! Take a pic so I can see the dress. Miss you x

22.11: Dont get toooo drunk, OK?

23.49: You just called me and hung up. Are you OK? Call me back plz xx

23.56: Cads? Pick up your phone xxxx

00.03: I never knew how hiliarous you are when your drunk OMG. You should get like this every weekend. CALL ME when you wake up so I can tell you all the stupid things you said. Love you to pieces, you drunkard.

I was so busy smiling at these texts that it took me a moment to realize there was another message from someone else waiting for me. I clicked on it, expecting Tarin, and saw Suzanne's name. For a moment I was confused, and then realized that her message was a reply to one from me.

'Shit,' I whispered out loud. A big part of me wanted to delete both messages without even looking at them.

23.46: Why do you have to be soooo perfect?

I felt a flush of pure embarrassment so acute I actually lifted a hand and tugged at my hair. Oh *God*. I tried to tell myself it could have been worse. Somehow.

23.59: Um. Thanks? :/

I felt a little sick, and not just because I was hungover. My fingers hovered over the keypad, trying to figure out how to respond. I couldn't just ignore it surely, much as I wanted to.

08.37: Oh God. I was drunk! I'm sorry, don't even know what I was talking about.

Her reply didn't come through for another couple of hours, when I was sitting in McDonald's with Mishka and Kesh. I had to force myself to look.

10.59: Haha, no worries. One day you'll get why I laughed so much when I saw it. Hope you're not too hungover! See you later x

So she got to be magnanimous *and* mysterious, and I was the drunken embarrassment. Great. I pushed my phone back into my bag without replying and took a sip of milkshake, trying to bring back the feeling I'd had from the night before, that sense of possibility in myself. It didn't work.

What I always thought of as the 'real' half-term — that is, the week that Rosie was also off school — was well underway when I stayed over at Rosie's house. It was the Tuesday night, and it was just the two of us. Suzanne planned to meet us the following day, with some of their other friends from school.

Rosie was in the bathroom, getting ready for bed, and I had seized the opportunity to do some quality stalking. As I'd hoped, she'd left her Facebook logged in. Squashing any guilt, I typed Suzanne's name into the search bar and then clicked on it when it appeared.

Her page unfolded before me, full of updates and pictures and messages. She'd changed her profile picture since I'd tried to look a few weeks ago; now it was just her, holding a dog. I scrolled down slowly, looking over the messages. Most were obviously from friends from her old school, because they were variants of 'miss you!' I noted that earlier that day Rosie had posted a photo of a rabbit wearing a pair of round sunglasses. For some reason Rosie had captioned this: 'It's you!' Suzanne had written, 'Oh, shush, you.' Five people had 'liked' it.

Directly below the photo, a message caught my eye.

Ellie Lewis Zanne, have you been watching Corrie?
Suzanne Watts Yes :/
Ellie Lewis ☹ Are you OK? I can't believe they didn't put a
    trigger warning on it or something!
Suzanne Watts Yeah. I'll call you, OK?
Ellie Lewis Oh yeah, sorry xxx

*

This was such an odd exchange that I read over it a couple of times. It made no sense to me, which was to be expected because I had no idea who Ellie was and I didn't watch *Coronation Street*. Plus I didn't know what trigger warnings were. I was about to click on Ellie's name to take my creepy jealous-friend stalking to a new level when I heard the shower turn off.

I clicked back on to Rosie's home screen and slumped back on the bed, pulling out my phone. I tapped 'trigger warning' into the search and scrolled through the results, which only confused me more. The top entry was, bewilderingly, something to do with feminism. A couple of entries below that, a Wikipedia entry for Trauma Triggers. I opened the page and scanned the first line.

'What are you looking at?' Rosie asked, coming out of the bathroom in her pyjamas, a towel wrapped around her head.

'Just Facebook,' I lied, turning my screen off. Trauma triggers: experiences that trigger traumatic memories. Trigger warnings: brief messages that appeared before content deemed to be potentially triggering.

I was turning these definitions over in my mind, trying to match them to what I knew of Suzanne, when Rosie flopped on to the bed next to me and grinned.

'Stalking a certain Jonny?'

'Guilty as charged,' I said, even though I hadn't thought about Jonny for days.

'You can do better,' she promised, which was nice if not exactly true. 'Here,' she said, pulling her laptop over and opening Facebook, 'let me show you Liam.' Her current crush, a football player from the year above who'd smiled at her during assembly.

I looked at the pictures and made all the right noises, but my mind was working overtime. *Trauma*. What kind of trauma? And what did it have to do with Suzanne? Surely finding out what was happening in *Coronation Street* would help me answer this, but when I tried quickly Googling it on my phone while I was meant to be brushing my teeth, the top results were all about an actor who'd just been arrested for drink driving. I couldn't figure out how to ask Rosie without giving myself away, so I decided I'd wait for an opening in the conversation the following day, when there was group of us to hide in.

I can try and pretend that I just didn't realize that bringing up a subject I'd learned was potentially 'triggering' for Suzanne in front of her friends wasn't a particularly nice thing to do.

But that would be a lie.

The following day Rosie and I arrived at the American diner on the seafront at lunchtime, a few minutes late because we'd missed the bus. Suzanne, Levina and Maya were already there, saving us a booth, talking animatedly. Suzanne was gesturing with her hands, and they were all laughing.

'Hello!' Rosie sang out, throwing herself into the booth.

'Hey,' Suzanne said, grinning at us.

'Charlie text me,' Levina said to Rosie. 'He's going to meet us later, with his friends.'

'Cool,' Rosie said. 'What were you guys talking about?'

'Suzanne's incredibly successful date with Alex,' Maya said, smirking.

'And by incredibly successful,' Suzanne said, taking a sip from her cup, 'she means a complete disaster.'

'What happened?' Rosie asked.

'He's just an idiot. I mean, we had an OK time. We just went to the beach, and he was telling me about his *band*.' She made a face. 'Who sound crap, by the way. They're modelling themselves on the Smiths. I was, like, aren't you a bit young to try and be the Smiths? And he got all huffy and said that Morrissey was universal.'

'That should have been your first clue,' Maya said.

'I know that now! Anyway, it turned out the band is actually his brother's, and Alex is basically the guy who carries the amps and stuff. So I was ready to forgive him for that, but then he started talking about *Grand Theft Auto* instead, and I just about died. I kissed him just to get him to shut up.'

'Oh, Suze,' Rosie said, rolling her eyes.

'It was worth it. He was actually pretty good at it. But anyway, that's not the disaster bit. So I go home, and later that night he texts me. At first he's being normal, and then, I swear out of nowhere, he says to me, "Send me a picture of your boobs."'

'*What?*' Rosie and I said at the same time.

'I know! It's, like, learn to read the signs, dude.'

'What did you say?'

'What do you think I said? I said no! And so he tried to be all "ohh, I won't tell anyone, please". Really pathetic.'

'God, this is so disappointing,' Levina said, looking sad. 'I thought he was cool. You're ruining the illusion.'

'Ruining the illusion is a public service,' Suzanne said just as the waitress arrived.

We ordered our food even though I'd barely glanced at the menu, and waited until the waitress was out of earshot before starting up the conversation again.

'Tell them about the Snapchat,' Maya urged. She was grinning.

Suzanne was pressing her lips together, clearly trying to suppress a laugh. 'So, after I'd said no a few times, he Snapchatted me a picture of his dick.'

'*What?*' Rosie and I shrieked this time, and our whole table burst out laughing, so loud that people at other tables turned to look at us.

'I *know*,' Suzanne said. 'I couldn't believe it either. And it was like *this*.' She held her hands in the gesture I recognized she'd been making when we first walked in, indicating, I presumed, a small penis. 'Definitely not picture material. Which I guess is why he Snapchatted it.' She sighed. 'The real sad thing is that it was a Snapchat, so I can't even show you.'

'What a shame,' Maya said, deadpan.

'And then he says, "You can Snapchat your boobs." And I said, "I'll Snapchat your face," and he thought I was *flirting* with him, because then he really did send me a Snapchat of his face. And then I gave up and just stopped replying.'

'Have you heard from him since?' I asked.

'He sent me a few after I stopped replying, basically calling me a bitch.' She seemed unconcerned about this. 'The moral is, I wasted my time, which would have been better spent with you guys.' She was looking at me as she said this, smiling her usual friendly smile.

I smiled back, but all I could think was, *Trauma triggers: experiences that trigger traumatic memories.* It just didn't make sense. How could anyone who'd been in any way traumatized be so bright and cheerful? I watched her face as she turned to Maya, lifting her hands to illustrate some new joke she was making, scanning for hints. But there was nothing. Just her, all smirks and eye rolls and wisecracks. The picture of ordinary happiness.

After our food arrived and the conversation lulled, I decided to go for it. 'So, what's going on in *Corrie* at the moment?'

'You don't watch *Corrie*,' Rosie said. I noticed, out of the corner of my eye, Suzanne lift her straw to her teeth and begin chewing on it, her face passive.

'I know,' I said. 'But I saw some stuff about it on Facebook. I'm just curious.'

'Yeah, there's supposed to be this big controversial storyline,' Maya said, 'but it's not that controversial really.'

'It's been building for ages,' Levina added. 'Weeks.'

Maya nodded. 'It was getting pretty boring. Denise has this new boyfriend, Dave, see, and her daughter, Clarise, who's, what, fifteen?'

'Fourteen,' Levina chirped.

'Fourteen. She doesn't like him. And he doesn't like her either. They've been having fights and stuff.'

'Clarise is a bitch,' Rosie said. She speared a chunk of tomato. 'Dave is trying really hard, and she keeps winding him up and stuff.'

'Anyway, on Thursday, they had this big fight when Denise was at work,' Maya continued. 'And Clarise said that Dave was . . . what was it?'

'Pathetic and past it,' Levina supplied without hesitation.

'And Dave slapped her,' Maya finished. 'That's the big drama they've been leading up to.'

'It was more of a punch than a slap,' Levina said. 'It was like . . .' She lifted her hand and made an odd punching motion, but without a proper fist.

Rosie laughed. 'What was that?'

'Yeah, it didn't really look like that, did it?' Levina grinned and shrugged. 'It was more than a slap though. That's why the producers made such a big deal about it.'

'Same thing,' Maya said dismissively. 'I think you're supposed to feel sorry for Clarise, but seriously? She deserved it. She's been such a bitch to him.'

My heart was pounding a strange, tense rhythm in my chest and my hands were clammy. I was starting to feel like I'd made a huge mistake bringing up this topic. The whole time they'd been speaking, Suzanne had sat in silence, watching them, her face completely blank – *too* blank. But when Maya made this comment, Suzanne's whole face flinched and she closed her eyes for longer than a blink.

When she opened her eyes again, she caught me looking at her. Her eyes squinted slightly, clearly taking in the odd expression that I must have been making, then relaxed. I watched her rearrange her face into something normal again, like the flash of pain hadn't even happened.

'You can't say things like that,' Levina scolded Maya, but her voice was playful rather than serious. None of them had noticed Suzanne's changed mood. 'He's a grown man, and he did hit her, even if it was kind of more a slap.'

'Oh, please,' Maya said, rolling her eyes. 'If she didn't want to get a slap, she shouldn't have wound him up.'

'That sounds like a horrible storyline,' I said.

Rosie reached over and took a fry from my plate. 'It's a soap – what did you expect? Do you know how many serial killers they've had in that one street? This is boring compared to those storylines.'

'Maybe it'll get more interesting,' Levina said.

'Maybe Clarise will finally shut up,' Maya said. The three of them laughed.

Suzanne stood up abruptly, which was a feat considering she was bunched up in the corner of the booth.

'I'll be back in a sec,' she said.

'Want me to move?' Levina asked.

'No, it's fine,' Suzanne replied, already climbing over the back of her seat.

I watched her walk past the toilets, through the restaurant and straight out the front door. My stomach dropped and for a moment I thought I might be sick.

'Can I have some of your milkshake?' Maya leaned forward, her hand already reaching for my cup.

'Sure,' I said distractedly. I stood up. 'I'll be back in a sec.'

Rosie raised her eyebrows at me. 'Everything OK?'

'Brain freeze,' I said, pointing at the milkshake. This didn't really make much sense, but I was away from the booth before any of them could question me further.

It was so windy my hair flew right into my face the second I walked outside. I tried to claw it back around my ears, looking around for Suzanne. For a few moments I couldn't see her, and then I realized she was on the other side of the road. Her back was to me, but her blonde head was unmistakable.

I crossed over the road with the usual crowds, trying as I went to think of the best thing to say. Should I open with an apology? Admit that I'd orchestrated the conversation but hadn't realized what the outcome would be? I'd never seen her angry or upset. What if she was the confrontational kind? What would I do?

When I was inches away from her back I still hadn't thought of what to say. She was leaning stomach-first against the railing, looking out to the sea. Her right hand was clutching her phone to her ear.

'Will you please come and get me?' she was saying. Her voice was strange, and it took me a moment to realize that that was because she was crying. I'd made her *cry*. 'I know, but I can't.'

As she said this, she glanced behind her, as if sensing my presence. When she saw me, she did a double take. Into the phone she said, 'Five minutes? OK, ten. I'll be there. Thanks.' She lowered the phone from her ear and slid it into the pocket of her jeans. Her eyes were still on me.

This was the moment I was supposed to speak, but my mind was still completely blank. I opened my mouth, but nothing came out.

'What do you want?' she asked. The wind ripped the words from between us, taking the intonation of her voice with it. I had no idea whether her question had been confrontational or genuine.

Tears were coursing down her face. Everything I associated with her – the confidence, the presence, the sparkle – was gone. It was mascara-stained to her cheeks.

'I'm sorry,' I managed.

'Why?' She looked, under the tears, confused.

'I . . .' I felt the words freeze on my tongue. She clearly had no idea that the orchestrator of her current situation was me, let alone that I'd basically done it on purpose. 'I didn't know that would happen. I just wanted to *know*.'

'What are you talking about?' She sounded frustrated, and it occurred to me that she probably wanted me to leave so she could cry alone. 'Know what?'

Too late to back out now, Caddy. Own your mistakes. 'I saw a message from someone on your wall,' I said. 'About . . . um . . . *Corrie* and trigger warnings? And I didn't know what it meant. So . . .'

Suzanne pressed her lips together, her eyes on me, blinking hard. She asked, 'Ellie?' When I nodded, she shook her head. 'I knew I should have just deleted that. I thought I was being paranoid.' There was a long silence. I wondered if it would make me the worst person in the world if I ran away.

'I don't get how you saw it,' she said finally. 'We're not even friends on Facebook.'

My whole body felt hot with shame. It stuck in my throat.

'You looked on Rosie's,' she said. When I nodded, she set her jaw, bit down on her tongue and shook her head. 'You know, when you first brought it up, I thought it must be a coincidence. That I was just being really over-sensitive, because I really am about anything to do with abuse. But clearly *not*.'

The word 'abuse' had snagged between us. I so desperately

wanted to say the right thing, something to make this better, maybe even absolve myself, but all I could muster was, 'I'm really sorry.'

'I *know* you are.' Suzanne's whole face was scrunched, partly against the wind, partly with pain. 'People are always so *fucking* sorry.' With these words, practically thrown at me, she turned and started walking away.

'Wait,' I said, hurrying to catch up with her. 'Where are you going?'

'Sarah's coming to pick me up,' Suzanne replied without looking at me. 'You can go back inside.'

'No, I have to . . .' I trailed off. Had to what?

'Have to what?' she asked, forced to stop at the traffic lights. 'You've said sorry; what else is there?' Then her face changed and she turned to me. '*Oh.* You want the story.'

'No,' I said quickly.

'You want me to spill it all out, right? You want answers? Is that why you looked at my Facebook even though we aren't friends?'

I had a horrible feeling I was about to start crying, but before I could speak she made a face and said, sounding frustrated, 'I mean friends on Facebook. We aren't friends on Facebook. Obviously we're *friends*.' She suddenly looked a little lost. 'I mean . . . right?'

'Right,' I said quickly. The lights changed, and we both stepped forward. 'You don't need to tell me anything.'

She was silent for a while, and neither of us said anything as we crossed the road.

'They're wrong, you know,' she said finally. Quietly. 'Rosie, I mean. And Maya and Levina. What they said.' She drew to a stop on the roadside and shoved her hands into her pockets.

'The whole thing about Clarise deserving it? And maybe now she'll shut up?'

'People say that kind of thing all the time. That's what people think. That you must have done something.' She kicked the toes of her Vans against the concrete. 'I wanted to keep it a secret as long as possible. People treat you differently when they know. They even look at you differently.' She gave me a meaningful look then, and I tried very hard to not look at her differently.

'Can I ask one question?' I asked carefully.

'One,' Suzanne said. For a moment I thought she was going to smile, but then she swallowed hard and exhaled, glancing away from me.

'Is that why you live with Sarah?'

She nodded. 'She took me away from them. My parents. Well, just my dad really. Stepdad. I call him "Dad". I mean, I thought he *was* my . . .' She stopped abruptly and took a slow breath in. 'Look, I'm really bad at this. Short version is, my dad – stepdad, whatever – used to hit me, like, a lot. And so my aunt came and took me away. And now I live here.'

A car appeared around the corner then, and Suzanne craned her neck hopefully. 'It's Sarah. Thank God.' She waved, and the car pulled up alongside us. She took a step forward and opened the car door.

For a moment I thought she was going to leave without another word, but she turned to me and said, 'Don't tell Rosie. I'll tell her myself, OK?'

'OK,' I said. 'Um, where shall I tell her you've gone?'

'That,' Suzanne said, folding herself down into the seat, 'is your problem.' She closed the door with a decisive clunk.

I stepped back, feeling heavy with guilt, ready to watch the car drive away. But then the window rolled down and Suzanne's face appeared.

'Sarah says that was rude,' she said.

'Oh,' I said.

Suzanne turned her head back into the car. I heard her say, 'What?' She looked back at me. 'I'm supposed to tell you I know it's not your fault any of this happened.'

I put my hand on my chest. 'Told.'

A brief, reluctant smile flickered across her face. 'I'll see you later, OK?'

'Yeah,' I said. 'I'm—'

'Don't apologize again. Bye, Cads.'

Before I could say anything else, she'd raised her window again and was waving through the glass as the car pulled away. I waved back, a little awkwardly, until it rounded the corner and disappeared.

When I got home hours later, there was a notification and a message waiting for me on Facebook. I knew what it was before I clicked, and sure enough: *Suzanne Watts has sent you a friend request*. Before I accepted, I clicked on the message.

> I hereby endorse all stalking under the name of Friendship. The Friend (CADNAM OLIVER) may at any time assert her right to:
>
> a) View the page of Me (SUZANNE WATTS)
> b) Send messages to Me, including i) life updates ii) article links (only good ones) iii) videos and/or pictures of dogs (no cats)
> c) View the information of my Other Friends, insofar as this information is publically available.

> Confirmation of the Friend Request
> will be taken as an extremely legally
> binding agreement to these terms.

I was grinning like an idiot.

> I, The Friend (CADNAM OLIVER), do
> hereby accept these terms. The Friend
> would also like to reaffirm her earlier
> apology for previous misdeeds.

Barely a minute later, my laptop pinged.

> These terms are predicated on a clean
> slate basis.

I felt light with relief and happiness. I clicked 'Confirm' by her name, and then refreshed my news feed to double-check. It was official.

Caddy Oliver and Suzanne Watts are now friends.

Part 2

8

The next time I saw Suzanne, four days later, with Rosie in tow, it seemed like nothing had changed. She was just the same as she'd been before the diner, chatty and friendly, peppering the two of us with questions about the days she'd missed. She'd spent the time in Cardiff, visiting her brother, Brian. I had no idea if the timing of the trip was a coincidence, or if she'd panicked after telling Rosie the truth and taken the opportunity to leave.

Suzanne had chosen to tell Rosie the morning after the diner incident and had done so, in Rosie's words, 'like she was talking about someone else'. For her part, Rosie seemed both unsurprised and unbothered. 'Well,' she said to me over the phone that same day, 'I'd guessed it must be something like that. If someone doesn't want to talk about something, it's obviously going to be something completely shit. So I wasn't going to push her to tell me or anything. But I'm glad she has, and off her own back, you know?' Which made me feel even worse.

'There's five of them that live there,' Suzanne was saying, talking about her brother's student house. She was holding two corners of a blanket in her hands and shaking it out. 'Can you believe that? Five? Wouldn't it be so much fun to live with your friends?'

We'd gone to the beach with the vague, optimistic hope of catching the last remnants of sunshine and had been rewarded with grey clouds and a definite chill in the air. Suzanne and Rosie seemed undeterred by this, and I'd been vehemently vetoed when I'd suggested giving up and going to my house. Even taking shelter in the Palace Pier arcade was out.

'Imagine if you fell out though,' Rosie said, wrinkling her nose.

'And what if you ended up with a housemate who pissed you off?'

'By the time you're twenty, you're like a grown-up,' Suzanne said. 'Maybe you don't fall out as much.' She settled the blanket on to the pebbles and then sat on it, pulling over a picnic bag. 'Sarah made us picnic stuff,' she announced, waving a Tupperware container at us. 'And Welsh cakes!'

'What are Welsh cakes?' Rosie asked, dubious.

'Kind of like scones. Squashed scones.' Suzanne reached back into the bag and pulled out a wad of paper plates.

'Oh wow, you came prepared,' I said, unable to keep the smile off my face and out of my voice.

She hesitated momentarily, her eyes sliding towards me, scanning for sarcasm. Then the smile returned to her face and she gave her hair a slight toss. 'Always come prepared for a picnic.'

The picnic had been entirely her idea. She'd messaged both me and Rosie late the previous evening, announcing her return and suggesting a day at the beach. I'd been nervous that she'd act differently around me after what had happened, but she was just herself.

Rosie had settled herself on to the blanket and started pulling the lids off the containers, peering at the contents.

'So what are your brother's housemates like?' I asked, taking what looked like a samosa and biting into it.

'Great,' Suzanne said. 'Really friendly. They didn't seem to mind this random fifteen-year-old turning up. They had a house party while I was there, and it was amazing. It made the ones we have look like children's parties.'

She crammed two tortilla chips into her mouth and crunched through them slowly, turning slightly to look out at the waves. The wind had picked up since we'd sat down, causing them to break with a fierce crash against the stones.

I tried to imagine myself at a student party, surrounded by twenty-year-olds. *Drunk* twenty-year-olds. Just the thought was enough to make my stomach seize with anxiety. I took another bite of samosa, trying to shake it off.

We worked our way through the food, which all tasted amazing, talking about not much at all. It felt like the perfect way to spend the last day of half-term, even though the sky threatened rain and the wind was cold.

'The rest of the term's going to be brutal,' Rosie was saying dolefully, teasing the layer of chocolate off a Jaffa cake with her tongue. 'So many deadlines. So much coursework.'

'Same,' I said, restraining myself from making a self-pitying comment about my private school workload.

'How did you get on with the English essay?' Rosie asked Suzanne. 'How long is yours? I went over the word limit by about three hundred words, but she won't notice, right?'

'Probably not. I haven't finished mine.'

Rosie's eyebrows scrunched. 'You haven't finished? You do know it's due tomorrow?'

'Yeah, but it's fine. I'll do it tonight.'

'So you're nearly done?'

Suzanne shrugged. 'Halfway, maybe?'

'Suze!' Rosie looked horrified. 'This is *coursework*!'

'I know.' Suzanne looked completely unbothered by this information.

'Don't you care?'

'Not really.'

Rosie looked at me, as if for help, but I had nothing to add to this conversation. I'd had my own deadlines, of course, and I'd got everything done in the first few days of the holiday. I was far away from being the type of person who could leave half an essay to the day before it was due, let alone be so blasé about it.

'I just think homework is kind of pointless,' Suzanne elaborated when neither of us spoke.

'But it's *not* pointless,' Rosie said slowly, as if talking to an idiot. 'You get that, right? Even if you can't be bothered, it still counts.'

'It's not that I can't be bothered. It's just the pointlessness of it kind of gets to me sometimes. I know it sounds stupid.' Her casual tone had hardened slightly with defensiveness. 'You know, when I was younger I used to do all my homework, all the time, right on time. And I'd get good marks, and the teachers said I was good, and it didn't make the slightest bit of difference at home, where it mattered. So I kind of stopped trying so hard, maybe a couple of years ago now, and you know what? Nothing changed. So homework? Pointless.'

Her face had reddened as she spoke, and when she finished she looked slightly dazed, as if she wasn't sure where the outburst had come from. She bit her lip, looking away from us, then let out a shaky, embarrassed laugh. 'Oh God, I'm sorry. Let's talk about something else.'

'We can talk about it more if you want to,' I said, a little nervously.

'No, no.' She shook her head emphatically. 'I don't usually talk about it. And that's fine – I don't want to.'

We all knew what the 'it' referred to. Rosie's eyes were wide and keen; clearly she had the same morbid curiosity I did.

'Maybe it would help?' Rosie suggested, transparently.

'Sarah says that all the time, and it doesn't. Help.'

'What does help?' I asked.

Suzanne smiled, but it looked a little forced, and gestured around her with a now-empty container.

'This.'

*

There was no magic moment when I started thinking of Suzanne as a real friend. Even accepting the friend request on Facebook had felt more like a relief than any confirmation of a real bond. In those first few weeks after the diner, she was still, in my mind at least, Rosie's friend.

That's not to say that we weren't both trying. We were. Whenever she made plans, like the beach picnic, she made sure to send us both a message. I did the same, gradually getting into the habit of waiting for two replies to my texts. I assumed at the time that her allowances to my existence as Rosie's best friend were as perfunctory as mine were of her. It wasn't until much later, when she'd refer to these early days of our friendship, that I realized I'd been wrong.

Rosie and I had been friends for so long that we had the luxury of not remembering the time before we knew everything about each other. Most of our best anecdotes were mutual; it had been in my garden that she'd broken her arm; her mum's wardrobe where we'd pretended to find Narnia.

Suzanne was brand new in this sense, and in contrast to Rosie's total familiarity, this was at times exciting and terrifying. It was so easy to say the wrong thing without realizing, particularly bearing in mind her fractured past. She was like a puzzle I was trying to solve, but the surprisingly complicated kind that looks shinier and easier on the box than it really is.

Not long after half term, she sent me a message on a rainy Wednesday, asking if I wanted to go to her house for dinner with Rosie. It turned out that Rosie hadn't been to Suzanne's house before either, and it wasn't a house, but a basement flat. It was on one of the steep roads that we used to sled down as kids in the winter.

'Careful on the stairs,' Suzanne said as we started down them, keys already in hand. The rain had been relentless all week and the stone steps leading down to the door were slippery.

The flat was large on the inside, stretching further back than the outside had suggested and containing a decent-sized living room and gigantic kitchen. We passed Sarah's room, which was towards the front of the flat, and walked the full length of the hall to Suzanne's, which was tucked away like an afterthought next to the bathroom.

Suzanne's room was much smaller than I'd expected, with a sloping ceiling and hanging fairy lights that made the whole room feel more like a fort. Almost every inch of the walls was covered not just with photos, like in my room, but with posters and magazine clippings and postcards and scraps of newspaper. Post-it notes were stuck haphazardly over the cracks between the paraphernalia, and when I looked closely I saw they each contained scribbles in Suzanne's handwriting. Poetry, maybe? Song lyrics?

'Wow,' Rosie said, taking it in. 'This is . . . busy.'

'Bare walls make me nervous,' Suzanne said casually, hopping on to her bed and sitting up on her crossed ankles.

The only thing left bare in the room was the window, looking out on to the garden. Even the windowsill was empty. Seeing me looking, Suzanne shrugged and said, 'Always leave an exit clear.' I couldn't tell if she was kidding.

'Didn't this take ages?' Rosie asked, still looking around.

I knew what she meant. The display looked like the kind you'd expect to have been built up over several years. Suzanne had only had about two months.

'Yeah, but I did it when I first got here. School hadn't started and I didn't know anyone, and it was like a project for a couple of weeks. Kept me busy.' She was still smiling, but there was a touch of anxiety on her face. 'Maybe it's a bit much, but I like it. Always have something to look at, you know?'

'I think it's great,' I said, meaning it.

Suzanne beamed at me. 'Sarah says it gives her a headache, so she stays out. Though she was the one who got me the Calvin and Hobbes prints.' She pointed to a large spot above the chest of drawers, plastered over with comic strips.

'You like Marilyn Monroe?' Rosie was looking at a black-and-white portrait of the actress I hadn't noticed. I realized there were postcard-sized replicas of old posters of some of her films dotted around the walls.

'I *love* her,' Suzanne replied.

'Wow, I had no idea you were such a cliché.' Rosie softened this remark by flashing Suzanne a mischievous grin over her shoulder.

'There are worse things to be,' Suzanne said with a shrug, smiling. 'I just think she was amazing. Do you know anything about her except her being a sex symbol? She had a really hard time, but she still became this *icon*.'

'A sex icon,' Rosie pointed out flatly.

Suzanne rolled her eyes. 'You should read up a bit on her – you'd probably be surprised. Oh! We should watch one of her films!'

I drifted out of the conversation, knowing Rosie would never agree to spend her evening watching an old film from the 1950s, and looked at Suzanne's mirror. It was almost full-length and bordered with photos and handwritten lists. I leaned closer to read one of them.

Brighton Rock
aka My Sister Moved To Brighton And All I Gave Her
Was This Lousy Playlist

1) Seaside Shuffle – Terry Dactyl and the Dinosaurs
2) End of the Season – The Kinks

3) Seaside – The Kooks
4) Waiting For The 7.18 – Bloc Party
5) Pinball Wizard – The Who
6) Brighton Rock – Elastica
7) Green Eyes – Suggs
8) Rumble in Brighton – The Stray Cats
9) Brighton Rock – Queen (NOT THE SAME SONG, DON'T SKIP!)
10) The Sea – Morcheeba (Apparently this song is about Brighton – who knew!)
11) You're Not from Brighton – Fatboy Slim

Bonus
12) Holes – Passenger

I'd lived in Brighton all my life, and I hadn't heard of some of the songs. I pulled out my phone and took a picture so I could look them up when I got home. Rosie and Suzanne were still sparring over what film they should watch – 'Some Like It Hot is a classic!' – so I glanced over a few more of the photos and playlists.

Hey Suze, Don't Get the Blues
aka Cheerful Songs For Sadful Days

1) The Life of Riley – The Lightning Seeds
2) Here Comes the Sun – The Beatles
3) Simple Song – The Shins
4) It's Time – Imagine Dragons
5) So Alive – Ryan Adams
6) Smile – The Supernaturals
7) The Diamond Church Street Choir – The Gaslight Anthem

8) *Fascinating New Thing* – *Semisonic*
9) *Uptight (Everything's Alright)* – *Stevie Wonder*
10) *Get Rhythm* – *Johnny Cash*
11) *Itchycoo Park* – *Small Faces*
12) *I'm a Cuckoo* – *Belle & Sebastian*
13) *Marvellous* – *The Lightning Seeds*

There was a cartoon of a duck wearing headphones in the bottom right-hand corner of this one. On another list – *Our Humble Beginnings, aka Look At All The Great Music Manchester Has Given The World* – the same duck was smoking a cigarette. I looked for the duck on another list and finally found him partially hidden by a photo of two children – presumably Suzanne and Brian – on a beach. The duck's head in this one was bandaged. This playlist was named *And Sometimes They Write Songs, aka Survivors Come In All Shapes And Guises*.

'Did your brother write all of these?' I asked, turning my head towards Suzanne and gesturing at the mirror.

'The playlists? Yeah.'

'He must really love music.' I said. What I meant was, *He must really love you.*

'Oh yeah.' She considered this, then smiled. '*I* really love music. We get it from our dad.' She said this casually, as if her father wasn't a loaded topic.

'I haven't even heard of loads of these songs,' I said. This was probably because I considered music one of life's background essentials, and so had never really played close attention to it. It was there, and that was nice, but in an added-extra kind of way.

Suzanne laughed. 'Don't give him too much credit. I think he Googles his themes and then picks the tracks he likes.'

I looked closer at the pictures on the mirror, realizing that a good half of them were of her and Brian at various ages. They looked nothing like each other: her, blonde and wispy; him, dark-haired and stocky.

'You guys were so cute,' Rosie said, taking one of the photos for a closer look. Out of the corner of my eye I saw Suzanne flinch, as if stopping herself from reaching out to take it back.

There were no photos that I could see of anyone else who looked like a family member. The photos on the walls contained people around our age, strangers to me but unmistakably friend-shaped. I wondered, for the first time, what it must have been like to leave them all behind and start over. To trust the strangers you met with the weight of the second chance you'd been given. I felt the responsibility, suddenly, surrounded by the blueprints of her rebuilt life.

'Excuse me,' Suzanne said, her voice light. 'We're still cute.'

Rosie grinned at her. 'Obviously.' She reattached the photo to the mirror. 'He looks cool. Is he a good brother?'

'The best,' Suzanne said. 'He's the only one who loves me.' She said this lightly, in the same matter-of-fact way I'd say I was five foot three. Like there wasn't even a question.

'Well, that's not true,' Rosie said, in the same tone.

Suzanne leaned back fully so she was almost lying on her bed, her head on her pillow, eyes on the ceiling. 'Do you think a dog knows it's a dog if it lives with people?'

Rosie and I looked at each other.

'Like, what if it had never *seen* another dog,' Suzanne continued, as if this was normal. 'How would it know?'

'Walking on all fours would probably be a clue,' Rosie said.

'Would it though? They're not *that* smart.'

Rosie blinked at her, then raised an eyebrow at me. I shrugged. She turned back to Suzanne. 'Do you think Brian'd make a playlist for me? I want one.'

'I'll make you one,' Suzanne offered. 'And I'll put *loads* of ABBA songs on it.'

Rosie laughed. This was clearly an in-joke I had no hope of getting. 'No playlist is worth listening to if ABBA aren't on it.'

Suzanne was grinning. She looked at me. 'Want one, Cads?'

'Sure,' I said. 'Go light on the ABBA though.'

They both cracked up as if I'd said something funny on purpose, when I'd actually been completely serious.

'You just wait,' Suzanne teased. 'I'll convert you.'

'You can try,' I hedged. 'So – *Some Like It Hot*?'

Suzanne bounced up off the bed, looking thrilled. 'Yes! See, Roz? Two against one. Now you can't argue.' She gave my arm a spontaneous squeeze. 'Caddy's on my side. Right, Caddy?'

'Right,' I said. I couldn't help grinning at Rosie's sour expression. 'Sorry, Roz. You're outvoted.'

'You're not supposed to gang up on me,' Rosie said sulkily. 'That's not how this works.'

'Except it is,' Suzanne replied. She went over to her shelf of DVDs and began searching through them. 'You just wait. You'll love it. I *promise*.'

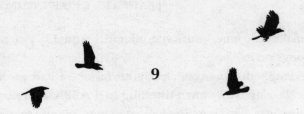

9

The following week was parents' evening, a rare evening with both my parents. On the short drive to Esther's, Dad attempted to cram in the six weeks' worth of information he'd missed while being Superstar Doctor of the Year, which I found irritating but Mum seemed to think was endearing. She kept making eye contact with me in the rear-view mirror and rolling her eyes in a misguidedly chummy way.

The evening went as I'd expected. I worked hard. I was pleasant. My grades were satisfactory. I should speak up more during lessons. I should get involved more in extra-curricular activities. These were the kinds of things Esther's teachers said to the filler students like me. Credit where it was due to those of us who kept the boat steady while others created waves. I'd never really minded being one of those. It only ever bothered me when I knew it bothered Dad.

I could see the vaguely frustrated look on his face while he sipped coffee and made small talk with other parents, introducing himself as Dr Oliver in a way that made me wonder if he was expecting applause. My mother kept putting her hand to my shoulder and squeezing gently.

'Your English teacher seemed impressed,' was all she could muster when we were finally back in the car and heading home.

'Mmm,' I said.

'It doesn't hurt to stick your head above the parapet occasionally,' Dad said. 'There's no shame in being noticed.'

'John . . .' Mum said, a soft warning.

'I try my best, Dad,' I said, knowing I was wasting my breath.

I heard his short exhalation of annoyance and tried to ignore the pang of hurt that he always managed to induce at times like this. He never actually said it, but he didn't need to. I was not the confident star he'd thought Esther's would turn me into, and this became more and more apparent each year, with every parents' evening and end-of-year report.

And it wasn't just him. I wondered if I'd ever be able to shake the feeling that, for all my opportunities and privileges, I'd never be as good as Tarin, who had shone her whole life on her own merit. All the money thrown at my education, and what did I have to show for it, apart from a handful of A grades I'd probably have had anyway and a good school name to put on my CV? What a waste I was. What a disappointment.

When we got home I took refuge in my room and curled up under the covers with my laptop and a bag of Skittles, hoping to be soothed by the combined comforts of YouTube and Buzzfeed. I had just started scrolling through a series of gifs entitled '17 Ways You Know You're A Private School Girl' when my bedroom door opened and Mum came in.

'He doesn't mean to be that way,' she said, forgoing both a greeting and an invitation. She sat down on the bed beside me, craning her neck slightly to look at my laptop screen. I pushed it down pointedly, and a flicker of disappointment passed over her face.

'Mmmm,' I said, deliberately noncommittal.

'It's because he loves you and wants what's best for you,' she continued. 'We both do.'

Making me feel inadequate isn't exactly a sign of love, I thought, but I kept the words inside my head, where they belonged.

On Saturday, I went to the Marina with Rosie and Suzanne, who were meeting a group of their school friends at the cinema. Rosie's mother drove us, even though we could have got the bus, and then insisted on paying for our tickets. Rosie, hunched inside her jacket, complained about her interference for almost the entire time after her mother left and before the rest of the group arrived, until Suzanne made a pointed comment about it being nice that she had a mother who loved her that much, which shut her up.

The rest of their friends turned up not long after, spirited and loud, and I felt myself begin to shrink inside, even as I pasted my most sociable grin on my face. Charlie, Levina's boyfriend, was leading the show as always. Everything was fair game.

'So how's Esther's, Caddy?' he asked me, the question deceptively friendly. He was looking at me, and he was smiling, but his eyes weren't even focused on me. It occurred to me that if I turned away and asked him to name the band on my T-shirt (Haim) or the colour of my eyes (brown), he wouldn't be able to say.

'Fine,' I said stupidly, because what else could I say? There's something unstoppable about being set up as the punchline to a joke. Even when you see it coming, there's no avoiding the inevitable.

'Got a girlfriend, yet?'

I felt my face flush scarlet, my heart seizing. 'What?'

'We all know the truth about Esther's girls,' Charlie's eyes were dancing. '*Lesbi*-honest.'

Almost everyone laughed, even Rosie, though she hooked her arm through mine and squeezed. But Suzanne, who was wearing an exaggerated not-amused expression, said, 'Is that the best you can do, Charles? A *lesbian* joke about a *girls'* school?'

Charlie's smile dropped, but only momentarily, returning with a slight strain. 'Who said it was a joke?'

Suzanne rolled her eyes at him, then looked at me, keeping her shoulders turned outward so she was still addressing the whole group. 'So *little* imagination. How many times have you heard that joke, Cads?' Her sparkling eyes were focused on me, steady and sharp and encouraging.

'Every time a guy thinks he's being funny?' I said, taking this unexpected gift of a chance to speak.

My voice wasn't as strong as hers or Charlie's had been, but it was enough. Everyone laughed, and even Charlie shrugged and grinned, accepting the shift.

As everyone turned to head into the multiplex, Suzanne bounced a little on her feet, taking hold of my free arm and hooking hers through it.

'Thanks,' I whispered, so no one else would hear.

She squeezed my arm rather than respond, a satisfied grin flashing across her face. We walked through the doors together, still connected, a happy line of three.

Suzanne and I were standing by the ticket machines not long after, waiting for the others, who were still queuing for popcorn. I took a sip of Coke, which already tasted a bit flat, and reached out to steal one of Suzanne's nachos.

'What's taking them so long?' she grumbled, angling the box towards me so I could swipe some salsa.

'Rosie's always like this,' I replied. 'She has real issues making decisions, especially when it's food.'

Suzanne smiled. 'Yesterday, at lunch –'

She stopped so abruptly I thought it was for effect, until I saw her face. The smile had disappeared, and she looked stunned. The bad kind of stunned. The horrified kind.

'Oh my God,' she said, and her voice was so flat it didn't even sound like her. Before I could ask what, she said, in the same flat voice, 'That's my dad.'

I turned my head to see where she was looking. The man in

her eyeline was not the figure I'd have expected even if I'd been prepared for the sight of him. I'd imagined someone huge, with broad shoulders and thick fists. This man was lean and average-looking, with dark brown hair flecked with grey. He was wearing a white shirt and jeans, like my own dad did when he wasn't working. He was laughing at something another man was saying, looking relaxed. Not at all like the kind of man who could hit a child. Could hit Suzanne.

In the few seconds it took me to take all of this in, and before I could even think of what to say to Suzanne, he must have felt our stares because he glanced over at us. For an instant his face registered shock, but just for an instant. I saw his eyes flicker slightly, taking in the full length of Suzanne, but then, his expression blank, he turned back to the people he was with.

I looked back at Suzanne just in time to see the agonized expression on her face before she shoved the box of nachos into my hands, turned and bolted.

The last few seconds had been so confusing it was all I could do to hold on to my Coke and the partially upended nachos. Suzanne had shoved the box so roughly a bunch of the tortilla chips had fallen on the floor and I saw a splodge of salsa on my jacket. I tried to right the items in my hands, but I felt strangely disconnected, as if my own world had itself been partially upended. Which was stupid, of course; it hadn't even happened to me.

I hesitated in the middle of the foyer, torn between going after her and getting Rosie for back-up. Despite myself, I glanced towards the man again. Now, he looked pained. Before he could turn and see me standing alone, I went to find Suzanne.

I found her bent double on a bench by the car park, arms clutched around her head. A woman sitting on the other end of the bench was looking at her half with worry and half with alarm, clearly wondering if she should say anything.

Before she could make a move, I kneeled on the concrete at Suzanne's feet, careful to leave a bit of space for her to breathe. Once, when Tarin had been rendered almost catatonic after a particularly bad panic attack, I'd moved in too close in my attempt to help and she'd headbutted me – completely by accident – when her head jerked back at the sound of my voice.

'It's me,' I said, keeping my voice quiet so the woman wouldn't hear. 'But take your time, OK?'

I heard a noise like a suppressed sob but she gave no other indication that she'd heard me, or that she even knew I was there.

'Caddy?' I jumped, turning my head to see Rosie's mum, Shell, standing behind me. She was holding two shopping bags and she looked confused and worried. 'What's wrong? What happened?'

The woman on the bench leaned forward slightly and said, directing the question to Shell, 'Is everything OK here?' She had an American accent and an imposing voice. Perhaps it was unintentional, but the question sounded almost accusing.

'Everything's fine,' Shell said, which was ridiculous. There were times when being polite was just not worth it, and this was one of them. Everything was clearly *not* fine. She should have just said, *No, it's not OK, but that doesn't make it any of your business*.

'Should I call someone?' the woman persisted.

This was such a bizarre thing to say that I couldn't stop myself. 'Like who?'

'Caddy,' Shell said, reproach in her voice. To the woman she said, with the same polite tone she'd used before, 'Thank you for your concern, but this is a personal matter.'

I saw Suzanne's whole body tense up further, her elbows crushing against her ears. Her hand seemed to spasm slightly and without thinking I reached up and took hold of it. Her fingers clamped down around mine almost instantly, squeezing tight. I heard her exhale a shaky, gasping breath.

'One time,' I said in the most normal voice I could manage, 'when me and Roz were about seven, my parents went through a phase where they wanted to keep chickens. In the garden, you know? Rosie thought this was really cruel, because we were taking their eggs away to eat, and if we didn't eat them they'd become chicks. She thought she'd save one, so she took one out of the chicken coop before my dad could get it and put it in our airing cupboard so it would keep warm. But then of course she went home and forgot all about it. Problem is, we didn't really use our airing cupboard that much, so God knows how long it was in there, but my dad eventually found it one morning before work, and he carries it into the kitchen, going to my mum, "Do you know anything about this egg?" and then it pretty much exploded all over his suit.'

I heard a snuffle of something like laughter from behind Suzanne's arms.

'One day I'll tell you about the time we tried to make a slide on the stairs out of a piece of tarpaulin and a bit of fairy liquid and vegetable oil.' I said.

'Oh God,' Shell said drily. 'I'd forgotten about that.'

Suzanne's elbows parted slightly and she peeked out at me. I put on my very best encouraging, this-is-a-safe-space smile and said, 'Hi.'

'Hi,' she whispered.

Shell moved around me and sat herself down on the bench next to Suzanne, putting an arm around her shoulders and squeezing. I saw Suzanne stiffen slightly, but she let herself be hugged.

'Shall I take you home?' Shell suggested in a quiet, kind voice.

Suzanne's fingers were bunched up inside her sleeves. She brought her fist to her mouth and bit down on her knuckles. 'I'm not allowed to be at home by myself.' Her face, which had steadied itself, crumpled again. 'And Sarah's at work.'

Shell looked worried. 'If you give me her number, I'll give her a call and explain the situation.'

A look of panic passed over Suzanne's face. She looked seconds away from retreating back into herself. 'But she's at work,' she managed.

'I'll go with you,' I said suddenly, surprising all three of us. 'Then you won't be on your own in the flat.' I thought of Rosie, probably still queuing for popcorn, wondering if she'd be mad at me for leaving her there with everyone else with no warning.

Shell looked at me for a moment, an unreadable expression on her face. Then she turned to Suzanne. 'How about that?'

Suzanne scrunched the end of her sleeves between her fingertips, her eyes scanning my face. 'Are you sure?' There was something childlike about her voice. A reluctant, cautious hope.

'I'm positive,' I said.

It wasn't until Suzanne shut her front door that I realized the two of us had never actually been alone together, unless you counted the confrontation outside the diner, which I tried not to. What did we have to talk about? Rosie was our mutual friend, and without her there to act as a buffer, were we really anything more than strangers? Rosie's response to my text – 'Sz had a panic attack, going to hers with her. Explain later? Sorry!' – had been a surprised but pleasant: 'OK! No worries, hope she's OK? Call me later x'

'Thanks for coming back with me,' Suzanne said softly, dropping her bag on the floor and walking into the kitchen.

'Oh, that's OK.' I could hear the awkwardness in my voice and it embarrassed me, but being aware of it didn't make it any easier. 'Um. Have you ever had a panic attack before?'

Stupid, idiotic, stupid question.

'Yes,' Suzanne replied, as if it had been appropriate for me to ask. 'I usually handle them better than that. But it was . . .' Her voice gave out and she let out a breath. 'It was a shock. Seeing my dad.'

'Yeah,' I said. Still the awkwardness. 'I guess it would . . . yeah . . . be a shock.'

'How did you know that that was what it was?' she asked, taking a couple of glasses from a cupboard and turning on the tap. She filled them both and handed one to me.

'Oh, Tarin used to have them,' I said, taking the glass even though I wasn't thirsty. 'You know she's bipolar, right?'

Suzanne shook her head. 'I didn't know they were part of that.'

'They aren't always, but she used to have quite bad ones sometimes, and her doctor said it was all related.' I glanced at the clock, wondering what time Sarah finished work. 'How come you're not allowed to be in by yourself?'

Suzanne looked at me for a long moment, her eyes just slightly squinting. If the earlier devastation wasn't still painted across her face in tear-stained blotches, I'd have thought she was amused.

'Sarah doesn't think it's safe,' she said finally.

'Oh,' I said, none the wiser.

We were silent for a while, both of us sipping from our glasses. I was frantically trying to think of something to say, any way to plug the silence with something other than either a comment on the fact that it was raining or a seriously heavy question about her dad.

Finally Suzanne let out a shaky laugh. 'You know, I just realized I've only cried twice outside of this house since I moved here, and both times it's been in front of you.'

I smiled, unsure if this was the right response.

'I hate crying in front of people,' she added, unnecessarily.

'I don't think anyone likes it,' I offered.

'Some people do. I had a friend who used to turn on the tears for attention. It was really annoying.' She rolled the bottom of her glass against the tabletop. 'But it's pathetic, crying like that. Like you can't control your emotions. It's so weak.'

'There's nothing wrong with showing weakness sometimes,' I said.

Suzanne made a face. 'You only say that because any time you've shown weakness people have responded with love.'

I tried not to let the annoyance I felt show on my face. 'You don't actually know if that's true.'

'Oh, it is,' she said, matter-of-factly, almost dismissively. 'I can tell.'

'You hardly know me.' I tried to say this in a light-hearted voice, but even to my own ears I sounded defensive and trite.

Suzanne looked at me, a strange half-smile on her face. The openness of the vulnerability that had come with breaking down in front of someone had gone. She was unreadable again.

'I don't need to know you to know that,' she said. 'It's not a bad thing. You should be pleased.'

I had no idea if she was trying to goad me, or if she really did think that way. Maybe it was both. I tried to think of how to respond, but before I could speak she spoke again.

'My dad hated it when I cried.' She ran her finger around the rim of her empty glass, her eyes fixed on it. 'It made him so mad. So I'd try to stop myself, but . . . sometimes you can't.'

And then of course there was nothing I could say.

Eventually Suzanne got restless sitting in the kitchen and we went to the cocoon of her room, where she wrapped herself in an afghan on top of the bed and hunched her chin down into her chest, looking at me as if expecting me to speak. The lack of other places to sit in her room made me perch on the end of her bed, half sitting on my shins. It still felt awkward between us, and I wasn't sure if she even really wanted me there. But it would have felt more weird to not have followed her, like I was her babysitter or something.

'Are you and Tarin really close?' Suzanne asked, surprising me.

'Sure,' I said. 'I mean, eight-years-apart kind of close.'

'I wish I had a sister. I always used to think it must be the best thing. Like having a best friend genetically hard-wired to love you.'

I had to laugh. 'Best friends love you without any genetic wiring.'

'Not in the same way though, right? And it's different with sisters than brothers?' She was earnest, like my answer really mattered. 'I mean, Brian is, like, my favourite person in the world, but he's always my brother, not my friend. Sisters are both.'

'I think you can get friends who are like sisters,' I said, thinking of Rosie. 'And sisters who are like friends. Maybe if Tarin and I were closer in age we'd be more like friends. But she's definitely a sister first.' I thought about it. 'Maybe you and Brian wouldn't have been as close if you'd had a sister.'

Her shoulders moved under the afghan. 'Probably not.'

'He's at Cardiff, right?' I asked.

She nodded.

'Where does he go when it's not term time?' I'd meant to broach the subject more innocuously, but it came out about as subtle as a plank.

'Home.' She said. Poker-faced.

'Is it . . . ? I mean . . . how is it there for him?'

'My dad never hit him, if that's what you mean.' Her voice was resigned, as if she'd expected this conversation. 'That was just for me.' She turned slightly, sliding her fingers under an old Lego advert, and pulled out a photo that had been hidden from view. 'Here's us,' she said, handing it to me.

I recognized Suzanne, looking maybe three years younger, first. Then Brian, from the photos on the mirror, and finally her father, from earlier. He, Brian and a woman – presumably Suzanne's mother – were standing by a Christmas tree, all smiles. Brian was leaning slightly as if to squat closer to Suzanne, who was sitting at their feet, arms hugging her knees. She was smiling too, but it was close-lipped.

'See how you could just cut off the bottom of the picture and it would be perfect?' she asked me. 'I kind of love that picture because it's so horrible but so *accurate*. The three of them, then me.'

'You still said us,' I pointed out. She looked confused. 'Just now. You said, "Here's us."'

A look of intense sadness passed over her face, and she turned quickly away from me again without answering, putting her fingers up to touch a piece of sheet music that was taped to the wall.

My shins were starting to hurt, so I rearranged myself, stretching out across the lower half of the bed.

'Did you see how he looked at me?' Suzanne murmured, still looking at the notes on the wall, her voice so quiet it almost didn't reach me. 'Nothing's changed. I'm still . . .' I heard her pause, then sigh. 'Just me.'

'How come he was here?' I wasn't sure if I should ask, but couldn't quite help myself. 'Did you know he would be?'

She shook her head vehemently. 'God, no. I can't . . .' She stopped, breathed in sharply, then continued. 'I don't know why he was here, or why I didn't know he would be. I guess it must be a conference weekend. He used to have those a lot, all over the country, for work, you know?' She closed her eyes for a moment, then opened them again and let out a sigh. '*God*, I can't get over how he looked at me.'

'Did you think things would have changed?' I asked carefully.

'Not really. But you always hope, you know?'

I absolutely did not know. Thank God.

'Was that why you moved here? So things would change?'

'No. We moved here because I'd have died otherwise.' She said this bluntly, still not looking at me. 'It would have been a bonus if things had changed, if he'd had this amazing change of heart and stopped treating me like I was the cause of all the problems in his life.' She closed her eyes briefly, shook her head slightly and sighed. 'But then again, "Penny Lane" is his favourite Beatles song, and I went and put the sheet music up on my wall. So maybe I'm just as fucked up as he is.'

'You don't seem very fucked up,' I said, trying to be reassuring, assuming that was my role in this conversation.

To my surprise she laughed. 'Oh my God. Thank you! Can you write that down so I can put it on my wall?'

I couldn't tell if she was being serious or making fun of me. Was I being ridiculous? How could I tell? I wished Rosie was here. Even when she was at her most prickly, talking to her was easy.

I was still trying to figure out how to arrange my face when Suzanne thrust a Post-it pad and a pen at me. She *was* serious.

I hesitated, then began to write, deciding as I did so to stop trying to fish for clues about her past and settle on a safe topic. I landed on, 'What's *your* favourite Beatles song?'

'"Here Comes the Sun",' she said without hesitation. 'But "Across the Universe" and "Blackbird" are high up too. What about you?'

'"Let It Be",' I said, more because it was the first song that came to mind rather than because it was actually true.

She looked almost disappointed. 'Really? Everyone says "Let It Be".'

'Only the people who don't say "Here Comes the Sun".'

'Touché,' Suzanne's whole face broke into a grin and she looked animated for the first time since we'd left the cinema. I mentally pocketed this nugget for future reference. *If in doubt, talk about the Beatles.*

She fixed the Post-it note to her wall, close to the sheet music for Penny Lane. She was still smiling.

'I'm flattered I'm going to be on your wall,' I said, looking at the jumble of her life spread across the room, which now, however inexplicably, included me.

Before Suzanne could respond, there was the sound of the front door opening and closing and then footsteps across the hall.

'Suzie?'

'We're in here,' Suzanne called.

Sarah's face appeared around the door. Her hair was wet and she looked anxious. 'How are you?' She came into the room and leaned her head slightly to shake droplets from her hair.

'You heard?' Suzanne asked, avoiding the question. There was something in her voice I couldn't translate.

'Your dad called your mother, and she called me.' Sarah glanced at me, and even though she smiled I could see the tension in her face. 'Hello, Caddy.'

'I should probably go home,' I said, realizing that Sarah probably wanted to talk to Suzanne without me in the way.

'I'll drive you,' Sarah offered.

'Oh, that's OK,' I said automatically. 'It's not far.'

'But it's pouring,' Sarah protested, pointing at her own wet hair. 'I can't have you walking home in the rain.'

'Why don't you stay for dinner?' Suzanne suggested. 'Maybe it'll have stopped raining later.'

'I'm sure Caddy needs to be getting home,' Sarah said pointedly.

Suzanne ignored this and fixed me with a surprisingly hopeful look. 'Stay for dinner?'

I thought of the way she'd squeezed my hand on the bench, like I was the last tether on a sinking ship. My handwriting on a piece of yellow paper on her wall.

I stayed for dinner.

There were two open evenings that week at Esther's, so I was too busy to see either Rosie or Suzanne until the following weekend. The open evenings fell on the Wednesday and Thursday evenings, and were the stressful highlight of the Esther's calendar. Everyone in Year 11 was expected to be there, polished and preened to perfection. Kesh and I were tasked with looking after a group of Year 9s, awkward and bolshie, in the English block.

When I got home that evening, exhausted and dry-mouthed from all the talking, I opened Facebook to see a long conversation underway between Suzanne and Rosie. They were making plans for the weekend. Rosie wanted to go somewhere; Suzanne wanted to stay put. I read through the messages until I was up-to-date and back down to earth, away from the Esther's bubble. They'd agreed to go out on Friday – a friend from school's birthday party, to which I was clearly (thankfully) not invited – and then stay in on Saturday evening. Suzanne suggested baking at her house, because that way Sarah could go out for the evening without worrying. The idea of baking on a Saturday evening was so unexpected it was almost charming.

This was the point when they stopped jabbering at each other and resorted to variants of 'Caddy? Are you in? CADDY!' until I typed my agreement, beaming to myself alone in my room.

10

When I got to Suzanne's on Saturday Rosie was already there, and the two of them were huddled together at the kitchen table, poring over the cookbook.

'You've got everything you need, Suzie?' Sarah asked for what can't have been the first time, judging by the look on Suzanne's face. It was weird to hear her be called Suzie. It just didn't fit right.

'Yes, we have everything we need,' Suzanne confirmed. She smiled at me and said, in a much brighter voice, 'Hey! Ready to bake?'

'That's a nice jacket,' Rosie said to me when I sat on the stool next to her. 'Tarin's?'

'Tarin's.' I leaned over and tilted the book so I could see it. 'What are we making?'

'Macaroons,' Suzanne said happily. 'The best things ever.'

'MacaRONS,' Sarah corrected distractedly, striding past us and poking her head into what had to be the pantry. 'Where's my purse?'

'Macarooooooooons,' Suzanne said, unruffled. She was grinning. 'Your purse is probably still on your bed.'

'Could you grab it for me?' Sarah reached into the pantry and pulled out, of all things, her car keys.

Suzanne went without complaint.

'You girls have fun, and feel free to call me any time if there's a problem. My number's on the fridge,' Sarah said to Rosie and me. She was smiling, but her eyes seemed anxious. She lowered her voice slightly. 'Make sure you don't leave Suzanne on her own for too long, particularly in the kitchen.'

She said this last point just as Suzanne walked back into the kitchen, brandishing the purse. For a moment I thought she hadn't heard, but then she looked at me and Rosie and said, head slightly cocked, completely deadpan, 'I'm not allowed to be left alone with the oven in case I stick my head in it.'

This was so clearly meant to be a joke that I laughed out loud, but I was the only one who did. Rosie looked confused and Sarah exasperated.

'You are a piece of work,' Sarah said, taking the purse from Suzanne and putting it into her bag. She sounded like she couldn't decide whether to be annoyed or amused.

'Caddy thinks I'm funny,' Suzanne replied. She flashed a grin at me.

'Caddy doesn't have to live with you,' Sarah said, but she was smiling now.

'Neither do youuuu,' Suzanne sang.

Throughout this exchange, which ended with Sarah draping a tea towel over Suzanne's head, Rosie alternated between looking from me to them with the same confused expression on her face. She would later ask me if I thought it was normal to joke about such horrible topics, a question that had never occurred to me. There was no 'normal', just Suzanne, who was spiky and self-deprecating and sardonic. It made sense to me that she dealt with her heartaches by making light of them, any time it was possible to do so. And really, what was the alternative?

By the time Sarah finally left — 'Please don't burn the house down!' — it had started to get dark. Suzanne turned the kitchen light on and then flipped open the laptop that had been left on the counter.

'Music?' she asked, tapping a few keys.

'Oh my God,' Rosie said in response. She was peering at the recipe for the macarons, her eyes widening with each step. 'I thought we were going to bake something easy! Can't we just make brownies?'

'But music.' Suzanne pointed at the laptop. 'Music first.'

'We have to whisk egg whites.' Rosie said to me, pointing. 'And pipe stuff.'

'It's really easy,' Suzanne promised. 'Is it OK if I play the Lucksmiths?'

'Who?' Rosie and I said at the same time.

'I'll take that as a yes.' The music started, bouncy and cheerful. 'OK, so . . . what's the first step, Roz?'

Rosie looked at her, her eyes narrowing. 'Haven't you made these before?'

'Nope,' Suzanne said cheerfully.

'Suze!' Rosie practically wailed.

'What? They're really easy, honest. Sarah said so, and I've watched her make them.'

'Let's make brownies,' Rosie said decisively, shutting the recipe book.

A flash of annoyance passed over Suzanne's face. She reached over and opened the book again, flipping through it to get to the right page. 'We're making macarons.' She pointed to the ingredients laid out across the table. 'I got everything ready.'

Rosie let out a huffing noise. 'Why does it have to be macarons? If we make brownies, we know they'll turn out good.'

They looked at each other, belligerent. I reached out and took the recipe book, sliding it towards me to see the first step. 'Egg whites and caster sugar in a bowl,' I read out in my firmest voice. 'Four egg whites, seventy grams of sugar.' I opened the box of eggs. 'How do you just get the white bit?'

Suzanne laughed, her face relaxing. 'You have to separate them.'

Rosie still looked mutinous, now with a side of betrayed. I avoided her gaze, opening the bag of sugar and weighing out seventy grams.

'Rosie and I used to make brownies a lot,' I said to Suzanne. 'Basically because they're really easy.'

'And they taste good,' Rosie said, a sulk in her voice.

Suzanne had cracked an egg against the side of a cup and was manoeuvring the yolk from one half of the shell to the other.

'Remember that time we tried to put treacle in them?' I said to Rosie.

'Oh my God,' Rosie said, dissolving into laughter. 'It was like sludge. Actual sludge.'

'When it came out of the oven it had turned into a brick,' I continued, grinning at the memory. 'We had to put it straight in the bin.'

'So they didn't *always* taste good?' Suzanne asked, her voice teasing. She was on to the third egg, her fingers deft and shiny with eggy remnants.

'The treacle was a mistake,' Rosie conceded. She seemed mollified by our reminiscing, and she leaned across me to look at the book. Her hair tickled my face. 'But usually they were great.'

'These will be great too,' Suzanne said. She poured the egg whites from the cup into the mixing bowl, gesturing to me to add the sugar.

'A new tradition,' I said, doing so. Suzanne's whole face seemed to lift at these words, making her look suddenly very young. She smiled at me, hopeful.

'They better be good then,' Rosie said.

They weren't.

The macarons we pulled out of the oven did not in any way resemble the beautiful, colourful treats I'd seen in books and patisserie windows. The circles we'd piped on to the tray had ballooned in the oven and merged into several gigantic cracked blobs.

'Oh,' Suzanne said. She looked confused.

'We piped them too big,' Rosie said.

'Oh, did we?' Suzanne's voice was sarcastic. 'What was your first clue?'

'It's just the first tray,' I said quickly, before Rosie could respond. 'We'll pipe the rest smaller, and with more space between them.'

We took no chances with the next batch, piping small discs of the mixture into lonely pink islands on the tray. They turned out perfect and they tasted like sugary almond heaven. We took the broken pieces from the first batch and, with the help of cream and raspberry sauce, salvaged them into a gloopy, delicious mess that we heaped into one bowl to share.

Together we squashed on to the sofa in the living room, Suzanne in the middle with the bowl on her lap, the two of us on each side with a spoon each.

'Did you know it's Suze's birthday in a couple of weeks?' Rosie said to me, and Suzanne made a face.

'No!' I said. 'Why didn't you say something? What are you going to do?'

'It's not a big deal,' Suzanne said.

'It's your sixteenth – of course it's a big deal,' I said, thinking about the hall my parents had booked for my birthday. 'Are you having a party?'

'Where would I have it?' She gestured around the living room, which was indeed too small for revelry.

'You could hire somewhere,' I suggested. I picked a piece of broken macaron off my spoon and nibbled at it.

'That costs too much.' Suzanne said. She shrugged. 'I really don't care. I don't want it to be a big thing.'

This made no sense. 'Why not? Your birthday is, like, the best day of the year.'

'Not for me,' she said tightly, and I finally got it.

'Oh.'

There was an uncomfortable silence, before Rosie adjusted herself on her side of the sofa and pointed her spoon at us importantly. 'I have an idea. How about you spend the whole of your birthday weekend with us? We'll both come to yours on Friday night, have dinner or whatever, and then on Saturday we can go to the beach, meet Lev and the others, have a few drinks and stuff, then crash at yours. Then on Sunday, on your actual birthday, we'll do things like have birthday cake and whatever. Sarah will make you a birthday cake, right?'

Suzanne nodded slowly. 'But, the beach in November?'

'Sure. We'll take blankets.' Rosie was in full-on planning mode. 'Say yes. You can't not celebrate your sixteenth. And you should celebrate it with us.' She caught my eye. 'Shouldn't she?'

'Definitely,' I said.

A small smile had lifted Suzanne's face. 'That sounds nice.'

'Of course it sounds nice,' Rosie said. 'It'll be great. Quiet but celebratory. With presents.' She looked pleased with herself. 'Are you in?'

'I'm in,' Suzanne confirmed. She took a spoonful of macaron gloop. 'I can't believe how good this tastes. Why do people even bother with proper macarons when you could just do this?' She licked a spot of whipped cream off her wrist. 'You know, this is what I want the rest of my life to be like.' She looked happy and relaxed, maybe more so than I'd ever seen her. 'Baking with my friends.' She grinned at us both.

'I am definitely on board with that,' Rosie said.

'What do you think, Cads?' Suzanne asked me. 'A new tradition?'

The macaron pieces in the cream were sweet and chewy and perfect.

'A new tradition,' I confirmed.

11

As soon as I got home from school the Friday before Suzanne's birthday I went straight to my room to pack my stuff for the weekend, something I'd been too lazy to do the night before, when I'd actually had time.

I was just flicking through my T-shirts, trying to find the one that featured Moomintroll, when I heard the phone ring. As it was the landline, I hoped immediately it was Rosie, and strained to hear Mum calling my name. When no shout came, I turned in slight disappointment back to my clothes. A few minutes later, just when I was pulling the Moomintroll shirt over my head, Mum poked her head in. 'Can I come in?'

'Sure,' I said, pulling my hair out from under the T-shirt.

'That was Suzanne's aunt on the phone,' Mum said, her voice cautious and measured. She let out a long sigh and then said, 'There's not going to be a birthday weekend. It's been called off.'

My first thought was that Suzanne had done something wrong, that she and Sarah had fought over something and Suzanne had lost. My second, far more ridiculous and yet right on the heels of the first, was that it was just me that had been uninvited, that Rosie would still be there. 'Why not?'

Mum didn't say anything for what felt like a long time. She looked like she was thinking hard. Finally she said slowly, 'Suzanne's finding things difficult at the moment, and she's just not in the right frame of mind for celebration. Does that make sense?'

Not even a little.

'What do you mean, difficult?'

Another silence. 'The word Sarah used was "sad". She's very sad, overwhelmingly so.'

'You mean like depressed?' *None* of this made sense. I'd seen Suzanne so recently; in fact we'd all three met up in Starbucks earlier that week, and she'd seemed fine. And Rosie hadn't mentioned anything about her being sad at school.

'I don't think it's like that. I think it's just the case that a weekend of joviality is too much to expect right now.' It was just like my mother to use the word 'joviality' in a sentence. Why couldn't she just say fun, like a normal person?

The thought of Suzanne being so sad she didn't even want to see her friends on her birthday was in itself so unbearably sad that I suddenly felt like I wanted to cry. Mum, seeing my face, reached out and gave my hip a reassuring rub. At least, I assumed it was meant to be reassuring. The fact that it was my hip diminished the comfort slightly.

'There'll be other weekends,' she said, missing the point entirely. 'Why don't you have Rosie here instead?'

'Maybe,' I said, though I knew that wasn't an option. There would be something callous about having Suzanne's birthday weekend without her, and in my house, not hers.

It struck me after Mum left my room that only a few weeks ago I would have been thrilled at the chance to have Rosie to myself for the weekend, especially at Suzanne's expense. But so much had changed in such a short space of time, and as surprising at it still sometimes seemed to me, Suzanne was as much as part of my daily life now as Rosie was.

I sent her a message saying I hoped she was OK and to let me know when she was feeling better. She didn't reply.

On Saturday, Rosie and I met up in town and settled down in Starbucks with hot chocolates and cake. It was pouring with rain outside and neither of us was in the mood to navigate the sodden crowds of Saturday's Brighton, let alone go to the beach.

'So what did your mum tell you?' I asked. We'd saved the most pressing conversation – Suzanne – until we'd secured the sofas.

'That Suzanne's depressed,' Rosie said, arranging our two plates in front of her and picking up a knife. She raised the blade above the Danish, biting down speculatively on her lip before cutting decisively down through the middle. Custard oozed across the knife and on to the plate. 'Does that look even?'

'Sure,' I said, picking up the smaller half and putting it on my plate. I watched as she cut the chocolate muffin in half. 'Did she say anything else?'

Rosie shrugged, already in the process of cutting her halves into bite-size chunks. 'Not really. What else is there to say?'

'Mum didn't use the word "depressed",' I said, not sure where I was going with this. 'She said Suzanne was *sad*.'

Rosie laughed, but not meanly. 'Isn't it annoying that she tries to sugar-coat everything for you like you're five years old?'

'Well, yeah, but I'm not sure that's what she's doing this time. I asked if that meant she was depressed, and she said this is different.'

'Different how?'

'I have no idea.'

'What difference does it make anyway?' Rosie picked up her first chunk of Danish. I'd already finished mine. 'The end result is the same.'

I had a feeling that it made quite a big difference, and that Sarah had used sad as opposed to depressed quite deliberately. But the nuances of the two words, the look on my mother's face and even the tone of Rosie's voice seemed to belong to a world I didn't understand, no matter how much I strained.

And then the answer came to me, so obvious I wasn't sure why it had taken so long. 'We should go and see her.'

Rosie paused, flakes of Danish still on her fingers. Her forehead wrinkled slightly. 'What do you mean?'

'We should go and visit Suzanne,' I said. 'Which bit is confusing?'

'But Sarah said not to.'

'No, she didn't, she just said the birthday weekend was off. We should take her presents.' We'd bought Suzanne's card together, along with a toy elephant and a hanging butterfly decoration for her wall.

Rosie exhaled a sceptical 'hmmm', then said, 'I don't think that's a good idea. She obviously doesn't want to see people. What if you go there and Sarah's like, "What are you doing here? I told you not to come"?'

'Then we can leave. But at least we'll have made the effort, and that might help.'

'Help with what? You don't even know what's wrong with her.'

I wondered if she was being obtuse on purpose. 'Well, obviously it's something to do with her family.'

'You shouldn't assume stuff like that.' Rosie picked up the last chunk of Danish and popped it into her mouth.

I tried to ignore my rising frustration and keep my voice level. It was a waste of time for me to try to argue with anyone, especially Rosie, because I lost every single time. I was too weak to hold my ground. Soft all over, too easily dented.

'It doesn't matter anyway,' I said, trying my best to regain control over the conversation. 'Either way, she's unhappy and we're her friends, so we should go and see her on her birthday.'

Rosie considered this, her brow still scrunched. Finally she said, 'I do see what you mean, but I still don't think it's a good idea. We don't know her like we know each other, you know?'

I didn't see what that had to do with anything.

'I just mean that maybe we should let this one go and wait until we see her again,' Rosie said. She was watching my face carefully. 'If it was you, I'd definitely go anyway, whatever you said. But it's *not* you, and I don't know how she'd react, so I really don't think we should risk it.'

Despite my rising certainty that I was right on this, I was touched. She did still like me best, after all. She did recognize what our friendship had that theirs never could.

'Well, I'm going to go,' I said, making up my mind. 'I'd rather you came with me, but I'll go by myself if you don't.'

Rosie's eyebrows had risen. 'Are you going to go today?'

'Tomorrow. On her actual birthday. Maybe I'll take cake!'

'Sarah will have baked a cake,' Rosie pointed out. She was still looking at me with a look of curious surprise, as if I'd announced I wanted to learn to play the accordion or take up poi.

'Oh, good point. Maybe flowers then. I wonder if you can get sunflowers at this time of year.'

'Sunflowers?'

'Sure, why not? They're the most cheerful flower there is.'

Rosie regarded me for a moment, an odd expression on her face. Then, cautiously, said, 'Can I ask a question that is going to sound weird?' When I nodded, she said, 'Why does this matter to you so much?'

The question did sound weird, and I wasn't sure how to answer. 'Well, why doesn't it matter to you?'

'It does. I mean, Suzanne does, obviously. But I'm happy to wait until school to speak to her. I don't think either of us needs to go above and beyond. Especially you – you only know her through me. We haven't been friends for that long, not really. I don't see why you can't just wait.'

Because Suzanne had no one else. Because I'd never really had the chance to go above and beyond for a friend before. Because she clearly needed friends who were prepared to do this. Because no one should be alone and sad on their birthday, even if they thought they wanted to be. Because, and I didn't know how I knew this, she would do the same if it was me.

'I think it would be a nice thing to do,' I said.

'Nice doesn't always mean right,' Rosie said infuriatingly.

'Well, it should,' I said.

I didn't manage to persuade Rosie to come with me, but she did help me find a florist that was stocking sunflowers in pots that didn't look half dead. When I took it home, Mum watered it and set it on the kitchen counter.

'Rosie thinks it's weird,' I said, looking at the yellow petals, even brighter against the cream kitchen tiles.

'Taking Suzanne flowers?' Mum asked.

I nodded. 'It would be better if we were both going.'

'It's a lovely thing to do,' Mum said. 'And I think it means even more that you're prepared to go by yourself.'

I was trying to remind myself of this as I walked to Suzanne's the following afternoon, carrying the sunflower in one hand and the gift bag in the other. I kept imagining turning up on the doorstep and both Sarah and Suzanne craning their necks, looking for Rosie behind me. Twice I almost turned around and went home.

It looked like the lights were all off in the flat, even though it was just starting to get dark. I was instantly seized by paranoia – what if they weren't even there?

Thankfully, Sarah opened the door almost as soon as I knocked. When she saw me, her eyes widened in surprise. And then an odd expression passed over her face, a strange kind of smile, almost like she was about to cry.

'Caddy,' she said. 'Caddy and a sunflower.'

'Hi,' I said. I could feel my face going red. 'Um . . . I just wanted to bring Suzanne her presents. And say happy birthday.'

She smiled properly then. A big, friendly smile. 'How lovely. That's really lovely.' She took a step back and gestured for me to come in. 'I can't promise you'll be able to see Suzanne though,' she added, closing the door.

'That's fine,' I said quickly. 'I can just leave this here. But I thought it was . . . worth a try, you know?'

'If you want to come into the kitchen, I'll go and see how she's feeling. Do you want something to drink?'

'No, I'm fine, thanks,' I set the sunflower down on the kitchen counter.

Sarah hesitated in the doorway, as if about to say something else, then smiled again and left the room. I glanced at some of the papers on the counter – all recipes for chocolate truffle cake – and then the small pile of cards that had been left, undisplayed, on the windowsill. I managed to contain my nosiness for about thirty seconds.

There were six cards in total. A standard niece card from Sarah; a dogs-dressed-like-the-Beatles card from Brian; three general sixteenth-birthday cards from names I didn't recognize. The final card said daughter on the front. I really did hesitate this time, knowing I shouldn't look, but my hand reached out anyway and flipped the card open. 'To Suzanne', the handwriting read, 'from Mum and Dad'. The card's text said 'Happy Birthday'. The card didn't even have a '16' on it.

My stomach felt queasy. I turned the card over, as if I was expecting to see a proper message on the back. Was that really it? The most basic of daughter birthday cards? It was almost worse than nothing at all.

I heard footsteps in the hall and I turned quickly, pushing the cards back into place, hoping to see Suzanne. But it wasn't her, and by Sarah's face I knew it wouldn't be later either.

'I don't think it's a good idea,' she said. 'I'm sorry.'

'Does she know I'm here?' I asked, just to check.

'She's asleep,' Sarah said. 'And I don't really want to wake her up. It's been a tough couple of days.'

I hesitated, then reached out my hand to touch the cards. 'Was it . . . ?' I let the sentence linger.

'You saw the card?' Sarah sighed and came over, reaching straight for the daughter card. 'Quite something, isn't it?' She looked angry, and she was shaking her head. 'I'd have ripped it up before she saw it, if I'd got to it first.'

She turned the card over in her hands, exhaled again and put it back. 'She took it hard,' she said quietly. 'I think she'd got her hopes up for more than this.'

'Was there any present?' I asked, almost afraid of the answer.

'Yes,' Sarah said, her expression grim. 'A bank transfer.'

'Oh,' I said. 'Well, that's something.'

'Yes,' Sarah said. 'It's something.' She paused, looking at me. Then, gently, she asked, 'What did your parents give you for your sixteenth?'

I thought about the comically oversized card shaped like a cupcake, my beloved laptop, the silver bracelet, the whole bunch of new clothes. My mother had stuck a photo of me as a baby in the card and written underneath: '16 years of joy!'

After a silence, Sarah reached for the gift bag I realized I was still holding. 'I'll tell her you came by as soon as she wakes up.'

'I could come right back if she wants me to,' I heard myself say.

A smile spread across her face. 'You're very sweet.'

'I just want to make it better,' I said, feeling helpless.

Sarah didn't reply. She didn't need to. I knew what she was

thinking, because I was thinking it too. It looped in my head as I walked back home.

You can't.

Later that evening, my laptop pinged. *Suzanne Watts has tagged you in a post.*

I clicked on the notification and a photo of the sunflower filled my screen. It was sitting on her bedside cabinet, beside the elephant toy. She'd written: 'Sunshine in a pot. Thank you SO much, Caddy.'

Not long after, my phone lit up with a text.

19.33: Thank you thank you thank you xxxx
19.35: You are welcome! xxx
19.36: Means the world. Can't even tell you x
19.37: :) Happy birthday!
19.38: Haha, thanks. Happier now :)

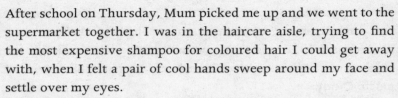

12

After school on Thursday, Mum picked me up and we went to the supermarket together. I was in the haircare aisle, trying to find the most expensive shampoo for coloured hair I could get away with, when I felt a pair of cool hands sweep around my face and settle over my eyes.

I jumped about a foot in the air, dropping the John Frieda bottle I was holding and letting out a noise that was somewhere been a shriek and a laugh. Trying to regain my composure, I picked up the shampoo and stood to face my attacker.

'Sorry.' Suzanne was laughing, almost doubled over with it. 'Oh my God, Caddy, I didn't think you'd react like that.'

My heart was still racing, but I was laughing too, the two of us in pieces in the middle of the aisle. An old woman with nothing but washing-up liquid and a pineapple in her basket eyed us warily.

'You can't sneak up behind someone in a supermarket,' I said between gasps. 'What did you think would happen?'

When we'd calmed down, she reached for the bottle I was holding and looked at it. 'You should go for the honey one,' she said. 'This is for platinum blondes. Yours is warmer.' She turned to the rows of bottles and located the one she was looking for, holding it out to me.

I was so happy to see her.

'This might be a stupid question, but what are you doing here?' I asked, taking the bottle and tucking it under my arm.

'Shopping. Obvs. Sarah's here somewhere. Are you here with your parents?'

As she said this my mother came around the corner, pushing the trolley in front of her. When she saw me, she let out a tut of annoyance and came to a stop next to me. 'There you are. Didn't I ask you to get lemons?'

'I'll get them in a minute,' I said, wondering for a second why she was ignoring Suzanne, before realizing they'd never actually met. 'Mum, this is Suzanne.'

Mum's face lit up, which was embarrassing. 'Oh! Hello!' She reached out her hand and Suzanne shook it, looking surprised but polite. 'I'm Carol.'

Sarah walked past the entrance to the aisle at that moment, then did a double take and turned her trolley towards us.

'Hello, Caddy!' she said enthusiastically as she approached. 'What a lovely surprise.'

It took barely a minute for Mum and Sarah to turn their enthusiasm on to each other, shaking hands and introducing themselves while Suzanne and I inched closer together in bemused solidarity.

'Isn't it weird how happy they both were to see each of us?' she muttered to me. 'Sarah never looks as happy to see me as she did to see you.'

Even if this was true, they both seemed to forget about us, barely noticing as we sidled off to wander the aisles together. Trust my mother to strike up a friendship among the shampoo bottles.

'Do you think they're talking about us?' I asked.

'Undoubtedly,' Suzanne replied. She picked up a lemon from the box and sniffed it. 'Waxed or unwaxed?'

'What's the difference?'

'Isn't the clue in the name?' She held out two bags for me, one in each hand. I selected the unwaxed ones. 'Have you spoken to Roz today? Did she tell you what happened in PE?'

When I said no, she launched into a complicated story I couldn't really follow that involved trampolines and an overenthusiastic somersault attempt. I watched her face as she spoke, searching for a trace of the previous weekend's sadness. There was none.

We meandered companionably around the supermarket for a while longer before finding my mother and Sarah in the frozen section. They were pushing their trolleys side by side, still deep in conversation. When they saw us, they stopped talking abruptly. Sarah looked a little guilty, while Mum wore a look of earnest sympathy. I knew this face. I called it her Samaritans Face.

Suzanne's cheerful expression faltered a little, clearly having spotted The Face and being all too familiar with what it meant. She shot Sarah a brief, sullen look and dropped the bags of pasta and rice she'd been holding into the trolley, which was much emptier than Mum's.

'Ready to go, love?' Mum asked me, seemingly oblivious. She took the lemons from me and placed them on top of a packet of dishtowels.

I nodded, watching Suzanne paste a smile back on to her face as she turned to me. 'See you later?'

'Yeah, maybe this weekend?'

She nodded. 'I'll text you.' She leaned over and hugged me, which was new, but nice.

Mum didn't say much until we were out of the supermarket and heading towards the car. Then it began.

'I had a lovely chat with Sarah,' she said, manoeuvring the trolley around an ineptly parked car. 'She seems like a lovely person.' The double use of lovely meant she must really be impressed. 'And I must say, what a saint – taking on Suzanne.' She stopped at the car, keys already in hand, and opened the boot.

I felt my forehead crease. 'What's that supposed to mean?'

'I mean, teenagers are hard enough work as it is –' Mum shot me a pointed look at this, beginning to load the bags into the car – 'but factor in the situation here and . . . well, it's a lot to take on, I'm sure.'

'It's probably worse for Suzanne,' I said flatly.

'Perhaps,' Mum said, only fanning my growing annoyance. 'Take the trolley back will you, love?'

When I returned to the car and slid into the passenger seat, clicking the seat belt into place, Mum continued where she'd left off.

'I hope she's getting regular counselling.' She adjusted her seat and tapped her keys gently against the steering wheel. She looked at me. 'Is she getting regular counselling?'

'How would I know?' I pulled my elbow up against the window frame and slouched a little in my seat.

'There's no need to take that tone.' Mum reached over and straightened my seat belt, which had twisted near my shoulder. 'I could recommend some fantastic therapists who work with teenagers. You should find out for sure.'

Like I was really going to ask my friend if she was having counselling, for God's sake.

'OK, I'll try,' I said.

'How does she seem to you?' Mum asked, oblivious to my sarcasm. 'Does she seem like she's coping well?'

'She's fine, Mum,' I said, trying to keep the irritation out of my voice. 'Can we go home now?'

'I'd be surprised if that were the case,' Mum said, making no move to put the keys in the ignition. 'Growing up in that kind of environment, it has a profound effect. Children rarely pass through their teenage years unscathed.'

Are you *a therapist now?* I wanted to say. I *so* wanted to say it.

'And this can have a negative impact on their relationships,' she continued. 'I did wonder if there was something strained about how she and Sarah were with each other.'

As opposed to what? How relaxed and open Mum and I were right this moment?

'Can we please go home?'

Mum ignored me. She was sat back in her seat, fiddling with her keys, her head tilted slightly upward, eyes on the ceiling. She seemed like she was thinking hard, and she didn't say anything for at least a minute.

'I hope you'll be careful in your friendship with her,' she said finally, delicately.

'What do you mean?'

'Damaged people—'

'*Mum!* You can't say things like that!'

'I'm trying to be frank with you,' Mum said, raising her hand to indicate she had more to say. 'And yes, it is upsetting and unfair, and I certainly don't want you using the term in front of her, but it's important that you recognize what damage has been done to her. And what effect that could have on your friendship and the way you interact.'

My face felt hot, and a big part of me wanted to get out of the car and bolt, just to get away from her. There was something horrible about what she was saying, and she either didn't recognize it or just didn't care.

'My priority is you,' Mum said. 'I worry about what effect this will have on *you*. People in pain can be very self-destructive. And sometimes they pull in the people who are close to them, often without realizing.'

'I'll be sure to be on the lookout for destruction,' I said, this time letting the sarcasm soak into my words. Mum looked at me for a moment like she didn't know me.

It worked though. She put the key into the ignition and turned it, finally letting the matter drop.

13

By the time December rolled around, I was up to my neck in exam revision and barely had time to see my family, let alone Rosie or Suzanne. I kept in touch with both of them by text, getting so used to their respective styles that I didn't even need to check the name any more. Rosie was full of her special brand of snarky cheer in her messages; Suzanne far more random and quick to joke. When I told her that I was revising for my Religious Studies exam, she went through a phase of messaging me with Deep And Important questions.

Caddy, is the green grass you see the same green grass as the green grass I see?

Caddy, would you be able to fly if you really believed you could?

Caddy, what is life?

Caddy, what if you're dreaming right now? WAKE UP CADDY.

And so on.

On a Wednesday evening in early December I was taking a break from revising, playing an unfeasibly addictive game on my laptop, when my phone began buzzing beside me. I reached distractedly over for it, keeping one hand tapping on my keyboard. I was about a minute from a new high score.

Fingers scrabbling, I found the answer button.

'Hello?'

'Hey, it's me.'

'Who's me?' I asked. In my attempt to pick up without interrupting my game, I hadn't even looked at the name flashing on the screen.

There was a slight pause. 'Me as in Suzanne?'

'Oh!' My eyes flicked automatically towards the time on my laptop – 21.57 – and that was all it took. There was a trumpet horn of doom and an unnecessarily large GAME OVER sign started pinging all over the screen. 'Oh, dammit.'

'Is this a bad time?' Her voice was bemused. 'Was that a trumpet?'

'No, it's fine,' I said, ignoring the second question. 'What's up?'

'I'm outside.'

'What do you mean, outside?' I asked, not following this.

'I mean, outside your house. Outside your window.'

I moved my laptop off my lap and on to the floor and scrambled across the bed to look outside. Sure enough, there was Suzanne. When she saw me, she waved.

'Can I come up?'

'Why don't you just use the front door?' I asked, confused.

'It's late. I don't want your parents to know I'm here.'

'OK, but how are you going to get up here?'

In answer, Suzanne ended the call, made a couple of pointing gestures I couldn't decipher and then disappeared from sight. Seconds later her head appeared over the garage roof, and then the rest of her.

I opened the window and she crawled through it, pausing to take off her shoes before sliding down on to my bed. She grinned at me. 'Hi!'

'Hello,' I replied, trying not to laugh. 'Nice acrobatics.'

'It's a handy skill,' Suzanne said.

'So . . . not that I'm not thrilled to see you . . .' I began.

'Obviously!' she interrupted brightly.

'Obviously,' I affirmed. 'But . . . why are you here?'

'I had a fight with Sarah, so I just wanted some space. Just for a bit. Is it OK if I hang out here? What have you been up to tonight?' She glanced around my room as she spoke, her eyes settling on my photo montage.

'Not much,' I started to say, but she interrupted me again, her eyes widening.

'Oh!' she exclaimed, actually saying the word. 'That's me!'

She seemed so genuinely surprised and pleased that I laughed. 'Why so surprised?'

There was just one picture with Suzanne in it in the whole bunch; the three of us on the pier, balanced on one of the benches, posing as the no-evil monkeys. I was see, Rosie was hear, Suzanne was speak. I loved the picture so much that I'd put it up weeks ago, back when it still bothered me to share even photograph space with her.

'I don't know.' Suzanne was smiling, leaning closer to examine the picture. 'I guess I didn't realize I was important enough for your wall.' She rolled her eyes. 'Oh God, that was a pathetic thing to say. Please forget I said that.'

We talked about nothing for a while as Suzanne roamed around my room, studying various photographs and running her fingers along the spines of my books. Finally she came across my collection of nail varnishes and held one up hopefully.

'Can I do your nails?'

We settled, cross-legged and facing each other, my back against the wall and my hand splayed out on the floor. We were both quiet for the first few nails.

'So you had a fight with Sarah?' I prompted finally.

She nodded. I thought about the first time I'd met Sarah, when she and Suzanne had picked me up on the way to Rosie's house, way back in September. The two of them had seemed like friends. What had happened?

'I thought you got along pretty well,' I said. Suzanne had chosen a teal nail varnish from a set Tarin had bought me a couple of years earlier that I hadn't even opened, loyal as I was to my spectrum of pinks.

'We did,' Suzanne said. The teal had sparkles in it. 'Sarah's really nice. I mean, it was kind of weird at first, but I think we were both getting used to it. But seeing my dad . . . you know, at the marina?' I nodded. 'It really got to me. I tried to shake it off, but it feels like it changed everything.'

I hesitated. 'Am I allowed to ask why?'

Her head was slightly bent, but I saw the smile quirk over her face. 'You can ask me anything, Cads.' There was a pause. After a moment, she looked up to grin at me. 'Go on, then.'

'Why has it changed everything?' I asked obediently.

Her head dipped again. 'Because it turned out she knew he'd be in Brighton. And she didn't tell me.'

'Oh,' I said quietly.

'She says they all decided not to tell me, because the chances of us, like, running into each other or whatever were so remote. Which I guess they were. But it happened. And it was like . . . I don't know. Just a really horrible shock, I guess. I mean, I trusted her, and now I feel like I can't. I thought she was on my side.'

'She is on your side,' I said immediately.

Suzanne shook her head. 'No, she's not.' She was quiet for a while, concentrating hard on my index finger, sweeping the polish across my nail. I was about to change the subject when she spoke. 'She wants us to go back to my parents' for Christmas.'

I was so surprised my head actually jerked, causing my hand to spasm.

'Hand still, please.' Suzanne said, not looking at me. 'And I know. It sounds bad, right? That was pretty much my reaction when she first said it, last week.'

'I don't get it. Why would she suggest something like that? You're obviously not going to go, right?'

'Well, for her it's not this terrible thing. She's been saying for a while that I should see my mother. Trying to arrange dinner, things like that. I've said no for a while. I've actually been worried that she's going to give up trying to convince me and one day I'll come home and Mum will be there.' She sighed and dipped the brush back into the bottle. 'Anyway, that hasn't happened yet thankfully. But Sarah's moved on from that now to say we should spend Christmas with them. Her reasoning is that all of us will be there together, her and me and my parents and my brother. Nothing will happen, she says, and it will be good for all of us.'

'But that's not the point, right?' I said carefully.

'What's not the point?'

'That nothing will happen.'

Suzanne stopped, the brush tip just above my finger. She looked at me, letting out a *tchts* of frustration. 'Yes, that's exactly it. See, *you* get it. Why doesn't she get it? She's been making me feel like I'm being completely unreasonable.'

'I don't get why she'd think you'd be OK with that.'

'She knows I'm not. But she says I probably never will be, that it's the kind of thing I just have to do. Otherwise I'll always feel like I can't. She says until we've all sat down together we'll never be in a position to move forward.'

'But what about when you saw your dad that time?'

At this, Suzanne smiled a humourless smile and resumed painting my nails. 'Sarah says that he says he ignored me out of respect for me. Apparently he thought that I'd "freak out" if he came over. Can you believe that?' She'd clearly meant this to be a flippant question, but it came out earnest, like she was really asking me.

I thought carefully about how to answer this. 'Um, I guess that would make sense, but I don't think it makes it any better.' I hesitated. 'What do your parents say? About Christmas?'

'They want me to come, Sarah says. I don't know if I believe her. I spoke to my brother and he said basically the same thing.'

'Well, that's good,' I said cautiously.

Suzanne shrugged. 'I don't know what difference it really makes now. The damage is done.' She started the second coat on my left hand. 'That's not what I'm really worried about anyway. Sarah said something about needing to think to the future, that we couldn't stay like this forever. But I actually thought this *was* a forever thing. That it would be me and her for the next few years, until I'm old enough to move out or whatever.'

I felt a stab of sadness, unsure of what to say. I couldn't even imagine living with such a temporary foundation. I'd assumed it was forever too. Wasn't Sarah supposed to be the great rescuer in this scenario?

'So, what – are you going to move back at some point?'

Suzanne looked troubled. 'Maybe. God, I hope not. But now I'm thinking that this is all some kind of groundwork that Sarah is laying, so she can say, "Oh, see, you're all fine now, you can go back to live with them and I can have my life back."'

'I'm sure that won't happen,' I said automatically, even though I wasn't even the slightest bit sure. 'Besides—'

She put her hand up to shush me, so suddenly that I did so without question. Her brow had furrowed and she was angling her head slightly towards my bedroom door.

'*What?*' I mouthed.

'*Sarah,*' she mouthed back. She pointed towards the door and mimed listening with her hand to her ear.

I strained to hear, and sure enough I could just about hear the sounds of my mother talking to another woman. I wouldn't have been able to place the voice as Sarah's by myself.

'Shit,' Suzanne said out loud through a sigh.

'Why is she here?' I asked, bewildered.

She made a face as if she really didn't want to answer this, then said, 'She made me give her yours and Rosie's addresses, when we first started being friends. She must have come here first because it's closer.'

'Why is she so overprotective?' I asked. 'She doesn't seem like the type.'

'It's not that she's overprotective. She's just trying to . . . get a grip on me, I guess. Maybe she thinks if I know she'll come looking for me, I won't leave.'

'Do you leave a lot?'

'Sometimes I just want to be by myself. I just walk for a bit, but I always come back. Usually she doesn't even notice I've gone.'

I thought of the bare window in her room. *Always leave an exit clear.* So she had meant it.

Suzanne looked towards my window now, twisting her lip thoughtfully. 'If I leave now, I can get home in ten minutes. Then she can wander around Brighton looking for me for as long as she likes, and I'll still be there when she gets back.'

'What if she's worried about you?'

'She's not.'

'What if you get in trouble?'

She laughed at this. 'What kind of trouble? Like ground me? I'll just go anyway. She can't do anything. Who cares?'

I hesitated, trying to think of the best way to play this. 'I wonder why my parents haven't come up here to look for you.'

'They must just assume I'm not here.' Suzanne had picked up the polish again and was finishing my last two nails. 'Because *obviously* if I turned up at your window, you'd tell them immediately.' She grinned at me.

'Obviously,' I said, but a little more weakly. 'But why's Sarah still here then?'

'Probably complaining about me. You know she and your mum have met up a couple of times since that day at the supermarket?'

'Really?'

'Yeah. I think it's the Samaritans thing.'

'Yeah, people like talking to her because they assume she must be a good listener.'

'No, I mean . . .' Suzanne trailed off, then smiled. 'Yeah, that must be it.'

She'd finished my nails and was twisting the lid back on to the bottle.

'I think you should go downstairs,' I said.

Her face fell a little and she looked at me warily. 'Why? Are you turning me in?'

'No, I just think that's the best way to play it. I'll come downstairs with you, and we'll say you came to see me. Maybe we can all agree that you can come and see me whenever without needing to ask. Then you've got freedom, and she won't check up on you.'

Suzanne smiled. 'As simple as that, huh?' She glanced towards my window again. 'It would be a lot easier to just go.'

'Not in the long run,' I said.

She was silent for a while, considering this. 'OK, fine. I'll try it your way.' She stood up. 'Will this get you into trouble?'

Possibly. 'Shouldn't do.'

We headed out of my room together and down the hall to the stairs. I could hear Sarah's voice more clearly as we started down them, her words suddenly decipherable. I tried to get into the kitchen as fast as possible to stop her saying anything bad about Suzanne, but we ended up walking through the door just as she said, 'The problem is, I thought she'd be grateful. But she's such *hard work*.'

There was a terrible silence as Sarah and my parents realized we were there. I glanced behind me at Suzanne, hoping that by some miracle she hadn't heard, but her face was hard and set. I looked towards Sarah, hoping to see guilt and contrition on her face, but her initial expression of surprise had faded into frustrated anger.

Apologize, I thought to her desperately. If she apologized immediately, things could still be OK.

But she didn't.

'Caddy,' Dad said, patiently but with a hint of annoyance, 'why didn't you tell us Suzanne was here?'

'I didn't think I needed to,' I responded, hearing my sullen tone and instantly regretting it. None of this was going right.

'So you *are* here,' Sarah said to Suzanne, her voice shaky with controlled anger. 'Why didn't you answer your phone?'

'I left it behind.'

'Don't you care that I can't get a hold of you when you do that?'

Suzanne looked her right in the eye. 'No.'

My heart was starting to pound, my hands clammy at my sides. Fights between my own family in my kitchen were bad enough. But a fight between Sarah and Suzanne? I had to fight a childish impulse to run away.

'I'm trying to look after you,' Sarah said slowly, angrily. 'How can I do that when you decide to disappear?'

'I'm right here,' Suzanne shot back.

'OK.' Mum stood up suddenly, one hand raised slightly. 'Let's calm down.'

'You see what I mean?' Sarah said to her, the worst possible thing she could have said. She seemed to realize it too, and her face faltered for the first time. 'Oh,' she said quietly, almost to herself. 'Oh, this is difficult.'

'You mean *I* am,' Suzanne said tightly. I could hear suppressed tears in her voice. 'Hard work, right?'

'I *worry* about you.' Sarah's voice was earnest and frustrated, rising with each word. 'How can I know, when you're not in your room, where you are? How can I be sure that this isn't the time you won't come home again?'

My mother took a step forward and said '*Sarah*' in a quick, warning voice, but she wasn't looking at Sarah, or even Suzanne. She was looking at *me* with an anxious, frustrated frown on her face.

For a moment, I still didn't get it. And then I did. Something in my head finally clicked; *Samaritans . . . won't come home again . . . I'm not allowed to be at home by myself . . .* . Sarah wasn't worried Suzanne would *get* hurt. She was worried she'd hurt *herself*.

'I *will* come home again,' Suzanne said, and then she started to cry, helplessly, right there in the middle of my kitchen. She pressed a hand to her mouth and turned away from us, her shoulders shaking.

If I'd been a better person, I'd have gone to her straight away, but I was frozen in place by confusion and worry. This was the bit I felt most guilty about later. The beat it took for any of us to move to her side that was just a little bit too long. Both Sarah and my mother went to her, finally, while I stood there clumsily and my dad rubbed his forehead with his fingers, shaking his head.

They left together not long after. The fight had gone from Suzanne, and Sarah seemed, finally, remorseful.

'Do you want to talk about it?' Mum asked me.

Maybe I'd have said yes if she hadn't used her Samaritans voice and face. But she did. And so I didn't.

I went up to my room and found my phone half-buried under a pile of schoolbooks on my bed. I tapped out a message to Suzanne and sent it.

22.49: I'm sorry. Next time I'll let you go through the window
xxx

22.59: Don't be sorry. Not your fault x

23.00: Are you OK? x

23.04: No.

23.05: Do you want to talk about it? x

**23.09: Never. Really never. Can we never talk about it?
Please?**

23.10: Talk about what?

23.11: :) Love you x

Part 3

14

One week before Christmas, Tarin and her boyfriend split up. I was the only one who seemed surprised.

'I had thought she was spending less time with him,' Mum said. The two of us were in the kitchen, wrapping presents for my younger cousins, while Tarin cried on the phone to her friend in the living room.

'But they were together for two years,' I said. 'Doesn't that count for anything?'

'They were happy for most of that time,' Mum said. 'I think that's what matters.'

I made a face. 'It doesn't seem worth it.'

'Why not?' Mum asked. She was smiling. 'Because it ends?'

'Well, yeah.'

'Maybe we shouldn't have Christmas then,' Mum said seriously. 'It'll have to end.'

I rolled my eyes. 'Sarcasm doesn't suit you, Mum.'

'My sweet girl.' Mum leaned over and put an arm around me. 'This is a good lesson to learn now, when it's happening to someone else: letting go is just as important as holding on, sometimes. It's a good thing that Tarin ended this relationship if she wasn't happy. I'm proud of her.'

'But she wasted her time,' I said, frustrated. 'And now she's miserable. What was the point if she just had to let go at the end? Isn't it better to be with someone worth holding on to?'

'People can spend their whole lives thinking that way,' Mum said. 'But people we love come and go, Caddy. That doesn't mean we loved them any less at the time.'

I tried to talk to Tarin about it, but she refused to talk about Adam, insisting instead that she wanted to spend time with me and Rosie, like we used to do when we were younger.

'And Suzanne,' I said.

'Oh yeah,' she said. 'It's three of you now. I keep forgetting.'

Suzanne was uncharacteristically shy around Tarin at first, letting Rosie and me do most of the talking when the four of us went to Nando's for a Christmas Eve-Eve dinner. It was the night before Suzanne was to go to Reading with Sarah, something she had almost completely avoided talking about, even when it was just the three of us. All I knew was that they'd 'compromised' and would be spending their Christmas in a hotel with the rest of Suzanne's family.

After the food arrived, Tarin moved into big-sister mode. I could almost see it happening.

'So,' she said to Suzanne, spreading butter on her corn, 'how's everything with you? How long have you been in Brighton now?'

'Fine,' Suzanne said, in a way that seemed automatic. 'Um, about five months.'

'Are you getting on OK?'

I recognized the instinctive concern in Tarin's voice, but Suzanne seemed, if anything, confused. 'Yeah, fine,' she said.

Tarin smiled. 'Really? You're a better person than me if that's true. I was a gigantic mess when I was your age.'

Something lit up in Suzanne's eyes. 'Really?'

'Oh yeah.' Tarin bit down on her straw. 'Right, Cads? Wasn't I a mess?'

'A big mess,' I confirmed.

'I used to sneak out and stuff,' Tarin explained. 'Trouble in school.' She grinned. 'I was a right cliché, me. I mean, I did have a mental illness. But still. Own your behaviour and all that.'

'My dad used to beat me up,' Suzanne replied, using the

same matter-of-fact tone as Tarin.

'That's shit,' Tarin said sympathetically. She reached out her fist and Suzanne bumped it obligingly. 'So's my mental illness. But look at me!' She gestured to herself with the chicken wing she was holding. 'I'm a totally functioning adult. I pay taxes and everything.'

Rosie caught my eye and grinned. The grin said, *Your sister is the best*. I grinned back. *I know*.

'I'm just saying it doesn't last forever,' Tarin said. 'Even if it feels like it will, you know? And you're still in the middle of it.' She smiled, encouraging and hopeful. 'But you'll be *fine*, love.'

This was how Tarin talked. Full of darlings and loves and gorgeouses. But the look on Suzanne's face; it was like no one had ever said that to her before. Such a simple statement with a casual endearment, the kind I barely registered when it was aimed at me.

'I hope so,' Suzanne said, and there was a warmth in her voice now, the wariness gone.

Christmas was fairly quiet that year. Both my parents seemed to be on high alert to any changes to Tarin's moods after the break-up, but she was fine, pointedly taking her medication while she had an audience of at least one of us. On Christmas Eve she slept in my bed, curling herself around me, telling me silly stories as if I was still four years old. I didn't mind.

I saw Rosie every day of the Christmas holidays, even meeting up on Christmas Day to exchange presents, as we had done for the last few years after her baby sister had died and she'd spent that Christmas with my family. I spoke to Suzanne over the phone every day except Christmas Day, when she enacted a communications blackout for twenty-four hours before resuming normalcy as if nothing had happened.

She came around to my house almost immediately after she

returned to Brighton, armed with my Christmas presents and a tin of homemade mince pies for my parents. Sarah was with her, and she sat downstairs with my mother drinking coffee while Suzanne followed me upstairs. Rosie was already in my room, stretched across my bed, playing *Mario Kart*.

'Hey,' Suzanne said, sitting down next to her and tapping her head.

'Hey,' Rosie said, not even looking away from the screen. 'Good Christmas?'

'Mmmm.' Suzanne pulled her feet up under her and rested her chin on her knees. There was something heavy in her shoulders, I noticed then. A sadness in her eyes.

'You OK?' I asked, pausing in the act of unwrapping one of my presents.

Suzanne nodded quickly, a reassuring grin sweeping across her face. 'Sure. Tired. Happy to be home.'

'How was Reading?' Rosie asked, still focusing most of her attention on her pixelated alter ego. She was looking away from Suzanne, clearly unaware just how unwelcome her question was.

'I don't really want to talk about it,' Suzanne said, her voice still light, just casual enough. She flapped a hand at me. 'Open it!'

I ripped aside the last remnants of wrapping paper to reveal a photo frame decorated with silver leaves and vines. The photo was the same one I had in my montage, of the three of us posing on a bench on Brighton pier.

'I gave the same picture to Rosie,' Suzanne said unnecessarily. I glanced at her, the smile I'd broken into still on my face, to see that her forehead had an anxious crease. 'Because I think it's so great. But you don't have to display it if—'

'I love it,' I interrupted, and her expression relaxed. 'It's going on my shelf. Thank you!' I sat up on to my knees and leaned over to hug her.

When we broke apart, I noticed the delicate chain she had around her neck, a tiny white bird hanging at its end. 'I love your necklace!' I said. 'Christmas present?'

She smiled. 'Thanks! Yes. From my mum.' She glanced down at the bird. 'It's a dove. Like a promise, see? It means, like, a fresh start.' She looked so pleased I suddenly felt choked. 'It's my favourite thing I've ever owned.'

Rosie tossed the Wii remote on to my pillow and adjusted herself so she was facing the two of us. 'It must have been good, then,' she said cheerfully. 'With your mum?'

Suzanne's face closed off. She looked away from us both, her fingers finding each other in her lap and twisting together. 'Really don't want to talk about it.'

Rosie shrugged. 'Well, it's a nice necklace anyway. And a promise? That must be good, right?'

'How was *your* Christmas?' Suzanne asked in response. Her voice was hard though, and the question came out antagonistic.

'Better than yours, clearly,' Rosie replied, rolling her eyes. 'Do you want me to be sorry about that?'

I just sat there holding the photo frame, watching them. Rosie was just being her usual self, all light snark and sniping, but Suzanne clearly *wasn't* herself. She was looking at Rosie with nothing but ice.

'Did you get any other presents?' I asked, attempting to lift the tension, even slightly.

Suzanne's head snapped towards me. 'For God's *sake*, Caddy, what part of *I don't want to talk about it* don't you get?'

'*Hey*,' Rosie's voice, suddenly sharp, cut through the room. 'Be a bitch to me if you want, but don't talk to Caddy like that.' She'd sat up a little on her calves, all traces of humour gone from her face. Protective-best-friend mode.

The tension burned, peaked and dissipated almost as soon as it had arrived. Suzanne's face relaxed and she looked at me. 'Sorry.'

'That's OK,' I said immediately.

'No, it's not. Christmas was just a bit shit, but it's over now, and it's not your fault. I just want to be with my friends.' She glanced at Rosie, reached out a hand and poked her shoulder. 'That means you, bitch.'

Rosie grinned. To her credit, she let the conciliatory moment pass without comment. 'Damn right it does.' She poked back. 'Takes one to know one.'

I felt the snake in my stomach uncoil and I let out a breath, relaxing. Suzanne flashed another tentative smile at me and I smiled back, trying to put all the friendly reassurance I had into it.

Rosie picked up one of the Wii remotes and waved it at us. 'Multiplayer?'

We arranged ourselves over the bed so we could all face my TV as the simplest *Mario Kart* track loaded on screen. Suzanne shifted herself so she was partly leaning against both of us, her head almost in my lap, her feet resting on the backs of Rosie's legs. We had the whole of my bedroom open to us but still that's how we stayed for the rest of the afternoon, the three of us tumbled and wedged together, until Sarah came upstairs to take Suzanne home.

That year started slowly, the first few weeks unravelling with new coursework deadlines and the results of the mock exams from before Christmas. I had a comfortable mix of As and Bs, results which would have been considered good in any normal school but were signs of inadequacy in the eyes of both my school and my parents.

'Maybe you should cut back on the time you're spending with your friends,' Mum said to me the evening I got my results.

'Why?' I asked, defensive immediately on their behalf. 'What's it got to do with them?'

'Well, this is an important year,' Mum said, as if I didn't already know. 'You can't afford to be distracted in the run-up to your exams, Caddy. You're capable of A grades. So we expect A grades. Whatever Suzanne has told you, your results *do* matter.'

It took me a second. 'Wait – what? Suzanne told me *what*?'

'I just hope she isn't passing her clear disregard for education on to you,' Mum said, either ignoring my question or choosing to interpret it to suit her own thought process. 'After all these years at Esther's, it would be tragic if you threw it all away in your final few months.'

Her words wound me up for two reasons. One, that she could be so preachily judgemental about a friend of mine that she basically knew nothing about, aside from whatever Sarah had chosen to tell her. Second, that she could think I was so impressionable that my just being friends with someone for whom school wasn't the highest priority would be enough to ruin the private-school investment they'd made.

'I guess it makes sense,' Suzanne said diplomatically, when I complained to her and Rosie about my parents' impossible standards, leaving out the fact that they partially blamed the two of them. 'It must cost a lot for you to go to Esther's, right?'

'It's *thousands*,' Rosie said. 'Like, literally thousands. Per *term*.'

I felt my face flush. 'I never asked for it.'

'So? You still got it,' Rosie said bluntly. She'd never had much time for my private-school complex.

'They must be expecting great things,' Suzanne said. 'Uni, right?'

'Oh yeah.' There had never even been a question. 'Law or something.'

She made a face and looked at Rosie, as if expecting back-up. 'Really? Law?'

'Should I be offended that you look so surprised?'

'You know that's basically arguing for a living?'

I had to laugh. 'Yeah, OK, it doesn't scream Caddy Oliver.'

'What do *you* want to do?'

It was such a simple question. 'I don't know. Law, I guess.'

'You guess?' she repeated, grinning. 'It's *your* life, Cads. What do *you* actually want?'

'Most people our age don't know what they want to do,' I said defensively. 'Do *you* know?'

'No, but I'm a mess,' Suzanne said matter-of-factly. 'I need to sort myself out first. I'll be lucky to make it to eighteen.'

'Don't be such a drama queen,' Rosie put in, rolling her eyes. She'd stretched out on her back, her head hanging off her bed, dark curls touching the floor. 'Any one of us could get hit by a bus tomorrow.'

'When did we start talking about death?' I asked. An image came to my mind of Sarah's face before Christmas, when she'd said about Suzanne not coming home again. I'd honoured Suzanne's request to never talk about it, but that didn't mean it wasn't in my head.

'*I'm* going to be a businesswoman,' Rosie said. 'Caddy, you could be my PA. You'd be a great PA. Organized and anal.'

'God, thanks,' I said. 'Organized *and* anal?'

'I think you should be a therapist or something,' Suzanne said, cutting in before Rosie could respond. 'Or a counsellor. Someone who listens.'

'That's a good idea,' Rosie said, swinging herself up and flipping on to her stomach. 'You've got that whole calm empathy thing going on.'

Calm empathy was surely just a nice spin on what I'd been

hearing since I was eight – *passive and a little too placid, though very sweet,* an old school report had said – but still, I was touched. It had never occurred to me that my flaws could be strengths in a different context.

'Anyway,' Rosie said briskly, sitting up properly and reaching for a folder beside her, 'we're not meant to be talking about your further-education prospects. We're meant to be making sure Suze has any.'

Suzanne smirked, rolling her eyes. 'Any further education?'

'Any education at all,' Rosie corrected, mock sternly. The three of us were spending our Sunday afternoon at her house, taking refuge from the January sleet that was rattling against the window. She had taken it upon herself to improve Suzanne's school performance, which had, apparently, been in steady decline for several months. I'd tagged along to help, but I'd mainly been sorting her DVDs into alphabetical order and eating Doritos, then distracting them both with complaints about my parents.

'Where do you live?' Rosie asked, flipping open the folder.

'Um . . .' Suzanne screwed up her face obediently in concentration. '*J'habite à Brighton, qui est un ville le sud de l'Angleterre.*'

'*Dans,*' I said.

'What?' they both said together.

'It's "*dans*" le sud,' I said. '*Dans le sud de l'Angleterre.*'

'How can you know that when you don't even have the answers in front of you?' Rosie asked, looking annoyed.

'I take French too, you know,' I said.

'Private school,' Suzanne said to Rosie in an exaggerated whisper. '*Dans* private school.'

I rolled my eyes, but laughed despite myself.

'What's private school in French?' Suzanne asked me.

'No!' Rosie said firmly, leaning over the bed to give Suzanne a reprimanding tap on the head. 'No distractions.' She looked at me. 'Don't distract her.'

'*Merde*,' Suzanne said morosely, giving me a beseeching look.

'Of course that's the word that sticks in your head,' Rosie said drily.

'It's one word; it's not difficult.'

'And this is just a few words strung together. OK, the next one is to describe your school.'

'Why are you asking the questions in English?' I asked. 'Won't you need to know them in French?'

'Baby steps,' Rosie replied. 'The answers are more important.'

'I don't need baby steps,' Suzanne protested. 'Don't baby me.'

'I wouldn't need to baby you if you'd learned all this when you were supposed to,' Rosie said starchily. She looked at me. 'Did you know Suze can say good morning and goodnight in twelve different languages?'

'Really?'

'Yeah. But apparently that's more important than learning *actual exam material* for French.'

'I learned them ages ago,' Suzanne objected. 'And it *is* more important than "My school has a large playing field". I mean, *really*? When am I *ever* going to need to say that?'

'That's not the point,' Rosie said. 'The important bit is the exam, not how useful the information is.'

'Say goodnight in Italian,' I requested.

'*Buonanotte*,' Suzanne said without hesitation. She grinned at me. 'When I was—'

'*Hey*,' Rosie interrupted, sounding exasperated. 'Can we at least get back to French? Come on. Try this one: describe your family.'

'Ugh, do I actually have to answer that?' Suzanne made a face. 'Isn't that discriminatory?'

'Just talk about Sarah,' Rosie said. 'Like, "My aunt is called Sarah and she works in a cafe," or whatever.'

'Won't that sound really weird if everyone else is talking about all their different family members?'

'I just talk about Mum,' Rosie said with a shrug. 'Be glad – it means you've got less to remember.'

'Maybe if I did actually talk about my family I'd get sympathy points. Maybe they'll just give me an A.'

Rosie frowned suddenly and reached forward. 'There's something on your face . . . Oh no, it's just your victimhood showing.'

Suzanne, who'd lifted her hand to her face in concern when Rosie started talking, broke into laughter. 'You're such a bitch,' she said with affection.

Rosie settled herself back against the wall, a barely restrained grin on her face. 'A bitch that's going to help you get some actual GCSEs. Now, can we *please* get back to French?'

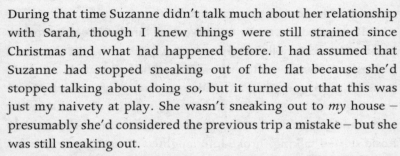

15

During that time Suzanne didn't talk much about her relationship with Sarah, though I knew things were still strained since Christmas and what had happened before. I had assumed that Suzanne had stopped sneaking out of the flat because she'd stopped talking about doing so, but it turned out that this was just my naivety at play. She wasn't sneaking out to *my* house – presumably she'd considered the previous trip a mistake – but she was still sneaking out.

It was a Wednesday evening in February when I heard a knock at my front door. It was almost 10 p.m., late for an unexpected visitor. I listened with one ear to see if I could tell who it was, most of my attention on the physics textbook in front of me. The realization that the voice was Sarah's hit me almost a whole minute later and I jerked my head up, the textbook falling closed in my lap.

I slid off my bed and crept along the hall, closer to the stairs, straining to hear actual words. Sarah's voice drifted up towards me.

'Not answering her phone . . . thought she was in her room . . . does this all the time now . . .'

I turned and hurried back to my room, scrabbling to find my phone from where I'd dropped it carelessly on the bed earlier. Finding it under my pillow, I tapped the screen and called Suzanne. It rang once, twice, three times.

'Hello?' Suzanne's voice was weirdly breathless. 'Cads?'

'Hey,' I said quickly, not bothering to ask why she sounded funny or where she was. 'Listen, Sarah's here. She knows you've sneaked out again. Better get back home quick, before she does.'

'Shit. Thank you!' She hung up immediately, as I'd expected she would.

'You're welcome,' I said to the silent phone. I tossed it back on to my bed, turned around and let out a shriek. Mum was standing in the doorway I'd left open, arms crossed, watching me.

Still keeping her eyes on me and barely moving her head, Mum called, 'She's not here, Sarah. But she's had a tip-off so she's probably on her way home already.'

Sarah appeared behind Mum, a frown on her face. 'A tip-off?'

'Why don't you repeat to Sarah what I just heard you say to Suzanne, Cadnam?' Mum asked. Her voice was deceptively calm.

I tried to remember what I'd said and in what timeframe, the barest amount I could get away with admitting.

'That she should get home, because Sarah's looking for her?' I said finally, more out of hope than expectation.

'Nice try,' Mum said flatly. She turned to Sarah. 'I'm sorry my daughter is turning out to be something of an enabler.'

I had no idea what this meant.

'I'm sorry my niece is turning out to be such a bad influence,' Sarah responded. She looked at me, her expression disappointed. 'I know you must think you're being a good friend by doing something like that, and I know she must have said things that make you think you *need* to do something like that, but I'm really not an enemy here.'

I shifted uncomfortably on the spot, hoping she'd leave so Mum could shout at me and get it over with. But when Sarah did leave, there was no shouting.

'Should I be concerned about you and Suzanne?' she asked me, coming right into my room and sitting on my bed as if I'd invited her in.

I paused before answering, surprised at this line of questioning. 'Um . . . no?'

'I know things are a little tense between her and Sarah,' she said, 'and I know that she has something of a habit of coming and going at all hours, but I didn't know any of that involved you.'

'It hardly *involves* me,' I protested.

'No?' She looked sceptical. 'Calling her with tip-offs?'

'Well —' I began, then stopped. 'Wait. How do you know about her coming and going at all hours?'

'Sarah told me,' Mum said, like it was obvious. Seeing my face, she let out a laugh. 'Adults are capable of forming friendships too, you know.'

I wasn't sure I liked the idea of this. 'So she's told you stuff about Suzanne?' I wondered if it was anything I didn't know.

'Some things, yes,' Mum said, giving nothing away. 'Now, let me say this.' My heart sank and I let out an involuntary sigh, which she ignored. 'I think it's wonderful that you want to be a friend to Suzanne. Really. It makes me proud that you're able to be that kind of a friend to someone who needs it.' As if Suzanne was some kind of charity case and my friendship was a gift instead of something we shared. 'But I do hope that you're going to be sensible with this. Don't get involved with this kind of behaviour. And, if you *really* want to be a friend, you should discourage it.'

'OK,' I said, hoping she'd leave.

'I'm not going to punish you for this,' Mum continued, and I bit my tongue to stop myself saying something sarcastic, 'but if anything like this happens again, it will make me rethink whether it's a good idea for the two of you to be friends.'

'It's not like I need your permission to be friends with someone,' I said without thinking.

Her eyebrows moved upward and stayed there, like a warning. 'I just hope you are as sensible as I think you are, and know better than to be swept along with a troublemaker, however charming she is.'

Not long after Mum had finally left me alone, my phone screen lit up with a message from Suzanne. 'BUSTED! But thanks for trying! You're the best xx'

I tried to call Rosie that same evening, but it wasn't until the next day that I managed to get a hold of her.

'Look at you, calling to give a heads-up,' was the first thing she said. She sounded impressed. 'Way to be on the ball.'

'An ineffectual heads-up,' I replied.

'Yeah, but still. Suze loved that you tried.'

'She told you all about it then?'

'Of course.'

'Did she happen to tell you where she actually was?' This was still bothering me. If she wasn't with me or Rosie, where else did she have to go?

'She was with Dylan.'

A pause. 'Who?'

'Dylan. Dylan Evers.'

'Who the hell is Dylan?'

'Calm down. He's the guy from our form that Suzanne's been . . . what's the nice word? Seeing? Hanging out with? You know, whatever.'

Despite the cold I felt a strange heat at the back of my neck. How could I not know about this? 'How long has that been going on?'

'Oh, since before Christmas?'

'*Before Christmas*?' I repeated, my voice coming out high-pitched.

'Well, yeah. Didn't she tell you?' Rosie's upbeat tone had changed to one of slight concern.

'No, she did not.'

'I guess she thought it wasn't important enough to say anything. She does talk about it like it's nothing. Don't be upset or anything.' There was an anxious thread in her voice now. 'You're not upset, right, Cads? I shouldn't have mentioned it. Have I messed up?'

'No, of course not.' I was the idiot who went to a different school. I was the moron who called to tell her to get home without even bothering to ask where she was. I was the one who thought I'd made myself matter.

'They aren't boyfriend and girlfriend,' Rosie offered, like this made a difference. 'They don't even see each other much, outside of school.'

I tried to think of the times Suzanne and I had seen each other since before Christmas, and the number of opportunities she'd had to tell me about this Dylan, boyfriend or otherwise. There were plenty.

'What's he like?'

'Dylan?'

'Yeah.' *Obviously*.

'He's OK,' she said off-handedly.

'Well, that was informative, thanks.'

She laughed. 'Sorry. I don't really know what to say about him. I mean . . . I kind of liked him.'

'What do you mean? Before Suzanne did?'

'Not before. More at the same time.'

'Did she know?'

'Oh yeah. But he liked her, so . . .' She let the sentence die. 'She's welcome to him anyway. I'm not sure he's that nice. I think he talks about her with his friends, and it gets around.'

I'd phoned Rosie feeling relaxed and happy, ready to share my story of attempted rescue, but the conversation hadn't gone how I'd expected, and now I felt lost in it. The image of Suzanne I'd had in my mind felt suddenly distorted. Had I got her all wrong?

'Are you two OK, though?'

'Oh, completely. We didn't fight about it or anything. I mean, it was kind of a surprise when she first went off with him, but that's just her. I love her, but she's a bit of a slag.'

'Roz!'

'What? She is! I don't even know how many boys from our year and above she's got off with since she been here. And it's only been, what, five months, if that.'

'You can't go calling her a slag though.'

'Well, I wouldn't say it to her face. But it's you. I can talk to you, right?'

This usually went without saying, and for some reason it bothered me that she'd voiced it this time. 'Of course you can talk to me. About anything.'

Rosie abruptly changed the subject, as she tended to do when the conversation veered towards the sentimental. She started telling me about two guys in her form who'd been caught smoking weed behind the science block – 'I mean, the *science block*, Caddy, what morons' – and then launched into a rant about *Animal Farm*, which she was trying to write about for English. This started with complaining about her essay topic – something I didn't catch about propaganda and parody – but she soon lost track of literary criticism and instead gave me a longer-than-Cliff-notes version of the story. Around the time she said, with impassioned outrage, 'and then they killed the horse!' I stopped trying to follow what she was saying and just listened to her voice, her familiar cadences, the lilts and jolts of a friend in full conversational flow, talking about anything.

It was closing in on 10 p.m. when I forced myself to click on Suzanne's chat icon on Facebook.

Caddy Oliver Hey

Suzanne Watts Hey! :)

Suzanne Watts What's up?

Caddy Oliver I have to ask you something

Suzanne Watts I'm all ears

Suzanne Watts Or hands.

Suzanne Watts All eyes?

Caddy Oliver Why didn't you tell me about Dylan?

Suzanne Watts Oh.

There was an agonizingly long pause. The text kept switching from blank to the tell-tale '. . .' that meant she was typing a message. My stomach was starting to knot.

Suzanne Watts There's not much to tell?

Caddy Oliver Really?

Suzanne Watts It's not like I actively didn't tell you. He just never came up.

I wrote, 'It's not like I can bring him up if I don't know about him', and then deleted it.

Caddy Oliver Don't friends tell each other stuff like this?

Suzanne Watts Don't make it into a big deal. It's not a big deal. That's why I didn't tell you.

Caddy Oliver So there is a reason?

Suzanne Watts God

Suzanne Watts This isn't the best way to talk about this.

Caddy Oliver ?

Suzanne Watts This is stressing me out. Can't we just talk about it when we see each other?

Caddy Oliver Fine

Suzanne Watts Are you pissed off with me?

I wanted to tell her that, yes, I was kind of pissed off with her. That friends told each other everything, even (especially?) things that weren't a big deal. That thinking that I'd called her while she was with a guy I didn't even know about to do her a favour made me feel like an idiot. I wrote, 'No.'

Suzanne Watts Are you sure?
Caddy Oliver Yes.
Suzanne Watts If you are, I'd rather you just told me.
Caddy Oliver OK
Suzanne Watts Wouldn't you want me to tell you if I was pissed off?
Caddy Oliver I guess
Suzanne Watts I'm pissed off.
Caddy Oliver What? Why? With me?

My stomach, previously knotted, had clenched painfully and my heart was pounding. My palms felt cold and clammy. I was absolutely useless at confrontation of any kind, digital or otherwise. The fact that Suzanne was in a different street made no difference to the effect the conversation was already having on me.

Suzanne Watts Why are you talking to Rosie about me behind my back?
Caddy Oliver We weren't talking about you.
Suzanne Watts Seriously??
Caddy Oliver That's not what I mean. Wait.
Suzanne Watts Waiting.

My throat had tightened. I flexed my fingers over the keys, wondering if she'd believe me if I disconnected my Internet and told her it had just gone down.

Caddy Oliver We were talking about last night and I just asked her if she knew where you were when I rang you.

Suzanne Watts Couldn't you just ask me?

Caddy Oliver Would you have told me?

Suzanne Watts Of course!

Caddy Oliver I didn't get a chance to ask you anyway

Suzanne Watts Phone? Text? Facebook?

Caddy Oliver I'm sorry

Suzanne Watts That's all you needed to say.

Suzanne Watts And just be honest. I know you're mad I didnt tell you about Dylan. Just say so.

Caddy Oliver I'm not mad

Suzanne Watts Caddy! Ffs, we're friends, you can say anything to me. If I know you're mad I can say sorry and we can get over it. If you don't say it, I'm just like . . . is Caddy mad at me?

Caddy Oliver I know.

Caddy Oliver Next time can you just tell me when it happens? So I don't hear it from Roz? And then make you mad?

Suzanne Watts Yes.

Caddy Oliver And don't be upset that Rosie and I talked about you a bit on the phone. That happens, right? I'm sure you and Roz talk about me when I'm not around.

Suzanne Watts Well, maybe we would if there was anything to say.

It was like she'd reached out a hand through my laptop screen and slapped me around the face. The shock of her words froze my fingers over my keyboard, a hot flush working its way up my neck and across my face. Ridiculous tears sprang to my eyes and I blinked to keep them at bay.

And at the same time I was thinking, You're overreacting, chill out, why are you crying, people say this stuff all the time. Don't cry.

Below her name, the '. . .' appeared. I panicked, not wanting to read another insult or even an apology, and closed the browser. For a few seconds I just stared at my desktop screen, the words she'd written on a loop in my head.

There's something uniquely upsetting about having your deepest insecurities not just laid bare by a friend but thrown in your face. I knew I was not in any way exciting, that there was nothing going on in my life that could be remotely confused with interesting. I'd always worried that this made me boring and that that was what people thought of me: Caddy Oliver – nice, but dull. And now, clearly, that was true.

What's more, I'd thought we'd reached the conclusion of our mini-fight and were in the conciliatory stage. I'd been even more unprepared than I would have been earlier. And, worst of all, I'd never thought that Suzanne would be so suddenly and unexpectedly mean. Not just bitchy or sarcastic with me, which was completely normal, but outright *mean*. I'd never say anything like that to her. What did it say about her that she would to me?

My phone buzzed. I glanced at it, hesitated, then clicked on the message.

'Shit. I'm sorry. I shouldn't have said that. I didn't mean it. Call me please? Suze x'

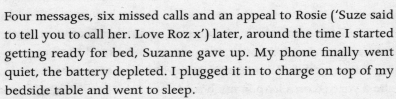

16

Four messages, six missed calls and an appeal to Rosie ('Suze said to tell you to call her. Love Roz x') later, around the time I started getting ready for bed, Suzanne gave up. My phone finally went quiet, the battery depleted. I plugged it in to charge on top of my bedside table and went to sleep.

I was startled awake a couple of hours later by the phone springing to life, buzzing in increments across the table towards my head. Blearily I reached for it, blinking against the sudden light. Suzanne. At 1.37 a.m.

I was half asleep and not entirely convinced I was really awake, so I answered it. 'Uh, hello?'

'Oh my God, I'm so glad you woke up. I thought – literally just now, and it would have been too late – that maybe your phone was on silent.'

'What are you talking about? Why are you phoning me?' My voice was croaky with sleep. Hers, in contrast, was bright and perky, like it was the middle of the day.

'I'm outside, come to the window, I'm by your window.' She said all this in a rush.

'You're outside?' I repeated dumbly. I sat up in bed but made no move towards the window.

'Yep.'

'Why are you outside?'

'You wouldn't answer your phone.'

'Do you know what time it is?'

'Of course. I would have come earlier, but I had to wait, to make sure Sarah was asleep. So she wouldn't hear me leave. Are you at the window? I can't see you.'

I went to the window. When she saw me, Suzanne, who was standing in the garden like it was completely normal, waved. Over the phone she said, 'Hi! Can you come out?'

'Are you being serious right now? Is this actually happening?'

'Yes, come out so we can talk.'

'You are an actual headcase. Did you know that? It's nearly 2 a.m. I am not coming out to talk to you.'

'Wow, you're much more assertive at this time of night. Come on, please? I really need to talk to you. And I brought you cookies.' She held up a box and waggled it in the air.

'I am hanging up on you now.'

'OK, fine, but only if that means you're coming out. I'll wait.' She hung up immediately, before I could, and then sat right down on the grass, clearly indicating her commitment to hunkering down and waiting for me.

I lay back down and tried to forget about her, but it was a wasted exercise. Less than three minutes after she hung up, I'd thrown a coat over my pyjamas and was crawling out of my bedroom window, heart pounding, trying to remember how she'd climbed up and over the garage last time she'd visited.

When she saw me coming, Suzanne leaped up and came over to the garage, leaving the box on the grass.

'There's a ledge here,' she said, her voice low, pointing. 'And the drainpipe is just to the left of where you are now. Climb down facing forward and try and get one foot on the ledge and your hand on the drainpipe.'

Needless to say, I missed the ledge entirely, and ended up in an ungraceful heap on the concrete.

'You OK?' She reached out an arm to help me up.

'I need a cookie,' I said, rubbing my scraped arm.

'You can have all the cookies,' Suzanne said, half laughing

with what sounded like nervous relief. 'I thought you wouldn't come down.'

'I don't know why I have,' I replied honestly.

'Because you're a good person and a good friend and you're giving me a chance to apologize in person?' Suzanne suggested hopefully. Before I could respond, she darted away from me, collecting the box of cookies from where she'd left them on the grass. 'Where shall we go?' she asked in a half-whisper over her shoulder. 'Beach?'

'Go?' I repeated, watching her return to me, tiptoeing over the grass in what looked like ballet pumps. She was wearing leggings and an oversized shirt, a woolly grey hat the only sign that she'd considered the February temperature. She had to be freezing, but you'd never have known.

'If we talk here, your parents might hear us,' Suzanne explained patiently. 'We should go somewhere else.' She raised both her eyebrows expectantly at me and, when I didn't speak, turned on the spot and began walking towards the road. Despite myself, I followed.

We walked for a few minutes in silence, her hugging her chest and me trying to convince myself I was really awake. This was not the kind of thing that happened to me.

Eventually Suzanne came to a stop at the end of the road running parallel to mine. She sat down on a stone wall and, after a moment's hesitation, I did the same. She opened the lid of the box and offered it to me. I took a cookie and bit into it: soft, chocolatey goodness. It almost made up for everything.

'I'm sorry for what I said,' Suzanne said as I chewed. She was looking down at the floor, playing with the sleeves of her shirt.

I swallowed. 'You came all the way here just to say that?'

She looked at me. 'Of course.'

'But it's the middle of the night,' I said slowly, as if speaking to a child. 'Couldn't it wait?'

'No.' Suzanne picked up a cookie and nibbled at the edges. 'I was so worried you'd had it with me and that you'd never speak to me again. That you'd given up on me.'

'Obviously I haven't given up on you. Don't be stupid.'

'But people have.' Her voice was quiet. 'They do do that. Sometimes.'

I didn't say anything, torn between reassuring her that I wasn't about to desert her and pointing out that she'd acted like a bitch.

'I know I'm hard work,' Suzanne said softly.

'You *are* hard work,' I agreed, rolling my eyes. 'I never thought I'd have a friend who'd wake me up in the middle of the night and take me for a midnight Brighton stroll.'

'Don't forget the cookies.' Suzanne nudged me with her elbow. 'Bonus, right?'

'Yeah, you can have that one. Definite bonus.' I took another cookie. 'I get that you're sorry, and I'm glad you came to *say* sorry, even if you did it in a kind of crazy way. But I still don't really get why you said it.'

She was quiet for a while. 'I don't know why.'

'I'd never say anything like that to you.'

'I know you wouldn't.'

'And neither would Rosie.'

At this she laughed. 'Oh, Rosie can get her claws out with the best of them. She's different at school than she is with you, you know.'

Wasn't this what I'd been afraid of the whole time? Discovering that the Rosie I knew and loved had the capacity to be a stranger to me? And that Suzanne, seeing both versions of her, would in the end know her better than I did?

'Anyway, will you forgive me?' Suzanne fixed me with her

most beseeching look. 'If I promise to try my best not to take my fucked-up-life's frustrations out on you?'

What else could I say? She'd brought me cookies and waited in my garden in the freezing cold just to apologize to me. She was crazy, and she was unpredictable, but she was also generous and open-hearted and like no friend I'd ever had before. 'I forgive you,' I said magnanimously. I nudged her back with my elbow. 'Hey. Maybe some of your Suze-ness will rub off on me, make me more exciting.'

'You don't need to be more exciting,' Suzanne said. 'People trust you. That's worth way more. I'm the troublemaker, right?' She made a face. 'That's not a good thing to be.'

'I don't think you are. You're fun. You make things *fun*. I'd like to be like that,' I said cautiously, wondering as I spoke if I was revealing too much. 'You know, just a little more.'

She smiled with one corner of her mouth. 'Ah. Like, something significant?'

For a moment I thought she'd read my mind, then laughed, realizing Rosie had mentioned my significant-life-event theory several months earlier. 'Yeah, exactly.'

'Well —' Suzanne broke off a piece of cookie and bit into it — 'I'll do my best.'

We ate the rest of the cookies and then took the long route back to my house, tripling the time it would normally take to make the journey. She told me a little more about Dylan, but still only the barest details. He was sixteen. He smoked. He was a good kisser. Yes, Rosie liked him too, but not enough for it to be a big deal.

'So am I going to meet him?' I asked.

She hesitated, moving her hand lightly along the stone wall we were walking past. 'I don't think I want you to.'

'Why not?' I asked, surprised and a little hurt.

'Because you probably won't like him, and then you might think less of me.' She glanced at me quickly, a flash of vulnerability across her features. 'Besides, it's not like he's important or anything.'

I tried to think of a way to tell her that there probably wasn't anything she could do that would make me think less of her, but I couldn't think of a way that wouldn't sound like I was trying to tell her I loved her.

'What do you mean, not important?' I asked instead.

She shrugged. 'He's just some idiot guy. I mean, really. He's just a guy.'

Then why are you sleeping with him? I wanted to ask.

And then, because there was nothing else I could say, and because she'd told me I could say anything to her, I said it out loud.

'Because . . .' The word started off confident, but then she trailed off. She looked unsure of herself, a rare thing. 'Because he can be so sweet to me. And, sometimes, the way he looks at me – he looks at me like I'm worth looking at.'

'Your view of yourself is completely fucked up,' I said bluntly, surprising myself.

She looked surprised too. 'Fucked up?'

'Yeah.' I decided to go with it. We'd almost reached my driveway. 'You're so *wrong*. It's so ridiculous that you could think for even a second that you're not working looking at. I mean, *God*, have you seen yourself?'

Suzanne said nothing. She looked away from me, chewing on her bottom lip, her fingers clutching the outer rims of her sleeves. I was just starting to wonder if I'd overstepped the mark when she turned back to me, a bright smile on her face. 'I'm really, really glad you don't hate me.' She reached over and gave me a sudden hug, squeezing tightly for just a second and then letting go. Before I could say anything, she stepped back, as if to start walking away. 'I'll message you tomorrow?'

'Wait,' I said, confused. 'Are you going to be OK, walking back by yourself?' I glanced at my house, which was reassuringly still dark and asleep as I'd left it.

'Oh, sure, it's barely ten minutes.' She backed away a few more steps, lifting her hand in a wave. '*Buonanotte*, my friend.' Her hand lifted further into a mock salute. Her shoulders were slightly hunched, a grin was on her face and she looked as far away from a troublemaker as it was possible to be.

'*Buonanotte*,' I replied. I saluted back. 'You fucking nutcase.'

'Hey, watch your fucking mouth.' She was still backing away. 'What do they teach you in that school?'

By now she was too far away to hear any response, so I just waved until she turned the corner and disappeared. I made my way over to the garage, panicking for a moment that I wouldn't be able to get back inside. But hoisting myself up turned out to be surprisingly easy, and I was through my window and into my bed in a matter of minutes.

The house was silent. My night-time exertions, which no doubt would have given my mother some kind of coronary, had gone undetected. I felt suddenly exhilarated, triumphant.

I fell asleep grinning.

17

Nothing strengthens a friendship like an argument survived. And nothing made me so sure of my friendship with Suzanne than the way she handled our first.

As soon as the very next day, our brief falling-out had become canonized, with Suzanne texting me after lunch with, 'Remember when I called you boring? GOD. What a BITCH! Xxxxx' and me replying 'Careful. I haven't forgiven you yet. (love you xxx)'. Her response – 'Oh please. I brought midnight cookies for you, I'm basically the Goddess of all friends' – made me laugh out loud on my way to art and almost got my phone confiscated.

The second time she turned up at my window, five days later at 1 a.m, she brought baklava and we sat together on my garage roof, huddled under my fleece blanket, talking about nothing. When she left she squeezed me into a hug and said, 'It's so great that you're here,' and I felt as if I'd won a contest I didn't even know I'd entered.

The third time she was angsty, agitated after an argument with Sarah about the increasing number of detentions she was getting at school. That time we left my house to wander around Seven Dials together while she ranted. The fourth time, close to 5 a.m on a Wednesday, she turned up dishevelled and happy, saying that she was on her way back from Dylan's house and just wanted to say hi.

'Do you ever actually sleep?' I asked, leaning out of my window, still half asleep myself. She'd plonked herself down on the roof and was sat hugging her knees to her chest.

She laughed, dismissive. 'Sometimes.'

I knew it was stupid. I knew it was reckless. I knew that walking around Brighton in the middle of the night was even a little bit dangerous. And I didn't care. Against all laws of circumstance and personality, I had somehow been chosen as the go-to friend by someone a little bit wild, a little bit crazy, a whole lot of fun. I was just grateful to be invited along for the ride.

I kept these midnight walkabouts a secret from Rosie, partly because I knew she wouldn't understand but mostly because I liked having something that belonged to Suzanne and me. To me, it felt like a fair exchange. Rosie got Suzanne in the daytime, and I got her at night. Our imperfect trio had, finally, found its balance.

'I feel like a tourist,' Suzanne said, lifting herself up on to her tiptoes and peering over the heads of the people in the queue in front of us. 'Isn't this a really touristy thing to do?'

'Yes,' Rosie said, taking a long sip of bubble tea through a thick orange straw. 'But actually, how many times you've been dragged around the Pavilion is a sign of a true Brightonian.'

'It's a rite of passage,' I agreed.

'I've been here four times,' Rosie continued. She was grinning. 'As a Brighton resident and a Pavilion virgin, Suze, you're way overdue.'

February had bled into March and the sun had finally started to feel warm against my skin. We'd taken the opportunity to spend a Sunday together in town, and the Royal Pavilion trip had been Rosie's idea. Suzanne had spent the previous night with Dylan and his friends drinking on the beach, and her eyes had the slightly red-rimmed smudgedness of the morning after. Despite the occasional twinge of hangover, she was her usual self: bouncy, chatty and excitable.

'It's so weird that there's, like, a *palace* here,' she said, her eyes scanning the domed rotunda of the Pavilion. 'Right in the middle of town.'

'You mean Reading doesn't have a palace?' Rosie asked, deadpan.

'How *conventional*,' I added, smiling. 'No wonder you left.'

I saw a grin break out over Suzanne's face as she looked back at us to screw up her nose playfully.

We paid our entry fee and headed in together, sticking close among the crowds of tourists. Rosie curved her arm companionably through mine. 'Remember the first time we came here?' she asked me as we headed down the first corridor, neither of us paying much attention to the displays. Suzanne was just ahead of us, the audio guide pressed to her ear.

'Yes,' I said. We'd been seven years old and under the supervision of Tarin who, at fifteen, had used the trip as a cover to meet her then-boyfriend, Jamie, who'd dumped her at the entrance. Tarin had spent the entire circuit of the Pavilion sobbing. It was one of my most vivid childhood memories. 'Wow, that was nearly ten years ago.'

'Shut up, don't say that,' Rosie shrieked, then laughed. 'God, Tarin did used to get landed with us, didn't she? I don't think I'd want to look after a couple of seven-year-olds on my weekends.'

'She loved us,' I said, which was true. 'I don't think she minded really.'

'I bet she – *oof*.' Rosie had walked straight into Suzanne, who had stopped abruptly in the middle of the Banqueting Hall and was staring upward. 'Suze!'

'Is that a *dragon*?' Suzanne asked, oblivious. She pointed up at the gigantic chandelier, which was hanging from the claws of – yes – a dragon. 'This place is so weird.' Her eyes were bright. 'I love it.'

'Wait till you see the music room,' Rosie said, an affectionate grin on her face. 'The wallpaper is ridiculous and there's a massive organ. I think you'll actually cry.'

I saw a familiar mischievous grin light up on Suzanne's face and she opened her mouth to make what I was sure was going to be a terrible massive-organ joke, but before she could speak her expression dropped and her mouth snapped shut.

Rosie and I glanced up just in time to see a woman with a mane of thick, coppery curls see Suzanne and do a very obvious double take. For an odd moment I thought she was going to just turn and walk away, but then she caught sight of me and Rosie watching. She looked again at Suzanne, who let out an audible sigh and then smiled, but it was tight and fixed. 'Hi.'

'Hello, Suzanne,' the woman said. She was friendly, her face open and kind. 'Nice to see you.'

'Yeah,' Suzanne said, not looking like she thought it was at all nice. She turned to Rosie and me. 'Um, this is Becca —' she waved a reluctant hand at the woman — 'and these are my friends Rosie and Caddy.'

'Lovely to meet you both,' Becca said, then added to Suzanne, 'I'll see you on Wednesday?' She was still smiling, but there was something in her face I couldn't read.

Suzanne nodded wordlessly, her expression tense. It was unsettling to see her red-faced and speechless, untethered from her usual poise. When Becca walked away I watched Suzanne's shoulders loosen, her face relax. She let out a breath and then smiled at us. 'Sorry about that.'

'Who was she?' Rosie asked.

'A friend of Sarah's,' Suzanne replied vaguely. 'Sometimes I babysit her kid.'

I frowned, the explanation jarring in my head like a Tetris block dropped too far to the left. Something about it didn't fit quite right. I had opened my mouth to say something when I felt

Suzanne's fingers close tight around my wrist, just for a second. I closed my mouth.

'Come on,' Suzanne said, the familiar grin back on her face. 'Weren't you saying something about a music room?'

I didn't quiz Suzanne about Becca for the rest of the day, restraining myself even when the distinctive copper curls appeared around a corner and Suzanne ducked behind me, out of view. I knew her well enough by then to know that pushing her for answers to anything was a useless exercise, likely only to bring out the stubborn, sullen side of her that she usually kept hidden. *Not* questioning her was the best way of getting her to talk.

Sure enough, I was woken just after 2 a.m by my phone buzzing on my bedside table. I opened my eyes, not moving for a second, just listening to the vibration. When it stopped, I threw on my joggers and a hoodie and climbed out of the window and over the garage roof, a manoeuvre I'd mastered after four tries. By this stage I could make it all the way out and down without making a sound.

Suzanne was waiting for me at the end of my driveway, slouched on the wall bordering my front garden. She was smoking, the cigarette already half burned down in her fidgety fingers. The smoking was just one thing that was different about Suzanne at night, a glimpse of the side of her I was only starting to get to know. At night she was quieter and more contained, the vulnerability she kept a careful lid on most of the time closer to the surface, peeking out.

When I came to stand beside her, she glanced up, attempting a smile. 'Good morning,' she said. 'Beach?'

'Sure,' I said. I'd already begun to understand what the different destinations meant on our midnight walkabouts. If she just wanted company, she was happy to sit on my garage roof and share chilly whispers for half an hour or so before heading home. If she was feeling restless, we'd wander Brighton's streets for a while, talking. The beach meant she needed to see the sea, in a way that wasn't usually good.

Brighton was quiet and still, like the whole city was taking a breather before the week started up again. We made it down to the seafront without seeing a single person. I went to walk down the steps to the beach, but Suzanne had stopped at the railings, leaning with her back to the sea. She'd pulled out a fresh cigarette and was flicking ineffectually at her lighter.

'Are you OK?' I asked. 'You seem tense.'

'I'm tense because I can't light this stupid thing,' Suzanne said between gritted teeth. A flame finally appeared and she touched the cigarette end to it. She closed her eyes and inhaled slowly, but the tension on her face didn't dissipate.

'You are such a cliché right now,' I said, because it was what Rosie would have said and Rosie wasn't there.

I watched in relief as an involuntary smile spread across Suzanne's face. She flicked her eyes towards me, her smile sliding into a smirk. 'The tortured soul, smoking away her blues?'

'No,' I said. 'The rebel teenager sneaking out in the middle of the night and – gasp! – chain-smoking in the dark.'

Suzanne laughed. 'The horror.' She rolled her eyes, but her shoulders had relaxed and she was still smiling. She looked at me, breathed in slowly and then sighed out a puff of smoke. 'OK. I wanted to talk to you about earlier, at the Pavilion.'

I nodded, not sure what to say. When she didn't continue, I prompted, 'The friend of Sarah's?'

I saw Suzanne bite down on her lip before moving her head in assent. 'That wasn't really the truth.'

'Right,' I said slowly. 'So who is she?'

'She's my social worker.' Suzanne had dropped her eyes to the ground so I couldn't make out her expression.

'Oh,' I said, surprised despite myself. 'I didn't know you had a social worker.'

'Well, no, that's the point.' There was a slight edge of irritation in her voice. 'I didn't want you to know. I wasn't exactly expecting her to turn up when I was with my friends.'

'So you lied?' I felt a delayed reaction of hurt creep up on me, tinged with anxiety. She'd lied to me. And it wasn't the first time. 'Why?'

'Because it was easier.' Suzanne crossed her straightened arms at the elbows, pressing the side of her chin into her upper arm. It didn't look comfortable.

'Easier?' I repeated. I thought about how she hadn't told me about Dylan for so long. What else was she lying about or hiding? How could I know?

'Don't be pissed off,' Suzanne said quickly. She sounded worried. 'That's why I wanted to talk to you, to try and explain, you know? I'm sorry. I just . . . didn't want to get into it there. I hate all of it, having a social worker, having to talk to people about stuff I don't want to talk about, and how they're all so *professional* about it. I hate it.' Her voice was picking up, agitated and tense. 'And they won't leave me alone; it's just the worst thing. Especially Becca. She tries to be like a friend, and I just *hate* it.'

'Yeah, but I'm your friend,' I said, trying to figure out why I felt so thrown by something that should have been so obvious. Of course she'd have a social worker. Wouldn't it be more weird if she didn't? 'Why can't you talk to *me* about that? Complain to me, that's what friends are for.'

'I can't,' Suzanne said, sounding on the verge of tears. 'I can't talk to you about her, because then I'll have to tell you why I don't like talking to her, and if I do that, I have to tell you what

I tell her.' Her words were starting to get difficult to follow. 'And then I'll have to tell you about getting hit and the stuff I used to do to try and get it all to just *stop* and trying to kill myself and how my dad used to just lose control sometimes and there was nowhere I could go because where could I go but there and no one stopped him, they just never did, and I don't—'

'Oh God, stop!' I managed to break in, panicked. She'd stood up, the cigarette crushed in her fingers, her eyes wild and wet, her breath coming in frightening short gasps. She turned away from me, raising her arms to her head. I could still hear her trying to breathe and I felt as lost and useless as a child. 'I'm sorry,' I tried. 'I was being stupid. I totally understand why you didn't explain earlier.'

She didn't reply, her back still to me, but she'd lowered her arms and was now hugging herself with them. I could see her fingers curled around the blades of her shoulders, squeezing tight.

I tried to think of something to say that wasn't the worst thing. In the end, I couldn't help myself. 'You tried to kill yourself?'

I heard a choked laugh before she turned around to face me again, wiping at her eyes with her sleeves. 'Oh God, did I say that out loud?' She blinked a few times, then drew in a long breath. 'My filter just goes to fuck when I freak out.' She winced suddenly, glancing down at her hand. 'Ouch. I think I burned myself on the cigarette.'

'Suze,' I said quietly.

She looked at me. 'Yes,' she said finally. 'Last year.'

I wanted to ask why, but even I could see that was a stupid question. 'Is that why you moved here?'

She made a face. 'No. But sort of.'

'OK . . .' I said slowly, waiting for more.

She let out a resigned sigh and sank back down on to the seafront wall. 'Things were really bad. At the time. At home, sure, but at school as well. There was some stuff with my friends. It was just too much, there didn't seem to be . . . much point, I guess. So I took some pills. But it didn't work, obviously. My dad found me before they could work properly. Sarah came to live with us after, to help try to make things better. But the short version is they didn't. Get better, I mean. So now I live here.'

'Sarah came to live with you in Reading?' I clarified, surprised.

Suzanne nodded. 'For about three or four months, I think it was.'

'Did she know before then?' I asked. 'That your dad was . . . ?' I trailed off, not wanting to say it.

Suzanne didn't say anything. She'd pulled out a fresh cigarette and was rolling it, safe and unlit, between her fingers, her eyes focused on it. After a long pause she nodded again.

'And she never did anything about it?' My heart was starting to hurt.

'It wasn't up to her,' Suzanne said. 'All she could really do was talk to my mum and try and get *her* to do something. But Mum, she's not . . .' She stopped herself, paused, then tried again. 'She's not very strong. I mean, emotionally. She couldn't . . . She couldn't have taken care of us by herself, without my dad. And she really loves him. So it was never really an option.'

I wondered who had told her all of this, who had made her believe it was true.

'My mum used to say —' Suzanne stopped herself abruptly, clamping her mouth shut.

'Say what?' I prompted finally.

'You'll think she's awful.'

'Suze, I already kind of think that.'

A look of distress passed over Suzanne's face. 'I shouldn't have said any of this. I'm not meant to.'

I sat next to her, the cold of the stone seeping through my

joggers. 'Says who?' I said carefully. 'There's only me here, and the only person I care about in any of this is you. And I want to hear it, if you want to talk about it. But if you don't, that's fine too.' I was almost disappointed that it really was only me and her there; I so rarely said the right thing at the right moment that it would have been nice if there had been someone else there to witness it.

'She used to say I was the strongest one,' Suzanne said slowly. 'That I was much stronger than her. That . . . well, that I could take it, basically.'

For a moment I couldn't speak. 'Wow. Wow, OK.'

'See, it sounds bad.' Suzanne's voice had quickened. 'But she meant it in a good way.'

When I'd heard 'abuse', that very first time I'd found out the truth about Suzanne's past, I'd thought of violence as being something simple. Awful, but simple. A violent man and a child who bore the brunt of it. I hadn't even considered the framework that supported it, allowed it to happen in the first place. The blind eyes turned, the excuses made, the insidious lies whispered into the ear of a child so desperate for love they mistook a gentle tone for truth.

Could I say that to her? Would that make me a good friend or a terrible one?

'Did you ever tell anyone?' I asked instead.

'No, I did everything I could to make sure no one knew.'

'Why?'

'I didn't want them to take me away,' Suzanne said. She wasn't looking at me, still rolling the unlit cigarette between her fingers. 'I know you won't understand. But they're my family. I love them. I just wanted them to love me back, that's all.' Her voice caught on 'back', but she gathered herself. 'I didn't want to be taken away. I didn't want that to be my life. I'd rather die than go into care.'

There were more things I wanted to say. I wanted to ask her why, if she was so against being taken into care, she wasn't trying harder with Sarah. Didn't it make more sense to try to be *good*? I wanted to know more about the family she'd left behind; where her beloved brother was during all of this; whether her old friends knew anything about what had been going on. But before I could voice any of it, she turned to me with a startling, full-bodied grin.

'OK! I've told you lots of really awful stuff it kills me to talk about. I'm done now.' She leaped up off the wall. 'What breed of dog do you think makes the cutest puppies? I think it's Newfoundlands. The puppies are like bear cubs. *So* cute! And they call them *Newfies*.'

'You can't beat a Labrador puppy,' I said, sliding off the wall and linking my arm through hers. We began walking away from the seafront, towards home. 'They're, like, *classic* puppy.'

'True,' Suzanne said lightly. She squeezed my elbow as we walked. 'German shepherds though. Oh my *God*.'

She kept this up all the way home and until she waved goodbye – '*Buonanotte!*' – and sauntered off down my street. It wasn't until the following morning – when I woke up dog-tired and achy – that I checked my phone to see that she'd sent me a text at 4.38 a.m., saying simply, 'Please don't tell Roz anything I told you'. The starkness of the words, so unlike her, jolted me properly awake. A second text had come through half an hour later: 'Thanks for listening. Sorry to offload on you. Next time will be more fun :) xx'

For the first time I felt a pang of unease. Had she even slept at all? I hesitated, then tapped out a reply. 'Offload any time. You did get some sleep, right? xx'

I was washed, dressed and halfway to school before she replied. 'Yep, just woke up. Too late for school OH WELL. Want to skip school with me? Sarah's at work. Netflix all day and ME! Say yes xx'

I was smiling, safe in my mother's car, the collar of my school blazer rigid against my neck. 'Private-school girls don't skip. Be good! x'

'What are you grinning at?' Mum asked. The Esther's school gates loomed in the distance.

'Nothing,' I said, reaching for my school bag and pushing my phone into my pocket. I leaned over and kissed her cheek. 'See you later!'

Later that week I met Rosie and Suzanne after school in Starbucks. The two of them were deep in an animated conversation when I arrived and I hesitated at the top of the stairs, looking at them. Both in school uniform and sipping from identical Frappuccino cups, they looked like a matched set.

'Hey,' I said when I approached, cutting into their chattering. 'No chair for me?'

Rosie gave me an odd look. 'There's literally one right there.'

'I always forget how green your uniform is,' Suzanne said. She scooped up some cream with her straw. 'Don't you hate them for making you wear that?'

'Hello to you too,' I said, pulling up an extra chair from the next table.

Suzanne grinned at Rosie. 'Caddy has third-wheel face.'

'Caddy is right here,' I said, irritated. 'But she doesn't have to be.'

'Oh, chill out, I'm just teasing,' Suzanne said lightly. 'How are you?'

I shrugged. 'Fine. You?'

'Average, three stars.' She was half perched, half sat on the sofa chair, one leg curled underneath her, her hair haphazardly plaited on one side of her head. She flicked one of the braids out of her face. 'I've decided to end it with Dylan.'

'Really?' I took a sip of hot chocolate, which was still too hot. 'Why?'

'I think I'm done with him. His dickishness doesn't balance out his hotness any more. So I think we'll break up.'

'How can you break up if you're not together?' I asked.

Rosie smirked. 'That's exactly what I said.'

'You know what I mean,' Suzanne said.

'So, basically —' Rosie pointed her straw at me — 'she's going to stop having sex with him.'

'That and other things,' Suzanne said, unruffled. She wedged her straw back into her Frappuccino. 'Maybe I'll find someone at Levina's party.'

'Oh yeah,' Rosie said, brightening. 'Me too! Do you think Liam will be there? That's who I want.'

'Probably. From what Lev says it sounds like the whole school will be there. But you actually have to try and *get* Liam this time. Like, actually talk to him. That'd be a good start.'

Rosie rolled her eyes. 'We're not all beautiful and confident, you know.'

'Oh, I'm sorry,' Suzanne said earnestly, her eyes wide. 'I didn't know the ability to speak was restricted to those society deems aesthetically pleasing to the eye.'

Rosie laughed. 'Shut up.'

I gave up waiting for one of them to let me into the conversation. 'Society deems aesthetically pleasing?'

'We had a talk at school about body image and society,' Suzanne said. 'The woman was a *raging* feminist. She said the aesthetically pleasing thing about five times.'

'I liked her,' Rosie said. 'I thought she was great.'

'She said that our self-worth shouldn't be dependent on

whether we're considered pretty by men,' Suzanne said. 'And I'm like, come on, that's all I have in the world; don't take it away from me.'

'You are *extremely* fucked up,' Rosie said grandly, leaning back in her chair to stretch. 'But, yeah – I do intend to make myself as aesthetically pleasing to the eye as possible for the party.'

Suzanne grinned. 'Me too. Shall we do it together?'

'Obviously.' Rosie glanced at me, saw the look on my face and laughed. 'Oh my God, Cads, you have epic third-wheel face right now.'

I tried to smile. 'Levina's having a party?'

'It's her birthday next week,' Suzanne explained. 'She's having a massive party on the Saturday. Her house is huge and her parents are loaded, so it should be fun. And they won't even be there!'

'They must be crazy,' I muttered into my hot chocolate, imagining the look on my parents' faces if I suggested they vacate the premises so I could have a party in their precious house.

'You should come,' Rosie said, but I could tell by the look on her and Suzanne's faces that they weren't expecting me to say yes.

'OK,' I said before I could second-guess myself. I was gratified by their stunned expressions. 'Sounds great. I'll be there.'

18

According to Suzanne, Dylan took the sort-of-break-up pretty well. She told me, via text, that his exact words had been 'yeah. whatever.' but that he was still texting her in the evenings as he'd used to, asking her to come over.

'And I haven't!' she said the following weekend, proud.

'Well done, you,' Rosie said, deadpan.

And then Tuesday happened.

Lunchtime was almost over and I was on my way to maths when I felt my phone buzz in my pocket. Thinking more about the fact that I should take the vibration off before I got to the classroom than anything else, I tapped the screen.

13.58: Fuck. HIGH DRAMA. Suzanne's been suspended.
13.59: What??? What happened?

I'd stopped right in the middle of the hall, staring anxiously at my phone.

'You OK?' Mishka asked, pausing between me and the departing backs of Allison and Kesh.

'Yeah, I'll catch you up,' I said.

She looked worried. 'Are you sure? Henderson hates it if we're late.'

'It's fine, I'll be there in a minute,' I said, already turning back towards the nearest toilets. When I got there, I locked myself in the first stall and sat on the toilet lid, waiting for Rosie's response.

14.07: OK, this might take a few texts so sorry. At lunchtime

Dylan and his friends were being dicks, trying to wind Sz up.

14.07: It was just funny at first. Dylan said she was easy and Sz was like, lucky for your ugly mug, you know how she is, everythings a joke. She seemed like she didn't care.

14.08: But then Dylan said give it easy, take it hard, and she told him to fuck off. And he called her a bitch, said she wasn't even good, just cheap.

14.08: Then he said damaged goods come cheaper and Sz LOST IT. She threw a chair across the room, we had to hold her back

14.09: She would've gone for him. Mr Daniels was next door in his office, & he came in yelling at us. Sz got taken to the head, now she's suspended.

I read the messages as they came through, one after the other, my heart pounding. My fingers angled over the keypad as I tried to figure out how to respond. I decided to text Suzanne first.

14.10: Here if you need me xxx

And then, to Rosie:

14.10: How come she got suspended? What about D?

14.12: They're really strict about destructive behaviour here. Plus she's on thin ice cos of all the detentions. D just got a detention.

14.13: That's unbelievable.

14.14: I know. Wait, how are you texting from class?

14.15: I'm in the toilets.

14.16: Are you skipping class???

I looked at the time. If I went straight to maths now, I'd be fifteen minutes late and in trouble anyway.

14.17: Yes. Can't believe any of this. Did you see her?
14.18: Wow, is that a 1st? Didnt see her. Lev did. Says she was crying, Sarah picked her up at the end of lunch.

Before I could reply to Rosie, Suzanne's name appeared on my screen.

14.19: Are you at school?
14.20: Yes x
14.21: What good is that then.
14.21: Sorry. Just leave me alone OK.

Stung, I read over the messages again, trying to understand her hostility. I considered sending her a message reminding her that it wasn't exactly my fault and I was only trying to help, but there didn't seem to be much point, so I texted Rosie instead.

14.23: Did you text her?
14.25: Yep, but she hasn't replied. Just told her to msg me whenever. All you can do.

Not replying was at least better than 'leave me alone', I thought. I was about to ask for more details, when I heard the main door open and then a tentative voice.

'Caddy?' It was Mishka.

I hesitated. 'Yeah?' I leaned over and released the catch on the door, letting it swing open to reveal Mishka's earnest, searching face.

'There you are,' she said, looking relieved. 'Are you OK?'

'Yeah, there's a big drama going on with Suzanne,' I

said, waving my phone as evidence.

'I told Mr Henderson you felt sick,' Mishka said, 'so you should probably go to the nurse now and get a note. That way you don't have to go back to class. I'll cover for you.'

'Thanks, Mish,' I said, meaning it. I pushed my phone back into my pocket and stood up. 'Tell him it's cramps.' It was cheap, but claiming cramps never failed with the male teachers.

She grinned. 'Will do.'

We headed out of the toilets together, going our separate ways at the end of the hall. As I walked towards the nurse's office, making sure to slow my pace and hunch slightly, it occurred to me that this was the first time I'd ever tried to skip class at Esther's. Surely a momentous occasion, never mind that it had taken me almost five years. I wanted to text Suzanne – *You're rubbing off on me!* – but I clearly couldn't right now.

As the nurse fussed over me, apparently not suspicious of my vague symptoms, I could only think about Suzanne. Suspension. What would that mean for her? Things between her and Sarah were strained enough already. If I was suspended, it would be a big deal, but for Suzanne it could be a disaster.

My phone buzzed again in my pocket, but I had to wait a few minutes until the nurse left the room before I could look.

14.38: Whoops. Sz jst txt me, v pissed off I told you. What did u say to her?

14.46: Literally just here if u need me.

14.48: Fucks sake, y does she have to be such a bitch. I didnt throw any chairs. As if I wouldn't tell u!

14.49: She told me to leave her alone.

14.52: !! Unbelievable. K I actually hv to do some work now. Call me after school x

14.53: Will do xx

19

22.31: Have you heard from Suze?
22.32: No, have you?
22.33: No, I left a message just after 6, no reply. I text her like an hour ago, but no reply.
22.35: :/

Wednesday 11.49
From: Suzanne Watts {suzyanne.whats@gmail.com}
To: Caddy Oliver {cadnam.oliver@gmail.com}; Rosie Caron {rozzlepops@outlook.com}

Hi guys,

Sorry for communication outage last night. I just really, really didn't want to talk. I'm rubbish, I know.

Just wanted to give you an update. Things are fine, really. Sarah is steaming mad, but not at me(!!!). She's at school right now trying to appeal the suspension. It probs won't work but nice that shes trying. I thought she'd be so mad at me but she says a suspension is completely unnecessary, because of the circs, esp as Dylan just got a detention. She was like, you should have just ignored him. Tbh I think she was kind of distracted by finding out I've had sex. I was so upset I told her what he said – not all of it, but enough for her to get it. HER FACE. GOD. Now we're both kind of pretending that bit of the conversation didn't happen.

So anyway. She's got a meeting with Mr Henriksen (thats our head of year, Cads), so we'll see how it goes. If it doesnt work the suspension is for the rest of the week, so I'll be back at school by Monday anyway. Sarah says I have to go to the cafe with her so she can keep an eye on me for the rest of the week, and I'm not allowed to see anyone, including you two. Thats basically my punishment, but it could be loads worse.

We're still on for Lev's party though, right? Thank God I didnt tell Sarah about it before, because she def wouldnt let me go if she knew. She just thinks I'm staying at yours on Saturday, Roz, which is basically true.

OK, that's pretty much it. Send me lots of texts and stuff until the weekend otherwise I'll be lonely :(

Lots of love xxxx

Wednesday 13.18
From: Rosie Caron {rozzlepops@outlook.com}
To: Suzanne Watts {suzyanne.whats@gmail.com};
Caddy Oliver {cadnam.oliver@gmail.com}

Are you sure it's a good idea to go to the party, Suze? Dylan will be there.

xx

Wednesday 13.20
From: Suzanne Watts {suzyanne.whats@gmail.com}
To: Rosie Caron {rozzlepops@outlook.com}; Caddy
Oliver {cadnam.oliver@gmail.com}

Why not?

Wednesday 13.22
From: Rosie Caron {rozzlepops@outlook.com}
To: Suzanne Watts {suzyanne.whats@gmail.com};
Caddy Oliver {cadnam.oliver@gmail.com}

Suze, come on.

Wednesday 13.25
From: Suzanne Watts {suzyanne.whats@gmail.com}
To: Rosie Caron {rozzlepops@outlook.com}; Caddy
Oliver {cadnam.oliver@gmail.com}

Why should I not go because of him? He shouldn't go
coz of me.

Wednesday 13.30
From: Rosie Caron {rozzlepops@outlook.com}
To: Suzanne Watts {suzyanne.whats@gmail.com};
Caddy Oliver {cadnam.oliver@gmail.com}

Maybe, but that's not what will happen.
What if you go and get really upset or

something? What if he's a dick again?

Wednesday 13.32
From: Suzanne Watts {suzyanne.whats@gmail.com}
To: Rosie Caron {rozzlepops@outlook.com}; Caddy
Oliver {cadnam.oliver@gmail.com}

I'm not going to talk to him or anything, I'm not an
idiot.

Wednesday 13.35
From: Rosie Caron {rozzlepops@outlook.com}
To: Suzanne Watts {suzyanne.whats@gmail.com};
Caddy Oliver {cadnam.oliver@gmail.com}

I know, but you'll be drunk, probs. What if he's all
nice to you and you think it's a good idea to get back
with him?

Wednesday 13.36
From: Suzanne Watts {suzyanne.whats@gmail.com}
To: Rosie Caron {rozzlepops@outlook.com}; Caddy
Oliver {cadnam.oliver@gmail.com}

Is that really what you think of me?

Wednesday 13.38
From: Rosie Caron {rozzlepops@outlook.com}

To: Suzanne Watts {suzyanne.whats@gmail.com};
Caddy Oliver {cadnam.oliver@gmail.com}

Don't be like that, I'm just worrying about you.

Wednesday 13.39
From: Suzanne Watts {suzyanne.whats@gmail.com}
To: Rosie Caron {rozzlepops@outlook.com}; Caddy
Oliver {cadnam.oliver@gmail.com}

Well don't.

Wednesday 13.40
From: Rosie Caron {rozzlepops@outlook.com}
To: Suzanne Watts {suzyanne.whats@gmail.com};
Caddy Oliver {cadnam.oliver@gmail.com}

Oh fine, forget it.

Wednesday 13.41
From: Suzanne Watts {suzyanne.whats@gmail.com}
To: Rosie Caron {rozzlepops@outlook.com}; Caddy
Oliver {cadnam.oliver@gmail.com}

Fine.

Wednesday 16.04
From: Caddy Oliver {cadnam.oliver@gmail.com}

To: Suzanne Watts {suzyanne.whats@gmail.com};
Rosie Caron {rozzlepops@outlook.com}

Um. So . . . are we still on for Saturday?

Wednesday 16.17
From: Suzanne Watts {suzyanne.whats@gmail.com}
To: Caddy Oliver {cadnam.oliver@gmail.com}; Rosie
Caron {rozzlepops@outlook.com}

Yeah. You two can be my chaperones.

Wednesday 16.41
From: Rosie Caron {rozzlepops@outlook.com}
To: Caddy Oliver {cadnam.oliver@gmail.com}

Argh I can't talk to her any more. You deal with her.
Tell her to come to mine for 6 on Saturday, if she stops
acting like such a petty bitch.

Wednesday 16.53
From: Caddy Oliver {cadnam.oliver@gmail.com}
To: Rosie Caron {rozzlepops@outlook.com}

Give her a break, she was suspended yesterday.
I'll tell her, but I'm sure you'll speak to her before then
anyway!

xx

Wednesday 16.55
From: Rosie Caron {rozzlepops@outlook.com}
To: Caddy Oliver {cadnam.oliver@gmail.com}

Hmmm.

Wednesday 17.01
From: Caddy Oliver {cadnam.oliver@gmail.com}
To: Suzanne Watts {suzyanne.whats@gmail.com}

Shall we go together to Rosie's on Sat? We should get there for 6.

xx

Wednesday 17.12
From: Suzanne Watts {suzyanne.whats@gmail.com}
To: Caddy Oliver {cadnam.oliver@gmail.com

OK, Sarah can pick you up? Would that be OK with your parents?

xx

Wednesday 17.15
From: Caddy Oliver {cadnam.oliver@gmail.com}
To: Suzanne Watts {suzyanne.whats@gmail.com}

Yeah, it'll be fine.

Any joy with your head of year?

xx

Wednesday 17.19
From: Suzanne Watts {suzyanne.whats@gmail.com}
To: Caddy Oliver {c.oliver@live.com}

Nope. So I'll be at the cafe tomorrow. Hey, if you're free after school you should stop by for cake :)

Wednesday 17.22
From: Caddy Oliver {cadnam.oliver@gmail.com}
To: Suzanne Watts {suzyanne.whats@gmail.com}

Amazing! I will if I can. I'll bring Roz, yeah?

Wednesday 17.23
From: Suzanne Watts {suzyanne.whats@gmail.com}
To: Caddy Oliver {cadnam.oliver@gmail.com}

OK.

xx

In less than twenty-four hours, Suzanne and Rosie seemed to have got over their snippiness and were back to their usual selves. I came home late on Thursday evening, after a Sixth Form information evening at Esther's, to find they'd both spammed my Facebook page with forty-eight photos and videos of Elton John.

If anything, Suzanne seemed to enjoy her three days off school and her time in the cafe. When Rosie and I visited on Friday afternoon she was behind the till, concentrating so hard on taking an order that she didn't realize immediately that we were there. She brought us millefeuille and chocolate milkshakes and we sat at the corner table together, people-watching and talking.

On Saturday, Suzanne texted me to let me know she was outside with Sarah and I went out to meet her. She was dressed in the most casual of Saturday clothes, the picture of a teenage girl on her way to a friend's house for a sleepover.

'Just a quiet night for you girls then?' Sarah asked as she drove.

'Yeah,' Suzanne said before I could try to lie. 'It's been such a weird week I couldn't face anything else.'

It was almost scary really. I knew she was lying, and even I was momentarily convinced. It wasn't just what she'd said or even the placid expression on her face, it was the relaxed way she was sitting in the front seat, her overnight bag containing her going-out clothes right there on her lap, her fingers tapping her leg to the beat of the music. She lied with her whole body and it seemed effortless.

I thought about asking her about it later, but I couldn't think of a way of doing it that wouldn't come out confrontational. The last thing I wanted after everything that had happened that week was an argument.

Levina's house lived up to its billing. It turned out to be much closer to my own house than Rosie's, near to the seafront and *huge*. Her older sister and brother – twins in the Upper Sixth – had invited their own friends, so even by the time we arrived you could barely move for people.

'Come and get a drink!' Levina squealed when we arrived, already giggly with alcohol. She was wearing a too-tight dress and a large hat in the shape of a birthday cake. 'Oh my *God*, Suze, I can't believe you came!'

'Happy birthday,' Suzanne said in reply, a tight smile on her face.

When we headed into the living room to find the alcohol, she turned to me and gripped my wrist momentarily. 'Oh my God, I need a drink.'

'Me too,' I said, already feeling self-conscious and out of place. Suzanne had done a good job making me up on the outside, but it hadn't had the transformative effect I'd hoped for on the inside. I was still me.

We took our drinks into another room which had a table covered in pizzas and a crowd of excitable teenagers and found a spot for the three of us on the bench that was built into the wall.

'Cheers,' Rosie said, angling her bottle towards me.

'Cheers,' I replied, more enthusiastically than I really meant, clinking my bottle against hers. Suzanne leaned over the two of us and jiggled her own bottle between ours.

'I see Dylan,' Rosie said quietly.

Suzanne took a sip from her bottle and made a face. 'Can we pretend he's not here?'

I was about to ask which one Dylan was, but there was no

need. As soon as he spotted us his face changed and he started to make his way over.

'Oh great,' Rosie muttered to me. 'Can't we at least get a few drinks in first?'

When both Rosie and Suzanne had talked about Dylan, I'd expected a good-looking lad-type. Probably a bit obnoxious, aware of his appeal; hot in an obvious way. But Dylan was tall and lithe with messy dark hair and the unlikeliest blue eyes. He was wearing skinny jeans, a Bon Iver T-shirt and, most unexpectedly of all, a lip ring. This was not in any way a description I would have thought to put on a boy my two best friends both liked.

But then he smiled. And it made a lot more sense.

'Don't even think about it,' Suzanne said.

He ignored this. 'Hey,' he said, looking right at her. 'You all right?'

Suzanne just looked at him. A fierce, furious glare.

'Want to come out for a smoke?' Dylan asked, undeterred. He pulled out a pack of cigarettes and waved them slightly, still with that smile on his face. The smile said, *Of course you do.*

Unexpected. That was the only word I could think of for him.

'Dylan, just go,' Rosie said, her voice exasperated.

'Aw, Roz,' Dylan said, surprising me again. He called her *Roz.* 'I'm building bridges here.'

I glanced at Suzanne just in time to see something flash across her face. She *did* want to go with him. Even if it was just for a second, she did.

'Run along, little boy,' she said instead.

Dylan slid a cigarette between his lips, a smirk crooked behind it. 'See you later then.'

After he'd gone, Suzanne's tensed shoulders relaxed against mine. Leaning on me, she turned to Rosie. 'Credit for that, please.'

Rosie grinned. 'Well done, I'm so proud.' She reached over

and adjusted the strap of my top. 'What did you think of him, Cads?'

'Is there an acceptable answer to that?' I asked.

'Let's not talk about him,' Suzanne said. 'Let's just have fun.'

'Yes,' Rosie said emphatically. 'The three of us getting drunk on a Saturday night. *Yes*. And *you* . . .' She gestured her bottle towards Suzanne. 'Are you going to disappear again?'

'No!' Suzanne said, looking hurt. 'I'm here with you guys. I'll stay with you. I *promise*.'

She didn't.

To be fair, she lasted for over an hour, and by the time I turned and realized she'd disappeared I was having too much fun to really care. I was sitting around a ridiculously grand oak table with a plastic cup of beer in front of me, playing a complicated drinking game that involved numbers. Four rounds in and I still wasn't certain of the rules. Levina's boyfriend, Charlie, had taken charge, but most of the people I was playing with I didn't actually know.

But that didn't seem to matter, all of a sudden. We were just having fun.

'Five!' the girl next to me bellowed.

'Six!' I said.

'Seven!' Maya realized her mistake as soon as she spoke, but we all booed anyway. 'Oh fuck. Shut up, OK.' She took a swig of her drink. 'ONE!'

We started around the table again, me trying to concentrate on the numbers people were saying over the fuzzy blur of the beer.

'I'm going to get a drink,' Rosie said into my ear. 'Want anything?'

'No, I'm good,' I said, lifting my cup as proof. 'NINE!'

Rosie rolled her eyes, but she was grinning. She put her hand on my shoulder to hoist herself out of her chair, squeezing affectionately.

I was so engrossed in the game that I almost didn't notice her return, until I felt a prod on my shoulder and turned distractedly to see her standing there, holding a bottle of WKD. She gestured to me with her free hand. 'You need to come and see this.'

I stood reluctantly and followed her through the living room. She stopped inside the patio doors and I looked out obediently. There were two figures kissing by the table outside. It took me a moment to realize it was Suzanne and Dylan.

Dylan was half sitting, half leaning against the table. Suzanne was standing between his partly open legs, her arms around his neck, his around her waist.

'What the fuck,' I said.

'I know.'

'Aren't you going to say something?' I asked. We were both whispering, even though it was unlikely they could hear us.

Rosie's eyebrows shot up. 'Is that a serious question?'

'Don't you think we should?'

'No. Not even slightly.'

'Isn't it our job as friends to stop her doing stupid things?' I asked.

'I'm sure she'd take that really well,' Rosie said, sarcastic. She took a sip of the WKD, her face set, a little too calm.

'Wouldn't you want me to stop you doing something that stupid?'

'I would never do anything that stupid,' Rosie responded. 'I have an ounce of sense. And self-respect.'

'Oh, Roz, come on.'

Rosie put her two hands palm up in front of her chest, as if physically distancing herself. 'Oh, you go ahead. Don't let me stop you.' She clearly didn't expect me to take even a step in their direction.

I hesitated. As much as I wanted to help Suzanne and prove Rosie wrong in the process, I was still very much myself. I definitely hadn't had enough alcohol to cancel out my life-learned aversion to conflict.

I was about to admit defeat and go back inside, leaving Suzanne to her own mistakes, when I saw Dylan move his hand away from her waist. He lifted his hand into the air above her head, making the OK sign with his finger and thumb. I heard a shout of laughter from the other end of the garden.

'What a dick,' Rosie muttered in disgust.

I stepped through the patio doors and walked over to them, my steps more decisive than I felt. I reached out and took a hold of Suzanne's arm.

'Suze,' I said.

She broke away from Dylan, looking towards me with a dazed expression on her face. I tried to gauge how drunk she was, how culpable.

'What?' she asked. The confusion had vanished, leaving annoyance in its place.

'What are you doing?' I demanded, trying to keep my voice steady.

'Who the fuck are you?' Dylan interjected.

'This is Caddy,' Suzanne said. She was looking at me with a less-than-friendly expression on her face, but still she said, 'Don't talk to her like that.'

I was still holding her arm and I squeezed it for emphasis. 'Come on, Suze. Come and get a drink with us.' I gestured to Rosie, who had come to stand behind me.

'She's got a drink,' Dylan said. 'And who are you?'

'Caddy's my friend,' Rosie said, before I could speak. 'She goes to Esther's.'

Dylan's eyebrows raised as he finally registered my name. He looked amused. '*You're* Caddy?' He took the entire length of me in at a glance, then laughed. It was the kind of laugh that made me feel like my skin had been peeled back, leaving every nerve on show.

If I could be anyone but Caddy Oliver, I would have been able to voice the words that had jammed in my mouth. Something confident and brazen, or even just 'What are you laughing at?' But I was me. Self-conscious and tentative. Cowed by the casual cruelty of teenage boys.

'Don't be such a knob,' Suzanne said, rolling her eyes.

She gave his shoulder a shove and he caught her wrist, grinning, and turned to me, his eyes mocking. 'Hey, hey, I'm just teasing.'

'I don't care,' I said, even though I definitely did. 'Come on, Suze,' I said again.

Dylan moved his hand up from Suzanne's wrist and entwined his fingers with hers, pulling her closer to him in one smooth movement. He looked at her, *that* smile on his face, and said, voice soft, 'You're all right with me, right, Suze?' He moved his free hand to her shoulder, curling around her neck, pulling her towards him.

Suzanne closed her eyes and leaned her head against his chest. I heard Rosie let out a groan. 'Let's go, Cads,' she said.

I didn't move. 'She got suspended because of you,' I said to Dylan. Something like rage was building inside me and it had nowhere to go but him.

'I didn't throw any chairs,' Dylan replied, smirking.

'You called her damaged goods,' I said. Suzanne's eyes, already closed, clenched further shut. 'You said she was cheap.'

The smirk had disappeared. He was watching me warily. 'She knows I didn't mean it. Now would you just fuck off?'

I waited a beat for Suzanne to open her eyes and say, again, 'Don't talk to her like that.' But she didn't move.

'You're such a dickhead, Dylan,' Rosie said after a silence. She took my elbow and began steering me back towards the house. Then she paused, turned her head slightly and added, 'And you're pathetic, Suzanne.'

We walked back into the warmth of the house together, Rosie's arm through mine. There was something comforting about the noise of the party and the anonymity of the drunken crowd, but I still felt as if I was about to start crying.

'I think I liked it better when it was just the two of us,' Rosie said.

For the next couple of hours I tried to forget about Suzanne. I drank enough to blur out the edges of my anger and turned my attention instead to the beautiful boy who had sat next to me on the sofa and offered to share his beer. His name was Tariq. We would have beautiful babies, I had already decided. Rosie would be my maid of honour; maybe Suzanne could come to the hen party.

It was nearing midnight when I went to find out if there was any alcohol left, leaving Tariq on the sofa – 'I'll be back don't run off I'll be back OK?' – with my bag. Rosie, who I would usually entrust with my possessions, was otherwise engaged with Liam on an armchair on the other side of the room. I was on my way past the kitchen when I saw Suzanne, her back against the fridge, kissing . . . who? I stopped mid-step, confused, looking at the boy. Not Dylan. Not anyone I knew.

I was about to turn away in disgust, I was maybe a second away from doing this, when I saw her hands. They were squashed in front of her, ineffectually but unmistakably pushing against the stranger. I was processing this when she moved her head away from him, stumbling slightly, and he pushed her – hard – back against the fridge.

'Hey!' I heard myself shout, the loudness of my voice startling even me. I was already moving forward, shoving him away. 'What are you doing? Get off her!'

Without anyone to hold her up, Suzanne staggered, and I reached out my hands to steady her. 'Are you OK?' I tried to make eye contact, but hers were unfocused. I couldn't tell if the redness was due to alcohol or if she'd been crying. 'Hey.' I shook her shoulder slightly. 'It's me, it's Caddy.'

'Hey, we were just—' the boy started saying, his voice slurred.

'Fuck off before I knock you out,' I snarled, because he didn't know me and I could have been a black belt, for all he knew.

It worked. He bolted out of the kitchen, looking far more terrified than a threat from me should ever warrant.

'Caddy?' Suzanne's voice was hoarse and quiet, choked with tears. So she had been crying.

'Suze,' I said in response, relieved. I squeezed her shoulder. 'You OK?'

She shook her head. 'I'm a mess, Caddy.'

'Yes, you are,' I agreed.

'Are you mad at me?'

'No.'

Her face crumpled. 'I'm sorry.'

'No, I said I'm *not* mad at you,' I said slowly.

'I messed up so much,' she said, like she hadn't even heard me. 'Everyone hates me.'

'No one hates you, Suze.'

Tariq appeared in the doorway then, a friendly, searching smile on his face, my bag in his hand. 'Hey,' he said to me, 'did you get lost?' He took in Suzanne, and his smile faded. 'Oh.'

'Who are you?' Suzanne squinted at him.

'It's Tariq,' Tariq said patiently. 'I'm in your English class, remember?' He turned to me. 'Is she OK?'

'I don't think so,' I said. 'She's out of it. I think we should go.'

'Go?' He looked disappointed, which was gratifying.

'I live really close,' I said. 'But I need to find Rosie.' The easiest thing would be for the three of us to go to my house. We could walk the fifteen minutes or so, which would surely help. 'Could you just . . . stay here for a sec while I get Roz?'

Tariq looked alarmed. 'Um . . .'

'I'll be right back,' I said quickly, bolting out of the kitchen before he could protest. I found Rosie in the living room where I'd last seen her, still curled on the armchair with Liam. I hesitated, wondering if she'd ever forgive me if I interrupted this unexpected success for the sake of the complete mess that was Suzanne.

I decided not, and went back to the kitchen without disturbing her. I'd text her instead. Neither Tariq nor Suzanne had moved; she was slumped against the kitchen counter, barely holding herself upright.

'Sorry,' I said to Tariq.

'That's OK,' Tariq replied. 'Um, can I add you on Facebook?'

'Sure,' I said casually, trying not to look too thrilled. 'Ready to go, Suze?' I tried to remember if she'd brought anything with her except the phone I could see wedged into her pocket.

Suzanne looked at me, and for a moment I thought she was going to say something important. Then she stepped away from me and vomited into the sink.

It's fair to say I was almost completely sober on the walk back to my house, which took a lot longer than the fifteen minutes it should have done. This was because Suzanne seemed utterly incapable of walking more than five steps without either slumping on to the floor and crying or throwing up into a bush. I had never seen anyone so completely, definitionally wasted.

Between the bouts of tears and retching, Suzanne would talk. She told me she loved me. She told me she was sorry. She told me her mother had once told her she was a disappointment. She told me she'd once tried to step in front of a bus, and had been yanked back by a passer-by, who'd then yelled in her face that she was an idiot. She'd lost her virginity to her best friend's brother when she was fourteen. She had never told anyone this. She loved me. Did I love her? No one loved her. She was a disappointment. She was sorry.

I gave up trying to respond to these proclamations and revelations when it became clear she was too much in her own head to really hear me. Twice I had to physically hold her up while she sobbed into my shoulder, her fingers clutching my arms tightly enough to bruise.

The walk home took us almost half an hour. I rooted around in my bag for my keys while Suzanne stood blinking under the sensor light. I glanced at her dishevelled figure as I eased my key into the lock as quietly as possible, suddenly remembering the first time she'd stood in my doorway. She'd seemed so together then.

'Caddy,' she whispered to me as I guided her over the front step and into the house.

'Yes?' I whispered back, pushing the door shut in increments.

'Nothing.'

I turned to look at her in exasperation. Even in the darkness I saw the wicked, mischievous grin that had spread across her face. I had to laugh, albeit quietly. 'Do you know how ridiculous you are?'

Before she could respond, there was a creak on the stairs. I froze, clenching my fist around my keys. I'd really hoped I wouldn't have to face my mother until the following morning, when Suzanne had sobered up and regained some semblance of her charming self.

'Caddy?' A whisper from the stairs. 'Is that you?'

It was Tarin. Thank *God*.

She turned on the kitchen light and gestured to us to follow her in there. She was still wearing day clothes, her hair loose around her shoulders. Her gaze took in both of us, an odd expression on her face. Was she amused? She didn't speak for a moment and then said, 'Christ. What happened?'

'My life,' Suzanne said morosely, before I could even open my mouth.

'Oh, melodrama!' Tarin said, her eyebrows raising. 'How lovely!' She was definitely amused, but there was something else in there too. It might have been sadness.

'Is it still melodrama if it's true?' I asked.

'Yes!' Tarin looked at me like I was crazy. 'Even more so.'

'Tarin,' Suzanne said earnestly, 'I wish I had a sister. I wish you were my sister.'

'Oh darling, you're wasted, aren't you?' Tarin's whispered voice softened. 'You poor thing.' She said this with no trace of sarcasm. The sincerity was almost painful.

Suzanne and I went up to my room as quietly as possible, Tarin following with a glass of water for each of us. She set the glasses on my beside cabinet and then looked at me expectantly. Suzanne sank on to my bed, pulled off her shoes and then curled herself inwards, umbrella-like, on top of the covers.

'You should get a bucket or something,' Tarin whispered to me.

'I think it's out of her system,' I said.

'Don't be so sure,' Tarin said, with the voice of someone who'd learned from experience. 'Make sure she doesn't fall asleep on her back. Just in case.'

I looked at my friend, her arms curved protectively over her face, lying on my bed, shoulders already slack with sleep.

'I don't want to be a downer,' Tarin added in the same low voice, 'but you do realize you're going to be in major trouble tomorrow?'

'I don't care,' I said, realizing that I really didn't. 'I couldn't leave her on her own there. And she wouldn't have been able to get home safely by herself.'

A look of something like pride passed over my sister's face, followed by a smile. 'Night, Cadders. If you need me, just come right in and get me, OK?'

I found a bowl in the cupboard by the bathroom and put it by the bed, just in case. I turned the light off and climbed carefully over Suzanne to get to the free side of the bed. I was just settling into sleep when her voice startled me awake.

'*Buonanotte?*' she whispered, almost like a question.

I smiled. '*Buonanotte.*'

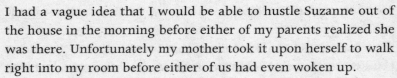

21

I had a vague idea that I would be able to hustle Suzanne out of the house in the morning before either of my parents realized she was there. Unfortunately my mother took it upon herself to walk right into my room before either of us had even woken up.

'Oh, you *are* here,' she said. I'd never noticed how loud her voice was before. 'I thought I saw your shoes by the door.'

I sat up, realizing as I did so that I was still wearing my clothes from the night before. Suzanne was still in the same position she'd fallen asleep in, on top of the covers, curled in a ball. She'd somehow slept through Mum's entrance.

Mum came further into the room and sat herself down on the corner of the bed by Suzanne's feet. The movement on the bed must have woken her, because Suzanne jolted, then sat straight up.

'What?' she said, looking at me. She reached up and brushed her mangled hair out of her face, blinking and confused.

'Um,' I said, a little helplessly. 'Morning?'

'Yes, good morning,' Mum said drily. Suzanne's head jerked towards her, her expression suddenly nervous. 'I'm a little surprised to see the two of you. I thought you were going to be staying with Rosie, Caddy,' she said, turning to me.

I tried to think of the best way to answer this. *Suzanne was dangerously wasted and Rosie was making out with a guy*, though truthful, probably wasn't what she wanted to hear.

'It was easier to come back here,' I said finally.

Mum raised her eyebrows, clearly waiting for more. I forced myself to resist the deep-seated impulse to tell her everything and stayed silent.

Finally Mum patted Suzanne's calf in a friendly way, then said, 'Why don't you both get a bit cleaned up and I'll make you some breakfast. Suzanne, I'm sure Caddy has some clothes you could borrow.'

After we'd both showered and I'd found some lounging clothes that fitted Suzanne, we went downstairs together. In the kitchen, Mum was frying bacon and eggs and Dad was sitting at the table reading the paper. Tarin was leaning against the kitchen counter, sipping tea. When she saw me, she threw me a knowing but supportive grin.

'How are you feeling?'

'I'm OK,' I said, even though my head was throbbing and my stomach had the persistent lurching sensation of a washing machine mid-cycle.

'I've spoken to Sarah,' Mum said to Suzanne, who blanched. 'She'll be here soon to pick you up. It's interesting – she wasn't aware there was a party at all. She was quite surprised to hear you'd come here.'

The only thing worse than being told off by your mother is your mother telling off your friend.

'Coming back here was my idea,' I said, the only thing I could think of.

Mum gave me a look and I shut up. 'Why don't you both sit down and have some breakfast?' she said.

When Sarah did arrive, not even ten minutes later and wearing the expression of someone deeply, deeply put upon, Suzanne didn't even bother trying to defend herself. She hunched her shoulders inside her leather jacket and looked down at the floor, avoiding Sarah's gaze.

'I'm so sorry, Carol,' Sarah said. 'I don't even know what to say.'

'I think they both share some of the blame this time,' Mum replied, putting her hands on my shoulders and squeezing.

Suzanne glanced up at me, a fleeting smirk of solidarity flashing across her face, before putting her head back down.

'Come on, trouble,' Sarah said with a sigh, reaching out and taking Suzanne's arm. 'Let's get this over with.'

When they'd gone, I tried to make my escape upstairs, but Mum blocked my way and pointed to the kitchen. 'In,' she said. 'Sit.'

I went in and sat.

'So,' Dad began, pressing his fingers together, 'I think it goes without saying that we expect a lot better from you. Behaviour like this, it's simply not acceptable.'

Less than a minute in and we were already two clichés down. It was just my luck that I'd ended up in trouble on one of the rare days my dad was actually at home. If it had been Mum, she'd have been disappointed and maybe a little shrill, but I'd have been contrite and it would soon have been over. Dad liked to be overly reasonable, like he was working through a checklist of How To Discipline Your Daughter. We could be here for hours.

'Shall we start with the alcohol?' Dad raised his eyebrows significantly. 'Or the fact that you walked across Brighton in the middle of the night while you were *drunk*? When we were under the impression that you were staying with Rosie?'.

'We were meant to be,' I said. 'But Suze was—'

'Right,' Dad interrupted. 'Yes. Your friend *Suze*. I was going to get to her.' He let out a sigh through his nose. 'This is the same friend who got thrown out of school for throwing a chair? The one with all the detentions – am I right?'

I hesitated. 'Well, yeah, but—'

'You may as well be honest,' he continued, talking over me. 'It's quite clear that she's the reason you came back here at all. Tarin said you were practically holding her up.'

I looked at my sister, stunned by the betrayal. 'Tarin!'

'Oh for God's sake.' Tarin looked annoyed. 'Don't twist that,

Dad.' She looked at me. 'I said that in an affectionate way, Caddy. The point of it was you being a good friend.'

'Well, you shouldn't be,' Dad said, his voice picking up. 'Not if it means doing things like this. If she wants to turn up drunk or high or who knows what else at all hours, that's her problem. Not yours.'

'High?' I said, confused. 'When was she high?'

'John,' Mum said pointedly. I caught the look she gave him, and it occurred to me for the first time that maybe Sarah really was telling her things about Suzanne that I didn't even know. The thought threw me, so I pushed it away. Mum turned back to me. 'We're very concerned about your friendship with this girl,' she said calmly. 'I've told you that before. If it's getting to this – drinking and not being where you say you are, well, that's a problem.'

'You can't blame her for me drinking,' I said. 'Everyone drinks.'

'You are *sixteen*,' Dad said slowly, enunciating each syllable. 'Do we really need to remind you of that?'

'Dad,' Tarin put in at this point, 'all sixteen-year-olds drink. I'm sorry, but they just do. You can't expect Caddy to go to a friend's party where there's drinking and her not to drink.'

'That is *exactly* what I expect.' Dad smacked his hand against the table, making us all jump. His voice had risen. 'We raised you better than this, Cadnam. You don't take the drink just because it's handed to you. You say *no*.'

I looked at him, trying to figure out how he could be so oblivious. I'd been drinking at parties with my friends since I was thirteen years old. My parents could have raised me however they wanted, but I'd still have grown up in the world.

'We've never had any concerns about your friendship with Rosie,' Mum put in, 'and I think that's significant. I thought you were sensible enough to not go along with this kind of behaviour. I'm disappointed to find out you're not.'

Tarin, standing behind Mum and still leaning against the counter, rolled her eyes at this.

'Some people are toxic, Caddy,' Dad said. 'Some people are more trouble than they're worth.'

I thought about Suzanne standing patiently at my side while she straightened my hair and talked to Rosie about Liam; showing me how to jerk the shot glass so I'd barely taste the spirit; clutching my arms and crying in the middle of the street.

'She's not toxic,' I said. 'She's just sad.'

'Well, that's not your problem,' Dad said again. My dad, the doctor. My dad, who'd caught spiders from my bedroom walls and released them with gentle fingers into the garden. 'I don't want to see her in this house again. She's not welcome here.'

I looked at Mum, feeling the sting of imminent tears in my eyes. She sighed. 'If you want better consequences, Caddy, you need to make better choices.'

There was worse to come.

Rosie turned up on my doorstep in the middle of the afternoon, a total surprise. Though she was polite to my mother, who let her in, I could see something simmering under her smile. Sure enough, when she and I were alone together in my room, it came out.

'I'm going to tell you straight away,' she said, her voice already shaky, 'because there's no point dancing around it. I'm really mad. And upset. With you.'

My whole body went cold with dread.

'Don't look like that. Don't make me feel guilty before I've even started.' Her face was red, her eyes blazing. But still she looked more hurt than angry, which was maybe the worst thing about it. 'Can I at least yell at you first before you make that face?'

I tried to calm my racing heart with rationalizations. This was Rosie. My best friend. Even if she was angry, even if she yelled, it would pass.

'Go on then,' I said, trying to steel myself. 'Yell at me. What did I do?'

I knew what I'd done.

'You know what you did!' Rosie burst out, her hands flailing awkwardly, like she wasn't sure what to do with them. 'You *left* me. You left me in fucking Levina's house and you didn't even say. I was *looking* for you.'

'Suzanne was—'

'I don't give a fuck about Suzanne. This is about you. You're my *best* friend. I'm supposed to be *your* best friend. And I'm the fucking *moron* walking around trying to find you, and then Tariq of all people finally tells me that you've gone. And you know, I actually didn't believe him. I was like, obviously they haven't gone. Caddy wouldn't go without me.'

'I texted you—'

'*So?*' she exploded. 'A *text*? I wasn't looking at my phone! Why didn't you at least tell me you were leaving?'

'I almost did,' I said quickly. 'I came to find you before we left, but you were with Liam, Roz, and I didn't think that I should disturb—'

'Oh for fuck's sake, Caddy,' Rosie interrupted, her voice suddenly snide. 'You're seriously trying to say you thought I'd be so wrapped up in Liam that I'd be fine with you disappearing with Suze, when you were supposed to be staying at my house? When Mum came to pick us up she was like, "Where are the girls?" And I had to say, "They left without me."'

I felt sick with guilt now. In the afternoon sunlight, in the normality of my bedroom, I could see how right she was. How wrong I'd been.

'I'm really sorry—' I tried to say, but she cut me off again.

'I don't understand this,' Rosie said, her voice strained with frustration. 'I literally don't. How are the two of you better friends than the two of us? How did that *happen*?'

'Of course we're not better friends than—'

'I mean than me and her. Not you and me. Don't even suggest that the two of you are better friends than you and me, because if you do, I might actually fucking die.' She was breathing hard, her jaw set. I could see how hard she was trying not to get upset.

I had no idea what to say. Anything that came to mind seemed hopelessly inadequate.

'You're my best friend,' I said finally, ridiculously.

'And what about her?' Rosie challenged. Her hands had balled into tight fists at her sides. 'What is she?'

What *was* she? I had no idea.

'I don't know.'

'Caddy . . .'

'I really don't. She's my friend, OK? Does it matter? Best means best, and that's you.'

'It does matter. Because she's supposed to be *my* friend, not yours. And now suddenly the two of you are all chummy, and she's turned you into the kind of person who'll leave me on my own at a party.'

'You weren't on your own.' It felt important to point this out. 'You were with Liam.'

For a split second I really thought she was going to slap me. But instead she reached into her pocket and pulled out her phone, tapping on the screen and then handing it to me.

'Look at this,' she said.

It was a string of text messages. Rosie had scrolled to where they began. Feeling apprehensive, I began to read.

09.39: What the hell happened last night? Where did you and Caddy go?

11.19: I don't know, total blank on it all. I woke up at Caddy's house.

11.24: You realize you both left me on my own?

11.29: Like I said, I'm blank on it. Ask Caddy.

11.31: Your stuff is still here.

11.34: Fine, I'll come and get it then. When?

11.36: Are you not even sorry?

11.39: Roz, I've got such a major headache. Can we save this please?

11.44: Your fault for getting so wasted.

11.47: Don't. Just tell me when to get my stuff OK.

11.49: I'll bring it to school tomorrow. Do you remember what you did with Dylan?

11.50: Fine. Yes.

11.51: . . . ?

11.52: What?

11.54: Nothing to say about that?

11.55: I'm trying so hard not to get mad at you, Roz. Can we drop this.

11.56: I'm already mad.

11.58: Then stop texting me.

12.02: Why are YOU mad? I'm not the one leaving you behind and taking your friends.

12.05: Grow the fuck up.

12.06: Wow. OK.

My fingers felt itchy, my throat tight. It felt as if each savage text was directed at me. I handed the phone back to Rosie, trying to figure out what to say. She was looking at me expectantly.

'You see?' she said.

'You were both *horrible* to each other,' I said.

'How was I horrible to her?'

'Oh, Roz.' I suddenly felt panicky, knowing that whatever I said was going to be the wrong thing. 'Please don't.'

Some people thrive on conflict. They enjoy the drama. I felt like I was being held underwater.

'I said I was sorry,' I added a little desperately, 'and I really, really am. Please don't be like this.'

I so wanted her to relax, laugh and make a joke about me caving so easily. But her face was still hard, her mouth an angry line.

'Don't be mad at Suze,' I continued, when it became clear she wasn't going to speak. 'It's really not her fault. I was the one who decided to come here instead of yours; she was totally out of it.'

'No one made her get that drunk,' Rosie pointed out, sullen.

'No, but she *was* that drunk. I was trying to look after her. And I guess that means I wasn't thinking enough about you, and I'm really sorry, you're right, I shouldn't have just left you there.'

Everyone says apologizing works, but it never really does. Not quickly enough anyway. Rosie looked away from me, her face pinched, but now her mouth was wobbling slightly, like she was about to cry. Rosie, who *never* cried.

'Do you like her better than me?' she asked in a rush, still not looking at me.

'*No*, Roz. God. Of course not.'

'You only really like her because she makes you feel needed.'

'That's not true.'

'Yeah, it is. You think I didn't notice that you only started being friendly after you found out about her being abused?'

There was a sudden guilty silence. I felt a bit sick, thrown by the truth of it. I *had* started liking Suzanne after the truth had come out. What did that say about me? Was it simply timing, or something else?

'That's not why I like her,' I said finally, but I could hear the uncertainty in my voice.

'*Sure*,' she said, long and sarcastic. 'Just like you didn't leave with her last night because you wanted to be the rescuer? Just like she doesn't only like you because you put up with her shit without telling her to get the fuck over it?'

I swallowed, close to tears myself now.

'You don't know her,' Rosie said, her voice hard. 'I can tell you think you do. But you don't. You only see her when she's putting on a face.'

My heart dropped. 'What? What do you mean?'

I saw Rosie bite down on her tongue, then look away from me. 'If you could see her at school. The way she is sometimes. Like she doesn't care. I don't mean, like, "Oh school's so fucking boring I don't care." I mean, she really *doesn't care*. About anything or anyone.'

I didn't see what that had to do with how she was with me.

'She's just putting it on with you. Because she can. Because you believe it.'

I felt tears starting in the corners of my eyes. I opened my mouth. Closed it again. Another long silence. Finally, when I was sure I'd be able to speak without my voice breaking, I said, 'Are you done?'

She nodded wordlessly, still breathing hard.

'You have no idea what she's like with me when you're not around,' I said, my voice shaky. 'No *fucking* idea, Rosie.' Her eyes widened. I'd shocked her for once. 'And the reason we're better friends than you thought is because sometimes she comes to my house at night and we talk. We probably talk more than you do. The one who's wrong about her is you.'

I had never – *ever* – talked to Rosie like this. But it didn't feel as liberating as I thought it might. It felt lonely.

'I said I was sorry that I left you there,' I said slowly, willing myself on. I *had* to say this. I *had to*. 'That was a crappy thing to do. But I like Suze. I like us being friends. And she's a really good one. I know she makes stupid decisions, but I just want to help. I would if it was you too. You know that, right?' I had let my voice soften, trying to ease the knife-edge tension between us.

She stared at me, her eyes searching my face.

'Can we hug it out?' I asked, not really expecting her to say yes.

Rosie shook her head slightly, but she no longer looked like she was about to burst into flames. Progress. Then, 'She comes to your house at night?'

Shit. That was something that should have stayed in my head.

'Um. Only a couple of times.'

'It didn't sound like a couple of times.'

'Just when she needed to get away for a bit. She just wanted someone to talk to.'

'That's not normal, Caddy.' Rosie's eyes were trained on mine. 'There's no "just" about sneaking out and going to wake up your friend in the middle of the night. Don't you get that?'

'What am I supposed to do? Turn her away?'

'*Yes!*' Rosie's face scrunched, incredulous. 'Yes, that's what you do. You say, "Hey, let's talk about this in the daytime. Go back home. Go and talk to the aunt who's trying to help you instead."'

The last time Suzanne had turned up at my window at night, almost a week ago, she'd brought me a magazine article about golf caddies that featured a picture of a girl who looked like me. 'Isn't it great?' She had been thrilled, her eyes bright in the darkness. 'I wanted to show you all day.'

How could I explain to Rosie what those visits meant to me? That they weren't just for Suzanne's benefit, but mine too? And that somehow Suzanne knew that, because she knew *me*? I couldn't. It would only make things worse.

'You're right,' I said. It wasn't exactly a lie. She *was* right. I just didn't agree. 'Are you still mad at me?'

Rosie twisted her lip, clearly torn.

'Do you forgive me?' I asked.

She made a non-committal noise, but I was sure I saw her mouth twitch.

'If it helps, my parents are both mad at me too,' I said. 'And they've banned Suze from coming over.'

'I'm not surprised,' Rosie said. 'God, she's such a fucking trouble-magnet. I wish she'd never moved here.'

'No, you don't,' I said, attempting a smile. 'You love her, remember? Even with all her dramas.'

Rosie raised her eyebrows. *Don't be so sure.*

'Plus, remember I'm the one who made us leave,' I added. 'Not her.'

She let out a frustrated sigh. 'Caddy, you need to stop making excuses for her. She's the one getting wasted and throwing herself at Dylan fucking Evers, dickest of all dickheads, who *just got her suspended*. And then she tells *me* to grow the fuck up!'

'What do you want me to say?' I asked. 'Do you want me to say that I'll stop being friends with her? Because I won't, Roz. Yes, she's a complete mess, but she needs us. We're like her best friends. Both of us.'

I watched Rosie nibble on her bottom lip, and her eyes slid away in the direction of my photo montage. I reached out my foot and nudged her ankle. 'Right?'

'I guess,' Rosie said. She paused for a long moment, then looked back at me, a resigned smile growing on her face. 'All right. One last chance.'

I grinned at her, flooded with relief. 'You're the best. Can I hug you?'

This time she let me.

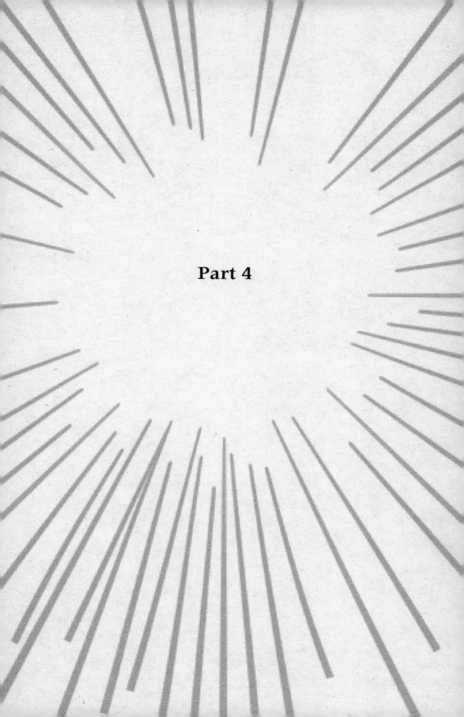

Part 4

22

It turned out that, for Rosie, 'one last chance' did not exactly mean forgiveness. For the next few days after the party she was even more prickly than usual, replying to my texts with one-word answers and skipping our after-school phone calls. I knew that things between her and Suzanne were even worse, a fact that wasn't helped by them having similarly combative personalities and a proclivity for the dramatic. For the first time ever, I was glad I was in a different school.

Just to make things worse for Suzanne, she and Dylan were all anyone at their school would talk about, meaning it was probably the worst time for her to lose her closest ally. By Wednesday, the rumour mill had gone into overdrive. 'God, now ppl are saying she went down on Dylan on Lev's patio. FFS!' Rosie texted me that lunchtime. 'This is getting stupid. I almost feel bad for her.'

I jumped on this hint of sympathy and managed to persuade them both to meet me at the beach after school on Thursday. It rained, so we took shelter in one of the cafes, sharing a plate of chips. Suzanne, wearing more make-up than I was used to and looking as a result a little scary and distant, was unusually subdued.

'I just wish they'd hurry up and find something else to talk about,' she said when I asked, tentatively, about school. 'I mean, it's not like I *care* what any of those knob-ends think of me. But it *is* fucking annoying.'

'What are they saying?' I asked.

She pursed her lips into a dry smile. 'The usual. "Did you *hear* about *Suzanne*, she's *such* a fucking *slag*, oh my *God*."' She put a voice on, exaggerating the disdain. '"Some girls are *so* pathetic."' She rolled her eyes. 'Like I don't know that already. I don't need anyone to tell me I'm pathetic.'

I thought instantly of Rosie doing exactly that. How drunk had Suzanne been at that point? Did she even remember? I glanced at Rosie to see her reaction, but she was already on it. 'Except me,' she said. 'You need me to tell you.'

'Do I?' Suzanne said mildly. 'You don't think that's something I can figure out myself?'

'Clearly not,' Rosie replied.

'Rosie,' Suzanne said, 'are you seriously sitting there calling me pathetic to my face?'

'OK!' I interrupted, putting my hand flat on the table. 'Shall we talk about something else?'

Suzanne's head snapped towards me. 'Aren't you going to tell her she can't call me pathetic?'

Rosie's eyebrows shot up. 'Yeah, Caddy,' she said, sarcasm saturating her words. 'Aren't you?' She looked at me expectantly.

I could have said, *I think you're* both *being pathetic*. Or, *I'm not responsible for her behaviour any more than I am yours*. Or even a simple, *I'd rather you kept me out of this, OK*?

I said, 'Um.'

'Oh, forget it,' Suzanne said, picking up the receipt with restless fingers and beginning to rip it into pieces. I wasn't sure if she was disappointed or annoyed.

'I don't think you're pathetic,' Rosie said, but she'd already won and we all knew it.

This was the dynamic I was working with as the weekend drew in. It seemed like a long time since my friendships had felt simple and uncomplicated, if they ever really had. Suzanne hadn't come to my window once since the party, which was perhaps the most worrying thing of all. I wasn't sure if she blamed me for her falling out with Rosie or the trouble she'd got into with Sarah, or if she was just trying to be good for a while. Either way, I missed her.

So when she texted me that Saturday morning, it felt like an opportunity. Or a test. 'Hey! I'm going to do something very stupid. But fun! Want to come? xx'

I dropped my spoon back into my cereal bowl and tapped out a reply. 'Sure! Details, please. xx'

Her reply was almost instantaneous. 'Yay hooray! Meet me at the train station in an hour. xx'

I arrived at the station just before eleven to find her waiting for me by the ticket barriers, all smiles. 'Congratulations,' she said by way of greeting. 'You are officially more adventurous than Rosie.'

'She said no?' I was surprised. It wasn't like Rosie to turn down that kind of invitation, even if they were still sniping at each other. 'How come?'

Suzanne's grin widened, mischievous and engaging. 'She asked more questions than you did.'

My stomach gave a kick I tried to disguise by smiling. 'Right . . . and what questions were those?'

'Where and what both featured quite heavily,' Suzanne said cheerfully. 'Come on! Train leaves in five.'

She turned to go and I grabbed her elbow. 'Wait a sec – don't I need to get a ticket?'

'Nope, you can have mine.' She passed me the strip of card. 'Don't worry. I've totally thought this through.' She grinned at me again, and despite myself I laughed. 'You go through first,' she said. 'Then hand the ticket back to me, but make sure no one sees. I'll see you on the train. Platform Five.'

Bemused, I followed her instructions, certain such a cheap trick would never work. I was pretty sure the ticket barriers were sophisticated enough to recognize a ticket used twice in five seconds. I glanced behind me as I walked towards the train, and sure enough, the barrier beeped. Suzanne pulled the ticket back, an exaggerated expression of confusion on her face.

'Damn,' she said, not bothering to lower her voice. She waved a hand at the member of staff nearest to her, a man somewhere in his thirties. Out of range, I couldn't hear what they were saying, but I saw the amused smile on the man's face, the grin on Suzanne's, before he shook his head ruefully and waved her through the gate. She came jogging up to me, triumphant. 'I said get on the train, not stand there admiring it.'

'How did you do that?'

'A little charm, a lot of style,' she replied, then laughed, giddy and happy. She handed the ticket back to me. 'Come on.'

We sat down just as the train began to move away from the station. Suzanne sat back in her seat, lifting her feet up to rest on the chair opposite. I did the same, nudging her thigh with my left foot. She grinned at me as my phone buzzed and I glanced down to see a text from Rosie. 'You didn't go with her, did you?'

'So where are we going?' I asked. I hadn't bothered looking at the departures board, or even the ticket she'd given me. 'It better be good.'

'The best,' she replied.

I waited. 'So? Where?' At this point I was still thinking Lewes or Eastbourne or somewhere within the same county. I glanced casually at the ticket and my heart lurched. '*Cardiff*?'

'Nope, Reading,' she said. She rested her head contentedly against the back of her seat. 'We're going to Reading.'

11.21: Yep, I'm with her right now!

11.28: You're an idiot.

11.32: I'm having an adventure :)

**11.35: No you're not, you're tagging along on someone
else's fuck up.**

I didn't know what to think. Reading wasn't as far from Brighton
as Cardiff, and it could conceivably be a day trip, but I was still
starting to regret going along with Suzanne quite so merrily.
Especially when the 'stupid' part of her original suggestion
became clear.

'I'm meant to be going to Brian's,' she said. 'Sarah's packed me
off there because she thinks he's the only one who can get through
to me or something. But I realized I don't really want to go to
Cardiff. And Reading's, like, right there on the same journey. It's
basically halfway. So why not?'

There seemed to be quite a few reasons why not, just off the
top of my head. But I couldn't face hearing her responses to any
of them, so I said, 'Why am I here then?'

She looked surprised. 'For company, of course. And it'll be
cool to show you Reading. I'd hoped Roz would come too, but
whatever. She can just have a boring weekend by herself.'

'Weekend?' I repeated, a shot of anxiety piercing my chest.
My exact words to my mother on leaving my house had been,
'Just going out for a bit.' *A bit*. Oh God.

'I mean, day,' Suzanne amended quickly. 'A boring day.'

I looked at her. She smiled, all innocence.

11.37: God, relax! What's wrong with you?

**11.39: YOU. I want my best friend back. Tell Suzanne
you're on loan and I want you back in one piece.**

11.51: Yeah, I'm really gonna tell her that. Chill out, will you?
Hey, remember who wanted us all to be friends in the first
place?

11.55: That was before.

11.57: Before what?

11.59: Before it actually happened.

At some point on that train journey I made the conscious decision to relax. It was too late to turn back now, I still had several hours before anyone would begin to wonder where I was and, most importantly, this could actually be *fun*. Suzanne was at her most lovable, all bounce and humour, trying to teach me 'The Clapping Song' with bright eyes and quick hands.

'What's happening with you and Tariq?' she asked me.

'Nothing,' I said.

She looked as disappointed as if she was the one who'd been rejected. 'Really? How come?'

'He said he'd add me on Facebook, and then he didn't.'

For a second she just looked at me, then started to laugh. 'Caddy, you know you can add *him*, right?'

I shrugged. 'I'm not that bothered.'

'Oh, go on,' Suzanne urged, tapping her Vans against my shin. 'He's really sweet. Will you just add him and see what happens? Please?'

I hesitated, looking at her open, clueless, unfairly beautiful face. She'd never understand. How could she?

'What is it?' she asked, her smile fading a little. 'He didn't upset you, did he? If he did, tell me so I can kill him.'

I couldn't help smiling. 'No, of course not. I haven't even spoken to him since Levina's party. It's just . . . I don't want to start something I'm not sure about.'

She looked blank. 'Why would you be starting anything? It's just Facebook. Then you can chat. Then maybe meet him at the beach or something, if you like each other.'

Just the words were making my heartrate jack up. 'Yeah, maybe.'

'I thought you wanted a boyfriend?' She nudged me again with her foot. 'Wasn't that one of your goals or something?'

Those stupid goals. I wished I'd never mentioned them to anyone. 'I guess.'

She bounced up out of her seat and sat next to me instead. 'He'd be seriously lucky to have a chance with you.'

'OK, stop it now.'

'What can I do to help? Want me to talk to him?'

'No,' I said. 'Just leave it, it's fine.' I could tell that she was about to speak again, so I quickly asked, 'What are we going to do when we get to Reading?'

'Not make plans,' Suzanne replied, arching an eyebrow pointedly. She grinned. 'Think you can handle that?'

12.01: What is your actual problem? Are you saying I can't be
     friends with both of you?
12.06: Would that work?
12.15: No.
**12.18: Fine. I'm saying when this fuck up catches up with
     you don't come crying to me.**
12:19: NOTED.

We got to Reading sometime after lunch, Suzanne as happy as I'd ever seen her, spinning round to face me as we walked out of the station. 'Welcome to Reading! Birthplace of Kate Winslet, dontcha know.' She beamed at me. 'OK, so there's no palace. But who really needs a palace?'

For the next couple of hours I let her play tour guide, the two of us meandering around the streets together. She told me stories about the seven years she'd spent living there, careful to leave out references to her parents but full of anecdotes about her friends and her brother. The confidence that came with being in a place you'd grown up in sat comfortably on her shoulders.

'This is my old street,' she said, turning a corner.

'Oh,' I said, surprised. I'd assumed we'd steer clear of her parents' house.

'It's OK,' she said, reading my mind. 'They're not here. It's their anniversary weekend, and they always go away for it.'

'What a lucky coincidence,' I said.

She looked at me. 'Sarcasm?'

'Never.' At least the timing of her 'spontaneous' trip made more sense.

Suzanne guided me around the back of the house into the garden, heading straight for a row of tomato plants along the right side fencing. I watched her kneel down and lift one of the pots, scrabbling with her fingers until she found what she was looking for. She sat back on her ankles, grinning at me, holding a key into the air.

'It's good you knew that was there,' I said, even though I wasn't actually sure whether it was good or not.

'I lived here for seven years,' she replied, heading for the back door. 'Some things don't change.'

The house was quiet and still. I paused by the back door, watching Suzanne walk into the kitchen and put her bag on the table like she still called this place home.

'Um. We're just stopping by, right?' I asked.

'Sure,' she said, her back to me. 'I'll show you around first though, right?' She walked around the kitchen, running her fingers along the counters. Her expression was unreadable. 'It's weird,' she said suddenly. 'I thought it might look different. But it's just the same as when I lived here. I guess it didn't all revolve around me after all.' She attempted an ironic smile, but it was a little shaky. She glanced at me. 'And you here – it's like two worlds colliding.'

'In a good way?'

I expected her to break into a proper smile, but she paused thoughtfully, her eyes falling on a calendar pinned to a cork board by the door. 'Look,' she said, even though I was on the other side of the room. 'They're in Edinburgh.'

'Do you have family there?'

'No. It's where they went to uni. That's how they met.'

A new titbit. 'What's your mum like?' I asked.

Suzanne paused, considering. This was one of my favourite things about her, I realized. How she always thought about my questions before answering, like they mattered to her. 'Sad,' she said finally. 'Kind of . . . small.'

'Oh.' It seemed like a strange way to describe your mother.

'She stopped working a long time ago, and she spends most of her time in the house,' Suzanne explained. 'It always felt a bit like she didn't really know what to do with us. Me and Brian, I mean. My dad was the only person who could really bring her to life.'

'Did she ever try to stop him hurting you?' It seemed safe, somehow, to ask the question in this house.

Suzanne shook her head. 'It's hard to explain, but it was always just something that happened. Like part of our family.'

'That's horrible.'

'Yeah. Lots of things are horrible.' She shrugged, like this was a normal thing to say, then turned away from me. Her fingers closed around the handle of the fridge, pulling it open to look inside. 'Now I'm older, I think I get it. I think she felt guilty. About cheating on my dad, you know.' She closed the door, holding what looked like a mini Scotch egg.

'She cheated on your dad?'

Suzanne pushed the Scotch egg into her mouth, whole, then chewed slowly. Swallowing, she said, 'Yeah. Didn't I tell you that he's actually my stepdad?'

'Well, yeah, but I guess I didn't—'

'It was just once,' Suzanne said, interrupting me. 'Apparently.'

I had absolutely no idea what to say to this.

'Hence —' Suzanne spread her arms, gesturing to herself, then posing momentarily like a blonde, female Freddie Mercury — 'my existence.'

'Did you always know?' I asked stupidly.

She returned her arms to her sides. 'Nope. Found out when I was fourteen. *That* was a fun revelation.' She rolled her eyes, determinedly unbothered. 'My dad had known for years. I mean, my stepdad.' Seeing my face, she shrugged again. 'My family is ten levels of fucked up.'

I thought of my parents, boring and ordinary, bickering about loading the dishwasher. 'How did you find out?'

A shadow passed over her face. 'I don't really want to talk about this.' As if someone else had brought it up. 'Come on,' she said, chancing a small smile. 'Want to see my room?'

I got the sense that she wanted to show me more than I actually wanted to see it, so I followed her despite my reluctance when she headed up the stairs, tapping the banister as she went. She turned to walk down a hallway, pointing at a closed door to her right. 'That's Brian's room,' she said as we passed. 'And that's my parents'. And . . . here's mine.' She pushed the door and walked in.

For an awful moment I thought we'd enter to find the room stripped of any trace of her, but it was unmistakably the room of a teenage girl, albeit one who didn't live there any more. The bed was made, there were still books on the shelves. But there was one glaring difference.

'It's so bare,' I said, surprised by how thrown I felt by it. 'No posters or anything?' I thought of her jumbled walls in Brighton, overflowing with life.

'My dad hates clutter,' Suzanne said, standing in the middle of the room and gazing up at the walls. 'Like, really. He's a neat freak.'

'A poster or two is hardly clutter,' I said.

'In this house,' Suzanne said, 'it's not worth it.' Her phone started ringing in her pocket and she pulled it out, her face lighting up when she saw the name on screen. She answered, turning slightly away from me. 'Hi!' Her voice was suddenly bright and animated. 'Oh my God. You'll never guess where I am! Reading!' She paused, and I heard the excited babble, tinny through the phone. 'Yeah! I'm literally standing in my bedroom.' She let out a laugh. 'I know! They're not here. I'm here with my friend.' She glanced back to beam at me.

I grinned back at her, proud to be there, proud to be her friend. I let her carry on talking as I wandered over to a shelf in the corner of the room that housed a collection of ornaments, similar to one I'd had when I was younger, though mine had been mainly woodland animals and hers seemed to be fairies and other faintly ethereal winged creatures. The light had cast an odd shadow on what could have been an angel, and I tilted my head to get a closer look. A slight but defined line separated the folded hands of the angel from its arms. I frowned, taking in more of the figurines, seeing that at least half of the collection had their own markings. Some were cracked, others were missing wingtips, a few showed scars where they had been stuck back together.

'Cool, huh?' Suzanne said, suddenly at my side. 'I loved collecting this kind of thing when I was, like, ten or something.'

'They're all broken.' I said.

She grinned at me, like she'd expected me to say that. '*What?* Are they?'

'I don't get it.' I said.

'They're fixed,' she corrected me. 'They *were* broken, but now they're repaired. And it didn't seem right to only keep the still-pretty ones, so I had to keep the broken ones too. They keep each other company.' She looked pleased. 'Besides, you can only tell if you look properly close.'

'How did they get broken in the first place?'

'Dad. Of course.' She didn't elaborate, to my guilty relief.

I had a sudden vision of a younger Suzanne bent over a pile of broken china, gluing the pieces back together. My heart ached in sympathy. 'So you put them all back together again?'

'No, it wasn't me.' Suzanne hesitated, then sighed. 'Dad did it. I was staying at a friend's house one night, and when I came back he'd done it. I went to my room and . . . well, there they were. That might be more why I never threw them out.'

I felt a confused sadness crinkle my forehead. 'Why would he do that?'

'Because sometimes he felt bad.' Her face had lost its sparkle. 'Sometimes.'

There was so much I would never know, let alone understand. A violent dad who repaired damaged fairy ornaments. A broken girl who kept them on display.

'How come you didn't bring them to Brighton?' I asked.

The grin reappeared, sudden and bright. 'Oh God, I don't like them *that* much.' She reached out impulsively and tugged on my sleeve. 'Come on,' she said. 'Want to meet my friends?'

We met up with her friends in town just as it started to get dark. They were excitable, loud and far more ordinary than I'd built them up to be in my head. I had imagined, given they'd been friends with Suzanne during her most formative adolescent years, that they would all be larger than life and intimidating, like her. But they were just people, with the same variations and similarities as any group of friends.

'Oh my *fucking* God.' This was practically shouted at us as we first approached the group by a tall, curly-haired boy who broke apart from the crowd to rush Suzanne with a hug. 'I wouldn't believe it till I saw you.' He was called Toby, Suzanne told me when they broke apart, flushed and happy.

In the confusion of introductions – which were themselves swallowed up by shrieks, hugs and greetings to Suzanne – I gave up trying to keep track of everyone's name. I decided to just keep a smile on my face and nod along if and when anyone spoke to me.

We headed as a group to McDonald's, spreading ourselves over one of the tables and sharing portions of fries and chicken nuggets. I stuck close to Suzanne, who was sat cross-legged on top of the table, ignoring the food and talking about Brighton. Every now and then she'd reach out a hand, tug playfully on my hair, throw me a huge grin and then return to her story. She talked about getting suspended, but she told the story with a slant, as if the whole thing had just been one big joke.

'I can't believe you got suspended.' One of the girls, Liz, whom I'd established was Toby's girlfriend, was laughing, but she looked a little concerned.

'This wasn't my fault,' Suzanne said. 'Was it, Cads?'

They all looked at me and I wished, not for the first time, that humans had some kind of control over their blushing reflex. 'Well,' I said, trying to make my voice as light as hers, 'you *did* throw a chair.'

She grinned at me and shrugged. 'True. But he deserved it.'

'Oh, totally,' I said, then hated myself as I caught an amused smile pass between two girls whose names I'd forgotten. *Tow-tar-lee.* My stupid private-school diction.

By the time it got dark we'd moved from McDonald's to a shabby-looking off-licence, which was staffed by an equally shabby-looking man, who barely glanced at us, even as we heaped bottles of vodka on to the counter. 'Do you want to share with me?' Suzanne asked, prodding me with a two-litre bottle of Coke and gesturing to a cheap bottle of vodka. 'We can mix.'

'Sure,' I said quickly, happy to follow her lead.

We ended up in a park that had absolutely nothing to distinguish it from any park in the country. I sat on my jacket, trying to tell myself I wasn't cold, listening to the happy shrieks of laughter around me. Suzanne had opened the Coke and was pouring some of it on the grass, her head tilted slightly, judging how much should be left. She set it upright, balanced between her knees, and poured the vodka straight into it. She screwed the lid back on, gave the bottle a careful shake, then passed it to me. 'All right?' she said.

It was so strong I almost choked. 'Great!' I said, my eyes tearing, and she laughed.

'It's just because it hasn't mixed properly,' she promised. 'It'll get better.'

Regardless, I took a couple of sickening gulps, hoping the vodka would go straight to my head and make this whole thing a little easier. Suzanne's friends were friendly enough, but this kind of situation would never be one I'd feel comfortable in.

Here I was, somehow, sitting in a random park in the middle of Reading with people I didn't know. I thought with a sudden, unexpected pang of Brighton beach, with the uncomfortable, cold pebbles I'd complained about for years. The sea stretching out in front, the city behind and the two piers like goalposts in the night. You always knew where you were in Brighton.

'What time is it?' I asked Suzanne.

'Just gone seven,' she said, glancing at her phone.

I took a more restrained sip from the bottle and passed it over to her, trying to calm the flutterings of anxiety in my stomach.

Just gone seven was still early. We had plenty of time to get home before my absence became noteworthy.

**Tarin 19.36: Hey, when will you be home? I want to watch
The Lion King. Watch it with me? :) xx**
19.40: Not till late. Sorry! xxxx
19.43: Where are you, btw?
19.58: Just out.
20.02: . . . my sister sense is tingling. Everything OK?
20.03: Haha yes of course! xxx

It wasn't. It was getting harder to ignore my nerves. It was just past 8 p.m., and the journey back to Brighton would take close to three hours. Suzanne was showing no signs of intending to leave, and neither was anyone else. Worse, my phone battery was getting dangerously low.

'Hey,' I said to Suzanne, dropping my voice so her friends wouldn't hear. 'Um . . . are we going to head off soon?'

'It's way too early to leave,' she said, her tone dismissive. She leaned forward, away from me. 'Hey, Toby, can you spare a cigarette?'

'Suze –' I touched her arm, waiting for her to look back at me – 'seriously. If we're not going to leave now, then when?'

Toby glanced at me, a packet of cigarettes in his fingers, then looked back at Suzanne, who held out her hand. 'Are you causing trouble?'

'Me?' Suzanne responded, half innocence, half mischief. Toby let out a short laugh, then handed her a cigarette. There was a moment of silence while she lit it before she turned to me. 'Hey –' her voice was suddenly upbeat, but a little too casual – 'you know, we could just stay the night here.'

I blinked at her. 'What?'

'Instead of going back to Brighton,' Suzanne said. She was smiling her fullest, most engaging smile. 'Why not just stay? My parents won't be back until tomorrow evening, and we'll be long gone by then.'

'My parents are expecting me home tonight,' I said slowly.

'So? Tell them you're staying out with me.'

'I can't.' I didn't even want to think about how my mother would react if she found out I'd upped and left Brighton for the night without even telling her. 'It'll make it worse if I say I'm with you.'

'God, Caddy.' She rolled her eyes, looking wearily amused in a way that made me want to pour the contents of the Coke bottle into her lap. '*So what?* Stay out, go home tomorrow. So they'll get mad – so what? Who cares?'

'I care,' I said. 'I'm the one who'll have to deal with it.'

'Deal with what? Them being "disappointed" in you?' She raised her fingers into sarcastic scare quotes. 'How terrifying.'

I bit my tongue. 'Don't be—'

'It's not like they'll stop loving you,' Suzanne interrupted, 'just for staying out *one* night without telling them. What are you so scared of?' She reached out and poked my shoulder. 'Come on, Cads. Nothing *significant* will ever happen unless you get out of your comfort zone every now and then.'

I caught her eye and looked at her levelly, waiting for the expression on her face to falter. Eventually it did. 'Did you do this on purpose?' I asked. The question was unnecessary. She had clearly done this on purpose.

She at least had the grace to look sheepish. 'Maybe a little?' Seeing my face, she added quickly, 'I didn't tell you because I knew you wouldn't come, and I wanted you to come. Oh, please don't be mad. It'll be fun.' Her eyes were full of sparks and mischief. 'Don't be mad. Are you mad?'

Was there any point in being mad? Had I *really* thought we'd go to Reading and back again in a day?

'Why did you bring me?' I asked. 'Why would you even want me here so much?'

Her forehead crinkled, the corner of her mouth quirking into a smile. 'Is that a serious question? Because you're my best friend and I love you? Because I have fun with you? Because I wanted you to meet my friends? And because you're a good influence. I'm much better with you.' She made a face. 'In a non-rom-com kind of way.'

'You're a *bad* influence on *me*,' I replied, but I was smiling despite myself.

She looked startled. 'Am I?'

'Uh, yeah? Didn't you notice?'

'I'm not a *bad* influence, I'm a *fun* influence,' Suzanne said confidently, but her expression was still a little troubled.

'Maybe we balance each other out,' I suggested, reaching for the Coke bottle. 'I'm good, you're fun. Or something.'

'Ooh, yes. That's good. What's Rosie though?'

'The spirit level,' I said. I'd meant to joke, but the image was so unexpectedly accurate I laughed. 'She is *definitely* the spirit level.'

'What's a spirit level?'

'The thing you use to check shelves are straight,' I said, still laughing. The vodka was clearly starting to work its magic.

She looked baffled, which only made me laugh harder. 'God,' I said, trying to calm myself down. I reached for my phone. 'Right. OK, so I'm staying here tonight. Shit, my battery's almost out.'

'That's good,' Suzanne said. 'No fallout till tomorrow. This is a *great* opportunity for you to learn to live in the moment.'

'Seize the day,' I said, flexing my fingers over my phone and trying to decide who to text first. 'Carpe diem.'

Battery: 5%

20.14: T, I'm going to crash at Rosie's tonight. Will you tell
   Mum? Be back tomoz x

20.17: ? Why not come home? Have you got stuff with you?

4%

20.18: Roz has pjs. Battery's about to die. See you!

3%

20.19: If anyone asks, I'm staying at yours tonight.

20.23: No you're not.

20.24: ??? Wtf Roz?

2%

20.28: Is the fuck up catching up with you?

20.29: ROZ seriously my batterys dying. Are you kidding?

20.36: Nope. Have a good night.

As I stared at the phone in genuine shock, the screen went black
as the battery died. I felt a moment of pure panic, imagining the
possible scenarios that could play out when I got home. And then
I let it go. It was done. I was either in the biggest trouble of my
life or I wasn't, and there was nothing I could do about it now.

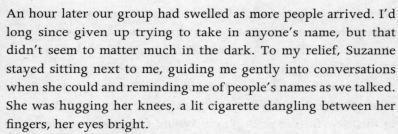

23

An hour later our group had swelled as more people arrived. I'd long since given up trying to take in anyone's name, but that didn't seem to matter much in the dark. To my relief, Suzanne stayed sitting next to me, guiding me gently into conversations when she could and reminding me of people's names as we talked. She was hugging her knees, a lit cigarette dangling between her fingers, her eyes bright.

'Did Suze tell you she had her first kiss here?' Toby asked me, grinning.

'Fuck off – no, I fucking didn't,' Suzanne said, laughing.

'Oh, shit, yeah – that was me.' He laughed too, loud and amiable. Out of all of the strangers here, Toby was definitely my favourite, with his cheerful brown eyes, quick smile and eyelashes that put mine to shame. 'But you were there.'

I looked at Suzanne, assuming this was an extension of a joke, but she just rolled her eyes and grinned at him, settling the cigarette back between her lips. She caught my eye and shook her head a little. *Don't ask.*

'How are things going with Liz?' she asked, a little pointedly. At some point – I had no idea when – Toby's girlfriend had departed from the group and not returned.

Toby flashed her a grin. 'Pretty good. How about you? Got a boyfriend down in Brighton?'

'Oh, please.'

'Brighton boys not good enough?'

'Not all girls need boyfriends,' Suzanne said. 'I'm a happy soloist, thanks.'

I took another sip from the Coke bottle and thought about this, zoning out of the conversation I had little to add to anyway. Technically Suzanne and I were both single, but I'd never thought of myself as 'happy' about it. Did it all come down to who had the power? Suzanne was single out of choice (she could clearly have anyone she wanted), while I was hindered by a lack of interested parties, let alone options. And even when there was a hint of interest, in the form of the sweet Tariq Laham, I chickened out.

I tried to imagine how different things could have been for me if I'd led a different, less sheltered life. Not going to private school, to start with, but maybe even growing up here, with Suzanne, in this city, instead of Brighton. Would I be more confident and extroverted? Or was my self-conscious introversion just part of who I was? Maybe it would actually have been worse to be surrounded by boys every day, who would probably have teased me relentlessly rather than fall in love with me.

Still, the thought process was an oddly unsettling one. I'd always thought of my personality as a fact of my life, a given, regardless of my circumstances or friends. But maybe it wasn't.

The word 'weed' jolted me back to my surroundings and I looked up, suddenly anxious. One of the newer arrivals, a boy with sweeping brown hair whose name I thought might begin with a *J*, was rolling a joint.

'Is that for me?' Suzanne asked, stretching out a hand towards him. Joe? Jack? Jay?

'Get your own,' Joe/Jack/Jay said, laughing. 'Dirty scrounger.'

'I am getting my own,' Suzanne said. 'From you. Go on.' She grinned flirtatiously at him, wide and dazzling. It was her usual winning smile set on fire. 'I'll make it up to you.'

'Oh, I bet you will.' There was a devilish smirk on his face. He wound up his arm and tossed the spliff into Suzanne's lap.

'Lighter?' she prompted.

'God, you're demanding.' He reached into his pocket and withdrew a metal Zippo. 'There's a cover charge, you know.' As he threw it at her, he glanced at me. 'Does your friend want one?'

'We'll share,' Suzanne said immediately. 'Caddy doesn't want to make anything up to you.'

The laughter seemed to come from all around me, and I wondered how many people were actually there. I tried to smile, but I felt so out of my depth I wanted to sink into the ground. I'd never felt so *private-school girl* in my life.

'Hey —' Suzanne had leaned her head close to mine and was speaking softly, directly into my ear so no one else could hear — 'that was just for show. You don't have to have any.' I could hear the protective affection in her voice, the reassurance, and the anxiety that had seized me at the first appearance of the joint disappeared.

'*Can* I try it?' I whispered back.

'Do you want to?'

'Yeah.'

'Are you sure?'

'Yes! Gimme.'

She laughed, putting her hand through the crook of my elbow and squeezing. 'I completely love you.'

'Watts!' someone called. 'Are you done yet?'

Suzanne fumbled with the lighter, cupping one hand around the flame as she lifted it to the joint between her lips. I watched her confident movements, the ease in the way she inhaled before tossing the lighter to whoever it was who'd spoken. I'd never seen her do this, yet how many times had she clearly done it before? I thought about Dylan and his friends. Maybe even Rosie?

She handed me the joint, smaller and lighter than I'd expected, and put her head close to mine again, in the pretence of leaning against my shoulder, her voice low. 'Make sure to breathe in normally.' Was this the dreaded peer pressure the professionally anxious had always warned about? Half drunk with a friend I loved and trusted in the middle of a park in Reading? It didn't feel like it.

I inhaled, trying not to think too hard about what 'normally' meant, given that I'd never even smoked a cigarette, and felt the smoke burn into my mouth, curling in my throat. It tasted thick and hot and *disgusting*. I choked out a cough, spluttering out a humiliated 'Sorry' as I pushed the joint back into Suzanne's hand. For all her whispered instructions, I'd made it pretty clear it was the first time I'd tried one, but I was gagging too much to really care.

I could see Suzanne trying not to laugh, her hand on my back, patting slightly. 'It's OK,' she said. 'It's not for everyone.'

'It's *exactly* like breathing in smoke,' I said, my voice hoarse. 'Why would anyone do that for fun?'

'It gets better,' she said. 'Want to try again?'

I looked at the little stub of a spliff caught in her fingers. 'Maybe in a minute,' I said, imagining a layer of ash coating my throat. 'Or, you know, maybe never, ever again.'

Suzanne laughed properly and reached an arm around me, squeezing my neck in a brief, tight hug. 'I'm so glad you're here,' she said.

By the time I'd stopped keeping track of time I'd finished the bottle of vodka and Coke and had taken four more 'experimental' puffs on the joint. My head felt spongy, my eyelids heavy, the world around me slightly blurred and sparkly. I was lying on my back on the grass, my head in Suzanne's lap, listening to her and the others talking. There were just six of us left now, slumped in a sort-of circle. Joe – his name was definitely Joe – had found a tennis ball under a tree and we were tossing it back and forth between us.

'What time is it?' a girl with dark brown hair asked. I thought her name might be Emmie. Or Ellie. *E*-something.

'Nearly one?' Hasan pulled his phone from his pocket and glanced at it.

'Is it? Shit.' She started scrambling to her feet. 'I have to go home.'

'What?' Suzanne's voice was an affected whine. 'No! Stay! You can come back to mine. It'll be like old times.'

E-something was already pulling the strap of her bag over her shoulder. 'Sorry, Zanne. Give me some more warning next time, yeah?' She came over and knelt to give Suzanne a hug. 'So amazing to see you.'

When she'd gone, the five of us that remained shared the last few dregs of alcohol between us – a cheap cider I mercifully could barely taste – then left the park.

'So are we going to yours?' Joe asked, his arm slung around Suzanne's shoulders. 'Like old times, right?'

Suzanne, who had her arm linked through mine, shrugged him off. 'Probably not a *great* idea.'

'Come on, just for a bit,' Toby coaxed. He grinned at me. 'You think it's a great idea, right?'

'Yeah,' I said, buoyed and bouncy. 'What are you so scared of, Suze?'

She laughed. 'You're supposed to be the good one.'

'Not tonight,' I said.

'I've got to head off,' Hasan said.

'Oh, what?' Suzanne stopped in her tracks. 'If we're going back to mine, you have to come, Has. Please?'

He grinned an easy, lazy grin. 'Next time. Promise. See ya.'

'Damn,' she muttered into my ear as he walked away. 'I thought you two might hit it off.'

'Really?' He'd barely looked at me all night. 'Why?'

'Because he's funny and nice. Plus he actually has a brain. And there wouldn't have been any pressure because you wouldn't have to see him again, so you could just relax and see what it's like.' She let out a sigh. 'Oh well. We'll get rid of Toby and Joe as soon as we can, yeah? Then we can stay up and talk.'

'It's so weird being back here,' Toby said when we got to Suzanne's, craning his neck to look up the stairs.

'Weird for you,' Suzanne said, flicking on the hallway lights. 'Imagine what it's like for me.' She looked at us, the cheerfulness gone from her voice and face. 'Don't smoke in here, OK? And don't spill anything.'

'Chill out, Snooze,' Toby said lightly. He swung an arm around her shoulder and squeezed. 'We know the rules.'

'I don't,' I offered.

'Make a mess and you're dead,' Joe said. He laughed. 'Right?'

Suzanne glared at him. 'Not you, fuckhead. Me. I'd be the dead one.' She paused. 'Maybe you should just go.'

'Relax,' Joe said, either missing her tone entirely or choosing to ignore it. 'Have a toke.'

'What's a toke?' I asked. It felt as if the vodka had infected my vocal cords. *Wozzatoke?*

'Jesus,' Joe said, his eyebrow raised. 'Where'd you find this one, Zanne?'

'That's not very nice,' I said, offended. 'I have a name.'

'A weird name,' he said. 'Hey, what's with the weird name?'

'Leave her alone.' Suzanne sounded exasperated. She glanced at Toby, who smirked at her. 'God, what am I doing here?'

'Chilling out and having fun,' Toby said. This time he put both arms around her, hugging her from behind like a bear, his chin on the top of her head. 'With your friends.'

No one had ever hugged me like that. It looked nice. Was *this* what I was missing out on, being in a girls' school? Not boyfriends, but boy *friends*?

'I want a hug,' I said abruptly. All three of them turned to stare at me. 'A hug,' I clarified, because they looked so confused.

'Cads, maybe you should sit down for a bit,' Suzanne said. She broke away from Toby and looped her arm through mine, guiding me into the living room. 'Want some water?'

'If you put some vodka in it,' I said agreeably. I felt fuzzy and happy, like I was seeing myself from the outside for the first time. Look how much better I was with the fuel of alcohol and drugs! No wonder people got drunk and stoned. I was like Caddy 2.0. Beta Caddy. I nudged her. 'Hey, Suze?'

'Yeah?'

'Am I doing OK?'

She stopped, right in the middle of the living room. 'What?'

'Am I doing OK?' I repeated. 'Like, am I cool? Do you think they like me?'

For a second I thought she was going to burst into tears, which confused me so much I almost tripped over my own stationary feet. She turned on the spot and then hugged me suddenly, so tightly I let out an involuntary *hnuh*, then let go. 'You're super, Cads.'

'Super Cads,' I echoed happily. I sat down on the nearest sofa, curling my back against the cushions. 'God, this is the most comfortable sofa in the entire world.'

'Right . . .' Her voice sounded far away. 'I'll go get you some water.'

I had lost track of time, lost track of myself, lost track of my senses. I had no idea where Suzanne was. The sofa, *so* comfortable, had me safe and cocooned, like a hug. I was burrowed into it, the armrest against the back of my head, and Joe Something lying on top of me, one leg in between mine, his hand up my top. Everything was beautiful. And hot.

Maybe I'd been confused earlier about why exactly I was here. Here being Reading, this random city I hadn't ever even given much thought to, and now the scene of my imminent devirginization. But now – *now* – it was clear. This was number two on that list I'd made all those months ago on a bus. This was the bonus of having a friend like Suzanne. She introduced me to boys. Boys who thought nothing of taking the virginity of girls they'd just met and would probably never see again.

There were three things I was thinking. One was, *So this is why people do this* (because, OK, it all felt pretty good). The second was, *Hnnnarrrgghhh* (because I was pretty much the most drunk I'd ever been in my life). The third was, *Sometimes you just want to get it over with*, in a voice that sounded a lot like Rosie's. I did want to get it over with. And wasn't Joe Something the perfect get-it-over-with guy?

'You're so hot,' he whispered into my ear, and my brain said, *Caddy, you're a lot of things, but you're not hot. Maybe you can pull off cute on a good day. Hot is a sex word. Hot is not you.*

A shot of panic pinged from my head right down to my feet. How was it possible to want something and not want it at the same time? Joe's hand moved to the zipper of my jeans, I thought, *Yes, OK,* and then the room flooded with light.

'Oh, for God's sake.' Suzanne's voice.

'Turn the fucking light off,' Joe's voice, loud against my ear. Hand still on my jeans.

'Are you kidding me?' She was angry, I registered with some surprise. 'Joe, get off my friend.'

For a few seconds nothing changed. Joe's weight was heavy and solid and exciting against me. For my part, I was still kissing him. And then he was suddenly wrenched away from me, and everything went south very fast.

Joe, regaining his footing after being pulled backwards by someone – Suzanne? – whirled around, furious. 'What's your problem?' he shouted. Suddenly loud, suddenly angry.

I sat up on the sofa, trying to take in the scene through the fuzz of my confusion. Toby had come through the door and was standing there, looking like he too was trying to make sense of what was going on.

'Go home,' Suzanne said, steady and controlled, but clearly simmering.

Joe stepped forward, shoved her shoulders with both of his hands. 'Don't be such a bitch.'

'Hey.' Toby was there instantly, stepping in front of her, pushing Joe away. 'Back off, OK?'

'Can't you keep her occupied?' Joe gestured at Suzanne, who was standing rigid behind Toby, one hand clenching her shoulder as if it had been burned by his touch. 'I heard it doesn't take much.'

I'd never seen boys fight. I'd seen *girls* fight, plenty of times. Hair pulling and slapping and nails clawing at skin. But when Toby went for Joe it was all fists and testosterone. It wouldn't exactly have been an equal fight; Toby probably outweighed Joe by at least a stone, but that didn't matter. It ended almost as soon as it had begun, and all it took was Suzanne, frantic, saying, '*Toby*.' Just once.

Toby, who'd only thrown one punch but was breathing as if he'd boxed three rounds, stepped back. 'OK,' he said. 'OK.' He reached out a hand to Joe, who'd stumbled to the floor on the first contact. Joe pushed his hand away, pulling himself to his feet.

'Fine,' he said. 'I'm gone.' He threw a hand up as he left the room, as a brush off or a wave, I couldn't tell. I heard the front door open and then slam. He hadn't even looked at me.

'Wanker,' Toby said. He took a step towards Suzanne. 'You OK?'

She flinched away from him. Even from across the room, I could see her eyes were ablaze. 'What the hell was that, Toby?'

He blinked. 'That was . . . He was . . . I just—'

'I don't need you to fight my battles for me,' she said. She was still holding her shoulder, her arm crooked against her chest like a shield.

'Well, yeah, you kind of do,' Toby replied, his voice suddenly tense. 'Maybe if you'd let me earlier, you'd never—'

'*Don't*.' One word, sharp and violent. But then on the next word her voice cracked, her face crumpled momentarily. 'Please.'

For whatever reason, my brain decided this was the time to remind them both I was there. It chose to do this by making me get up, abruptly, from the sofa, and then just stand there.

'Um,' Toby said after a moment. He was looking at me, but still he directed his words at Suzanne. 'Is your friend OK?'

'She's just drunk,' Suzanne said. She sounded tired. 'Come on, Cads.'

'Did you two have sex?' I asked.

Toby let out a noise that could have been a laugh or a snort. Suzanne rolled her eyes. 'Oh, for God's sake.'

'I like your friend,' Toby said to her, a grin back on his face. 'She's good value.'

'She has sex with everyone,' I said, by way of explanation.

'Shut *up*, Caddy,' Suzanne ordered through gritted teeth. 'Can you sober up, like, now, please?'

'I didn't mean that in a bad way,' I told her. 'I mean, I would too, if I looked like you.'

She was looking at me like she'd never seen me before. 'Is

this what your head sounds like all those times you don't say anything?'

'You're very pretty,' I said, confused that she didn't look more pleased. 'Like, not even real, you know?'

Suzanne looked at Toby. 'You should go.'

'Don't you think?' I asked Toby. 'You know what I mean, right?'

'Don't answer that,' Suzanne said before he could speak. 'Just go.'

When he finally did leave, after hugging us both three times and returning twice for his coat and his phone, I'd drained a glass of water on Suzanne's command and was leaning against the hallway wall, counting my split ends.

'So did you?' I asked her, almost as soon as she'd closed the door.

'Did I what?'

'Have sex. With Toby.'

'*No*, Caddy. *God*.' She looked horrified. 'Why would you even think that?'

'Because he clearly loves you,' I said. 'And I know you like it when boys are like that.'

'Like what?'

The sober me would have noticed the dangerous note in her voice. The drunk me did not. 'You know, being nice to you.' When she didn't say anything, I added helpfully, 'Like Dylan. You went back with him even though he was so shitty to you, just 'cause he smiled at you.'

'God.' Suzanne's voice was flat. 'You really think I'm pathetic, don't you?'

'No,' I said, surprised. I really didn't.

'When who was it, out of the two of us, on her back with some guy she doesn't even know?'

Far, far too late, I finally picked up on that dangerous note. My stomach lurched, violently.

'What's his surname, Caddy?' She'd rounded on me, sparks all but coming out of her eyes. 'How old is he?'

'Don't yell at me,' I protested. 'I thought you'd be proud of me.'

'*Proud* of you? *Why*?!'

'For living in the moment. For, you know, doing something fun. You're meant to be encouraging me to do fun stuff.'

'Yeah, fun stuff, not idiot stoner guys. Do you even know how out of his league you are? You'd be totally wasted on him.' Her eyes went wide. 'Oh my God, please don't tell me you were going to lose your virginity to him.'

It could have been the tone of her voice or the incredulous look on her face. It could have been the vodka, or the weed, or the fact that I was somehow in Reading with this girl who was suddenly a stranger again. Whatever it was, the tears had spilled before I'd even realized they were coming.

'Oh, Cads,' Suzanne said, instantly softer. 'Don't cry.'

I hiccuped, a humiliating, double-gasped hitch of a noise that made me think of a toddler mid-tantrum. 'Sorry,' I choked out, sinking down on to the floor and pressing my forehead into my knees.

I felt rather than saw her slide down beside me, her arm curling around my shoulders and squeezing me in close to her. There was a softness to being hugged by Suzanne, I thought through the drugged, drunken fog of my mind. At arm's length she was jagged edges and fire, but in her close affection she was cosy and warm. *Which one is real*? my fuzzy brain asked. *Which one is you*?

'Don't be sorry,' she said. Squeeze. '*I'm* sorry.' She pushed her head momentarily against mine. 'I'm being a bitch. It's not you. Blame me.'

'I just wanted to have fun,' I said. The words were meaningless. 'I wanted to know what it was like.'

'Sex?'

'Well, yeah, but I mean not being so . . . quiet and crap. I wish I was more like you.'

Her smile was sad. 'You really don't.'

'I do,' I insisted, my voice coming out petulant and ever so slightly slurred. 'You're confident and like . . .' I tried to find the word, sure it was somewhere there in my mind. 'Like . . . *more*.'

The sad smile quirked; amusement flickered in her eyes. 'Confident? Me?'

'Don't say you're not,' I snapped, a sudden anger welling in me. 'Girls like you – you don't *get* it; how it feels to *not* be confident.'

Her brow furrowed. 'You mean confident, like, with boys?'

I nodded.

'Oh, Cads, that's all crap,' she said. 'They're the easiest. Honestly. They just want you to smile at them, act like you want them. That's all.'

That's all.

'*You're* confident,' Suzanne continued. Her head tilted slightly, nudging mine again. 'I get that you think you're not. But you are. In your life. In yourself, you know?'

Like that means anything when you walk into a party full of people you don't know and all you want to do is hide in a corner until it's over.

'I'm a massive wuss,' I said, then hiccuped again.

She laughed, but it was friendly. 'You're not.'

'I am.' I felt tears start to rise up again.

'You came here, didn't you?'

'Because you *tricked* me.' I felt my face scrunch up, as the vodka and the weed and the weight of my own inadequacy spilled down my face, salty and hot. 'Oh God, I'm such a *loser*. I'm such a loser even my best friend has to trick me into doing fun stuff.'

I could tell Suzanne was trying not to laugh again. 'Caddy. *Caddy!* Calm down. You're not a loser. You're so *not*.' Her breathy chuckling stopped abruptly. 'Did you just call me your best friend?'

'Oh God!' My voice came out as a wail. 'I didn't mean to say that. Don't tell Roz I said that. I didn't mean it.'

'Oh, great, thanks.' Suzanne's fingers pinched into my side. 'Now I feel super-special.'

'You're like . . . sort of best.' I scrabbled for sense. 'You know? Like second best.'

'Do you think a shovel would help with this digging?'

'No, Suze,' I said earnestly. 'No, I mean really. Like, if it wasn't for Roz, you'd totally be my best friend. 'Cause you are, like, the *best*. But just not *my* best. 'Cause Roz is my best. My very best.'

'I am so very, very flattered,' Suzanne said drily. 'Nothing's better than a drunk friend telling you how much they love you. As *second best*.'

'I do think you're brilliant though,' I insisted.

'OK, Cads. Time for bed.'

'I thought you wanted to stay up and talk.'

'I think we should save that for a time when you might actually remember the conversation afterwards.'

The rest of the night passed in a foggy haze. I'd forgotten most of the details by morning, but I retained a clear memory of throwing up into the toilet, the bathroom tiles pressing into my knees, Suzanne's hands holding back my hair. Slumping on to her bed, looking up at her spinning ceiling.

When I woke up on top of the covers on her bed, feeling an awful lot like death, the sun was bright through the open curtains, hurting my eyes. I lay there for a while, trying to sift through the jumble of blurry memories in my head, before giving up and going to find Suzanne.

I found her in the living room, curled up asleep on the sofa. When I touched her shoulder – as gently as I could – she jolted up, pushing my hand away. 'What?'

'It's me,' I said quickly. 'It's just me.'

She relaxed back against the cushions, letting out a breath. After a moment she smiled. 'Oh yes. Super-Cads.'

'Oh God,' I managed. The first memories were starting to unblur. Me, standing in her hallway, announcing that I wanted a hug. *Oh God.*

'It's OK,' she said, laughing. 'Trust me, it could have been a lot worse.'

Joe, sitting next to me on the sofa, telling me I had a pretty face. Me, telling him I went to a girls' school. Complaining that I'd only kissed three boys. Him: *Want to make it four?*

'Aargh,' I collapsed next to her, tucking my head against her shoulder. 'Is this what the morning after feels like?'

She laughed again. 'Yes. Enjoy it. Remind yourself it means you must have had a good night.' She glanced at the clock on the wall. 'Do you mind if we head off soon? I know it's early, but I just want to get out of here. We could head into town? Get some food?'

'OK,' I said.

'You can use the bathroom upstairs if you want. I'll meet you back down here in half an hour.'

After I'd washed my face and dosed up on paracetamol, I felt vaguely human again. I brushed my hair with a hairbrush I found in Suzanne's room and headed downstairs to meet her. In the kitchen, she was folding up a piece of paper and setting it in place with the key she'd taken from the back garden. She smiled at

me. 'Just going to grab my hat.' When she was gone, I gave into
curiosity and unfolded the paper to read what she'd written.

> *Mum and Dad –*
> *It's me! Just to let you know I came by with*
> *a friend, so if you see anything out of place,*
> *that's why. Hope you had a good anniversary*
> *weekend.*
> *Lots of love, Suzie xx*

I'd expected something sullen, maybe even overtly sarcastic, but
the ordinariness of the note hit me right in the chest. I closed the
paper back up and stepped into the hall, biting on my tongue to
contain the sudden impulse to cry.

Suzanne's footsteps sounded on the stairs and she appeared,
pulling her hat over her head and tucking stray hairs under the
rim. 'Ready to go?' she asked me.

I was just about to nod when the unmistakable sound of a key
turning in the lock jolted us both. I saw a look of total, complete
panic pass over Suzanne's face. As if by instinct, she moved closer
to me, her hand clenching over my wrist.

She relaxed as soon as the door opened to reveal a figure I
recognized from the photographs on the mirror in her Brighton
bedroom. When he saw us, his face dropped in shock. He stopped
in the doorway, one hand still on the handle, mouth open. Then,
'Fucking hell, Zannie.' Suzanne's brother walked forward, leaving
the door open, and lifted her right off the floor into a hug.

'Hi,' she said, her voice muffled against his shoulder. 'What are
you doing here?'

'Looking for you!' Brian set her back down on the carpet and
let out a breath. 'God, I was worried sick.'

'Really? Why?'

'You don't appear at Cardiff station and no one knows where you are? Yeah, I was worried.' The relief had faded from his face and he looked faintly annoyed for a moment before his eyes fell on me. 'Oh! Are you Caddy?'

I nodded mutely.

'I recognize you from Facebook pictures.' He actually held out his hand, and I shook it. 'Right.' He reached out and hooked his arm around Suzanne's shoulder, pulling her in for a second hug. 'Seeing as I'm here, I guess I'd better take you both home.'

As soon as we'd got in the car, Brian pulled out his phone and dialled a number before he even started the engine. 'Hey, Sarah.' His voice was relaxed and easy; it was the voice of someone used to smoothing situations over. 'I'm in Reading . . . Yeah . . . No, that's why I'm calling. She's here.' He glanced to his left at Suzanne, who glowered. 'She's fine . . . No, totally fine.' His eyes moved to the rear-view mirror, catching my gaze.

I answered the unspoken question with a vigorous, horrified shake of my head. There was still at least a *chance* that my parents didn't know what had happened or that I'd ever been out of the city. He grinned, an understanding ally. 'So we're heading back now,' he said into the phone. 'We'll be in Brighton in a couple of hours probably.'

When he hung up, he tossed the phone on to the dashboard and started the car. 'So –' he said, still upbeat. He executed a perfect three-point turn, throwing his hand into a wave at the house behind us, as if there was anyone there to see it – 'want to explain yourself?'

'What's to explain?' Suzanne asked.

'Oh, I don't know, Zanne,' Brian said, deadpan. 'Maybe start with why the three of us are in my car driving from Reading to Brighton on a Sunday morning?'

Suzanne muttered something I didn't catch, but whatever it was made Brian laugh. She looked at him, a grin appearing on her face. He reached out a hand and ruffled her hair. 'I've missed you,' he said.

After a respectful fifteen minutes, Brian tried again. I sat in the back, fiddling with my hoodie cuffs, hoping they'd forget I was there.

'There I was, thinking you *wanted* to see me,' he said, easing into the roundabout and then taking the second exit on to the motorway.

'It's not about that,' Suzanne replied. 'It would have just been nice to be included in the decision.'

'OK. One: when Sarah and I talked about it we thought you'd be thrilled, so asking your opinion didn't even come up. And two: you can't just up and leave just because you don't like a decision someone's made.'

'Why not?'

In the rear-view mirror I saw Brian roll his eyes. 'Because it's bloody annoying. I don't get my kicks driving from Cardiff to Reading to Brighton and back again, you know. We could've just had a nice weekend in Wales. I was going to take you to the rugby.'

Suzanne made a face. 'Wow, I'm so sad I missed it.' It was strange for me to see her like this, somehow diminished in the presence of her older brother. She was transformed from my cooler, worldly friend into Brian's Little Sister. Sulky and slouching against her seat.

'Plus,' Brian added, ignoring her comment, 'you really should tell me before you turn up at Mum and Dad's. What if they'd been there?'

'I wouldn't have gone in if they were. And why would

telling you make a difference?'

'Oh, Zanne, come on.'

'No, go on, tell me.' She shifted a little in her seat so she was facing him. 'Spell it out.'

I saw Brian tense his shoulders against his seat, tilting his head back slightly. 'I just worry, OK? You know that.'

Suzanne leaned her head around her seat to look at me. 'That's Brian's speciality,' she said, a touch of sarcasm in her voice. '*Worry.*'

'Is it?' I said, not sure what to say.

'Yeah, it's a great filler for where the actual helping should be.'

'*Jesus!*' Brian let out a sharp exhalation. 'That's not fair.'

Suzanne sat back, her face disappearing from view. 'Is it fair that you get to act really put upon? Oh, poor you, having to drive to come and get your stupid, tearaway sister?'

'You don't get free reign to act however you want because you've had a rough time,' Brian said. 'The world doesn't work that way.'

'*Doesn't it?*' Suzanne's voice was earnestly sarcastic. 'That changes *everything*. I'll be perfect from now on.'

'For God's *sake*.' Brian's calm exterior was faltering. 'Do you have to make this so hard?'

'Yes. Consider it payback for all those years I was being abused and you weren't.'

The words sliced through the car, stopping my breath for a second. I watched Brian lift a hand from the wheel and wrench it through his hair.

'I *tried*—'

'Hey,' Suzanne interrupted, her voice suddenly, disarmingly conversational, 'remember when I was, like, nine or something, and you were sick and tired of all the yelling, so you locked yourself in your room? But I didn't know you had? And I went running away from Dad and ran smack into your door? And I was crying for you, but you didn't open it? Remember that?'

In profile, I saw Brian's jaw clench so hard I could see the muscle twitch.

'I do,' Suzanne added, still in that bright, cheerful voice, like she was sharing a happy memory instead of one that was utterly devastating. When he didn't respond, she reached out and poked his arm.

'I was thirteen when that happened,' Brian said, quiet and tense. '*Thirteen*. I know it's life-fuckingly awful that it happened to you, but it was completely shit for me too, OK?'

'I have stories from when I was thirteen too,' Suzanne said.

I heard Brian let out a *hrumph* of frustration. 'When did you get so bitter? Was it around the same time you started acting like some kind of delinquent?'

'Oh, fuck you.' Suzanne snapped, twisting in her seat to face the window, then changing her mind and turning back to him. 'Maybe it was when I realized that you're not some kind of hero?'

'For God's *sake*,' Brian's voice had suddenly got louder. 'None of this is my fault, OK? I'm doing the best I *fucking* can.'

I was starting to feel panicky. The tension in the car felt like electricity sparking out of control from a wire ripped free from its moorings. It felt like it could catch at any minute and set us all aflame. The cars and lorries and coaches and buses roared past us, steady and controlled, while Suzanne and Brian battled in the front seats.

They'd both reached full volume now, Brian leaning back against his seat, one hand on the wheel, the other sporadically leaping up into the air to gesture wildly. Suzanne, her face twisted with rage and pain, both hands waving in the space in front of her as if trying to shape it into something she could control.

'What is it you *want*?' Brian was yelling, bashing his fist against the wheel for emphasis. 'Whatever it is, you actually think you'll get it like this?'

'I don't want anything!'

'Right, sure. So you're just going to act like a total lost cause until you become one? How's that working for you so far?'

'Lost cause?' Suzanne threw herself back in her seat, her fingers scrabbling at her seat belt. 'Fine. *Fine*.'

Brian's head jerked between her and the road. 'Stop it. What're you doing? Sit down.'

'Why wait?' The seat belt pinged back into its casing. 'It's going to happen anyway. Might as well make it interesting.' From the back seat I saw her fingers move towards the door handle.

Brian's free hand had reached for her, his fingers clenched tight around her arm. 'Calm the fuck down, Suzanne. Sit down.' I watched his other hand lift from the wheel and scramble at the buttons beside it, locking her door from his side. I was too scared to move, clutching my seat belt tight to me as if it would save me when we got steamrolled by a lorry.

'Get *off* me!' Suzanne tried to wrench herself free from him, pulling at the door handle. '*Stop trying to act like you care.*'

Brian looked properly at her. 'Of course I—' The car swerved, a dozen horns sounded. Despite myself, a strangled shriek of panic escaped my throat. '*Shit.*' He let go of Suzanne, put both hands on the wheel and guided the car across the left lane into the hard shoulder.

When we stopped, I realized just how much my heart was hammering. My hands, released from their death grip on my seat belt, were shaking.

But it still wasn't over.

In the sudden silence of the stopped car, I saw Suzanne's panicky rage flame. 'Open my fucking door, Brian.'

'Just calm down.'

Suzanne's fist slammed against the door frame. '*Open it.*'

Instead, Brian opened his own door and got out, closing it behind him and hurrying around the car to open Suzanne's. He caught her as she lunged out, his hand closing securely over her arm, pulling her away from the road to the grass beyond. I opened my door and watched them argue, listening to the words that carried in the wind.

'Why won't you just let me . . . ?'

'Worried about you . . .'

'I just *hate* . . .'

'What about . . . ?'

I let my feet touch the tarmac, my hand on the open door, wondering whether to go over and intervene. I didn't really think Brian would ever hurt Suzanne, but how could I know for sure? What exactly was my role here? Because, surely, I had one.

After a few minutes watching the argument escalate – Suzanne getting more worked up, Brian easing off, trying to calm her down – I forced myself to slide out of the car and make my way over to them. I paused a few metres off, thrusting my hands deep into my pockets. Brian glanced at me.

'Why are you even here?' Suzanne was yelling at him, seemingly unaware of my approach. 'You're *useless*. You're so *fucking* useless.'

'You're right,' Brian said. His voice was calm now. Controlled. 'I am useless. I'm sorry.'

'No.' Suzanne's face screwed up, her hands clenching into fists. 'No, that's not OK. You can't do that.'

'I'm sorry,' Brian said again. He held up his hands, palm up, away from his chest. 'You're hurting, and I'm sorry.'

Suzanne bridged the gap between them and smacked her closed fist against his chest. 'I hate you.'

'I know. It's OK.'

Another punch. 'I *hate* you.'

'I know, Zannie.'

'Shut *up*.' She pummelled his chest, her frustration almost palpable in the air. He let her, holding out his hands away from her, waiting.

I could see what he thought he was doing. I recognized this moment from the earnest, moralizing TV shows I'd watched that took on an Issue and solved it in forty minutes. This scene was ubiquitous – the unhappy person taking out their frustration on someone who loved them, before collapsing in tears into their chest, all that rage spilled out, purged. The healing always came next.

But that wasn't what would happen here. I had no idea if Brian could see it too, but as I watched Suzanne smacking her hands ineffectually against her brother I saw it clearly. He was steady and solid, so together and unbroken. Her fists, her shouting, her fury, had no impact on him, not really. Nothing she could throw at him would dent or bruise him. She, in contrast, was so unbearably fragile. A house of cards on the verge of collapsing. She'd already been pummelled by closed fists and someone else's rage, and it had broken her. All Brian was doing was forcing her to see this unbridgeable difference between them.

She did break down, of course. The tears took over and she pressed herself against him, letting him settle his arms around her shoulders. I heard him saying, 'It's OK, it's OK,' and I wondered how he could lie like that. Why did people do that? Where did that impulse come from, to tell someone so clearly far from it that things were OK?

'Let's go,' Brian said, quietly but firmly. Still with one arm around Suzanne's shoulder, he started walking back towards the car. He met my eye and smiled reassuringly, understanding and secure.

In the car, Suzanne curled herself into her seat, facing away from us both. We were all silent as Brian eased out of the hard shoulder and into the traffic. After a few minutes, Suzanne's tentative, shaky voice broke the silence. 'Caddy, tell me something good.'

I thought she'd forgotten I was there.

'In Iceland,' I said, keeping my voice light and steady, 'there's a waterfall that always has a rainbow in front of it. Like, guaranteed. You can go and stand under it. Or at the end of it, you know, like a leprechaun.'

'An Icelandic leprechaun?'

'Of course. They're the best kind.' I waited for a moment. 'Do you want another one?'

'Yes. Please.'

'Last year, during the Brighton marathon, my uncle tripped and twisted his ankle three miles from the end. So another guy, who was running for Mind, I think, gave him a piggyback the whole rest of the way, so he'd still finish and get the full money for the charity. He was, like, a total stranger.'

I heard a smile in her voice. 'That's a nice story.'

'Hey, Zannie,' Brian said. His voice was gentle. 'You want to pick some music?' He reached across her and pulled an iPod from the glove compartment. She took it from him and began scrolling through it. He squeezed her shoulder, solid and steady, before returning his shaking hand to the wheel.

24

We drove most of the way home without talking after that, listening to an album called *August and Everything After* twice through. I'd never heard any of the songs before, but Suzanne and Brian clearly had a *lot*, because at random intervals they would both sing along to a single sentence, or even just a word, making me jump each time. It was the kind of music where even the happy songs felt sad. Or that could just have been my mood.

By the time we pulled off the motorway and began winding through the familiar Brighton streets, Brian and Suzanne were talking comfortably, not quite as if the argument hadn't happened but more like they'd consciously left it behind. It occurred to me that being able to smile so soon after crying was something you learned.

'So how much trouble are you going to be in, Caddy?' Brian asked, throwing me a knowing smile as he slowed for a red light.

'Don't say that,' Suzanne said. 'You'll make me feel bad.'

'You should feel bad,' I teased. 'We're not all as used to it as you.'

She turned in her seat slightly to grin at me. 'Am I a Bad Influence?' she asked, waving her fingers and making a face of exaggerated fear.

'The very worst,' I said, laughing more with relief than anything else.

When Brian pulled up outside my house, Suzanne unbuckled herself and got out of the car, coming to join me on the pavement. She reached out her arms for a hug. 'I'm sorry,' she said, surprising me.

'What for?' I asked, hugging her.

She laughed into my ear. 'You want a list?' I moved to end the hug, but her arms tightened around me, just for a few seconds longer. Her hair smelled like cigarettes and last night's party and Suze. 'Good luck.' She released me, lifting her hand in her favoured mock salute before heading back to the car.

I threw a wave over my shoulder as they drove away and then turned back to my house, taking a second to just look at it. Was I caught or not? I had no way of knowing. It was Schrodinger's house. I was bad Caddy and good Caddy, all at once. I curled my fingers around my keys and walked towards the door, bracing myself for the answer.

It was bad.

Maybe the worst thing about it, at least for me, was how close I'd come to getting away with it. My parents had no reason to question my late-night decision to stay at Rosie's house, and even my dishevelled, same-clothes-as-yesterday appearance could have been written off as the harmless Saturday-night fun of a sixteen-year-old. What got me caught was the fact that I had a great sister who loved me. It's funny how the world works.

Tarin, innocently helpful, had called Rosie not long after I sent my last text, trying to get a hold of me to tell me that she was heading into town to see a friend and did I want her to stop by Rosie's house with my phone charger and a change of clothes? Rosie, seeing her opportunity, told her I wasn't there and that I was, in fact, with Suzanne somewhere that wasn't Brighton.

'It's not even that you did something so reckless and irresponsible,' Mum said, spitting nails. 'It's that you *lied* to us.'

Except it clearly was a lot about me doing something so reckless and irresponsible. And also my 'clear lack of respect', my 'failure to consider the consequences' and 'Jesus Christ, Cadnam, did you *smoke*?!'

Suzanne, previously a point of concern, had become the devil incarnate overnight. (Rosie, in contrast, was the saint who'd alerted them to the truth.) Never mind that I'd gone with her quite happily – albeit with a blinkered idea of where we were going and how long it would take – and had lied to them off my own back.

'That's it now,' Dad said. 'You can't be friends with her any more. You're grounded for the foreseeable future anyway, but in either case you just can't see her again. She's not welcome here, and you're not allowed to visit her; we'll speak to Sarah to make sure.'

He said this with all the gravitas of a person who'd cultivated their friendships before the Internet.

'And we're taking away your phone,' Mum added, as if she'd read my mind. 'And your laptop.' When my face dropped in horror, she shook her head. 'This behaviour isn't acceptable, Caddy. We expect so much more than this, *especially* this year, when you've got your exams coming up. These are your consequences.'

As bad as it all was, it wasn't the worst thing. When they were finished shouting at me, I went upstairs and knocked softly on Tarin's door before pushing it open and poking my head into the room. 'Am I allowed in?'

She was sitting on her bedroom floor, surrounded by coloured bits of paper, a book open in front of her. Origami was her hobby of the moment, a colourful distraction.

'Sure,' she said, but she didn't look up and her voice was flat.

I crept into the room and stepped carefully over her creations, taking a seat on her bed. 'Um,' I said, intelligently, 'I'm really sorry.'

'Thanks, but I don't think it's me you need to say that to,' Tarin replied. She still wasn't looking at me, her eyes focused on the yellow paper she was holding. Her fingers moved carefully, folding and turning.

'I feel like it is,' I said.

'I'm on the list, yeah,' Tarin said. 'Me and Mum, Dad, Rosie, Sarah, Brian.' I wondered how she knew about Brian. 'And Suzanne too.' She shook her head, almost to herself. 'That little fucked-up friend of yours. She probably thinks she's hit the jackpot with a friend like you, the poor kid.'

My heart twisted. 'What's that supposed to mean?'

'You're steady. And you're nice. You won't understand what that means because you've never needed it yourself. You don't realize how important it is.' With one hand Tarin lifted the bird she'd made into the air so its sharp-cornered wings caught the light. It made me think of the dove on Suzanne's necklace, always around her neck. 'And so you think you're being a good friend by going along with her and not saying, "Stop, you're hurting yourself."'

'You don't even know her.'

'No, but I know what it's like to feel like you've lost control of your life. And I know *you*. Helping someone who feels like that isn't in saying *yes*, Caddy. It's in saying *no*.'

Part of me understood what she meant, but the other part, the obstinate part, was sure she was wrong. If I *had* said no, what difference would it have made? Suzanne would surely have gone to Reading with or without me. It was hardly like she needed my permission or approval to do anything.

I wasn't sure what to say, so I said the only thing I could. 'I'm sorry.'

Tarin looked at me. The disappointment on her face was worse than anything Mum or Dad could ever say to me. 'I know, Cads.'

'Do you still love me?' I asked. I'd meant to tease, but as I spoke I pictured Suzanne the previous night, the look on her face when she'd reminded me that no one would stop loving me because I'd stayed out for one night.

I saw the reluctant smile break out on Tarin's face. 'Of course I still love you, you minge. Here.' She angled her wrist and tossed the origami bird towards me. It landed, small and delicate, safe in my lap.

Rosie called later that evening, and was allowed to speak to me because she was The Good One. I could hear in her voice that she was nervous, even as she tried to sound bold.

'Did you get in trouble?' she asked me.

'Yes,' I said shortly. 'Happy?'

'No,' she said, her voice quietening. 'What happened?'

'They yelled. I'm grounded. Did you want anything or were you just calling to gloat?'

'Of course not,' she said, sounding hurt. 'Look, I'm sorry you got in trouble. But that's not actually my fault. You were the one who went. And you were the one who lied.'

'The only reason you did it was to get back at me,' I said, 'which is really petty, Roz.'

There was a short silence. 'Well, we're even now,' she said eventually. 'Maybe I was a bit petty, but you were stupid. So.'

'*Even?*' I repeated, incredulous. 'You just *ratted* me out to my *parents*. Who does that?!'

'Who leaves their friend at a party?' Rosie shot back, fire back in her voice. 'And anyway, I spoke to Tarin, not your parents.'

'*Rosie*,' I said sharply, 'why don't you just apologize?' As I spoke, I realized she'd already sort-of apologized, but I carried on anyway. 'You haven't just got *me* in trouble; you've completely screwed things up for Suze. My parents are saying we can't even be friends any more.'

'*God*, Caddy! Suze has screwed things up for *herself*. AGAIN. I can't believe that even after something like this, you still can't see that.'

Almost without warning, I felt tears springing to my eyes. How had we got here? Rosie and I had never been the kind of friends who argued. And now here we were, fighting two Sundays in a row.

'You both brought all this on yourselves,' Rosie said. 'If you don't like the consequences, that's not my fault. But I'm your best friend. I'm not going to tell you everything's fine when it's not. I think your parents are right, OK? She's clearly a bad influence on you.'

This was when something in me snapped. 'Why do you all think you know me better than I know myself?' My voice was suddenly louder than normal. 'Do you really think I'm so stupid I can't make my own decisions?'

'Caddy—'

'You're just *jealous*, Roz. It's so obvious. And you know what? You should just get over it. Really.'

Tarin had appeared in the living-room doorway, her eyes wide and incredulous. I turned away from her, pressing the phone so hard against my ear it was starting to burn. 'And actually –' I stopped. There was a dial tone on the other end of the line. Rosie had hung up. 'Oh,' I said.

'Do you want to talk about it?' Tarin asked.

'No,' I said, getting up and walking past her, the tears finally breaking free and spilling down my face. 'I really, really don't.'

Here's the thing though. For all the talk of consequences, nothing *actually* happened. Yes, I was grounded, but I knew it wouldn't be forever. True, I was fighting with my best friend, but I was sure that too would pass. My parents were disappointed in me, but Suzanne had been completely right about one thing: they weren't going to stop loving me.

I'd stayed out drinking and smoking in a park with a bunch

of relative strangers in a city I didn't know, and I was *fine*. Everything was the same. I woke up on Monday morning and went to school, and nothing had changed. It made no sense, but I felt buoyed by the weekend's events. I'd done something wrong, I'd got caught, and the world had carried on turning and my cereal tasted just the same in the morning. All these years I'd been so worried about being good. The taste of the alternative was caramel sweet. I wanted more.

The problem was Suzanne. With all methods of communication severed between us, I had no way of knowing how she was, and I worried for her. If Rosie was angry with me, she'd surely be furious with Suzanne, the catalyst for all the changes she didn't like. And what about Sarah, who'd sent Suzanne to Brian in the first place because she didn't know how to handle her behaviour?

I used my lunch break to send her an email. I kept it short, hoping she'd had the same idea and would reply before I had to go to maths. But no response came until Thursday and it only made me feel worse.

Thursday 13.23
From: Suzanne Watts {suzyanne.whats@gmail.com}
To: Caddy Oliver {c.oliver@live.com}

Cads,

Sorry for late reply. No access to anything. No phone, nothing. God, everything is so shit, Caddy. I ruined everything. I'm so sorry you got in trouble with your parents, and Roz. Are you sure ur not mad? I'd be mad if it was me. I don't know why you put up with me. When I got back on Sunday Sarah just cried, and then

I cried and Brian got all awkward and then left. I don't know why I do this. What's wrong with me? Why couldn't I just go to brian's like I was meant to? Sarah says she doesn't know what to do with me. No, Roz and I aren't fighting. She's just completely ignoring me. It's horrible.

Better go. I love you and I hope you're not in too much shit. I haven't come to see you coz no way am I risking getting you in more trouble. I'm not really sleeping, though. My head won't shut up. I miss our little walkabouts and talking things over with you. That really helped.

Anyway. Sorry.
Lots of love
Sz xx

I printed the email out and read it over a few times more that evening, sitting on my bed with nothing else to do. She sounded so empty and lost it was almost frightening.

Folding the paper in my hands, I went to my parents' room, knocking softly on the door and poking my head around it. Mum was sitting on the bed watching the news. When I appeared, she smiled at me and muted the TV with the remote. 'Hello,' she said. 'Come and sit with me.'

I sat down next to her, crossing my legs underneath me. 'Can I talk to you about Suze?'

'Oh, Caddy . . .'

'I mean properly,' I said. 'No shouting or anything.'

She sighed and rubbed the edge of her forehead. 'I've spoken to Sarah,' she said. 'At length. And your father and I have discussed it. I really don't think there's anything you can say that will change things.'

'But —' I unfolded the paper, ready to show it to her, knowing its contents would probably get me into more trouble but not caring.

'I know this is hard,' Mum said, as if she hadn't even noticed I was trying to speak. 'I know you want to help your friend. But your actions *aren't* helping her, and hers certainly aren't helping you. Some distance between you two will do you the world of good, I'm sure. You'll come to understand where we're coming from.'

I gave up. Why had I thought for even a second that she'd listen to me? I folded the paper back up, this time into quarters, pushing it into my pocket out of sight.

I retreated back to my room, lying flat on my back on my bed and staring at my ceiling. My anxiety had gone into overdrive, thinking about Suzanne's email. *My head won't shut up . . . I'm not really sleeping*.

And what was I doing to help? Absolutely nothing. Lying on my bed and worrying. I hadn't even made any real effort to change my mother's mind. So much for being trustworthy and dependable. I was just as useless as everyone else. Too worried about getting in trouble to do anything. Too passive, too scared to act.

By the time the house had quietened and everyone else was in bed, I hadn't got anywhere. My thoughts were still a tangled, guilty mess. I forced myself to get up and brush my teeth, then collapsed back on to my bed, crawling under the covers and trying to turn my brain off. I couldn't help but think of Suzanne, most likely doing the same. She was probably wishing she could just take off for a while to clear her head, but couldn't now because it had caused so much—

I was jerked out of my thoughts by the sound of my bedroom door creaking open slightly. I closed my eyes instinctively, feigning sleep, and heard my mother's whisper: 'She's here.'

After she'd gone, I actually laughed. The situation was so ridiculous. Six months ago the idea that my mother would feel the need to check I was in my bed after midnight would have been ludicrous. It still *was* ludicrous. As if I'd risk further trouble by sneaking out again.

And then, suddenly as a slap, I realized something. There was no further trouble. I had surely reached peak trouble. I sat up and gave my head a frustrated shake, trying to sort out my thoughts. But there was no need. The idea had crystallized in me and it was clear what I needed to do.

25

It was scarier by myself.

The moment my feet touched the ground beneath our garage I felt a rush of nerves so strong I almost climbed back up again. Maybe I was wrong; maybe I wasn't brave enough to do this alone. I hesitated, my hand still on the rough wall of the garage. I closed my eyes, took in a slow breath and then let it out, counting the beats. Then I opened my eyes and started walking away from my house.

My heartbeat picked up further as I walked, to the point where I found myself breaking into a run. There was no one around; the streets were deserted. I wasn't sure if this was better or worse. With each empty street corner turned, the need to see Suzanne, to validate my recklessness, increased.

I was breathing hard by the time I reached her door, realizing too late that as her bedroom was at the back of the house I would have to double back on myself and then try and find my way, in the dark, into her back garden. This was when it started to rain.

I stood there for a moment, feeling raindrops begin to trickle down the back of my collar. There was a reason girls like me didn't do things like this. It was because we were crap at it. I had none of the fuck-it spirit that Suzanne possessed in spades. I was all nerves and second guesses.

But you don't have to be, I told myself, clenching my hands into fists and feeling my nails dig into my palms. Maybe we have a degree of choice in how our personalities are formed. I could be brave. I could be reckless. I could be trouble.

It took me a while, but I eventually found the wall that I was sure backed on to Suzanne's garden. On tiptoes, I recognized the pink of the Judas tree that had always caught my eye from their living room. I made it over and crept across the grass.

I crouched by the window I knew to be Suzanne's, hesitated, then knocked softly. Nothing. I bit down hard on my lip, then knocked again.

For another agonizing minute the stillness remained unbroken. I was just wondering whether I should give up on this ridiculous exercise and go home when the curtains twitched, then moved aside. When she saw me, Suzanne's mouth dropped open in shock, then shifted into an enormous grin. As her fingers scrabbled at the window, I felt my nerves subside. I'd been right to come here, of course I had. I was pretty sure that no one, in my entire life, had ever been that happy to see me.

'Oh my *God*,' Suzanne whispered once she'd opened her window. She leaned out of it, reaching out to hug me. 'Oh my Gooodddd, Caddy!!!'

'Who did you think it would be?' I asked, attempting a joke and hugging her back.

'I thought I was imagining it!' Suzanne replied. 'What are you doing here?'

'I came to see you,' I said. 'Obviously. Want to go somewhere?'

'Did you climb over the garden wall?' she asked, her voice incredulous.

'Yeah, of course.' I was starting to feel unsure of myself again. Did she have to be so surprised?

'Why?'

'To come and see you,' I said.

'Oh my God,' she said again, this time sounding a little nervous. 'Everyone's right. I am a bad influence on you.'

'Oh, don't you start,' I said, annoyed. 'I thought you'd be pleased.'

'I am!' She laughed a little, but her eyes were still anxious. 'I really don't want to get you in more trouble though. Maybe you should go home, before they realize you're gone.'

I shook my head. 'It's fine – my Mum already checked on me. Let's go somewhere. Let's actually do something, instead of just sitting on the beach. What about the pier?'

She shook her head. 'You can't access it at this kind of time. It's completely locked up.'

'You've tried?'

'Once.' She smiled coyly. 'With Dylan.'

It had never occurred to me that she and Dylan had ever actually gone anywhere at night. I'd kind of thought that was our thing. Why did I assume so much about people and their lives? Why did I think that if it didn't happen in front of me it didn't happen at all?

'I have an idea,' she said.

Suzanne had the intelligence to bring an umbrella with her, and we huddled together underneath it as we walked away from our two houses.

'So go on, tell me,' she said, tucking the umbrella closer to us as we walked under a particularly low hanging tree, 'what made you come to get me?'

'What made *you* come and see *me* all the other times?' I asked, thinking I was being clever.

'Loneliness,' Suzanne said simply.

'Oh,' I said, thrown.

She looked at me expectantly.

'I tried to talk to my mum,' I said. 'To try and explain. But she basically made it clear that nothing was going to change. And I kind of thought . . . fuck it.'

For some reason she smiled. 'Really? Is that what you thought?'

'Yes!' I said, defensive. 'Fuck. It.'

'But seriously, have you thought about what you'll do if you get caught?' she pressed.

'Stop it, you're spoiling my buzz,' I said.

At this she outright laughed. 'I love you so much.'

'Then stop patronizing me,' I said, wiggling the umbrella so the water dripped on to her face. 'Don't forget I'm older than you.'

'By about three months,' she said, grinning. 'That hardly counts.'

I decided to ignore this. 'I kind of want to get caught,' I said instead, realizing as I spoke that it was true. The feeling of recklessness that had propelled me out of my window and over the garage roof welled up inside me again.

'Hmm,' she said, noncommittal.

'Then they'll see that trying to stop us being friends is never going to work,' I explained. 'They'll have to accept that part and move on to helping you.'

I felt her bristle beside me. 'Helping me?'

'Yeah.'

'I don't need help,' she said. 'What you mean is, they'll accept that we're going to be friends no matter what and just deal with it. Right?'

I paused, trying to think of a way to respond. It didn't seem like a good idea to say what was in my head, which was that she clearly did need help, and she was the one with the problem, not me.

'You're the troubled one,' I said, making my voice as light as possible so she'd know it wasn't a judgement.

Suzanne took a step backwards, out from under the umbrella. I stopped walking and turned back to look at her. 'You're as bad as they are,' she said, her voice fierce. 'That stupid word. I hate that word. *Troubled*. What the fuck does that even mean?'

Shit. 'That you've had a hard time. It's not a bad thing.'

'Of course it's a bad thing! *Look* at us!' She gestured between us; me standing helplessly under the umbrella, her already half drenched just outside it, then upward, presumably towards the 2 a.m. sky. 'You want to fix me, just like everyone else. You want me to be better, so you can be all proud of yourself.'

I was about to object, then reconsidered. 'Well, yeah, of course I want you to be better. But I'm not trying to "fix" you, and I'm not trying to be proud of myself.'

Her expression was dubious.

'Come back under the umbrella, you headcase,' I said, determinedly upbeat. 'You can yell at me and be dry at the same time.'

She smiled reluctantly. 'I wasn't yelling at you.'

'Little bit,' I said. When she still didn't move, I let out an exaggerated groan and moved towards her instead, holding the umbrella up over us both.

We started walking again, this time in silence. After a while she said, in the voice of someone not yet completely placated, 'Did you have to try out your rebellious streak while it was raining?'

'It wasn't raining when I left,' I said. 'And I didn't check the forecast before I climbed out the window. *Sorry.*'

'Rookie error,' she replied.

'Well, I'm not proud of myself,' I said.

She laughed. 'OK, OK. I'm sorry I said that. I just get it a lot.'

'Isn't people trying to help a good thing?'

'Not if it starts to feel like that's the only way they know how to talk to you. Like everything else about you is erased because you're the poor sap who got hit. And they *tell* you how you're feeling, instead of asking. Like, *you must be feeling awful. You must feel like it's your fault. It must be just terrible being you.* And then they tell me I should be in therapy! Where – what – we can pay someone to carry on telling me how crappy my life is and how bad I should be feeling about it?'

It took me a moment to realize she'd finished talking because I was trying to remember our conversations over the last few months. Did *I* do that?

'Yes,' she said.

'What?'

'Yes, you do it.'

'Did you just read my mind?'

'No, I read your face.'

'Oh.' What was I supposed to say? 'Well, sorry?' I still wasn't convinced that caring about someone was a bad thing. What did she expect? That people wouldn't try to empathize?

'You know who doesn't do it?' Her voice had started to relax. 'Rosie.'

I felt a flash of hurt. *Rosie?* Who'd called her pathetic and made jokes about her victimhood showing?

'She said once that I should just get over it,' she continued.

'But that's a horrible thing to say,' I said, frustrated.

'At least it's honest. And it's true. Hey, we need to go left here.' She'd taken hold of the umbrella and was gesturing in the opposite direction to the one I'd gone in, towards the railway line.

None of this made any sense to me. I followed her, ducking my head under the umbrella, unsure what to say.

'So I should be more like Rosie?' I asked eventually.

'Oh God, no. I didn't mean that. And don't make it about *you*. It was just a passing comment.' She hooked her arm through mine. 'Let's talk about something else.'

I'd never known anyone who could flit from mood to mood as lightly as she did. In fact, if I hadn't had a sister with an actual diagnosed mood disorder (where the changes between moods were in no way 'light'), I'd have thought she had one.

Maybe it was a self-defence thing.

We were both silent for a while. As we walked, I watched the droplets falling in front of us, gentler now.

'Do you know that quote?' I asked. 'The one about rain. Something like, "in every life there'll be a little rain," or something?'

'Oh, that shit can fuck off,' Suzanne said, surprising me with her vehemence.

'What? Why? Isn't it a nice quote?'

'No, it's total bullshit. I hate it when people make sadness all deep and beautiful and, like –' she waved her hands helplessly – 'profound. That's the word. It's not profound. It's not beautiful. It *sucks*. It sucks *balls*.'

'Well—'

She interrupted me. 'I think it makes non-sad people feel better. Like, they think it must be a good thing to be sad, because you're getting all this insight into real life and pain or whatever. Like how people say tears are like rain. Fuck off. Tears are just tears and they make your eyes hurt and they won't stop when you want them to and *ugh*. You get all those arty photos of girls crying – it's always girls, have you noticed? – and it's so beautiful and tasteful and moving. When the reality is your face goes all blotchy and your nose runs and you can taste it every time you breathe.'

'Taste what?'

'*It*. Pain. Sadness.' She let out a breath through her nose and twisted her lip. 'I'm just saying that sadness isn't beautiful. And if it looks that way, it's a lie.'

'Liiike . . . you?' I couldn't not say it. She'd basically given it to me on a plate.

She looked at me, half proud, half bitter. 'See, Cads? I knew you'd get there in the end.'

*

I wasn't sure exactly where we were going, but I followed Suzanne through Brighton's slick, winding streets, happy to let her lead. She'd cheered up, something about the freedom of the city at night having its usual effect on her. She'd got bouncy again. 'So, if I'm the troubled one,' she was saying speculatively, after we'd been walking for about fifteen minutes, 'and you're the nice one, what's Rosie?'

'The sarcastic one,' I said. '*Nice*? Really? Why do I get the dull word?'

'I'm sarcastic too,' Suzanne said, 'so she can't be that.'

'Well, you're both nice as well. So . . .'

'We're not nice.' She was grinning. '*You're* the nice one.'

Before I could give her hair a sort of playful tug, she'd moved away from me, swinging the umbrella back to her side.

'Here we are!' she sang, gesturing to a huge, derelict building I'd assumed we were walking past. It was surrounded on all sides by dark blue fencing that was covered in graffiti.

I looked up. 'Seriously?'

'Yeah!'

'I think I'd rather go to the beach.'

'Nooo.' She shook her head. 'We can go up on the roof and watch the sunrise. It'll be great.'

'The roof?' I repeated. My last shred of bravado vanished and nerves set in. 'You want me to go into an abandoned building and climb up on to the roof in the middle of the night?'

'Yeah!' she said again.

'Hi, I'm Caddy,' I said, stretching out my hand. 'I don't think we've met.'

She laughed. 'Don't be like that. You said you wanted to do something fun. We can go to the beach if you want, but there's nothing to *do* there. Plus, no sunrise.'

'What part of this is fun?' I asked.

'Oh.' Suzanne's face fell. 'I didn't think you'd be this against it. I'm sorry.' She took a step back towards the road. 'Let's just go to the beach.'

It was the immediacy and sincerity of her acquiescence that made all the difference. If she'd tried to convince me or guilt-trip me I'd have carried on disagreeing.

'No, you're right,' I heard myself say. 'The beach will be boring. And wet.'

She looked thrilled. 'Really? Great! If you don't like it, we'll leave.'

'What's to like?' I asked, but still I followed her around the corner of the building. 'What is this place anyway?'

'I think it used to be a factory?' She didn't sound sure. 'Or maybe something to do with the railway? I don't know. It's been abandoned for years though, apparently.' She twisted her lip thoughtfully. 'On the Internet it said one of the fence panels is loose, so we just need to find it . . .'

'What if we can't actually get on to the roof?' I followed her as she ran her hand along the fencing, pushing slightly on each panel.

'You must be able to, because there were skylights up there in the pictures,' she said. 'You wouldn't have skylights if you can't access them.'

'When did you see pictures?' I asked, confused.

'This is it!' The panel had moved against her hand and she eased it forward, creating enough space for us both. She turned her head to grin at me. 'Come on.'

It was completely dark inside the building, and the dusty air tasted and smelled like something left to decay. I stopped by the doorway, ready to let my eyes adjust, when a stupidly bright light lit up right beside me.

'Fuck!' I closed my eyes instinctively, turning my head. 'Thanks for the warning!'

'Sorry,' Suzanne said, not sounding very sorry. 'Better than the dark though, right?'

I opened my eyes, still shielding them with one hand, and looked over at her. 'Is that your phone?'

'Nope. This is a silly little torch thing I have on my keys. Useful, right?' She sounded pleased with herself. 'Ooh, stairs!'

'Do they look like the kind that will collapse when you're halfway up them?' I asked, my heart clenched tight by anxiety.

'I don't know. I can't tell from here.'

How could she be so blasé about this? Didn't she get a little nervous?

'This is starting to feel like an episode of *24 Hours in A&E*,' I said.

'Don't worry.' She managed to sound both sympathetic and amused. 'People come to this building all the time.'

'Definitionally untrue,' I said.

'Trust me.' She turned away from me, along with the light, and I watched her shadow rise up along the wall. 'Come on. We'll take it really slow.'

There was a little more natural light once we got to the roof, which was surprisingly (worryingly?) easy to access through an extra set of stairs and a door. The rain was starting to ease off and the clouds had mostly cleared, leaving the stars and a crescent moon in full view. The roof was almost completely flat, with surprisingly low rails around the edge. In the dark I couldn't make out much of the surface, but I could feel something like gravel, crunching but squelchy with mud.

'Now what?' I asked, imagining the mulch soaking into my shoes. That would be interesting to explain to my mother.

Suzanne darted away from me, skipping over the roof as lightly as if it was solid ground, and peered over the edge. My stomach lurched.

'It doesn't seem as high as I expected,' she said cheerfully, her voice carrying easily with the wind. 'But a good view, right? You can see most of Brighton. Do you know which way the sun will come up?'

I took a cautious step, trying not to think about the emptiness beneath my feet. The beams and floorboards left to rot. *Stop it, Caddy*.

'East,' I said. Another step.

'So . . . that way?' She pointed first towards the sea, then turned herself left so she was pointing east.

I smiled at her back. 'Yep, that's east.'

'Cool.' Suzanne put her arm back to her side. 'So I guess we just wait.' She leaned forward again and I resisted the urge to grab her arm. 'Do you think you'd die if you fell?' she asked conversationally.

'OK, time to move away from the edge,' I said. My voice sounded a little shrill and she glanced over her shoulder at me, flashing a grin.

'Would you rather I stayed in the middle?' She took several unnecessarily bouncy leaps into the centre of the roof and spun around on the spot. 'Hey! It's raining, and there's no one around. This is a perfect opportunity.' She opened the umbrella with a dramatic flourish, then began twirling around, raising the umbrella high above her head. 'Have you ever seen *Singin' in the Rain*?'

'Oh God,' I said. 'Please don't.'

'"What a glorious feeeeeeeling",' she sang, deliberately off-key. '"I'm haaaappy again."'

I rolled my eyes, smiling, and turned to look out across

Brighton. It *was* a good view. I could see right out to the pier.

'How did you even know about this place?' I asked, turning back around and taking a few more tentative steps across the roof.

'Brian,' Suzanne said. She was still moving her feet in some approximation of the steps from *Singin' in the Rain*, twirling the umbrella like a fencing foil. 'He likes to think he's a photographer, and he sent me a list of links to buildings he wants to photograph when he visits. Properly visits, I mean. Last weekend doesn't count.'

'When's he coming?' I asked.

Suzanne lifted the umbrella over her shoulder and began sashaying around with it. 'Not sure – it keeps getting postponed. Hopefully soon though.'

It had finally stopped raining completely, but her performance with the umbrella had left me open to the elements enough that I was pretty drenched. I gathered my wet hair in my hands and scraped it into a temporary ponytail.

'You know, I don't really get why you talk about him differently.'

Suzanne stopped mid-spin and looked at me, the umbrella balanced on her shoulder. 'What do you mean?' Her face was suddenly anxious. 'Didn't you like him?'

'Well, yeah. But that's not what I meant. That story you told in the car? About him locking his door? That was horrible. I just think . . . Isn't he just as bad as your parents? He's older, and you said your dad never hit him. Couldn't he have done . . . something?'

Suzanne made a face, then moved closer to me, light on her feet. Her hair was stuck to her face in wet tangles. 'When I was ten I fell against a radiator after Dad hit me. It was one of those really old ones – you know, the fat round ones? – and it had a jagged edge. I must have fallen weirdly, because it cut my shoulder really badly.

Blood everywhere. Brian tried to clean it and patch it up, but it was too deep. He was barely fifteen at the time. He said I had to go to the hospital, that it would need stitches. He tried to get my dad to drive us, but Dad said no. He'd been drinking anyway, so it probably wouldn't have been safe.'

She drew in a slow breath and glanced up at the sky, closing the umbrella. 'He tried my mother next. Mum was in one of her moods, when she'd barely get out of bed for weeks at a time, you know? She said no too. But Brian wouldn't let her off. I don't know what he said, but eventually she came downstairs and got her keys. She just put a coat on over her pyjamas and got in the car. Brian sat in the back with me, holding a towel to my shoulder and testing me on Beatles lyrics to distract me. When we got to the hospital, Mum said she'd wait in the car—'

'*Wait in the car?*' I interrupted. 'Are you serious?'

'She could barely talk to *us* when she was like that. She'd have been useless. Plus, like I said, she was wearing pyjamas. Anyway, Brian took me into the hospital and talked to the doctors and told me jokes and held my hand when they did the stitches. He said I'd have a battle scar forever, and when I said I hadn't been in any battles he told me I was going to be a warrior queen one day.' She paused. 'He looked after me. He was the one who'd hug me if I was crying. When he got his driving licence he used to take me on drives in the evenings if my dad was going off, and we'd listen to music and it was so *safe*. When my dad told me I was worthless, Brian was the one who'd tell me it wasn't true.' She looked at me, and even though she'd just told me an unbearably sad story, her eyes were clear. 'That's why I talk about him differently.'

'OK,' I said simply.

But it wasn't, not really. I still didn't get it. So he'd hugged her and said she wasn't worthless. Didn't those things constitute the bare minimum of what he should have been doing? Her adulation of him seemed to be entirely undeserved. Sure, in comparison to her parents he was a saint. But it wasn't exactly a high bar.

'I'm not saying he's perfect or anything,' she said quickly, her voice a little defensive, answering a question I hadn't actually asked. 'And, I mean, it would have been nice if he'd visited me properly since I moved here. But, you know, he's got uni and stuff. And, if you're going by *numbers*, there *are* two of my parents, and just one of me, so really it makes more sense for him to go to Reading.'

'You seemed pretty angry with him,' I said cautiously. 'In the car last weekend, I mean.'

'Oh, that.' She shrugged dismissively, but she'd looked away so I couldn't see her expression. 'I'm sorry you had to see me lose it like that.'

'No, I didn't mean it was bad of you,' I said. 'I guess I think it's OK to be angry about that kind of thing. And sad. You know that, right?'

She looked at me then, but she didn't say anything for what felt like a long time. 'Yeah, I know. I just . . . I don't want it to affect me like this. I don't *want* to be like this.'

I hesitated, unsure what to say. I was surely unqualified to have this conversation. 'What do you mean, "like this"? Like hurting?'

Her hands moved to clutch her elbows in a gesture of self-protection I now recognized. 'It's over. I know that. But it still hurts as much. I just wish that would go away. What if . . . what if it never does? What if I always feel like this?'

'Well, it probably makes it worse if you tell yourself you're not meant to be feeling it,' I said. I didn't know quite where I was getting that from, but it sounded right so I carried on. 'I mean, being hurt by your parents? That's awful. You're allowed to feel awful about it.'

'But, see, it's not even that.' She breathed in a deep sigh. 'It's not so much that they hurt you; it's that they don't care that you're hurt. That's the bit that . . . stays.' She made a face, like she thought she wasn't expressing herself well enough. 'I mean, bruises fade. Obviously I remember how it feels to get punched, and that's completely shit, but the bit I really remember is sitting on the edge of the bath, by myself, trying to clean up my face. And I was in the house with my family, you know? But I was doing it by myself. They just . . . left me to do it by myself.'

I both understood and didn't understand what she was saying. What I did know was that I was the wrong person to hear it.

'You need to talk to someone, Suze.'

Her voice was soft, fragile. 'But talking about it hurts.'

I felt a wave of a helpless kind of sympathy rise in my throat. 'Well, what about Brian? Do you ever talk to him?'

'Yeah, I always used to. But ever since I moved here it's been different. Like, I can't pretend that things are the same for the two of us any more. He's got a normal life, at uni and everything, and I . . . don't. And I think he feels like that too. I'm just this crappy burden for him, getting in trouble all the time and whatever. He used to try and help me out when I needed space and stuff, but now he's all, like, "Stop fucking around, what's wrong with you?" You know? Like he misses me being this little kid who didn't realize how bad it actually was. Because you don't, when you're a kid. It's just your normal.' She let out a sudden choke of breath. 'God, this makes him sound awful, doesn't it? He's not. He's really not.'

'You don't have to defend him.'

'Yeah, I do.'

He didn't defend you, I almost say, but I stop myself just in time and choose a less cutting response. 'But why hasn't he visited you?'

'He helped me move,' she said. 'He came with me and Sarah and stayed for a couple of days. I was still pretty bashed up, so I couldn't really leave the flat. He was a big help.'

I knew I would regret this. 'What do you mean, bashed up?'

'I . . . Well, I didn't move out with a hug and kiss.' Her smile was pained. 'There was no sunshine; let's just put it that way.'

I wanted to know. I didn't want to know. Despite myself, I tried to remember all the snippets of information she'd revealed over the last few months. Hadn't she said that Sarah had lived with them for a while? So what had she been doing? There was something about hospital as well, wasn't there?

'Well, it's good you got out,' I said, stating the obvious because I didn't know what else to say.

'Is it?' She turned away from me again, taking a few steps closer to the edge. 'Maybe things would have got better. You know, if I'd been better.'

'It wasn't anything to do with how good you were,' I said.

'How do you know? You weren't there.' She was still facing away from me.

'I don't have to have been there to know that.'

She shook her head. I caught a glimpse of the frustration wrought on her face. 'You're saying that because that's what you think you have to say. But I *know* it was me.'

'*What* was you?'

'Why I had to leave. It was me.'

'What are you talking about? Of course it wasn't.' The conversation was getting so confusing, and she was so close to the edge my heart was hammering. 'Do you have to stand there?'

She turned on the spot, which made me relax a little. At least being able to see her face made me stop worrying that she was about to throw herself off the roof. She opened her mouth like she was about to speak, then closed it again.

'Have you ever actually talked to anyone about this?' I asked. 'It sounds like you really need to.'

'I try not to even think about it,' she replied. 'But I do, all the time. I can't shut it off.' She put her fist to her forehead and closed her eyes. 'God, I'm sorry. This was supposed to be fun.'

'Oh, this is just as fun as I'd expect visiting an abandoned building's roof would be,' I said seriously, and she smiled a little. 'Look – why don't you tell me why you think it was your fault? Then you can go back to umbrella-dancing if you want to. But we've basically got the rest of the night here, and it's *me*, so you might as well.'

Suzanne bit her lip and looked away, considering. When she looked back, apprehension had clouded her face. She looked like a child. 'If I tell you, I can't take it back.'

I didn't say anything, just looked at her levelly, waiting. I was sure she'd start speaking eventually and, sure enough, she pushed her fingers into her pockets and started.

'You know how I told you that I tried to kill myself? Well, the doctors wanted to get social services involved because they said I was still a suicide risk, but my parents said no, it was fine, they'd handle it. That was when Sarah came to live with us. And it's true that my dad stopped hitting me, but nothing was *better*. Nothing was fixed. No one talked about what had happened, no one said sorry. It was just my dad keeping out of my way, basically. And the longer it went on, the worse it felt. It was like the only difference was that everyone was on eggshells around me, like it was my fault.

'Then, one night, it was just too much. I overheard my dad say to my mum, "One day she'll move out and we can have our lives back." Like it was all *me*. Like *I* was the problem, like I'd ruined *his* life. And so I went into the kitchen when it was just him, and I . . . I fucked everything up. I could have just stayed away from him, which was what I was supposed to do. But I was so *mad*. It was so *unfair*. I wanted to get a rise out of him; I know it was stupid, but it's the truth. I *wanted* him to hit me, so they'd all see what the problem really was. I said a bunch of stuff, I can barely remember it now, but I think it was something like that he was weak and pathetic. I can't really believe it now. I'm probably making it sound like saying that stuff to him was nothing, but I was terrified of him, Caddy. I don't remember ever not being scared of him. But at that moment I was more angry than scared. And when he lost it and punched me, this is fucked up, but I was *pleased*. And then he hit me again. And then he wouldn't stop.'

Neither of us said anything. All I could think about was how he'd looked when we'd seen him at the marina. So *ordinary*.

'You're not saying anything.' There was a catch in her voice, a note of panic.

'I don't know what to say,' I said honestly. 'But nothing you just said makes me think it was your fault.'

'Well, what did it make you think? You can tell me. Just say it.'

'It made me feel really sad for you,' I said, treading carefully. 'That you can go through something as awful as that and come out of it blaming yourself.'

'But if I hadn't goaded him . . .'

'Suze, he *hit* you. That's all him. And it wasn't even like that was the first time, right? How old were you when it started?'

'Seven.'

God. 'Well, then. There you go.'

'But he never hit Brian,' she said. Her voice was soft. 'It was always me. So it has to have been because of me.'

'No.' I suddenly felt like I might start crying, but I tried to keep my voice light, so she wouldn't shut down. 'Inaccurate. Try again.'

'Sarah says he has problems,' Suzanne said. 'With anger, and control, you know? She says he doesn't mean it. And it's true – he did used to go into these rages, where it was like he was a different person – but he could be really *mean*, even on normal days. And only to me.'

'It definitely sounds like he has problems,' I said.

'But people say that about *me*.' Her voice cracked. I could tell she was near tears. 'That I have "problems". So what am I going to turn into?'

'You're going to turn into an older version of my friend Suze,' I said. 'A headcase, yeah. But the best kind.'

She did start crying then. I stepped forward, the closest I'd been to the edge of the roof, and pulled her in for a hug. I looked out over her shaking shoulders to the rest of Brighton, still and quiet, oblivious to us. Was it my imagination, or was it starting to lighten?

'What if I turn out bad?' she asked, so quietly I almost didn't hear.

I squeezed my arms tighter around her, trying to put the weight of our friendship into a single hug.

'You won't.'

We stayed like that for a minute or two more, before I deliberately disentangled myself and reached for the umbrella.

'You want to teach me the moves?' I offered.

She wiped her eyes, nodding. 'You've really never seen *Singin' in the Rain*?' Her voice was raspy, but regaining its normal strength.

'Oh, I've seen it.' I said, gliding away from her with my poor excuse for grace. The gravel crunched under my feet. 'How does it go, like, "doo de doo do"?' I opened up the umbrella and started twirling it above my head like she'd done earlier.

'Yeah, see, you don't even need me.' She was grinning

now, watching me from the side.

I grinned back, covering more of the rough surface with each twirl. I tried to pinpoint what I was feeling, the strange giddiness of dancing on a roof in the middle of the night. It wasn't a simple happiness, because the anxiety I'd been carrying all night was still weighing in my stomach, but in a way that wasn't exactly *bad*. It was an odd kind of freedom, something I wanted to be able to remember. A new version of myself.

'This is all thanks to you, you know,' I called to her, as my foot found a section of roof that felt different.

'What do you mean?' She was still smiling.

'Me, being here, doing this.' I moved my feet around on the new surface, wondering where the gravel had gone. 'I'd never done *anything* interesting before I met you. And now –'

There was a cracking noise, so loud we both jumped.

'What was that?' Suzanne asked, looking worried.

I had frozen in place, too scared even to look down at my feet. 'Um.' My voice was shaking so much I almost couldn't speak. 'I think I might be standing on a skylight.'

The instant look of horror on her face scared me even more. I could hear a faint crackling noise, emanating from below my shoes. My heartrate was ratcheting up, roaring in my ears.

'Don't move,' she said, and despite the panic on her face her voice was calm. 'I'm coming to get you, OK?' She started towards me.

I knew I was going to fall an instant before it happened. There was a split second when the glass beneath my feet gave way before gravity caught up, and it was in that moment my brain selected an image for me. As I fell in a shower of glass and mud, I couldn't hear the screaming coming from my own mouth or Suzanne's. I couldn't see the rush of the floor below as it rose to meet me.

I saw Rosie, aged five, breathless and triumphant, holding out a ribbon to me. Her voice, lilting with excitement, before sarcasm dried it out, 'And now we're best friends.'

And then the ground.

When

26

Here's one good thing about the aftermath of a twenty-foot fall through a glass sheet: memory loss.

Not total memory loss, of course. But just enough to minimize the trauma. My brain is kind to me that way.

Even some time after I had the full use of all my limbs back and no longer felt a sickening dizziness when I stood up too quickly, I still couldn't remember most of what happened in the first twelve hours after the fall. All I had were scraps of memory, flashbacks that could be triggered by a chance phrase or sound or touch.

The rough scrape of the neck brace wrapped around my throat.

The sound of someone, a girl, sobbing.

A light shone into my eye.

A patient, calm voice. 'Caddy?' And me thinking, Who?

A strip of lights along a ceiling, whizzing by.

And pain, oh there was pain. Mercifully brief, as I moved in and out of consciousness, and then helped by drugs. But the memory of the pain struck me at odd moments, even months later. Like every nerve in my body had sounded an alarm: SOMETHING IS WRONG.

Which it was, of course. Aside from the severe concussion – which the doctors thought could be brain damage for what my mother says were the worst five hours of her life – I had a leg that was broken in two places, a wrist all but shattered and three broken ribs.

But I lived, conquering the odds of twenty-foot falls with an innate determination I didn't know I possessed.

My parents were by my side in the hospital for most of

the morning and afternoon, but I retain no memory of any conversations we had during that time.

'That's probably for the best,' Mum said later. 'You weren't exactly making much sense. You kept telling me that you'd ruined your shoes.' She laughed a little tearfully. 'Like I cared about your silly shoes. But you kept saying it!'

The first lucid conversation I had was later that same day, when I woke up to find Rosie sitting in a chair pushed right up to my bed. She had *Cosmo* magazine open on her lap.

'Hey,' I said.

Rosie's head jerked up. As soon as our eyes met her face broke out into a grin, and the sight of it almost brought me to tears. It was the smile of a friend who has known you for over ten years, the kind of friend who forgives you for your idiocy, the kind of friend where the word 'best' is unnecessary.

'Hey,' she said, reaching out to squeeze my shoulder. 'Oh my God.' She pressed her lips together, then took a deep breath and smiled again, a little shakily this time. 'Caddy, oh my God.'

'I know,' I said, because I did.

She attempted another smile. 'I've never had such a good opportunity to say I told you so.'

'You're not mad?'

She shook her head. 'Too scared to be mad. Maybe later. I'll save it.' She put the magazine on my bedside table and leaned forward in her chair. 'How are you feeling?'

'Oh, I'm fine,' I said automatically, but even as my mouth formed the words a foggy confusion descended on my head, turning down the volume on her voice for a moment. I blinked, trying to clear it.

'Cads, you broke your leg.' Rosie was saying sternly. 'That is not fine. Mum told me that your mum said it's a really bad break as well. Plus there's the concussion thing. You're lucky you didn't break your neck.'

At her words, the memory swooped into my head, unbidden. The feeling of the world giving way underneath me. The sharp sting of shards of glass on my head. The flash of remembering must have shown on my face, because her expression immediately became anxious again. 'Are you OK?'

I tried to nod, which was a mistake. 'Yeah,' I said instead. 'Just . . . whoa. I feel really woozy.'

'That's probably the drugs. You must be on loads. I bet—'

'Where's Suzanne?' I interrupted.

Rosie's mouth snapped shut. She glanced towards the door, twisting her lip, as if she thought the answer might come through it. She looked back at me. 'I don't know. At home?' There was an edge in her voice. Something cold.

'Why isn't she here?' My heart gave a jump of fear. 'Is she OK?'

Rosie's eyebrows scrunched, then slowly rose. 'Caddy, come on. You know why she isn't here.'

'She's not in trouble, is she?' The fuzziness in my head was making it hard to think. I tried to gather the snapshots of memory into something complete. The umbrella. Suzanne crying. Me hugging her, telling her she wouldn't turn out bad.

'*Not in trouble?*' Rosie repeated. 'Caddy, you almost *died*.'

'That's not her fault,' I said. 'We were both . . .' More fog. 'I mean, I was the one who . . .'

'Of course it's her fault,' Rosie said, her voice tense. 'After everything that's happened, she did it again, she snuck out *again*, and made you go with her, again, and now look what's happened.'

'No,' I said, trying to inject some strength into my voice. 'That's not right. Didn't she tell you? I went to see her, not the other way around.'

Rosie's expression faltered slightly and I watched her digest this information for about half a second. Then she regrouped. 'You would never have snuck out of your house before you met her,' she pointed out, which was true. 'You'd never have done something so fucking *stupid*, Caddy. You were on a *roof*. In the middle of the night!'

'We were going to watch the sunrise,' I said, feeling tears begin to gather in the backs of my eyes. 'How could we know this was going to happen?'

Her expression softened, but she still looked more exasperated than sympathetic. 'Don't cry. I'm sorry, I shouldn't have got arsey. But the thing is, you *should* have known that something like this could happen. Like, that's pretty much exactly why people don't do things like this. Because this happens.'

I felt the tears start making tracks down the sides of my face, prickly against my skin. I bit my tongue and tried to breathe in through my nose. The magnitude of what had happened was starting to hit me. And oh *God*.

'You have to go and see Suze,' I said, the tears making my voice shake. 'You have to check she's OK.'

'She's totally fine, Caddy,' Rosie replied, the edge of impatience sharpening her words. 'You're the one with serious injuries. You're the one who nearly *died*.'

'But why isn't she here?' I was starting to feel panicky. 'Didn't she come here with me? Did someone make her leave?'

'How would I know? I only found out when my mum called me at lunchtime. Which was the weirdest conversation of my life, by the way. First no Suzanne at school and then, "Don't panic, Rosie, but Caddy's in hospital because she fell through a skylight." And of course I *did* panic.'

I was barely listening. 'She told me some stuff about her family. It was awful.'

'Hey,' Rosie said, and the tone of her voice was so unfamiliar I jolted out of my own head and looked at her, 'I'm right here, you know.'

Before I could reply, the door opened and we both jumped. Rosie's mother had come into the room, holding a small bouquet of yellow flowers.

She smiled at me. 'Hello, Caddy. You're awake. How are you?' She put the flowers on the table and a gentle hand on Rosie's shoulder.

'I'm OK,' I said, because there's no answer to that question that doesn't sound sarcastic when your face is peppered with cuts and your leg's in pieces.

'We need to be getting going,' Shell said to Rosie. 'Caddy needs to spend time with her family.'

'*I'm* family,' Rosie said grumpily, but she was already starting to stand up. She turned to me. 'I'll come back tomorrow after school. And I'll see if I can find out about Suze, OK?'

I felt a grin of relief and affection break out over my face. 'You're the best, Roz.'

'Yeah, yeah.' Rosie rolled her eyes, but she was smiling too. 'And don't you forget it.' She folded her hand twice in a wave. 'See you.'

For the rest of the evening my family dropped in and out of my room while I drifted in and out of drug-assisted sleep. Tarin painted my nails a hideous shade of luminous green – 'Because you can't stop me!' – and told me stories about when she'd been hospitalized around the time of her diagnosis. Mum flapped and faffed and arranged the flowers she'd brought, talking mainly to herself about the dangers of inadequately protected buildings and teenagers with 'absolutely no sense'. Dad stood for a while in the corner, studying my chart, glancing at the various machines around me, nodding every now and then to himself.

When he left, he kissed my forehead for the first time in about ten years. 'Get some rest. The morphine will help you sleep. I'm on shift tonight, so if you need me, just buzz and one of the nurses will come and get me, OK?'

'OK,' I said, touched.

But then he paused in the doorway and looked back at me. 'Ah, I do mean only if you really need me, you understand? I will be working, after all.' He smiled at me and then left without waiting for a response.

The drugs sent me into a strange, uneven sleep, where my dreams were spongy and featured morphine-induced reimaginings of some of my most random memories. I kept falling asleep and waking up with a start, shocking myself each time with the unfamiliar room and how empty it was.

Until it wasn't.

'Hey.'

Suzanne was wearing an old pair of grey jogging bottoms and an oversized black hoodie. Her hair was haphazard around her face, unbrushed and wild. I had no idea how long she'd been there, but there she was, standing so close to the door she was almost pressed against it. Her voice, even on the short word, was shaky.

'Hey,' I said.

She crept closer, her fingers clenched together. Her eyes were scanning my face, and she looked so agonized I wanted to cry.

'Are you OK?' she asked finally, still a couple of steps from the bed.

'Yes,' I said, as definitively as I could, waiting to see her face relax into a smile.

'Caddy –' she took another step and reached for the bedpost, her fingers gripping so hard I could almost feel it myself – 'I'm so, so sorry. I'm so sorry.' Her voice broke, and her free hand flew to her mouth. 'They wouldn't let me see you last night, they wouldn't let me stay, I wanted to come. And today, oh God it's been so awful, today, everyone said no, they said I shouldn't, that I'd make it worse.'

'Suze—'

'But I couldn't not come, I had to say sorry, because it's all my fault, I ruin everything.'

At this I gave up trying to break into her frantic monologue and reached out my uninjured arm, curving it towards me in a hug gesture. Suzanne hesitated for just a moment and then bolted around the bed. At first she half crouched, half leaned into the hug, but it was so awkward she eventually sat her full weight on the bed, and then climbed on completely.

It occurred to me as she curled herself carefully between me and the edge of the bed, her limbs a tangle above the covers and mine stretched out clinically straight, that Rosie and I weren't really huggers. Even when we were very young we hadn't been the type of twosome who shared changing rooms at the swimming pool or beds at sleepovers. I wasn't sure which one of us had the greatest influence on this facet of our friendship, but I did know that Rosie would never have even thought to climb up on to my hospital bed beside me.

'You don't ruin everything,' I said inadequately.

'Are you basing that on the evidence, or . . . ?'

'I think you've just been unlucky.' I injected as much cheer and positivity into my voice as possible, hamming it up to show just how OK it was. 'The only way is up. There's a light at the end of the tunnel.'

'It's always darkest before dawn?' At last I heard a smile in her voice.

'Things are never as bad as they seem.' I tried to think of some more. 'Uh, *que sera, sera.*'

There was a pause and then, at exactly the same time, we both said, 'What doesn't kill you makes you stronger.' And then we both cracked up.

'Shhh,' Suzanne said through giggles. 'I'm not supposed to be here, remember?'

'Oh yeah, what *are* you doing here? How did you get in? And what time is it?'

'Nearly midnight. I had to wait until Sarah went to sleep.'

My heart sank, the laughter gone suddenly. 'Suze. Really?'

'I told you, I needed to see you,' she said, and even though her voice was calm there was defensiveness there. 'I haven't told you about today yet. You'll get why when I'm done.'

'So you sneaked out of your house – again – and then sneaked into a hospital?'

'It wasn't hard,' she said dismissively. 'That kind of thing is always so much easier than people think.'

'Didn't anyone see you?'

'Sure they did.'

I waited a moment, but she didn't elaborate. She sat up and slid off the bed, easing herself into the chair that was there, wincing. 'I banged my leg climbing over the garden wall.'

I couldn't help rolling my eyes. 'Only you could say something like that like it's completely normal. And did I mention that my leg is *broken*?'

Suzanne's face crumpled and I felt a surge of guilt. I'd meant to tease, but the veneer of I'm-fine-I'm-so-very-fine that she wore was just that, a veneer. In the instant after I spoke I saw her real emotional state flash across her face. She looked broken. Broken in a way that frightened me.

'I'm sorry,' I said quickly. 'That was meant to be a joke.'

'I know.' She looked away from me, wiping her eyes with her sleeve. 'Sorry. I'm kind of . . . off balance right now.'

I waited until she'd gathered herself before speaking again. 'So what happened today, on your end?'

'Nothing good. You should have seen Sarah's face when she opened the door to me and the police – the way she looked at me. It was horrible. And the police kept talking and talking, it was unbearable, they were just delaying the inevitable, you know? I didn't go to school, Rosie probably told you that. Sarah didn't go to work. The thing is, she didn't yell. She cried though. And that was worse.' She wiped her eyes again. 'What about you? Is everything OK with you, except the leg?'

'And the face?'

'Well, yeah, that too.'

'The leg is pretty bad apparently. And they were worried about my concussion for a while. But they all seem to have calmed down now. I'll probably be out in a few days.'

'That's good.' Finally she smiled a proper smile. 'I'm so relieved. All day I kept imagining the worst. Sarah said something about you maybe being paralysed, and oh God, can you imagine?'

Watching her babble away, I felt the slow creep of anxiety starting in my stomach. Something was wrong. There was something she wasn't telling me. There had to be a reason why, after everything, she'd sneaked into my hospital room at midnight to talk to me.

'Why are you here, Suze?' I asked.

She picked at a thread on her hoodie sleeve, avoiding my eyes. In the silence, my anxiety grew.

'I came to say goodbye,' she said eventually.

The anxiety, already at my chest, seized. 'What do you mean?'

'They're sending me away. Well, Sarah is – Sarah and social services. I'm being put into care.' She was still not looking at me.

'No.'

'There wasn't even a question. Sarah said it straight after

the police left. She didn't say it in a mean way, she just said it. Like there was no other option. She said this was the final straw. Actually she said a whole bunch of stuff that was horrible, but true.'

'But she'll calm down.'

'Not this time, no. She's already spoken to Becca.' Seeing my face, she added, 'My social worker, remember? So I guess she'll get it sorted out. Sarah tried to . . .' Still not looking at me, Suzanne seemed to choke on the words, then gather herself. 'She tried to get them to take me away straight away. But they can't do it that way, apparently.'

'What does it mean?' I asked. 'Where will you go?'

She closed her eyes briefly. 'God, I don't know. I don't know how the fuck this works. Probably some kind of group home?' Her voice wavered. 'You know, with all the other unloved fuck-ups.'

'Oh, Suze . . .' I ached with worry and sympathy. 'Look, maybe if you explain—'

'Explain what?' She looked at me now. 'What is there to explain? She tried. She tried really, really hard. But I'm just . . . What was it she said? I'm beyond help. I just cause pain for other people, and she's had enough of having to be responsible for my destructive behaviour. That's a direct quote, by the way.'

'But . . . care? Will that help?'

'Of course not. But it won't be her problem. *I* won't be her problem.' She studied her sleeves, bunched into her fists. 'Part of me wonders if I'd have been better off if she'd just never got involved.'

'You mean staying with your parents?'

'Yeah.'

'But they were hurting you. You could have died.'

'Maybe that would have been better.'

'What?'

'Nothing.' Suzanne let out a long sigh then, straightening her shoulders and tilting her head back. She closed her eyes for what felt like too long, then opened them again, smiling determinedly at me. 'Anyway. I brought you something.' She reached into her pocket and pulled out a necklace, which she held out to me.

When I took it, I realized what it was.

'Oh no, I can't have this.' I tried to push it back into her hands, but she held them clenched against her chest. 'It's yours.'

'I want you to have it,' she said simply. 'To say thank you.'

'Thank you for what?' I looked at the necklace closely, the delicate chain, the curve of the dove. It was even prettier up close.

'You know for what.' Her lips curved into a soft, sad smile. 'I think you're the best friend I ever had.'

'I won't tell Rosie you said that,' I said, trying to keep my voice light, because it felt like I was about to start crying.

'No, do. Tell her she was brilliant too. And tell her I'm sorry. I probably won't see her again. Before I go, I mean.'

'Do you know when that will be?'

She looked away from me. 'Oh, a couple of days, maybe?'

'Maybe you could come and stay with me,' I suggested, a little desperately.

Suzanne laughed out loud. 'Oh, I'm sure your parents would just love that.' She let out another sigh, but she was smiling this time. 'Face it, Cads, I'm a certified lost cause. A walking, talking fuck-up.' Her voice was light, in line with her smile, but I noticed that her hand, which she'd raised to wipe her face, was shaking slightly.

'You're not,' I said.

'I really am though.'

Before I could protest again, she looked over at the clock and made a face. 'I should probably go.'

'Why don't you stay until it gets light?' I suggested. 'You shouldn't walk all the way back to your house in the dark by yourself.'

'I'll be fine,' she said dismissively. 'You should be resting anyway; I've kept you awake long enough.'

'If you go by yourself I'll be too worried to go to sleep anyway,' I countered.

She looked at me then with an expression that was impossible to read. I couldn't tell if she was angry or sad, if she was annoyed by my statement or pleased.

'OK,' she said finally, 'but only if you promise that I won't keep you awake. You'll sleep, right?'

'I'm barely staying awake as it is,' I said, blinking.

She smiled a little. 'OK. I'll stay till it's light.'

As lies went, it was a kind one.

27

The next time I woke up, it was abrupt. My subconscious jolted me awake so suddenly I was disorientated for several moments, trying to take in my surroundings and simultaneously work out what had woken me. The two realizations stuck me at the same time, and I sat bolt upright in bed, causing a spasm of pure agony to ricochet around my body and a yelp of pain to escape.

The first realization was that Suzanne was gone, even though it was very much still dark. The second was that I had remembered something in my dream, something so frightening it had forced me out of sleep.

The memory was of Suzanne, weeks earlier, rolling an unlit cigarette around in her fingers. *I'd rather die than go into care.*

On the back of this memory, in my newly hyper-alert awake state, snippets of our midnight conversation came into sharp focus.

I came to say goodbye.

Maybe that would have been better.

She says I'm beyond help.

And then, the final clue I'd been too dense to notice: the necklace currently resting on my bedside table. Her favourite thing. Her prized possession. She had *given* it to me.

A sweep of panic rushed through me, causing my ears and fingertips to burn. The panic felt solid, like something had taken hold of me and shaken me. For a moment I was paralysed by it.

Dad, I thought. I'd get Dad to come, and he'd go and find her, and everything would be fine. I reached out towards the button by my bed, then paused. What would actually happen if I pressed it? A nurse would come, and then what would I say? My in-disgrace friend who was sort-of responsible for my current state had sneaked into the hospital to give me a necklace and now I thought she was going to kill herself? Wouldn't that sound stupid? What were the chances of the nurse actually getting my father?

So I'd have to go and find him myself. I looked around the dark room, my eyes settling on the outline of the wheelchair maybe two metres away. I pulled back the covers and looked at my leg. How bad could it be, really? It was still in the basic leg shape, even if the bones weren't as securely attached any more. The cast seemed like it would at least hold it together.

I hesitated, then swung my legs slowly, slowly around the side of the bed. The broken one stuck out comically straight in front of me, the other already bending to the floor as if in expectation. Bracing myself, I put all my weight on my uninjured arm and lowered myself down.

Even though my arm and my left leg were taking most of my weight, an instant shock of pain swept through me as soon as my feet touched the floor. When had I had my last dose of painkillers? What if I passed out before I made it to the wheelchair? I closed my eyes for a moment, gathering myself, then lifted myself completely off the bed.

It wasn't far, but making it across that room was the most painful thing I'd ever done in my life. My leg felt like a dead weight of pain dragging along behind me. I was almost at the wheelchair, tears streaming down my face, when my working leg buckled and I collapsed on to the floor. I crushed my hand across my mouth to stop myself crying out, waited a few seconds for the panic of intense pain to leave my body, then pulled myself up into the chair.

I rolled myself out of the room and into the empty hall, my heart cantering, hoping I'd find a lift close by. When I found one around the first corner, I pushed the right button, rested my head against the wall and cried all the way down to A & E.

When the doors opened on the ground floor, two doctors were standing there, presumably waiting for the lift.

'Oh,' the male one said, looking stunned. I saw his eyes move to the space behind me, as if expecting someone to materialize there and explain my presence.

'I'm looking for Dr Oliver,' I tried to say, but my throat was tight with pain and fear and the result was barely comprehensible.

'Dr Oliver?' the other doctor said slowly, her eyes moving from my leg to my arm to my face. 'Are you on the right floor?'

The doors started to close, and I shot my hand out to keep them open. I stumbled slightly out of the wheelchair, put too much weight on my bad leg and let out an involuntary howl of pain. The eyes of the two doctors went wide, and they both reached out automatically to grab my arms.

'He's my dad,' I started to say, just as the unmistakable broad figure of my father appeared at the other end of the corridor. He wasn't looking at us, and was talking animatedly with the nurse beside him, gesturing to the chart he was holding. 'Dad!' I yelled.

His head jolted up, and he looked around with the confused expression of someone hearing a familiar noise completely out of context. Then he saw me, and a look of shock overwhelmed his features. Shoving the chart at the nurse, he almost ran towards me, covering the corridor's length in seconds. 'Cadnam,' he half shouted, half gasped.

When he got closer, I realized his expression was almost panicked. He reached for me, his fingers gripping into my shoulders. 'What is she doing here?' His voice was raised almost to a yell, and it was full of an anger I'd never heard before. He was directing the question at the poor doctors who'd been holding on to me.

'We were just waiting for the lift and she appeared,' the woman said, her voice steady and calm.

Dad looked down at me and gave my shoulders a shake. 'What are you doing out of bed, Cadnam?'

'I need to talk to you,' I said. His panic was catching, and my voice sounded pitched and breathless. 'It's really important.' The words were so inadequate. I sounded like a schoolchild out of her depth.

'Tell me – what's wrong? What's happened?' His eyes were darting all over my face. He still looked half terrified. 'Did something happen?'

'No, it's not me.' I could feel tears at the back of my throat again. My desperation was building because I knew what would happen as soon as I mentioned Suzanne's name. I had to make him listen to me, and when had that ever worked? 'It's . . . it's Suzanne.'

The effect was immediate. His panicky expression vanished, his grip loosened. He let out a frustrated sigh and actually rolled his eyes. 'Oh, for Christ's sake.' Another loud exhalation. '*Jesus*, Cadnam, I thought something had happened. You frightened the life out of me.'

'No.' I tried to make my voice firm. 'No, Dad. It's not like that. You have to listen to me. I think she's—'

'Whatever it is, we can talk about it in the morning,' Dad said briskly. 'Right now it's important that you get your rest. Claudia, would you please take my daughter back to her room?'

'No,' I said again. 'No, you have to listen. I think –' My voice caught. 'I think she might hurt herself.'

Dad set his jaw, closing his eyes briefly. 'Cadnam. You need to calm down and go to bed.' Had he even heard me?

The female doctor was watching me closely. 'Who's Suzanne?' she asked.

'She's a troublemaker,' Dad said, before I could even open my mouth. 'She's the reason Caddy is here at all.'

'And why do you think she might hurt herself?' The woman directed the question at me. Her voice was gentle.

'She came to visit me tonight, said she wanted to say sorry. And she said she was being taken into care, but she said once before, ages ago, that she'd rather die than go into care.' I said all of this in a torrent, trying to get it all out before Dad could interrupt me again. 'And she said stuff like she's beyond help, and – and! – that she'd come to say goodbye. And she gave me her necklace, which is like her favourite thing – she never takes it off.' At some point during my rambling I'd reached out and grabbed hold of the woman's sleeve. I only realized when I'd finally stopped speaking, and I let go, embarrassed even in my panic.

There was a silence. Had I been convincing enough? 'Daddy,' I heard myself say. 'Please.' Tears were coursing down my face. The image of Suzanne handing me the necklace was looping in my head. 'It doesn't matter what you think of her.'

He looked at me for a long moment. 'Do you have a telephone number for Sarah?' he asked me finally.

'No,' I said. My voice was starting to shake. 'I don't have my mobile, remember?'

'When did Suzanne leave here?'

'I don't know, I fell asleep. She told me she'd stay until it got light. When I woke up and it was dark and she was gone, that's when I realized. I should have got it earlier –' a sob escaped – 'but I didn't . . .'

Dad put his hand on my shoulder again, this time gently. 'Calm. Down. OK? Calm down.' I bit down on my lip, trying to steady myself. 'What is the fastest way for us to get in contact with Sarah? If I call your mother, will she have a number?'

'Yes.' But what if she protested? What if she was as dismissive as he had been? 'Call Rosie's mum.' The answer came to me in a rush of relief. All those times calling Rosie's landline; aside from my own, it was the only number I knew by heart. 'She'll have it.'

I recited the number twice as he scribbled it down on to his notepad, checking it three times to make sure it was right.

'You'll call Shell right now?' I pressed. 'And then Sarah? Straight away?'

'I will call them both,' he promised. 'But you have to go back to your room and go to bed. Right now. Claudia, will you take her back upstairs?'

The nurse moved around the wheelchair, giving my shoulder a reassuring squeeze.

'I'll come and see you in the morning,' Dad said. 'Let you know everything's fine, OK?'

'She's tried before.' I blurted this out as Claudia reached for the handles of the wheelchair. She paused, her eyes swivelling towards my dad.

This time they all exchanged glances. I noticed Dad's fingers tense over the notepad. 'Don't worry,' he said, but by now even he seemed worried. He looked at Claudia again. 'Thanks, Claudia.'

It was 3.27 a.m. when I made it back to my hospital room, and it was Claudia who spotted the note. Next to the empty box of Jaffa Cakes, written on the back of a leaflet about juvenile diabetes.

> *I'm sorry for everything.*
> *Buonanotte.*
> *Love, Suze xx*

This is the image I have:

Around the time I was hobbling across the hospital tiles, Suzanne sat herself down on Brighton beach. She swallowed the pills in groups, three handfuls in total, pausing between each to force down the vodka. When she'd finished she took the empty bottle and half buried it in the stones, so it wouldn't get smashed or blow away. She slid her earphones carefully into her ears and scrolled through her iPod albums until she found *Abbey Road*. She listened with her eyes closed, and she didn't even cry.

And then, during the second chorus of 'Octopus's Garden', she fell asleep.

After

Part 5

28

I hadn't expected to sleep at all after Claudia left the room, but the drugs in my system, the pain and the panic caught up with me and pulled me under. I woke up more than once, drowsy and disorientated, convinced I could hear voices, before sinking back into sleep.

I dreamed snapshots of confusion and colour: sunflowers that towered over me, blocking out the sun, bending on impossibly long stalks; dancing kites with yellow tails, the string biting into my hands; Suzanne on the other side of the road, standing with her back to me at the seafront railings, blonde hair tousled in the wind; Tarin surrounded by origami birds, painting the bedroom walls green; pebbles on Brighton beach rolling under my feet like a waterfall cascade, carrying me away; Rosie, her face close to mine, saying, 'Caddy? Caddy?'

And then the unmistakable reality of a hand on my shoulder. I opened my eyes; the world lurched and righted.

'Caddy.' My father's voice, unusually soft. Not a question, not a request, not a reprimand. Just my name.

When I spoke, my voice came out cracked and husky, like I'd been crying in my sleep. 'Did you find her?'

'Yes.' He looked tired. His hair was dishevelled, like he'd been running his fingers through it. 'We found her.'

The terror that seized me was absolute. I felt instantly cold, my throat closed up. I tried to speak, but he got there first.

'We found her in time,' he said, inclining his head and meeting my gaze with a steadiness that made me let out my breath, my heart rate calming. 'It's OK. We found her in time.'

*

Relief is a flat word for an emotion that feels so boundless. I felt at once full and emptied by it. I cried, of course, but once the tears were done I wasn't sure quite what to do with myself apart from grill my parents for details, which I did, at length. They were unusually patient with me, answering all my questions until I had the fullest picture I could of what had happened.

As promised, Dad had called Rosie's mother and then Sarah, who'd called the police. Once she'd finished talking to them, her phone rang again. This time it was Rosie's mother on the end of the line, relaying possibly the six most important words Rosie had ever said: 'Tell them to try the beach.'

Would anyone but Rosie have known how much the beach meant to Suzanne? I thought I did, but it hadn't occurred to me that that was where she would choose to die, which was why I couldn't shake the queasiness of knowing how easily things could have been different. If I hadn't woken up. If I hadn't got my dad. If I hadn't made him call Shell to get Sarah's number. If Shell hadn't woken Rosie. If any of these steps hadn't happened, who would have been there to save her? No one.

We found her, Dad said, and in a way it was true. But it wasn't a reassuring sequence of events, not a montage-worthy pulling together of heroes, racing against the clock to find Suzanne in time. It was just a couple of lucky phone calls, and a girl who knew her friend.

After the drama came the anticlimax. I felt as if I'd spent the last few months being swept along a river and now, suddenly, there I was, dropped over the waterfall into the sudden calm of a plunge pool. The noise and motion and panic were gone. Everything was still. It was disorientating.

I wasn't allowed to see Suzanne, who'd been brought to the

same hospital I was in but was, apparently, in no state to see anyone who wasn't a medical professional or family. I worried about her, of course, but it was a different kind of worry than before. Now at least I knew she was in safe hands. The hardest part was over, the worst had happened; it was surely all good things from here. And that was, at least in part, because of me. I'd saved her, just as I'd been so scared I'd lose her. It wasn't just relief I was feeling, it was pride.

I left the hospital four days after my fall, my leg and arm in plaster and stitches twinging in the side of my face. 'It might scar,' the doctor said. 'It's too early to tell.' Secretly I hoped it would. A small scar by my hairline, between my cheekbone and my ear, seemed like the kind of souvenir I was owed after everything that had happened.

I was given only the barest details about Suzanne, even after I was settled at home. I knew that they'd got her to the hospital quickly enough after she'd taken the pills that there would be no lasting physical damage, but that her mental state, not so easily measured with monitors or fixed with drips, was the biggest concern.

'Is it like a breakdown?' I asked my mother.

'We don't really say breakdown any more,' she said.

I took this to mean yes.

One week after the overdose, Suzanne was transferred to an in-patient CAMHS unit in Hampshire called Gwillim House, a specialist facility for teenagers with serious mental-health problems. It was the best thing for her, I was told, and way overdue. A safe environment with trained professionals and no expectations of her except that she could be helped. As much as I knew this was true, and as glad as I was that it was finally happening, it made me feel strange to think of Suzanne being labelled as having 'serious mental-health problems'. Technically I knew it was correct, but it wasn't *her*. The four words seemed so scary and huge, painting the image I had of my friend in colours I didn't recognize or understand.

'Yeah, it's almost like having mental-health problems doesn't actually change your personality or something,' Tarin said sarcastically when I tried to talk about it with her. 'Ye gads! A clinical diagnosis! She is an entirely different person now.'

'That's not very helpful, Tarin,' Mum said drily.

'Try me tomorrow,' Tarin said. 'I'll probably have changed my mind by then, what with being bipolar and everything.'

'All right, I get it,' I said, rolling my eyes. 'Stereotypes are bad. Mental health is complicated. You can stop now.'

I had my own physical recovery to deal with, which at the very least was a useful distraction from worrying about Suzanne's emotional one. I was out of school for two weeks after the accident, resting my head and learning how to navigate my surroundings with two of my four limbs out of action. By the time I returned to Esther's and something like normality, I felt like a different girl than the one who had last walked through the school gates. No one noticed.

For the next few weeks I waited to hear from Suzanne, convinced at first that it would just be a matter of days and then revising that estimate as time went on. But before I knew it April had turned into May and brought with it exams. Having been all but bed-bound for so many weeks, I'd had plenty of time to revise and had also developed a healthy dose of perspective. I went into my exams with a new kind of confidence I'd never before experienced; I knew I would do well, but if I didn't, that was fine too.

'That's all right for you, Miss Private School,' Rosie said over the phone, our primary method of contact during her self-enforced revision exile. 'Want to swap brains for a while?'

The day after my last exam, as well timed as if it had been planned, I finally heard from Suzanne. It had been seven weeks since I'd last seen her, and I'd started to forget what her voice sounded like. She'd sent me an email, so brief I actually tried scrolling down, expecting more words to appear below her name. *Hi Caddy*, it read, as if we were mere acquaintances. *I know it's been ages but . . . hello! Hope all's good with you. Are you free some time soon to come and visit? There's some stuff I want to talk to you about. Sarah knows the visiting hours so just give her a call to arrange. Love, Suze.*

It didn't seem like much after so long apart, but I understood. After seven weeks, there was too much to say or nothing at all. The most important thing was that — finally — I was going to see her again. I emailed back immediately, using far too many exclamation marks in my enthusiasm, then called Sarah. I arranged to visit Suzanne at Gwillim House that coming Saturday.

I could have been nervous, but I wasn't. In the weeks Suzanne had been away I'd had plenty of time to worry and overthink every aspect of our friendship and what it would be like when we finally saw each other again. Now it was actually going to happen, I was just excited. More than anything else, I really missed her.

'You should come too,' I said to Rosie on the Thursday. She'd finished her exams almost an entire week before me and had spent the interim time applying for summer jobs. The two of us were sprawled across her bed with a bag of tortilla chips between us and Frank Turner on Spotify.

'Not this time,' Rosie said easily. 'I think this kind of thing is better one on one. Don't want to crowd her, right? Hey, do you think I'd get to eat a lot of doughnuts if I got a job at the pier?'

'Yes,' I said. 'And you'd probably get sick of them in about a day.'

In Suzanne's absence, without discussion or articulation, Rosie and I had found our rhythm again. Something had changed between us, there was no doubt about that, but it felt like a change that was positive. It was as if Suzanne had wedged herself in between us, squeezing in to create her own little niche in our twosome, and when she'd gone she'd left that space empty. The space felt like breathing room.

'I don't think it's physically possible to get sick of doughnuts,' Rosie replied, her fingers flying over her keyboard. 'I'm going to go for it.'

'You do that,' I said. 'But seriously. Suze. Gwillim House. Is it OK that I'm going without you? Wouldn't two of us be better?'

'I think if she thought it was better, she'd have asked us both,' Rosie said. She wasn't looking at me, her eyes focused on her laptop screen. 'And she hasn't, and that's fine. It's great that you're going though.'

'I'm going to take presents,' I said. 'What should I take?'

Rosie's fingers stilled on the keyboard, her eyes swivelling towards me. 'Honestly? I think you should just take you.'

I frowned. 'What do you mean?'

'Maybe save the presents this time. Just go and see how things are.'

'Who wouldn't want presents?' I asked, confused. 'I wasn't thinking anything big, just something small from me. Us. Something from us.'

'I think that's probably the last thing on her mind, to be honest,' Rosie said. Her fingers started tapping again at her keyboard.

'You're not still mad at her, are you?' I ventured. It seemed like a ridiculous question, after so long, but still . . .

To my relief, Rosie laughed. 'No, I am not still mad at her. What kind of monster do you think I am? When your friend almost *dies*, being mad at them seems kind of redundant.' She shook her head.

'Bloody Suze. Ruining my righteous anger by being all tragic and traumatized.' She was grinning. 'So selfish.'

I had to laugh. 'You could have just left it at no.'

'I *could*,' Rosie agreed cheerfully. 'But then I wouldn't be me, would I?'

Saturday was one of the most beautiful days I could remember for months. The sky was cloudless, the sun hot and bright.

'Hello, June,' Tarin said, grinning. She'd offered to drive me to the unit and I'd jumped at the chance, the alternative being my mother. 'What perfect weather to sit in a car in for an hour and a half.'

'Could be worse,' I said, pushing my seat as far back as it would go so I could stretch out my plaster-encased leg. On my lap I was holding on to a purple florist bag, containing a sunflower pot, a charm bracelet and a box of macarons. Despite what Rosie had said, I couldn't imagine turning up to see Suzanne empty-handed. 'You could be at work.'

Tarin slid her sunglasses up on to her face. 'True, true.' She turned out of our road, the satnav tracing a route for us. 'So how are you feeling?'

'Good,' I said, smiling. There was no other answer to give on a sunny June day, in a car with my sister, being driven to see someone I loved and missed, someone I'd started to worry I'd lost. 'Maybe a little nervous. But I'm good.'

Tarin glanced at me. 'What's making you nervous?'

'The whole thing, I guess. It's a weird situation.'

'Yeah, but it's still you and her at the end of the day,' Tarin pointed out. 'And think of it this way: she wouldn't have asked to see you after all this time unless she was ready.'

'That's true,' I said, feeling a jolt of relief for my wise, generous older sister and the fact that it was her in the car with me rather than my mother. 'I guess I'm just not sure what I'm meant to say. What do you say to someone who's so depressed they're suicidal?'

'Tell them you love them,' Tarin said, like it was nothing. Like it was everything. 'Be supportive. Look, what you need to understand is, you won't be able to single-handedly stop her wishing she was dead, if that's even what she still thinks, which I doubt. What you can do, as her friend, is make sure she knows you're glad she's not. Does that make sense?'

'It doesn't seem like enough.'

'There is no *enough*.' Tarin flicked her indicator on, the clicking noise filling the car as she merged on to the motorway. 'You seem to be forgetting that she's in a clinical facility getting professional help. Which is great, obviously. Let *them* worry about how to deal with depression. You're going to visit your friend, remember? Yes, she's a patient, but she's not *your* patient. So for God's sake, don't treat her like one.'

We got to Gwillim House a little after 2 p.m. It looked more like a residential community centre than the hospital I'd been expecting, which made me feel much better about Suzanne living there. At reception, a friendly Scottish woman called Yvette signed me in, talking too fast for me to really follow what she was saying. She led me down a corridor of magnolia walls and propped-open doors, taking it slowly because of my crutches, until we came to an empty room furnished with aggressively bright sofas.

'Make yourself comfortable,' Yvette said, then glanced at my leg. 'If you can. I'll go and tell Suzanne you're here.'

Suddenly alone, I stood uncertainly in the doorway for a few seconds before hobbling over to the window, which looked out on to a large, beautifully landscaped garden. I pressed my forehead against the glass, taking in the flowerbeds and ornate, mosaic path winding away from the building and into the distance, trying to figure out why this garden was such a surprise to me. I felt the wedge of my crutch digging into my skin as I stood, thinking of gardeners and flowers and Suzanne and unexpected things.

'I planted the irises,' a voice at my side said. 'Those blue ones.'

'They're pretty,' I said, even though I could see at least three different blue flowers and I had no idea which ones she was talking about.

'It's not exactly subtle, as therapy techniques go,' Suzanne said. Her voice was casual, musing, as if we were picking up a conversation we'd been right in the middle of. 'Plant something, watch it grow. But you're right – they are pretty.'

Keeping my forehead up against the glass of the window, I turned my head slightly so I was looking right at her. She smiled at me, the spontaneous, instinctive smile of a friend to a friend. 'Hi.'

'Hi,' I said.

29

My immediate thought was that she hadn't changed at all. Her hair was pulled back from her face in a simple ponytail, slightly longer than I remembered but still the whiter shade of blonde that I had come to associate with her. Her eyes still sparkled, her smile still shone.

But after the first happy kick of familiarity, I registered that there was a slight strain in the corners of her mouth when she smiled; that she wasn't wearing any make-up and her face was pale. Where her hair was pulled back at the sides of her face I could see darker roots that were almost, but not quite, hidden by the rest of the blonde. She was thinner than I remembered, the simple black T-shirt and grey zip-up hoodie she was wearing hanging slightly loose around her. Her neck, for so long framed by her dove necklace, was bare.

As I took all of this in, I could see her eyes searching my face and then dropping to my plastered arm and leg as she ran the same checks on me. We stood in silence for at least a minute, just looking at each other, each of us half smiling in the sudden awkwardness of reunion.

'Last time I saw you, you had cuts all over your face,' Suzanne said.

'Last time I saw you . . .' I began, then stopped. What was the right way to end that sentence? She looked at me, waiting. For God's sake. Not even two minutes in and I'd already shoved my foot right into my mouth.

'It's OK,' she said finally, a small smile hovering on her face. 'I know. Do you want to sit down?' She gestured to one of the sofas.

'*Can* you sit down? With the leg, I mean.'

'Yeah, it's fine,' I said, adjusting my hand on my crutch and then starting towards the sofa. 'I'm used to it now.'

'How much longer will it be before you can walk properly again?' Suzanne asked. She sat down and then pulled her knees up to her chest, hugging them close with both arms.

'The cast will come off my leg in about a month,' I said, settling myself back against the sofa. 'And then I'll have physiotherapy and stuff. But I get the one off my arm next week.' I smiled. 'Progress!'

Suzanne rested her chin on her knees. 'That's great.'

I waited for her to say more, as she would have done before, but she just smiled a little at me, quiet. I felt a wave of nervous sadness I didn't quite understand, remembering how she'd lifted the umbrella above her head and danced around on a roof, so dauntless and vibrant and bright. It was like I was remembering a different person entirely. I had never really been able to tell where the front ended and she began. Now that front was gone, and I wasn't sure exactly who was left.

'Maybe by the time you come home I'll be fine,' I said hopefully. At these words, her expression faltered slightly, so I added, 'Do you know when that will be?' She didn't reply, chewing her lip between her teeth. 'We should plan something,' I said, trying to smile. 'Me being mobile, you coming home.' She was still silent, so I picked up the bag I'd set on the floor and put it in front of her. 'Here, I brought you stuff.'

'Caddy.' Suzanne opened her mouth, then closed it again slowly. I saw her teeth catch a hold of her tongue. 'Caddy, I . . .'

There was something in her voice that stopped my breath.

'This isn't why I asked you to come here,' Suzanne said, her voice shaky. She put her hands on the top of the bag without even looking inside it. 'God, I'm sorry.' I watched her face crease as she lifted her sleeve to her eyes. 'I'm so sorry, Caddy.'

'Stop it,' I said, my sudden, all-encompassing anxiety fraying my voice. 'At least tell me why you need to be sorry before you say it.'

'I'm not coming home,' she said. 'I'm not going to come back to Brighton.' Her eyes were steady on me, the handles of the bag twisted around her fingers. 'I asked you to come here so I could tell you that. Not for presents, or anything like that. To say . . .' she hesitated. 'To say goodbye properly. Obviously I'm going to be here for a while, but even after I leave, I won't go back to Sarah's.'

Something had stuck in my throat. I tried to swallow. 'Why not?'

'I'm going to go into foster care,' she said carefully, like she was weighing out every word. 'There are, like, specialist foster carers for teenagers like me, who have been in places like this but don't have families to go home to.' She shrugged a little, but I could see the crease of pain on her forehead. 'There's a couple in Southampton who are going to take me. I've met them. They're nice.'

'Southampton?' I repeated, understanding starting to seep in. Southampton was a two-hour drive from Brighton. 'But that's . . . that's miles away.'

'I know,' she said, 'but it's good. They've taken in girls from Gwillim before, so they'll know what they're doing with me. Way more than Sarah did anyway. Nuru, one of my key workers, says she thinks they'll be good for me. They—'

'But why Southampton?' I interrupted without thinking, seizing a glimmer of hope. 'Don't they have those kinds of foster carers in Brighton?' I had no idea how this kind of thing worked, but I ploughed on anyway. 'Even if you don't live with Sarah any more, you can still come—'

'No.' She was shaking her head. 'No, you don't get it. I don't *want* to go back to Brighton. Sarah was ready to give it another go, but not going back is my choice. I need a clean break, away. I need to start again.'

The words died in my throat. 'Oh.' A hollowness was starting to work its way from my stomach to my chest. 'I . . . Oh.'

The tears that had been gathering in Suzanne's eyes finally spilled. 'I'm sorry, Cads. I know how that sounds. It's not . . . it's not *you*, or anything. You and Roz are the reasons I would want to go back, but deep down I know I need to do this. I need to try again, by myself, and I need to do that somewhere new, where there isn't someone I'm already depending on. I use people, Caddy. I lean on them, way too much. And then I get so panicked that I'll lose them that I make myself be what I think they want. I did it with you. I so wanted to be that person you thought I was. I tried *so* hard.' Her voice caught and hitched, and she pressed her sleeve to her mouth, like she was trying to hold something in.

She took a deep breath, shaky and jagged. 'If I go back, I'm scared nothing will change. What if I just fall back into the same stupid habits, make the same mistakes? Even if it's not straight away, give it a few weeks and I'm crawling out of the window again. Going to you when I want to feel good, Dylan when I want to feel bad. It's what I do, and it's so destructive, and so painful, and then, one more year down the line, I'm swallowing pills again. I don't want this to be the pattern of my life until one day there's no one there to save me.' She looked at me, anxiety etched in every line on her face. 'Do you know what I mean?' She was really asking me, I could tell. 'Does any of this make sense? I'm trying to be sensible –' she tried to smile – 'and you know that's not exactly my default mode.'

I knew I was supposed to smile back, say something reassuring, let her know I understood. But my ears felt hot, my chest was pounding. This was all wrong. This wasn't why I'd come here. She finally chose to be sensible and it was a decision that was going to effectively end our friendship? How was that fair? 'I don't get why any of this means you can't come back home.'

Suzanne's face dropped. 'Because it's *not* home,' she said. 'I don't have a home, Caddy. That's the whole fucking problem.'

'I thought you liked Brighton.'

'It's not about *liking* −' She stopped herself, letting out a frustrated breath. 'God, Caddy. Are you really going to do this?'

'Do what?' I could feel tears building and I forced myself to hold them back. 'Aren't I allowed to talk about this with you?'

'*No!*' she burst out. 'No, because it's not *fair*. You're talking about this like you *know*, like you've got the first fucking idea what any of it was like half the time. Do you still not get it?' It was almost a relief to see the anger spill. 'Do you want me to spell out how much I hid from you? You think because you saw me freak out maybe two or three times that you saw me at my worst? That's not even close. You want to hear about my birthday? My fucking sixteenth birthday, when my parents treated me like they didn't even know me, and I couldn't deal with it, so I had a meltdown and smashed up Sarah's kitchen? And then, when Sarah tried to calm me down, I sliced my arm open with a broken plate?' Tears were streaming down her face, but I felt frozen. I couldn't speak.

What was it Mum had said? *She's very sad. Overwhelmingly so.*

'Twelve stitches in A & E, Caddy. And did you have any idea? No. Because I hid it from you, like I hid most of the fucked-up things about me. Are you getting it now? And here. Seven weeks of *therapy*. Psychologists and nurses and being under observation and taking fucking medication and everyone being all, *Listen to us, Suzanne, we're trying to help.* Do you know how long it's taken me to get to a point where I finally accept that I have to do this?

And then you come here, you who's supposed to be the good, unselfish one, and you're making me doubt myself?'

I opened my mouth to speak – to defend myself or apologize, I wasn't sure – but instead I burst into tears. The horrible, uncontrollable kind you have no hope of disguising or minimizing. In the seconds it took for the tears to steal my vision, I saw the part-horrified, part-enraged look on Suzanne's face and I had the dim sense that I was doing exactly the wrong thing, exactly what she'd been afraid of. But this wasn't how stories like this were meant to end. She was meant to get better and come home, not leave completely. Not after everything. I trusted in happy endings, and this felt too much like sadness, like something lost.

'Caddy,' Suzanne said, her voice tense.

My name resounded in my head. *Caddy,* I thought, *this is not about you.*

'I'm sorry,' I managed. I pushed my hands up against my face, forcing myself to calm down. I drew in a sharp breath, then let it out slowly, closing my eyes. When I opened them again, Suzanne's head was tilted slightly, her eyes trained on me.

'Do you understand now why I need to do this?' she asked, her voice suddenly steady and quiet again.

I took a deep breath. 'I don't *want* to.'

'But do you?'

I nodded. I knew that I had to turn this around. If I couldn't pull this back, something would be lost. 'Fuck your life,' I said.

It worked. For a split second she looked startled, then her face changed and she laughed out loud. 'I know, right?' she said. The smile disappeared almost as soon as it had arrived, her face falling sad and flat again. She twisted the bag handles in her fingers, letting out a sigh. 'God, this is hard.'

'I'm sorry,' I said again. Her words had started to register and now I had guilt flooding into my head as well as everything else.

The last thing I wanted to do was make her question seven weeks' worth of progress.

'What for?'

'Everything.' I wiped my eyes with my sleeve, wishing I was better at this. 'For being so useless.'

'No, Caddy. No. You're the best person I know.' She dropped the gift bag's handles and took a hold of both my hands, squeezing for emphasis. The gesture was so adult-like, but also somehow so *her*, it brought on a fresh wave of tears. 'The best. OK? I don't think you'll ever know what you've done for me, and how much it means that someone like you would care so much about someone like me.'

'Someone like you is brilliant and amazing,' I said. 'Why can't you see that in yourself?' The unfairness of it was starting to sink in. If she could only see herself like I did, there wouldn't be a problem. But she didn't, and she never would, and that was so many levels of wrong and unfair I almost couldn't comprehend it.

Suzanne's chin quivered slightly and I saw her bite down on her tongue again. 'You know why,' she said softly. 'Please. Don't do this.' She let go of my hands and sat back slightly, letting out a breath. 'Look . . . Knowing that *you* see that is everything. Really.' She chanced a smile, shaky but there. 'And I can take that with me, you know? To Southampton and wherever else I go. I know that there are good people and that they can be good to *me*. I just have to find them. And, you know, not take them on midnight walkabouts and up on to roofs of abandoned buildings.' She looked guilty and I got the sense that this was probably an area she'd covered multiple times with the therapists.

'But I had more fun doing those things with you than I've basically had ever,' I said. 'Doesn't that matter?'

She made a face. 'That's kind of my point. People said I was a bad influence on you, and I was. But I didn't mean to be. I didn't *want* to be. But just because I didn't want it and you didn't see it, doesn't mean it wasn't true. You know? And I really, really don't want to be that kind of person. Which is why I need to do this, like I said. Start over, but properly this time. Find out who I want to be, find good people to be it with, yeah?'

I looked at her, my brilliant, beautiful, battle-scarred friend. So recently a stranger. So almost a ghost. *You can be it with me*, I wanted to say. I could convince her, if I tried. I knew she trusted me, that she'd listen, if I pushed this.

'Anyone you meet will be lucky to know you,' I said instead.

A smile broke out over her face, sweet and soft and genuine. 'Thanks.'

'I'll miss you.' Three inadequate words.

'I'll miss *you*.'

'Will you come back and visit?' I asked.

Suzanne hesitated. 'Maybe one day. But not for a while, OK?'

'Well, maybe me and Roz can visit you,' I said. 'In Southampton.'

She was silent for a while, but I could see the truth on her face and I could feel it in the space between us. There was no need to make her say it, so I didn't.

'Are you going to see Rosie? Or do you want me to tell her about . . . all this?'

Suzanne brushed her hair back from her forehead, a wobbly smile chancing on her face. 'Rosie already knows.'

'What? How?'

'I emailed her a few days ago. I wanted to talk to her before I talked to you. Plus I had a lot I wanted to say to her that I wanted to get right, and with email I got the chance to think everything through.'

'She didn't tell me.'

'I asked her not to.'

Rosie had said, *Just go and see how things are*. Oh God. More tears.

'Things with Roz . . .' Suzanne continued, then hesitated. 'I felt like she was one of the people I'd messed things up with the most. We had so many stupid fights near the end. But the thing with her is that she always kind of . . . got me. Like, she understood the crappy side of me and she'd call me out on it every time, and it was kind of tough to deal with sometimes, but it was the right thing for her to do, especially when it came to you. She used to tell me that she couldn't stop me fucking up my own life, but I couldn't drag you down with me.' She shook her head. 'I hated that she was so right. And I think I was jealous of what you two had, if I'm really honest. I wanted friends like that.'

'You do have friends like that,' I said. 'You have us.'

'That's exactly what Rosie said.' For a second I thought she was going to start crying again, but she sighed instead. 'God, the two of you.' She almost laughed. 'I don't think I even knew what "best" *meant* until I met you both.'

'How come Rosie isn't here?' I asked. It had been bothering me. 'How come you just wanted to see me?'

'Because . . .' She paused, chewing on her top lip. 'I didn't need to see Rosie to say all of this, and she didn't need to see me. We kind of understand each other in that way. We've been emailing a lot, and her emails are brilliant. Like, they actually make me laugh, and I haven't been doing much of that recently. But we talked about it, and she was the one who said I had to see you in person to explain, because it was going to hit you hard. I told her she could come too, but she said this kind of thing would be better one on one.' She looked at me. 'She's not one to say it, but you know how much she cares, right? She really loves you.'

The tears had clogged up my throat, so I just nodded. *Rosie*. When I got home and saw her I would tackle her with a hug, whether she wanted it or not.

'And I do too,' Suzanne added, smiling a smile that was as happy as it was sad. 'Just so you know.'

'I love *you*,' I choked out. 'And I –' I stopped, trying to find the words that could explain to her how much she meant to me, how she'd brought sparks and surprise and light and layers to my life, how every broken bone and all the tears had been worth it, for her. 'You're just the *best* . . . *my* best . . .'

She interrupted me by leaning over, putting her arms around my shoulders and hugging me. I let my forehead rest against her shoulder, her familiar blonde hair bunching against my face. I wondered how many times we'd hugged in the short time we'd been friends. How many times we'd hug in the future.

'Hey,' she said. 'Talk about significant life events, right?'

I smiled, trying to regain my composure. 'Oh God – that feels like a million years ago.' I thought of my former self, limbs intact, wishing for significant things. A year earlier I'd been planning my sixteenth birthday and playing 'where will I be when' with Rosie, entirely oblivious of what was to come. So much of what I had thought would be important then had turned out not to matter. Here I was, weeks from my seventeenth, still boyfriendless and in full possession of my virginity, and I didn't even care.

'Oh,' I said, suddenly remembering. I reached into my pocket and pulled out the small box I'd been carrying her necklace in. 'I brought this back for you.'

The dove at the end of the chain dangled between us. She looked at it, her brow furrowing. 'I gave it to you,' she said after a pause.

'But it's yours,' I replied. 'I can't keep it.'

'What if I want you to?'

'What if I don't?'

We looked at each other, stalemated.

'You said it was like a promise,' I reminded her, as if she'd have forgotten.

'A broken promise,' she said, and something in her face cracked. 'It hurts to look at it.' She looked at me. 'You have it, Cads, please?'

'How about this?' I said with a flash of inspiration. 'We'll share it. You take it now, and next time I see you, you can give it back.'

She was silent for a while, her eyes moving from the necklace to my face.

'Like a promise,' I added.

'Between you and me?'

I nodded, holding out the necklace towards her. After a moment, Suzanne opened her palm to me and I dropped the chain into it.

'And if anyone asks where you got it,' I said, watching her unclip the catch and reach up behind her neck, 'you don't even have to mention your mother.'

'I won't,' Suzanne said. She glanced down at the necklace then back at me, a grin breaking out across her face, brief but wide and so familiar. 'I'll say my best friend gave it to me.'

Acknowledgements

Beautiful Broken Things has been a long time in the making, and I am lucky enough to have many people to thank for their help and guidance, or just for the simple act of being there along the way.

First and foremost thanks to Claire Wilson, my brilliant agent, who made all this possible. Thank you for your patience and unfailing encouragement, for believing in this book and for believing in me. I got really, really lucky. Thanks also to the team at Rogers, Coleridge & White, particularly Lexie Hamblin.

Thank you to my wonderful editor, Rachel Petty, and everyone at Macmillan Children's for their enthusiasm and support at every stage of this book's creation. I'm so proud to be able to call myself an MCB author.

To everyone involved in the Authors for Philippines project in 2013, particularly Keris Stainton, thank you. You did such good, and in doing so set in motion small ripple effects like me and this book. Sara O'Connor, who went above and beyond the call of duty, I am inexpressibly grateful for your advice and encouragement. I will do my best to pay it forward.

Thank you to Claire's Coven, especially its intrepid leader Alexia Casale, for being so welcoming and supportive and for continuing to make me laugh every single day. Particular thanks to Alice Oseman, Lauren James and Catherine Doyle. I feel so lucky that I got to achieve a dream and make such amazing friends at the same time. Tusen takk, Melinda Salisbury: my dinobro, my friend.

This book has involved a lot of research over the years of one kind or another, but I am particularly indebted to the generous folks on Twitter, who responded to my incredibly niche questions with the generosity I'd usually associate with my closest friends, not near strangers. Particular thanks go to Rosie Claverton and Joanna Cannon, who understand how to balance accuracy with storytelling, and helped me with both.

Thank you to Erin Hanson, for writing such beautiful poetry and for allowing me to use the perfect four lines at the opening of this book. Anyone who is interested in finding out more or in reading more poems can visit Erin's website at thepoeticunderground.com.

Thanks to Rachael, who read this book when it had no title and has championed it ever since, and my other early readers, Lauren, Emily, Rebecca and Catherine. The fact that you wanted to read this story before it became a book meant the world.

Mum and Dad; James and Monika; Anna and Richard; Holly, all the Barnards and beyond: thank you. What a family I have. You're wonderful. Dad, I could never have been a writer without your example, advice and support. I said that to you once and you looked so surprised. Thank you for that, and for so much else.

Thank you to Tracy, for the photos, the advice, the pep talks and above all your friendship. If everyone had a friend like you, we'd have a smarter, funnier, kinder world. Jane, thank you for your wisdom, your empathy and your time.

A special thank you to DT – there are no words to explain how much your support, humour, enthusiasm and kindness have meant to me. You have made me a better feminist, a better writer, a better person. I am grateful beyond words for your friendship.

Thank you, Tom, for everything. For your patient rereading of draft after draft, for saving Suzanne when even I had almost given up, for looking after the cat and not complaining (much) when I disappeared with the laptop for hours on end. Thank you for giving me Brighton and for not being the slightest bit surprised when any of this happened.

And finally, but most fittingly, to Lora, who was my best friend then and remains my best friend now, who continues to bring sparks and surprise to my life. I don't know who I'd be without you, but I know this book would not exist. You are brilliant. I would climb out of a window for you.

Author's Note

When I set out to write what would, many years down the line, become *Beautiful Broken Things*, all I had in my head was a girl. I knew she had a dazzling smile and sad eyes. I knew she'd been hurt, but that for all her wild spirit and fury she was full of warmth and love. I wanted to tell her story, because it felt like a story that needed to be told.

Many stories about abuse end with the rescue or escape of the victim (a loaded term in itself), because that is the best thing about stories: they end when we want them to end. But in real life a child who escapes a violent home carries that experience with them. With *Beautiful Broken Things* I wanted to talk about what happens next. Who do you become after trauma, when you are still learning about yourself? How do you tell the people you meet in your new, safe life about your past, or do you not tell them at all?

This is Caddy's story because trauma is not just something that happens to one person; it touches the lives of everyone they love and are close to. Being a friend to someone in pain can be difficult and upsetting, but it is invaluable. We all have opportunities to be darkness and light in the lives of those we love, and in the truest friendships there will always be both.

Friendship is at the heart of this book. It is a love story without a romance, because there's no love quite like that shared between teenage girls. When I think back to my teenage years, I can barely remember the names of the boys I had crushes on, the faces of early boyfriends gone blurry. But I can tell you about the time my best friend and I carved peppers instead of pumpkins at a 'fake

Halloween' sleepover when we were thirteen. I can remember entire conversations we had while sat on a wall down the road from our school.

I wanted to honour this kind of relationship – because it is a relationship – with the story of Caddy, Rosie and Suzanne. I really do believe that, for all the arguments and misunderstandings and fallouts and tears, the best thing you can be to someone is a friend.

To anyone who is suffering, whether this is due to experiences similar to Suzanne's or to something entirely different, hold on. Better days will come. You wouldn't believe the number of people who are waiting to love you.

Don't be afraid to talk to someone that you trust, whoever that may be. Know that asking for help is a sign of strength, not weakness. If the thought of speaking to someone you know feels like too great an obstacle, there are many wonderful organizations and charities that exist purely to help those who are struggling, even if that is just to offer a friendly word. If and when you are ready, here are some people you can reach out to, but until then, their websites have a lot of very useful information.

Centrepoint
http://www.centrepoint.org.uk
Tel: 0800 23 23 20
Email: supportercare@centrepoint.org
Central House, 25 Camberdown Street, London E1 8DZ
Help for young people who need a safe place to stay. Advice and information for those forced to leave home.

Childline
http://www.childline.org.uk
Tel: Freephone 0800 1111
Weston House, 42 Curtain Road, London EC2A 3NH
Lines open: 24 hours, 7 days a week. Provides a confidential counselling service 24 hours a day.

Eighteen and Under
http://www.18u.org.uk/
Tel: Freephone helpline 0800 731 40 80
Text/Whatsapp: 07707531976
Email: lormac1053@aol.com
1 Victoria Road, Dundee DD1 1EL
Works with young people to identify their needs and provide them with the ability to empower and survive personal traumatic experiences.

National Society for the Prevention of Cruelty to Children (NSPCC)
http://www.nspcc.org.uk
Tel: 24-hour helpline 0808 800 5000
Text: 88858
Email: help@nspcc.org.uk
Weston House, 42 Curtain Road, London EC2A 3NH
Text phone: 0800 056 0566. Call via ISDN videophone: 020 8463 1148. Online via IP videophone or webcam to: nspcc.signvideo.tr. Monday to Friday 9 a.m.–5 p.m. A free 24-hour service which provides counselling, information and advice to anyone concerned about a child at risk of abuse. Provides support in Welsh and five Asian languages.

Sane
http://www.sane.org.uk
Tel: Helpline 0845 767 8000.
Email: info@sane.org.uk
1st Floor Cityside House, 40 Adler Street, London E1 1EE
Information and support to those experiencing mental health problems.

TheSite.org
http://www.TheSite.org/selfharm
An online resource offering advice and support for young people concerned about self-harm.

Youth Access
http://www.youthaccess.org.uk
Tel: 020 8772 9900
Email: admin@youthaccess.org.uk
1–2 Taylors Yard, 67 Alderbrook Road, London SW12 8AD
Lines open: 9.30 a.m.–1 p.m./2 p.m.–5.30 p.m. The national membership organization for young people's information, advice, counselling and support services (YIACS)